Willing Sacrifice

"Sizzling love scenes . . . emotionally intense."
　　　　　　　　　　　　　　　　—*Publishers Weekly*

"A story of second chances in a world where staying alive is a daily struggle. The reader is pulled into an engaging and suspense-filled story line where a human places a stranger's life above her own."　　　　　　　　　—The Reading Cafe

"Throughout a number of Butcher's previous Sentinel Wars novels, the heart-wrenching drama of Theronai warrior Torr and the all-too-human Grace has been previewed. . . . Their incredible struggles showcase all of Butcher's exceptional talent for plot, characterization, and storytelling!"　　—*RT Book Reviews*

Falling Blind

"A taut mixture of action and suspense."　　—Smexy Books

"Prime entertainment."　　　　　　　　—*RT Book Reviews*

Dying Wish

"A superb paranormal suspense."—Genre Go Round Reviews

"Butcher's rise to the top of the paranormal and romantic-suspense genres has been swift. . . . Her hallmark is consistent superior storytelling that combines emotional punch with high-adrenaline danger—a recipe that can't miss!"　—*Romantic Times*

Living Nightmare

"There's only one way to describe this book to me: fabulous!"
　　　　　　　　　　　　　　　　—Night Owl Reviews

"[An] action-packed story of the brooding and angry warrior Madoc and his journey to the future. This series rocks!"
　　　　　　　　　　　　　　　　—Fresh Fiction

continued . . .

"Utilizing her ability to combine excellent characterization with riveting danger, rising star Butcher adds another fascinating tier to her expanding world. You are always guaranteed generous portions of pulse-pounding action and romance in a Butcher tale!" —*Romantic Times*

"Ms. Butcher's written word began to grab hold of my imagination and lead me on a ride unlike anything I have read before." —Coffee Time Romance & More

Running Scared

"What an entertaining and thrilling series! The characters are forever evolving, secrets are revealed, powers are found, new details come to life, and love is the cause of it all. I love it!" —Fresh Fiction

"Superb storytelling. . . . I am amazed how Ms. Butcher's intricacies and subplots continue to expand the story without bogging down the overall plot." —Romance Junkies

"This book jumps right in the fray and keeps you hooked till the end, and I was unable to put it down. Emotionally dark, this is a wonderful blending of paranormal romance and urban fantasy [with] many twists and turns." —Smexy Books

Finding the Lost

"Exerts much the same appeal as Christine Feehan's Carpathian series, what with tortured heroes, the necessity of finding love or facing a fate worse than death, hot lovemaking, and danger-filled adventure." —*Booklist*

"A terrific grim thriller with the romantic subplot playing a strong supporting role. The cast is powerful, as the audience will feel every emotion that Andra feels, from fear for her sister to fear for her falling in love. *Finding the Lost* is a dark tale, as Shannon K. Butcher paints a forbidding, gloomy landscape in which an ancient war between humanity's guardians and their nasty adversaries heats up in Nebraska." —Alternative Worlds

"A very entertaining read. . . .The ending was a great cliffhanger, and I can't wait to read the next book in this series. . . . A fast-paced story with great action scenes and lots of hot romance." —The Book Lush

"Butcher's paranormal reality is dark and gritty in this second Sentinel Wars installment. What makes this story so gripping is the seamlessly delivered hard-hitting action and wrenching emotions. Butcher is a major talent in the making."

—*Romantic Times*

Burning Alive

"A wonderful paranormal debut. . . . Shannon K. Butcher's talent shines." —*New York Times* bestselling author Nalini Singh

"Starts off with nonstop action. Readers will race through the pages, only to reread the entire novel to capture every little detail. . . . A promising start for a new voice in urban fantasy/paranormal romance. I look forward to the next installment."

—*A Romance Review* (5 roses)

"This first book of the Sentinel Wars whets your appetite for the rest of the books in the series. Ms. Butcher is carving her way onto the bestseller lists with this phenomenal nonstop ride that will have you preordering the second book the minute you put this one down." —*Affaire de Coeur* (5 stars)

"Absorbing. . . . Butcher skillfully balances erotic, tender interactions with Helen's worries, and intriguing secondary characters further enhance the unusual premise. Fans of Butcher's romantic suspense novels will enjoy her turn toward the paranormal." —*Publishers Weekly*

"Ms. Butcher offers fresh and delightfully creative elements in this paranormal romance, keeping readers engaged as the story unfolds. *Burning Alive* is a well-crafted beginning to this exciting new series, and will have fans of the genre coming back for the next adventure in the Sentinel Wars." —Darque Reviews

"An exciting romantic urban fantasy. . . . Shannon K. Butcher adds her trademark suspense with plenty of tension and danger to the mix of a terrific paranormal thriller." —*Midwest Book Review*

"*Burning Alive* is Shannon K. Butcher's first foray into paranormal romance and what a doozy it is! Filled with sizzling love scenes, great storytelling, and action galore, fans of paranormal romance will rejoice to have Ms. Butcher finally join the genre!" —ParaNormal Romance

"A different twist on the paranormal genre. . . . Butcher has done a good job with *Burning Alive*, and I will definitely be reading the next in the series." —Fallen Angel Reviews

BINDING TIES

THE SENTINEL WARS

SHANNON K. BUTCHER

A SIGNET BOOK

SIGNET
Published by the Penguin Group
Penguin Group (USA) LLC, 375 Hudson Street,
New York, New York 10014

USA | Canada | UK | Ireland | Australia | New Zealand | India | South Africa | China
penguin.com
A Penguin Random House Company

First published by Signet, an imprint of New American Library,
a division of Penguin Group (USA) LLC

First Printing, March 2015

ISBN 978-0-451-24083-5

Printed in the United States of America
10 9 8 7 6 5 4 3 2 1

For Glen

Character List

Drake Asher: Theronai warrior, bonded to Helen Day
Briant Athar: Sanguinar
Connal Athar: Sanguinar
Logan Athar: Sanguinar, blood hunter, Hope Serrien's mate
Aurora: Athanasian servant
Cain Aylward: Theronai warrior, Sibyl's protector, bonded to Rory Rainey
Brenya: Queen of all Athanasia, the Solarc's wife
Angus Brinn: Theronai warrior, bonded to Gilda
Gilda Brinn: the Gray Lady, Theronai, bonded to Angus
Maura Brinn: Theronai, Sibyl's twin sister
Sibyl Brinn: Theronai, Maura's twin sister
Canaranth: Synestryn, Zillah's second in command
Meghan Clark: blooded human
Helen Day: the Scarlet Lady, Theronai, bonded to Drake Asher
Eron: Athanasian prince
Neal Etan: Theronai warrior, bonded to Viviana Rowan
Madoc Gage: Theronai warrior, bonded to Nika Madison

John Hawthorne: blooded human

Mabel Hennesy: blooded human

Lexi Johns: the Jade Lady, Theronai, bonded to Zach Talon

Justice: nomadic woman hunted by Ronan

Dakota Kacey: the Turquoise Lady, Theronai, bonded to Liam Lann

Nicholas Laith: Theronai warrior

Ronan Laith: Sanguinar

Liam Lann: Theronai warrior, bonded to Dakota Kacey

Samuel Larsten: Theronai warrior

Tynan Leygh: Sanguinar

Lucien: Athanasian prince, father of Jackie Patton

Andra Madison: the Sapphire Lady, Theronai, bonded to Paul Sloane

Nika Madison: the White Lady, Theronai, Andra's sister

Victoria (Tori) Madison: Theronai, sister to Andra and Nika

Torr Maston: Theronai warrior, bonded to Grace Norman

Beth Mays: blooded human, Ella's sister

Ella Mays: blooded human, Beth's sister

Jake Morrow: human, member of the Defenders of Humanity

Blake Norman: human, Grace Norman's stepbrother

Grace Norman: the Lavender Lady, bonded to Torr Maston, Blake Norman's stepsister

Jackie Patton: the Golden Lady, Theronai, daughter of Lucien, bonded to Iain Terra

Andreas Phelan: Slayer, leader of the Slayers, Lyka's half brother

Eric Phelan: Slayer, Andreas's brother, Lyka's half brother

Lyka Phelan: Slayer, Andreas's half sister

Rory Rainey: the Amethyst Lady, Theronai, bonded to Cain Aylward

Joseph Rayd: Theronai warrior, leader of the Sentinels

Viviana Rowan: the Bronze Lady, Theronai, bonded to Neal Etan

Hope Serrien: Logan Athar's mate

Cole Shepherd: blooded human

Alexander Siah: Sanguinar

Paul Sloane: Theronai warrior, bonded to Andra Madison

Carmen Taite: blooded human, Gerai, cousin to Vance and Slade Taite

Slade Taite: blooded human, Gerai, cousin to Carmen, brother to Vance

Vance Taite: blooded human, Gerai, cousin to Carmen, brother to Slade

Zach Talon: Theronai warrior, bonded to Lexi Johns

Iain Terra: Theronai warrior, bonded to Jackie Patton

Morgan Valens: Theronai warrior

Zillah: Synestryn lord

Chapter 1

"That woman needs to be restrained or someone is going to get hurt."

Joseph did his best to stay focused on what the concerned human parents were saying, rather than on just how much the idea of restraining Lyka Phelan appealed to him. "I'm sure she's being careful with her lessons."

"Our son broke his arm," said the mother, Joann, her lips tight with irritation.

"I'll see to it that one of the Sanguinar heals him."

"Lyka already took care of that, but that brings us to the next issue," said the father, Darren.

"Which is?" asked Joseph, bracing himself for yet another problem added onto the already impressive pile he had on his plate today.

His patience had worn thin. His head throbbed and his chest ached with the strain of the magic growing inside him. Unlike the men under his command, who were free to roam, he was usually trapped behind a desk, unable to enjoy the physical exertion of battle. Without even that small outlet, the power he stored within his body continued to build, causing the kind of pain he could have only imagined a few years ago. The one thing that would ease this ache was to find a woman who could wield that power, channel it out of him and free him from it.

And he sure as hell wasn't going to find her sitting behind a desk inside a fortified compound, deep in the rural Midwest.

The human woman sitting across from him tightened her lips until they were bloodless with irritation. "Lyka didn't even ask us if we wanted one of the Sanguinar treating our son. She had no right to let one of those leeches touch him."

Joseph bit back the harsh reprimand that surged behind his teeth at the woman's use of the derogatory term for the Sanguinar. "When we found your son hovering at death's door, you didn't seem to mind the Sanguinar healing him."

"That was before we found out what one of them did," said Darren. "We always knew they were a shady lot, but stealing children? It's unthinkable."

Since word had gotten out that one of the Sanguinar had turned traitor and stolen a human woman and her child to use their lives as a bargaining chip with the enemy, everyone inside the walls of Dabyr had become suspicious of them.

Every day fewer and fewer humans offered the Sanguinar their blood to help fuel their efforts to heal the sick and injured. And every day the Sanguinar grew weaker.

"We found the traitor," said Joseph, with as much patience as he could muster. "He's dead. He can't hurt anyone ever again."

"You found *one* traitor," said the man. "For all you know, there could be more of them waiting for an opportunity to strike. They can read minds, you know. Twist your thoughts and make you believe they're telling the truth."

Joseph pulled in a deep breath and let it out slowly. Pain stabbed behind his eyes, and the lighting in his office felt as if it were slicing his retinas. "I understand your concern, but I assure you that Tynan has used all his massive mind-reading ability to ensure that none of his people were working with the traitor."

"And you believe him? Our son can't leave this place. If he does, Synestryn demons will find him and he'll be as good as dead. This is the only place he'll ever be safe. That's what you promised us when we agreed to live here."

"Your son *is* safe here," said Joseph. "The Sanguinar aren't going to hurt him." He'd had this conversation or one just like it a hundred times in the past week. At least that's how it seemed.

All he wanted to do was get back to his job. Lead the Theronai in the war against the demons. Keep the humans under his care safe and sound. Calming worried parents was not in his job description, but it was all he seemed to be doing lately.

"Our son broke his arm," said the woman slowly, as if Joseph were a small, stupid child. "That's hardly safe."

Most of the nearly five hundred people Joseph housed at Dabyr were reasonable folks. They were grateful for the safety the magically enhanced walls around the compound provided. Unfortunately, these two people had forgotten the hysterical terror they'd faced three years earlier, when their son had been stolen by demons and rescued before he'd been exsanguinated for the traces of magical blood flowing through his veins. They'd forgotten how desperate they'd been at the time, and how willing they'd been to do whatever it took to keep their baby safe.

But Joseph hadn't forgotten. He knew what they would face outside these walls, and the fate that awaited their son if Joseph wasn't able to appease them.

Synestryn demons wouldn't care what the boy's parents thought or felt. All they cared about was draining as much blood as possible from their son before tossing his remains to their beasts to pick his bones clean.

It took considerable effort, but Joseph managed not to growl at them when he said, "Perhaps you'd be happier if your son didn't attend Lyka's class. It's not required, you know."

"But he loves it," said Darren. "The only way he'll stop whining at us is if you shut the class down altogether."

"Surely the other parents have complained," added the mother.

"There aren't a whole lot of parents here," Joseph felt the need to remind them. "Most of them died trying to protect their children. You are among the lucky ones."

The way her mouth turned down made it clear she didn't see herself as lucky right now. "It's teaching violence. The kids are too young to learn such horrible methods."

"I'm sure it's not all that bad," said Joseph. "A little self-defense training is a good idea."

The parents shared a meaningful look before the father spoke up. "A little self-defense? That's what she told you she was teaching?"

"It is."

"Have you watched her lessons?" asked the mother. "At all?"

Joseph shook his head. "No, but I have a feeling that's next on my list of things to do." The list was already a mile long, but the lure of seeing Lyka again was one he couldn't resist.

He dismissed the parents and went to the outdoor play area that had been set up for the kids. By the time he made it through the twisting halls of Dabyr, he'd been stopped three times and told about new issues that demanded his attention.

The grinding pain behind his eyes—his constant companion—grew worse with each problem heaped on the pile. He wasn't even halfway through his twenty-year term as leader of his people, and the strain was already tearing at him. He bowed under the weight of all the lives that depended on him to be smarter, stronger and deadlier than their enemy. Of all the hundreds of things he needed to accomplish, dealing with a petty human squabble over a children's class should have been so far down on his list of priorities that he couldn't even see it.

And yet here he was, drawn to it—not by a sense of duty to the human parents, but instead by the idea of seeing the female Slayer who took up far too much space in his thoughts.

Lyka's class was nearing its end by the time he finally made it outside. The sun was high overhead, making her hair look like spun gold. Even though she was a Slayer and practically immune to the cold, she still covered everything but her face and hands under a layer of clothing. The fabric clung to her skin, outlining curves that had kept Joseph awake and aching more nights than he cared to admit with the need to touch her. He'd never once laid a finger on her in any way, not even in greeting. Every time he got within arm's reach of her, she would back off so fast he was afraid she'd hurt herself trying to get away from him.

He would have taken it personally if not for the fact that she treated all of his men the same way. No one got close to Lyka Phelan. Period.

She was a Slayer, sent here to serve as a hostage to guarantee that her brother would honor the treaty struck with Joseph. In return, Joseph had sent Carmen, the young woman he'd claimed as his own daughter, to stay with the Slayers. It was an old-fashioned way of ensuring both sides upheld the treaty, but one that had worked well for centuries.

And like it or not, there really was no other choice but to end their hostilities. Their two races had been at odds for too long, sacrificing too much time and too many resources fighting each other when their real enemy was growing stronger every day.

If Joseph was honest with himself, having Lyka here was no hardship. As touchy as she could be, the distraction she offered was a welcome respite from the weight of his station.

The high glass ceilings and openness of the central dining and living areas had been recently renovated. The colors were earthier now, with plenty of warm golden tones and rich, gleaming wood. Colorful tablecloths brightened the dining hall, where people gathered over meals or a cup of coffee. The magically enhanced glass let in sunshine without the risk of its summoning the Solarc's deadly wardens if it touched the skin of a Sanguinar. Cozy alcoves were filled with comfortable leather sofas where kids could study, watch TV or play games.

The second he was through the glass doors leading outside, he saw her. As always, Lyka drew his complete attention, glowing like sunshine incarnate. He wasn't sure why such a prickly woman would appeal to him on such a deep level, but there wasn't much he could do to stop it.

Heaven knew, he'd tried.

As he watched her talking to the kids, the searing pressure behind his eyes began to fade. There was something magical about a beautiful woman, and Lyka was about as beautiful as they came. Long golden hair. Soft golden skin. Bright golden eyes. He couldn't stare at her too long without feeling the need to shield his eyes from the glow.

Every move she made was filled with the sinuous grace of her kind. She took after her mother, showing off decidedly feline attributes beyond her catlike eyes. There was an alertness about her—a kind of intense awareness of the people around her. He knew that if he got to within twenty yards of her, she'd sense his presence.

He didn't want that yet. He liked looking at her too much for her to know he was doing so. Maybe staring at her wasn't appropriate, but he couldn't seem to help himself. And he sure as hell wasn't about to tell her that she was so beautiful that merely watching her had the power to ease his pain.

He only wished he could find a way to stop wanting her. There was nothing quite like groping a man's sister to ruin a perfectly good peace treaty.

As he continued to watch, he realized that she was directing children in the open play area, though what was going on there was like no form of play he'd ever seen.

The kids were grouped by size. The largest four were in the center of a clearing, being watched by several smaller children. The big kids were clustered together, snarling at one another and grappling for supremacy as they tried to knock one another out of the rope bound-

ary laid out around them. They used teeth and fingernails, elbows and knees. The blows were real, leaving
behind both bruises and blood.

It was a small wonder that a broken arm had been the
worst of the damage these kids had suffered—at least
the worst Joseph knew of.

Lyka stood at the sidelines, shouting instructions to
the kids. After a few seconds, she put two fingers in her
mouth and let out a shrill whistle. "Time's up!"

The kids stopped what they were doing and scrambled to line up at attention. One of them was limping. All
of them were bloodied, even the young girl who'd been
fighting right alongside the boys.

Joseph's first instinct was to rush over and see to their
wounds, but he forced himself to stay where he was, out
of Lyka's sight. It was the only way he was going to see
exactly what she did when he wasn't watching.

Lyka strolled in front of the kids, studying them. She
lifted the girl's arm, inspecting her wounds. One of the
boys raised the hem of his shirt to show her where he'd
been bloodied. After she was done looking at them, she
pointed at each of them as she counted. "Four, three,
two, one."

The boy who'd been labeled one thrust his fist in the
air, jumping in victory. The girl beamed at her second
place, while the other two boys were clearly unhappy
with their ranking.

Lyka addressed the rest of the class. "What did Hank
do right?" she asked. "Why did he win?"

The kids started discussing moves and strikes, but
Lyka deftly steered the conversation more toward battle
tactics and the combatants' traits.

"He wasn't afraid," said one of the kids—a new girl
who'd only recently arrived at Dabyr.

Lyka turned to Hank. "Were you afraid?" she asked.

"Yes, ma'am. Mary's got a wicked bite."

The kids laughed, but Lyka kept going. "He didn't let his fear make him lose. We're all afraid sometimes. The key is not letting it control us. Fear is just a bunch of chemicals tricking your brain. The good news is they can make you stronger, faster. All you have to do is let them."

"But it's not the same," said a boy about ten years old, with a messy mop of dark curls. "Mary isn't one of the Synestryn. They bite for real. And they're poisonous."

"True," said Lyka. "That's why I tell you all to fight like you mean it. Don't hold back, because one of these days, you might be fighting for your life. You get strong here so you can survive out there when no one is around to save you."

Joseph braced himself, waiting for the kids to start crying, for their chins to wobble in fear or their eyes to shine with tears. Every one of them had suffered at the hands of the demons. Some had lost their parents and siblings. A few had been held hostage by the Synestryn for months, tortured and terrorized. Surely being told in such blunt terms that they might have to fight the demons on their own one day had to be scaring them shitless.

And yet not one of them so much as trembled.

"When I get big," said one little girl, "I'm going to chop their heads off with a sword, just like the Theronai do."

Lyka grinned. "I'm sure you will, but for now let's just stick to your bare hands and teeth. I don't think the Sanguinar can reattach your classmates' severed heads quite as easily as they heal teeth marks." She turned back to the four kids who'd been fighting. "Speaking of which, Logan and Hope are waiting for you inside. Go get yourselves patched up."

They took off, the limping boy trying to keep up like a trooper.

"The rest of you get a good dinner and go to sleep early. We have a lot of work to do tomorrow. Final exams are coming soon. You all need to be ready."

The kids started to race off back toward the main building.

Lyka raised her voice, shouting after them. "And no fighting outside of class, or you're benched for a week."

The kids all cleared out, leaving Lyka to pick up the rope that had been laid out to mark their sparring area. She hadn't seen Joseph yet, and that was just as well. He had no idea how he was going to deal with what he'd just witnessed.

But he did have to deal with it. Shut her down. Keep her from upsetting more parents, or, worse yet, traumatizing one of the children.

A cold breeze swept past him, ruffling the hair at the nape of his neck.

Lyka sniffed the air and froze in the act of winding the rope around her forearm.

He wondered if she'd ever let him tie her to his bed with it, binding her there so he could get his fill of her without her darting off like a frightened rabbit. He could finally get close enough to see if she smelled half as good as she looked, if her skin was even close to being as silky smooth as it appeared. She'd fight him—of that there was no doubt—but once she wore herself out, he was almost certain he could find a way to make her purr.

As soon as the thought entered his mind, he banished it. The leader of the Theronai didn't restrain and fuck the baby sister of the leader of the Slayers. Not unless he wanted an all-out war on his hands to add to the one he already had with the Synestryn.

Her gaze met his. Her shoulders tensed, moving up toward her ears. "Spying on me?"

"A little. There have been some complaints about your class. I wanted to check it out for myself."

The clouds overhead parted, allowing sunshine to spill over her. He was once again stunned by just how beautiful she was. Her pale golden eyes caught and held the sunlight, making them look like they were glowing from within. Her pupils constricted until only a narrow oval remained, showing off proof of the Slayer blood flowing through her veins.

"And?" she asked. "What did you think?"

He'd always been a diplomatic man, but it was a stretch to keep his mind sharp and focused on his words when his body was responding in such an acute way. It had been a long time since he'd wanted a woman, but he was definitely making up for lost time now. As cold as it was outside, his blood was pumping hot, bringing a fine sweat to his brow as he struggled to keep his cock under control.

It took him several seconds to word his response carefully. "I can see why there was concern."

She muttered under her breath. "Fucking pussy adult humans."

"Excuse me?"

She glared at him and spoke slowly and clearly. "Fucking. Pussy. Humans. If they don't want their kids to get eaten, they should pull their heads out of their asses long enough to teach them how to fight. The Synestryn demons aren't going to stand back while a kid runs off to let mommy kiss his boo-boos. They're going to tear the meat from his bones and use them for toothpicks."

The truth of her words only made them that much more appalling. "Is that what you told his parents?"

"Would you rather I have lied?"

Now he was stuck between agreeing with and encouraging her or lying himself. Instead he settled for, "That probably didn't win you any points for Teacher of the Year."

"Maybe not, but when I think about the work I do with these kids, I sleep fine at night."

And just like that, he could picture her in her bed, her golden hair spread across her sheets, her long, sleek body stretched out naked and warm beneath the covers. With the coiled rope dangling from her hand, it was all he could do not to add that particular prop to the already potent mix of his inappropriate fantasies.

He had no idea what it was about this woman that made him ache for her, but he did. All the way down to his bones.

Joseph exerted his substantial will and dragged his mind back to where it belonged. "Those children got hurt, Lyka. They were bleeding. You can't let it happen again."

"I made sure that there were two Sanguinar waiting in the wings to heal them. I know the kids were in pain, but it will help toughen them up. Besides, they need to know how to fight, and no one else is bothering to teach them."

"We make sure they get a good education."

"Sure you do. They'll all be able to do calculus in their heads while the demons rip their throats out. A lot of good it will do them."

"You're scaring the parents."

"Good. They should be scared. Their kids are demon food. If these humans stopped for even one second and thought about it, they'd realize that what I'm doing is right. I'm trying to keep the kids alive. Give them a fighting chance."

"I'm sorry, but I can't let you keep teaching them to fight like this. It's too dangerous for them and too upsetting for their parents."

"You said I could teach a class. If I got a sponsor to make sure I wasn't brainwashing them into siding with we evil Slayers, you said I could do this. Are you going back on your word, Theronai?"

"I never agreed to this," he said, waving his hand at the bloodstained dirt. "I can't believe you found anyone who would think this is a good idea."

Her pupils narrowed, giving her a decidedly feline appearance. "Are you calling me a liar?"

"Put away your claws, kitten. All I mean is that I'm wondering exactly what your syllabus looks like. Does your sponsor know what you teach?"

She took a step toward him before stopping herself. Her hands balled into fists, and her voice went lethally soft. "These kids have had their lives stolen from them. They feel weak and powerless. They're trapped here, with no hope of ever leaving, and as nice as the accommodations may be at Dabyr, it's still just a comfy prison. What I'm giving them is hope—hope that they might survive another run-in with the demons. Hope that maybe one day they can walk out of these walls and have some kind of a real life. If that bothers you or anyone else here, then that's just too fucking bad. These kids need me, and I'm not giving up on them just because a couple of parents are too scared to see reality."

"I'm not saying you can't teach them. Just teach them not to break the skin. Stop leaving bruises and breaking bones."

"That's the way I was taught. Are you saying that our Slayer ways aren't good enough for your precious humans?"

"These kids aren't Slayers. They're human. They don't heal as fast as you do. They're easier to break."

"That's why I've bargained with Logan to heal them."

The idea of Lyka giving anything to a man that stunningly beautiful rubbed Joseph the wrong way. "What was the bargain?" he asked, his voice rougher than he'd intended.

"None of your business."

"Everything you do here is my business. You're my guest."

"Guest? More like your prisoner."

"You agreed to stay of your own free will."

"That's a bit of a stretch. My brother convinced me it was the only way our races would survive. We form an alliance. You keep me here as a prisoner to guarantee his good behavior, just like Carmen staying with him guarantees yours. If I'd been even a little stronger and able to best my brother in combat, he'd be the one here and I'd be out there, running our people, free and happy."

The thought that she was unhappy here gave him pause and deflated the head of steam he'd built up. "You're not happy?"

"Everything I do is suspect. I'm constantly being watched by your men. And when they're not around, there are so many damn cameras in this place, I feel like I'm getting a colonoscopy just walking down the hallways."

"After what happened with Connal—"

She held up her hand. "I know, I know. There was a traitor in your midst, and you don't want a replay. I get it. Just don't stand there looking like I kicked your puppy when I tell you that I don't want to be here. It's not my home. It never will be."

"I've tried to make it feel like home for you."

"You've given me a beautiful suite, comfortable surroundings, all the food I can eat and something to do with my time. I'm grateful for that. Really, I am. But those things mean nothing to a woman who has no choice but to stay behind these walls. Like it or not, I'm your prisoner."

"I don't want you to feel that way."

"Then stop watching my every move. Back off and let me teach the kids my way. If you give me a chance, you might even like the results. The kids sure as hell do."

He knew he was making a mistake the second he opened his mouth, but the desire to see her content was far stronger than he could fight. "I'm not making any promises, but I'll talk to the children, the parents and your sponsor. I'll let you know what I decide in a couple of days."

"Until then I can teach?" she asked, sounding hopeful.

"Teach? Yes. Allow them to shed blood? No."

"You're just stringing me along, aren't you? Pretending to consider it when you've already made up your mind."

Joseph refused to budge. "Two days, Lyka. Come to my office and I'll give you my decision."

"And expect me to obey like a good little girl?"

He took a step forward, watching her nearly trip over her own feet to back away from him. "That's exactly what I expect, kitten. You're honor bound to follow my rules for as long as you're inside my walls."

Her eyes narrowed in fury. "You're as bad as my brother."

He grinned. "I'll take that as a compliment."

"Don't," she said. "I nearly killed him once, and I *love* him. You, Theronai, don't stand a chance."

Chapter 2

The second Joseph had left Lyka alone, she let out a long sigh of relief.

She'd survived another close encounter with the man and managed to keep her distance. He hadn't touched her. He didn't know what she really was.

She didn't know how much longer she could keep her secret, but every day that went by without one of the Theronai learning it was another victory. She'd take every one she could get.

She watched him walk away, admiring the way his jeans hugged his muscular ass. She couldn't see the magical sword strapped on his belt—it was invisible until drawn—but she could detect the slight dip in his waistband where its weight hung. The Theronai were deadly with their blades, and that was the kind of thing that made a girl like Lyka squirm with want.

It didn't help that Joseph was nearly six and a half feet of hard, kick-ass warrior. Sure, he was their leader and spent most of his time behind a desk, but that didn't mean he wasn't deadly. She was certain that if the shit hit the fan, he'd use every bit of that muscular bulk he carried around to thwack some demon heads clean off.

It was enough to make Lyka wake in a sweat at night, wet and desperate for those rough hands of his to ease her need.

As if she'd ever let that happen.

The man got under her skin, making it itch and tingle. She kept having to remind herself that he was the enemy—or at least had been until very recently.

Sure, it was a bad idea to be fighting a war on two fronts. And yes, things were easier now that the two races had teamed up, but that didn't mean she had to like it. Everyone else got to enjoy the benefits of the shiny new treaty while she was stuck here, unable to fight alongside her people.

Not fair. Not even close.

But that was life for you. Nothing was fair, which was exactly why she was pouring her heart and soul into teaching those kids how to survive. Fighting wasn't pretty. It wasn't civilized. What use was it trying to make the kids pretend that it was?

Then again, there was some value in pretending. She'd been doing so for weeks and it had served her well.

She finished picking up the gear and headed inside.

The unbelievably beautiful Logan and his even more stunning wife, Hope, were waiting inside the doors. The kids had all been tended to and had gone on their way, which meant that two Sanguinar were waiting for her.

Not a good sign.

"What's up?" she asked.

Logan threaded his fingers through Hope's in a move so casual, Lyka didn't think he was even aware of the act. "Joseph wasn't pleased that we were healing the children. Or, more accurately, he wasn't pleased that they needed healing."

"I know. His royal highness already expressed his displeasure with me."

"We can't afford to upset anyone right now," said Hope, sliding her honey-blond hair behind her ear. "Everyone is too uneasy about what Connal did."

Logan's expression darkened with anger. "Even we Sanguinar still can't believe what he did. Stealing a child? It's unconscionable. But she's right. We have to ease the fears that run rampant here. Nothing we do can upset anyone."

"So you're just going to bend over and do what Joseph says?" asked Lyka.

"Aren't you?" said Hope.

"I want to make nice, but it's hard to do when he's so very wrong."

"He told us he would let us know his decision in a couple of days," said Logan.

"And he expects us all to sit on our hands until then? I don't think so."

"Whatever you're planning isn't worth a war," said Logan.

"I'm saving lives. Every lesson those kids learn might be the one that keeps them alive someday."

"And what about all the lives we'll lose if the treaty between your people and the Theronai is broken? What about all the young Slayers who will be down one powerful group of allies because you couldn't wait two days for Joseph to think about what you're doing and realize you're right? Give the man a chance to see your side of things. Convince him to rule in your favor."

As much as Lyka hated it, Logan was right. She hadn't thought her actions all the way through. As usual, she was letting her hot-blooded Slayer side rule her emotions. "How am I supposed to do that? I've already stated my case. He knows where I stand. The ball is in his court now."

Logan scoffed. "Hardly. If you think you've made all the moves available to you, then you have a lot to learn."

Always open to learn new strategies, Lyka asked, "What do you suggest?"

"He's a man. You're an attractive woman."

"And?" asked Lyka.

Hope hid a grin. "He's telling you to use your feminine wiles to sway Joseph to your way of thinking. A man is much more inclined to do what a woman wants if he thinks it might get him laid."

Lyka let out a bark of laughter. "Really? That's your big play? Let him fuck me?"

"That's not what she said," said Logan. "I'd never suggest exchanging sexual favors for a ruling on your behalf. That's not to say you shouldn't do it. I'd simply never suggest it, for fear such advice would come back to haunt me."

Lyka shook her head. "I'm not sleeping with Joseph just to get my way."

"You don't have to. Just make him think you might."

"Hell, no," said Lyka. "I'm not teasing him or leading him on, either." She couldn't get that close. He might touch her. She didn't know if he'd be able to tell what she was if he did that, but she wasn't taking any chances.

"It's not like that," said Hope. "All you have to do is befriend him. Make him like you. He'll want to make you happy if you're friends."

Lyka shook her head. "It's no wonder everyone is suspicious of you guys. You ride that gray area pretty hard."

"There's nothing wrong with what we're suggesting.

And, as you said, what you're doing is saving lives. Is spending a few hours with Joseph really such a hardship that it's not worth the lives of those children?"

"Now who's playing dirty?" she asked. "Why the hell do you care so much whether or not I get to teach my classes? What's in it for you? You do all this healing without asking for my blood to fuel your efforts, and all I have to do in return is make sure that it's either you two or Tynan who patches them up. Aren't you supposed to demand payment in blood?"

"Hope and I sustain each other now. We have far less need for blood than the rest of our kind."

"That doesn't answer my question. What's in it for you?"

The two shared a secret look that spoke volumes— volumes Lyka couldn't even begin to understand.

Finally, Logan spoke, but it was clear he was choosing his words carefully. "Most of these children are wounded beyond what you can see. Their emotional scars run deep. Every time we heal their bodies, it gives us the chance to touch their minds and work toward healing that part of them as well. It's a slow, delicate process— one made much faster by the sheer frequency of opportunities to heal that your little lessons provide. Baby steps, as it were."

"That's it? You're doing all of this as some kind of magical therapy?"

"These children are blooded. The lives of our kind depend on them growing up and having children of their own. Without a continuation of their bloodlines, the Sanguinar will starve. Emotionally damaged children do not tend to live long enough to become parents. And those that do often pass on their scars. If we heal them now, we prevent all of that pain and loss."

Lyka stared at the couple. "There's more to it than that. What aren't you telling me?"

"Part of our arrangement with you was that you don't ask a lot of questions. This is where that clause activates."

"Fine. I'm being too nosy. I get it. Just promise me you're not doing anything that will hurt the kids."

"I swear it," said Logan.

"So do I," added Hope.

The weight of both vows settled over Lyka, reassuring her. They were bound to their word now. That alone was enough to put her mind at ease.

"Okay. Let's go back to the problem at hand. Clearly you two know Joseph better than I do. What do I do to sway his decision without resorting to naked time?"

Logan smiled, and it made him almost too beautiful to look at. "That, my dear, is simple. If you do what we say, he'll be putty in your hands by midnight."

The idea of getting Joseph in her hands was far more appealing than she dared admit, which was all the warning she needed to tread carefully.

One misstep and she could singlehandedly send their races back to war against each other. And she would be trapped behind enemy lines.

At sundown, Tynan eased from his bed in his suite beneath Dabyr.

He was ravenous. His bones felt ancient and brittle. His vision was clouded over with a hazy red film that nearly blinded him. His skin was fever hot, burning with fatigue that no amount of sleep could remedy.

He needed blood. Gallons of it. Oceans of it. He needed to gulp it down and let it ease the grinding hunger that prowled through his limbs, weakening him.

He swayed on his feet, flailing to find something to grasp.

"Easy, brother," said Logan, grabbing his arm.

Tynan hadn't even known his Sanguinar brother was here. His senses had dulled to the point that he couldn't even detect the presence of one of his own kind a few inches away.

Logan eased him back to sit on the bed. He pressed his wrist against Tynan's mouth and willed his skin to open.

Sweet, hot blood flowed over his tongue, rousing the hungry beast within him. He grabbed Logan's wrist, holding it tight enough to break bone if the man tried to pull away. Power surged through him, relieving the parched cells rattling around in his veins.

"That's enough," came a soft, feminine voice.

Hope. Logan's mate.

His skin closed, blocking the flow of blood. Tynan tore at the man's skin with his teeth, but he wasn't fast enough. Wasn't strong enough.

Logan ripped his arm away, flinging Tynan down onto the bed.

Both men were panting. Tynan's vision had cleared enough for him to see his brother slumped on the floor. Hope was over him, her delicate throat pressed to his mouth.

"I'm sorry," said Tynan, once again himself.

Sadness shone in her clear eyes. "We understand. You're doing all you can."

And he was.

Joseph had ordered him to scour the mind of every Sanguinar housed under Dabyr's roof, searching for signs of treachery. Most of his kind abhorred the violation of their privacy, resisting his efforts. Some intentionally. Others without even realizing just how thick and wide their mental barriers were. In both cases, the sheer power it took to overcome those defenses left Tynan weak. Utterly depleted.

If not for Logan's daily dose of blood, Tynan would have already failed in his task. And if he did that, his people could be banished from this place of refuge with nowhere to hide from the sun.

He feared that if that happened, the weaker members of his race would succumb to the lure of the Synestryn and the power their tainted blood could provide.

Logan stood, positioning himself between Tynan and his mate. "Is it enough?"

He nodded, giving no voice to his lie. "Thank you."

"Two more of our kind returned home after you retired. They're waiting for you in their quarters."

Tynan had no choice but to do his duty, but he couldn't face it yet. "Any other news?"

"I checked on the Theronai pregnancies. All is well there."

"That is a relief."

"Madoc isn't pleased. He thinks we're meddling."

"Madoc is never pleased. As long as he doesn't break your neck, assume he still likes you. What else?"

"Ronan still seeks the woman who saved his life. He regrets his inability to return."

"Did you tell him it wasn't a request?"

"I did. He didn't seem concerned."

"Do we know anything about this woman he's seeking?"

"She apparently enjoys fast cars. Ronan is unable to catch up with her."

"But he can still sense where she's gone?"

"He can."

"We need to find her. If she's anything like Hope . . ."

Logan tightened his hold on his mate. "Ronan is aware of the stakes."

"Anything else? Any sign of Torr?"

"No. He is still missing. Many of the Theronai have been searching for him ever since his disappearance."

Tynan ran his fingers through his hair. "Have you heard anything from those working on Project Lullaby?"

"No. Everyone is being particularly cautious since Connal's betrayal."

With good reason. If the Theronai found out that the Sanguinar had been matchmaking blooded humans and encouraging them to produce offspring, they wouldn't be pleased. With as little Athanasian blood as there was left on the planet, the Sanguinar had no choice but to resort to some unorthodox methods to strengthen the remaining bloodlines. They saw it as necessary coercion, ensuring that the humans they convinced to help them lived long and happy lives filled with many children.

The Theronai would doubtlessly see it as interfering with the free will of humans and react accordingly. In their centuries-long history together, more than one Sanguinar head had rolled for lesser infractions.

"We can't slow down our efforts," said Tynan. "There is no time to waste."

"We're all aware of the giant ticking clock, brother. I'm sure that the men are doing everything they can to further our efforts. That may be why some of them have refused to communicate with us. Once they do, they know you'll be forced to order them home for interrogation. That will waste valuable time and energy that none of you have."

Tynan nodded, praying Logan was right. "I'm scheduled to meet with Joseph tonight to report on my progress."

Hope smiled. "You might want to arrive a little late."

"Why is that?"

"Joseph has a date."

Tynan blinked. "Excuse me?"

"It's not really a date," said Logan.

Hope lifted her brows. "Yes, it is. Haven't you seen the way he looks at her?"

Ah. Lyka. "But she hates him," said Tynan.

"*Hate* is a strong word. And he now has something she wants. We simply gave her some pointers on how she might get it."

"You know this will end badly, don't you?" asked Tynan.

"It's possible," said Logan. "But I, for one, plan to enjoy the show."

Chapter 3

Joseph was still in his office, working, long after sundown. He should have stopped hours ago, but his mind kept going back to Lyka, making every task he did take twice as long as necessary. Because of that, he still had hours of work left to do before he could rest.

His stomach rumbled, reminding him that he couldn't remember the last time he'd eaten. The drawer where he usually kept snacks was empty, telling him that he'd been skipping far too many meals lately.

Not that he had much choice. There was so much to do to keep a place like this running. Even the help he had from a dozen humans wasn't enough to keep everyone here clothed and fed. On top of that, he was fighting a war against the Synestryn, working to lead his men to where they needed to be. One wrong move on his part, and countless humans would die.

The map on the far wall reminded him of just how much ground they had left to cover. Even though they cleared the demons out of every cave they found, collapsing each behind them so no more nasties could find shelter from the sun, it was never enough. There were always more caves, always more demons to kill.

The threat that the walls here at Dabyr would be breached was a constant worry. Even though Lexi had magically reinforced the stone perimeter that kept the Synestryn at bay, she was only one woman, fueled by one man. Their combined power was formidable but not limitless.

After centuries of sterility, Theronai babies were once again being conceived. They would be born here soon, and that meant there could be no more breaches in security. More now than ever, Dabyr was a tempting target. If he were the enemy, he'd be searching for some way past the walls.

Or through them.

Explosives had been used against Dabyr before. There was no way to know just how much damage the walls would take before they buckled, even with Lexi's efforts.

On top of that, Joseph had just learned that one of his men had been zapped away through a portal. Nicholas had seen Torr disappear with his own eyes. No one knew where he'd gone, who'd stolen him or whether he was even alive. He was completely out of reach, leaving Joseph helpless to offer any kind of assistance.

It was that sick sense of helplessness that made him wish he could be out there fighting rather than trapped behind a desk, dealing with all the things that kept hundreds of people clean, clothed, fed and protected. What he did here was important, but without some kind of physical outlet for his magic, he wasn't going to survive much longer. The leaves on his lifemark—the living image of a tree that stretched across his chest, shoulder and down onto his thigh—were falling faster every week.

Too fast.

Once his lifemark was bare, his soul would rapidly decay, twisting him into a selfish, violent shadow of his former self. He'd end his life before it got that bad, but he knew that doing so would only leave one of his brothers in this position: burdened by duty, bound by honor and tied behind a desk with no hope of finding the woman who could save his life before he, too, succumbed to the destructive power of the magic he housed.

Joseph's skin tingled in warning an instant before he heard the light knock on his open office door. Lyka stood there, a food tray in hand.

She was so beautiful, all golden and glowing, that he forgot to breathe.

"I didn't see you at dinner," she said. "I thought you might have been stuck here, working late again."

His mouth watered, but not for anything that was on the tray. He wanted her. Bad. In that intense kind of way that would render him stupid if he wasn't careful and completely in control of his emotions.

"Thank you," he said, letting none of his want come through his tone. He was polite, but that was it. Calm. Cool. Not fighting a raging hard-on at all. "That was kind of you."

She stepped over the threshold and he caught a glimpse of golden skin beneath her skirt. It was modest, falling well below her knee, but that didn't change the fact that her legs were obviously bare beneath the fabric. He'd never seen her in anything other than long pants, so this change of attire was both surprising and ridiculously arousing. He could imagine the warmth of her skin beneath his palms if he got the chance to slide his hand over her knee and up her thigh.

Not that he'd ever indulge in such fantasies. Down

that path lay one pissed-off Slayer brother with the power to inflict far too much damage. No, thank you.

"Come to bribe me with food?" he asked, teasing.

She smiled as she set the tray on the conference table that filled one side of his office. "It *is* steak. What else could it be but a bribe?"

"You should have opted for a salad. Way less obvious."

"I've never been a subtle kind of woman." She shrugged one slender shoulder, drawing his eye to the delicate line of her collarbones. The shirt she wore wasn't cut low, but it did show off more skin than he'd ever seen before — smooth, golden skin that appeared too flawless to be real.

He forced his eyes up to hers before she could catch him leering.

She removed the metal covers from the plates, revealing dinner for two.

"You're going to join me?" he asked, shocked that she'd want to be this close to him.

"I'm trying to win you over. I can't exactly do that from my suite. Unless, of course, my absence is worth something to you?" She sounded hopeful, as if she wanted him to dismiss her.

"Not at all." He watched as she positioned two chairs as far apart as the space would allow. "But I have to warn you that while I appreciate your efforts, I can't be bribed. I'll make my decision based on what I think is right, not on what you feed me." *Or what you wear.*

"Would you rather I leave? I'm happy to go if you'd rather eat alone."

"No." He rushed toward her, everything in him demanding that he keep her here for as long as possible. The pain behind his eyes was easier to bear when she was here. He didn't understand why that was—some kind of innate Slayer magic, no doubt—but he accepted the gift gladly and refused to let it go until he had no other choice.

She shied away, retreating to the open door before he reached her.

Joseph stopped dead in his tracks and raised his hands. "I'm sorry. I didn't mean to scare you away."

Her spine straightened until she was standing tall and proud. "You couldn't scare me on your best day, Theronai."

"Then why do you always back away when I get close? Do you think I'm going to hurt you?"

She snorted. "I'd like to see you try."

He sighed. "Sheathe the claws, kitten. You don't have a thing to prove to me. Let's just sit down and pretend you can stand to be in the same room with me for more than two minutes."

She looked longingly at the door for so many seconds that he thought she might just bolt and be done with it. Instead, she surprised him by coming to the table, smoothing her skirt, and sitting down as if the disastrously cluttered confines of his office were the finest restaurant in the state.

"You know I only came here so I could convince you to let me keep teaching my class, right?" she asked.

"I assumed as much."

She picked up her steak knife and gripped it in her fist. He could see her wavering on the edge of indecision, as if she had something she wanted to say.

"Just spit it out, Lyka. Whatever you've got to say, say it."

She stared at him for a second, sucking him into the glowing depths of her eyes. He got so lost looking at her, he was almost surprised when she finally spoke. "I was told to dress like this and put on makeup and perfume so you'd want to fuck me."

He choked on the bite of steak he'd taken, coughing to clear his throat. "Wow. Okay. Points for honesty, Lyka."

"I thought it was a stupid idea, too."

It wasn't stupid. Not even close. In fact, whoever had given her that advice had probably seen Joseph watching her. He was going to have to be a lot more careful about letting his desire for this woman show in public. "I can't let you sway my mind, no matter how beautiful you are."

"And I can't sit here and suck up to you, leading you on and letting you think you're going to score." She hit him with a hard, golden gaze. "You're not."

"I honestly never thought it was a possibility." Though he wished like hell it was. Maybe sex would help him release some of his building power and ease his pain just a little. It worked for some of the men.

And sex with Lyka? It would probably blow him away. He'd wanted her for too long, and despite his best efforts, had built up quite a set of fantasies about her. They were all wildly inappropriate, and more than one of them was doubtlessly illegal, but he couldn't seem to purge his thoughts of her.

She rose to her feet. "I'll go and let you eat in peace, then. Sorry for wasting your time."

"I'd like it if you'd stay."

She frowned. "Why? I already told you I'm not going to fuck you."

"That doesn't mean you can't stay, does it? You are capable of sharing a meal, knowing that's all it will be, right?"

"Of course."

"Then sit and eat. Tell me about your work with the kids. I don't get to spend as much time as I'd like with them these days. It would be nice to hear how they're doing from someone who is pathologically incapable of sucking up to me."

She stared at him for a moment, considering his request. Slowly she set her plate down and lowered herself into her chair. "You want the truth?"

"Absolutely."

She gave him a nod. "Okay. You got it." She went on for an hour, giving him a detailed report about the strengths, weaknesses and progress of every child that had crossed her path. She outlined which ones she thought were emotionally stable and healthy, and which ones were on the verge of collapse or explosion. She explained her strategy for helping each one of them grow stronger and more confident.

By the time she was done talking, he was impressed by how much thought and care she'd put into her teaching. She wasn't just using her class to pass the time. She really wanted to help these kids. Her methods were different from what he was used to, but maybe there was some value in her way of doing things, however violent.

"What about the injuries?" he asked. "Isn't there some way of teaching them without damaging them?"

"They need to learn to deal with pain. They need to know they can push though it and keep functioning even after they're hurt. It might make the difference in a life-or-death situation."

"I hate knowing that they're in pain."

"So do I, but we have to face facts. These kids are never going to lead normal human lives. They'll always be one step away from being some demon's snack. And they know it. Every injury they get and work through teaches them that they can take more. Be tougher. Keep going. If you start adding in pads and helmets, they'll always think they need them to fight and freeze up if they're not available."

"But they're so young. If you were only teaching the teens, it wouldn't be as hard to swallow."

"And waste all those years helping them learn what they're capable of?" She shook her head. "By the time they're teens, it's too late. Their hormones are raging. They either think they're immortal or wish they were dead. Teaching them is like trying to teach a crazy person with no ears and genitals for brains."

They'd had more than one teen kill himself inside these walls—the ones who couldn't deal with the terror of what was done to them. Poor little Tori had been half-mad—violent and deranged—from what she'd suffered. And she'd had the benefit of being a Theronai—stronger than a human child would have been—but even she'd had to be sent away in the hopes that beings more powerful than the Sentinels could purge the demon blood from her veins and heal her.

"I'm not reinventing the wheel here, Joseph. This is how I was taught. We were forced to push our limits, take the pain, grow stronger. All the Slayers learn the same way."

"But these kids are human."

"So? If you stop telling them that's a limitation, maybe it will stop being one. I know you've taken a vow to protect humans, but if you just stop and think about it, you'll see that's exactly what I'm doing."

"Your ways are violent."

"But they work. Generations of Slayers have been raised exactly like this. And we're survivors. Fighters. Just like those kids need to be."

"What would your brother say?" asked Joseph.

She rolled her eyes. "Who cares? I stopped worrying about his opinion the minute he dropped me off on your doorstep."

"I care. He's the leader of your people. He was the one with the guts to walk into the home of his enemy, completely unarmed and naked, asking for a truce."

"With me draped over his shoulder," she added. "Don't forget that part. The bastard."

No chance of that. She'd been naked, too, though Andreas had gone to the trouble of wrapping her up in a sheet. To this day, Joseph still regretted not insisting that they unroll her and check for weapons.

"The point is," said Joseph, "that your brother is not the kind of man I want to piss off. I don't know a lot about him, but I'm fairly certain that if anything happened to you, it would be my balls getting ripped off first."

"A trick he learned from me," she said. "You should remember that."

"Is that a threat, kitten? Care to have a little sparring match of our own? Prove who has the bigger pair?" What the hell was he doing? He couldn't spar with her. What if he hurt her? What if he got his hands on her and couldn't let go?

"You think you can beat me?" she asked, teeth bared.

He couldn't seem to stay quiet. His mouth dug a deeper hole. "I know I can."

"You're out of practice. You spend all day sitting on your ass, doing paperwork and listening to people whine. Face it, Theronai. You've gone soft."

Joseph normally kept a tight hold on his anger. It didn't serve him well in his position of leadership. But right now he was furious, his blood heating with more than mere lust. He knew it was a mistake, but she got under his skin, and before he could stop himself, he was rising to her bait. "I'll show you soft."

He reached for her, planning to grab her hand and force her to feel his body. Sure, he spent long hours behind a desk, but his body was still toned, thanks to a set of kick-ass magical genes and the few sparring sessions he managed to fit into his schedule. And even if he didn't have a genetic advantage, he never would have let himself go soft and weak. Too many lives depended on him being able to protect them with fast, brutal violence when needed.

Before he could so much as wrap his fingers around her wrist, she darted away, scurrying out through his office door. "Don't you touch me. Don't you ever fucking touch me."

Joseph immediately realized what he was about to do and let his hand fall to his side. "I'm sorry, Lyka. I lost my head for a minute. It won't happen again."

"Damn right it won't." She inched down the hall, backing away from him. "Let me teach the class or not— I don't care anymore. If you want those kids to die, then it's on your head, not mine. I've done all I can unless you get out of my way."

Once she was out of reach, she turned and ran, her skirt flying out behind her.

Joseph went back to his office and slumped into his chair. He wanted to run after her so badly his guts ached, but he knew that if he did, he'd probably just freak her out more. Though, honestly, he wasn't sure how that was possible.

Had something happened to her that made her detest being touched? Or was it just Joseph she didn't want touching her?

That thought was like a kick in the balls.

He scoured his memory for some kind of pattern, and it became clear that it wasn't just him. She didn't let any of the grown men touch her.

The list of things that might make a woman skittish like that wasn't very long, but it was grim. Just the idea of someone hurting her was enough to make his hand stray to the hilt of his sword.

He needed to talk to Andreas. Find out what had happened to her so he could . . . what? Help her heal? Keep her from panicking? Warn the other men to stay the hell away from her?

He liked that last one. Too much.

Jealousy was a bad sign that his attraction to her had gone off the rails somewhere. It was one thing to think she was beautiful or even sexy as hell. It was a much different thing to want to possess her all for himself.

Not going to happen, he reminded himself for the hundredth time. *Put your dick in a drawer and get to work.*

His dick didn't cooperate, but he moved to the next stack of demands waiting for him and went to work.

Tomorrow, when she was calm, he'd apologize again for losing his temper and reaching for her. He would find some way to appease her so she could be happy here and maintain the peace between their peoples. And, last but not least, he would learn to look at her without wishing his cock was buried in her as deep as it could go.

Somehow.

It took less than fifteen minutes for him to realize that tomorrow wasn't going to be soon enough. He couldn't concentrate knowing she was upset. He had to go to her now. Make peace.

He shoved away from his desk and the mountain of work waiting for him and went to find Lyka.

Chapter 4

Lyka shivered, hugging herself as she huddled against the inside of the door to her moonlit suite.

Joseph had almost touched her.

His hand had been only inches from her wrist—so close she could feel the heat of his skin and a warning tingle of danger.

She scrubbed at the spot, but it did nothing to erase the memory of that strange sensation. It did even less to remove her from the danger that lurked here inside the plush, comfortable surroundings of Dabyr.

She knew what that tingle meant. She'd heard the stories all her life about the way Theronai recognized their mates. It wasn't through scent, like her kind, but through touch. When skin met skin, a man and woman could both feel a buzzing tingle that told them they were compatible—that the woman would be able to wield the power raging inside the man. That's when he would claim her. Collar her. Tie her to him irrevocably for the rest of their lives.

Lyka didn't want that. Not with Joseph. Not with anyone. She wanted to be with her own kind and choose a Slayer mate.

Or none at all.

She was tired of having the men around her decide what she could and couldn't do. Even her brother, who was enlightened for one of their kind, still believed in the old ways. He still believed he had a right to use her as a tool to end the war with the Theronai. He even had the gall to say she should be happy to be so useful—that she was saving the lives of their people by staying at Dabyr and behaving.

As if. Behaving wasn't her strong suit, and he damn well knew it.

And look where it had gotten her. She'd nearly been touched tonight by a man who could uncover her secret and destroy her life. If word got out that her mother had diluted her Slayer blood by screwing one of the Athanasians, no Slayer would want her. There were strict laws about breeding among her kind, and the children resulting from unapproved unions were often shunned. Sometimes even exiled.

She couldn't see Andreas doing that to his own sister, but it would be his right. No one would question him.

Maybe that's what he'd been trying to achieve by sending her here. Maybe he'd intended for her parentage to be discovered so she'd stay here and he wouldn't have to deal with her anymore. Heaven knew she hadn't been as easy to get along with as her mother had warned her to be.

Another shiver of fear raced through her, stealing all her warmth. What if Joseph had felt that tingle, too? What if he knew what she was and was on his way here right now to demand that she give up her life and start flinging magic around like some kind of freak?

It was possible. Terrifyingly possible.

A soft knock sounded on her door. "Lyka?"

Joseph. He was here, and the only reason she could think he'd come was because he knew what she was. Her secret was out. Life as she knew it was over.

Fear expanded in her chest until there was no room left to breathe. She tried to fight it, but her mother had warned of this moment far too often for Lyka to think she'd escape unscathed.

Don't let them know what you are, sweetheart. One of their kind will claim you and never let you go. You'll belong to the enemy. A slave to their power. Forever.

She couldn't let that happen. She'd seen the way Theronai women looked at their mates, dreamy-eyed and docile. They might have access to untold power, but the cost was far too high. No power was worth a lifetime of bondage to the enemy.

Lyka was a Slayer. She would always be a Slayer. No amount of tainted blood could change that.

"Are you in there?" asked Joseph. "All I want to do is talk. I won't even step inside."

She didn't trust him. It was a trick to get her to open the door. He *knew*.

Fear grew inside her chest until it became a living, breathing beast. It trembled through her limbs and forced a sour sweat to form on her skin, making it go cold.

The animal in her reacted to that fear, rising to the fore. Her teeth and fingernails began to burn and lengthen. Even though her suite was dark, everything became as clear as day as her feline eyesight kicked in.

She could see the pale, soothing colors, along with the soft contours of the furniture her captors had provided. Small personal items dotted the space—gifts given to her to lull her into a sense of false peace.

They wanted her to trust them. Become one of them.

The taste of blood filled her mouth. The hair on her body stood on end, and a desperate growl surged up her throat.

She couldn't let him know that she was capable of shifting. Not only was it forbidden to tell outsiders that her kind was regaining their powers, but a sudden shift toward her tiger form might also end up being her only hope. The advantage of surprise might be the only thing standing between her and death once the Theronai decided to break the tenuous peace between their peoples. When that happened, she'd be trapped with the enemy. Her hidden strength and speed might be her only means of escape.

She tried to fight the shift, but she'd never been in control of it. Her Slayer side had always come out to play at the worst possible moments.

"I'm not leaving until you at least tell me you're okay. I can't stand the thought that I upset you." His voice was quiet, low, and sexy as hell. She could smell his scent leaking beneath the door, hear his strong heart beating on the other side of the wood.

She wanted to open it for him. Let him in. Taste him.

No. That was her animal side—instinct and emotion. She couldn't let it take over, not when there was so much at stake. The animal in her would want to kill him or fuck him. Possibly both. She had to lean on her Theronai side now and use it to keep her from making a disastrous mistake.

All she had to do was let him see the ring-shaped birthmark on her arm, and he'd know exactly what she was. No more worries. No more hiding. He'd claim her for his own and end all the fear of being found out. As desperate as the Theronai men were for mates, they might not even care that her loyalty would always lie with her own people.

She scrambled away from the door and curled into the smallest space possible.

"I can hear you breathing, Lyka. I know you're in there."

She held her breath, but all it did was lock his scent inside her nose. She could feel it becoming a part of her, tempting her to just let go. Those sword-roughened hands of his would feel so good sliding over her naked skin. As tough as he was, he would be able to take it if she got a little carried away with her claws and teeth.

Just the thought made her moan.

"Lyka? Are you hurt?"

She ached. Wanted. Hungered.

This wasn't normal for her, not even during a full moon. She was always a little more easily aroused during that time, but she'd never felt anything like this before.

This was what she'd heard her kind talk about. *This* was the need.

"That's it," he said. "I'm popping the electronic lock on your door if you don't open it."

She dug her claws into her palms, struggling for control. She closed her eyes to block out the moonlight. All her focus went into the pain until nothing else mattered. She let it consume her world, and reveled in the sharp sting.

Slowly her body eased and the storm passed. Her hair settled and lay flat once again. Her teeth and fingernails returned to normal.

She took deep breaths in an effort to calm her nerves. The next breath she pulled in smelled like Joseph—a combination of leather and steel, spring rain and lightning.

"You're hurt," he said, only this time his voice wasn't muffled by wood. He was inside her dark suite, crouched less than two feet in front of her.

His fingers were clenched into fists, as if he had to struggle not to reach for her. The magical, iridescent necklace he wore shimmered in the moonlight bathing her suite. His gaze was on her bloody palms, and concern ridged the skin between his brows.

She looked at her hands, realizing just how deep the wounds went. "I'll be fine in a minute. I just need to wash the blood away."

He held out his hand. "Can I help you up?"

She looked at his wide palm, easily twice the size of hers. Scars crossed his skin as proof of the battles he'd survived. Pads of rough flesh showed evidence of his work with a sword. He didn't reach for her or try to hurry her. Instead he stood there, patiently waiting for her decision.

She'd never wanted to feel a man's hand wrap around hers before. And she'd sure as hell never wanted to accept an offer for help. She didn't need help. From anyone.

Why, then, was she so desperate to feel his fingers wrap around hers now, when she knew how high the stakes were?

"I won't hurt you," he said, his tone the same one he reserved for speaking to frightened children.

Lyka shoved herself up with her legs, using the wall at her back to support her. She didn't want him to know just how unsteady she was on her feet, how much his presence had affected her. The second she could, she turned her back on him and inched into the kitchen to wash the blood from her palms. Her skin had already begun healing, thanks to her Slayer genetics.

"How did you get hurt?" he asked from behind her.

"Paper cut."

"You don't want to tell me? That's fine. But keep in

mind that it's my duty to see to your safety for as long as you're in my care. If I think you're at risk of getting hurt again, I may have to assign one of my men to guard you."

The idea turned her stomach. The last thing she needed was some brooding Theronai all up in her business. "No, thank you."

"I wasn't asking for your permission. Tell me what happened."

Her chin lifted in defiance. "It's none of your business."

Joseph started typing on his phone.

"What are you doing?" she asked.

"Texting Morgan Valens to come and guard you against further injury. You won't so much as get a hangnail while that man is glued to your side."

She barely resisted the urge to grab the phone away and smash it into a wall. "You have no right to treat me like a child."

He gave her a level stare. "I have every right to see to your safety. If I don't make sure you stay in one piece, then how can I expect your brother to do the same with my daughter? He holds her life in his hands. I didn't want things to turn out that way, but, like you, I wasn't given much choice. We're both just going to learn how to deal." He paused with his finger over his phone, presumably about to send the text that would end her last shred of privacy.

What did it matter if she told him what had happened to her? Slayers were private people in general, choosing to keep to themselves, but if outing a few family secrets was going to help sell him on leaving her alone, then it was worth it. Besides, it was Andreas's rule about not spilling the beans on her ability to shift. If he hadn't wanted her to give away family secrets, then he shouldn't have sent her into their enemy's hands. She had to survive here. If that meant breaking one of Andreas's precious rules, then so be it.

She let out a long sigh, wondering how Joseph was going to make her regret what she was about to divulge. "I assume you're aware that we Slayers have been breeding with humans for enough generations to weaken the gene pool?"

"Yes. Andreas has put a stop to that, from what I understand. He placed strict laws around breeding."

She didn't comment on that. Better to stick to what was already public knowledge. "Centuries ago, Slayers could all shift into their animal form. Now . . . not so much."

"That's one of the reasons Andreas wanted the treaty. He needs the help of the Theronai and Sanguinar to help protect those of your kind who are too weak to defend themselves."

"Even the wimpiest of our kind could kick your ass in a fair fight all day long, so don't go getting a big head."

He held up his big hands. "Wouldn't dream of it. But how does that explain what happened to your palms?"

"My family comes from a long line of purists. Andreas's father and my mother didn't have their bloodlines diluted as much as most of the others." It was more her mother than his father, but her stepfather always claimed all the credit for winning the genetic lottery.

"So, you can shift?" Joseph asked, sounding impressed.

"-Ish. I don't go all the way, and I have absolutely no control over it, but yeah. I can shift—just enough to get me into trouble, mostly."

"And that's what happened now?"

She nodded.

He took a step toward her, and his arm twitched like he was going to reach for her hands. He stopped himself. "Does it hurt?"

She hadn't felt a thing since his scent had invaded her head. Whatever cologne he was wearing was lovely, powerful stuff. "I'm fine."

"I could get one of the Sanguinar to look at your hands."

"No," she said too fast. "I mean, no sense in bothering them. I really am fine. Speedy healing, remember?"

He stared at her for a long minute. His hazel eyes surveyed her as if he was taking mental notes of her condition. She squirmed under his scrutiny, but even as she did, her skin began to warm and tingle.

This man wreaked havoc on her peace of mind. He was dangerous in the same way that playing with matches near broken gas lines was. One false move, and she knew everything she'd worked to protect would go up in flames. *Kaboom.*

"It's late," she said. "I really should go to bed."

His pupils flared wide at her statement. She could smell a faint thread of lust trailing from him.

He wanted her.

Some deep, primal part of her woke up and stretched. A slow, steady burn started low in her belly and began to spread.

Lyka stumbled away from him, nearly falling over her own feet. "You should go now."

His mouth flattened and his wide shoulders seemed to droop. "Are you sure you don't need a guardian to keep you from hurting yourself?"

"All I need is some time alone. Please go." *Before I change my mind.*

He nodded once. "Sweet dreams, kitten. Try not to ruin the furniture with those claws."

It was all she could do not to purr at the way his deep voice stroked across her senses.

A second later, his phone rang, playing an old Duran Duran tune.

Instantly, he went on alert, heading for the door as he answered the call. "What's up?"

She could hear a man's voice on the other end of the line. It was her brother, Andreas. She couldn't distinguish the words, but she knew that tone. There was trouble.

"Are they on your heels now?" asked Joseph.

A string of four-letter words filled the line. Those were easy enough to hear.

Joseph shook his head. "I'm sorry, but you can't come here. We have too many humans to protect, not to mention several pregnant Theronai women. We can't risk their safety. You know that."

Andreas's tinny voice rose as he issued commands to whoever was with him. Then he spoke again to Joseph, and the Theronai's face went pale.

"You brought her with you?" asked Joseph. "Is she hurt?"

Her brother said something else, and she could see Joseph's mind change before her eyes. Whatever Andreas had told him was bad news all the way through.

"I get it. You're coming in hot. We'll be ready. Just hang on." Joseph hung up, turning to her as he pressed buttons on his phone.

"What's going on?" she asked.

"Trouble. You stay here, understand?"

She didn't so much as nod. Instead, she stood there, her face blank, letting him interpret that as he wanted. Whatever got him out of her way the fastest.

The second he was out of her suite, she flung the closet door open and started strapping on leather and weapons. Her big brother was in trouble, and there wasn't a thing Joseph or anyone else could do to stop her from going to his aid.

Chapter 5

This was so not good.

Hell was screaming Joseph's way, and he couldn't stop it. He couldn't even keep it out, not with his adopted daughter out there, too.

Madoc met Joseph on his way toward the gates of Dabyr. The rest of the warriors he'd summoned were on their way.

"What the fuck is going on?" asked Madoc, his perma-scowl in place.

"Andreas and his men fell under attack. I don't know all the details, but they have several wounded men. Synestryn may be on their tail."

"And you're letting them come here? We've got pregnant fucking women here, including my wife."

Joseph refused to let the man's ire upset him. "I'm aware."

"Tell him to veer off. We'll come find him."

"I can't. He's got kids with him. And Carmen. There's no way I'm letting my daughter sit outside the walls with demons nipping at her heels."

"We need to go intercept them," said Madoc. "It's too fucking dangerous to open the gates."

"I didn't ask for your opinion," said Joseph. Headlights bobbed in the distance. "Besides, it's too late. They're here. Now stop bitching and draw your sword."

"Fuck!" spat Madoc, but he rolled his shoulders and drew his sword.

Joseph's phone began singing again about hungry wolves. He answered to Andreas's voice. "There's no sign of any demons on our tail. Will you open the gate?"

"I'd rather make sure you're right about not being followed before I do that."

"I understand, but the kids are scared to death." Andreas's voice lowered to a whisper. "And my cousin is about to bleed out. He doesn't have much time."

Joseph scanned the area, searching for Tynan. He was nowhere to be found, but Logan and Hope were jogging across the lawn toward the commotion.

"Head toward the gate," ordered Joseph. "Incoming wounded."

The couple moved so fast they seemed to blur. Joseph still wasn't entirely sure how the two of them remained so powerful without Athanasian blood, but so far their luck seemed to be holding out.

Joseph addressed the rest of the men who had gathered. "You three go outside the walls and make sure there are no nasty surprises trailing behind Andreas. If there are, shut them down. You three go to the back of the compound and make sure this isn't a distraction for something worse. The rest of you stay near the gate. We may need muscle to move the wounded."

The men hurried off to take their places. Joseph put the phone back to his ear. "We're ready for you. The gate will be open. Don't slow down. Got it?"

Tires squealed in the distance. "Yeah. Not slowing down won't be a problem."

Joseph hung up and called Morgan, who was manning the control room that operated the giant mechanized gate at the main entrance. "Get ready to open it."

"On your go," said Morgan.

Joseph calculated the time it would take Andreas to reach the gate at top speed. As soon as he was within range, he told Morgan, "Now."

The heavy metal bars rolled open slowly. The engines of several trucks growled at top speed. They flew through the opening, kicking up a cloud of dust in their wake.

"Lock us down," said Joseph. "Check the perimeter cameras. Everyone stays on high alert until I say otherwise. If you see anything at all, call me."

"Will do," said Morgan.

Hope and Logan were already at one of the trucks. He'd crawled inside with whoever was wounded. Hope stood nearby, her hand on his ankle.

Blood dripped onto the pavement beneath the truck, proving Andreas hadn't been exaggerating. His cousin was bleeding out.

Joseph hoped it wasn't too late for Logan to save him.

Andreas got out of the truck and limped across the lawn toward Joseph. He was a tall, muscular man with a brawny build and tawny coloring, much like Lyka's. His jeans were shredded and bloody. The leather coat he wore hung in tatters where claws had ripped it apart. One sleeve had three long slits slashed through it, revealing more blood beneath. His arm swayed from his shoulder, limp and lifeless. The fingers dangling there were turning blue.

Joseph hurried over to save the man the obvious pain of walking. "What happened?"

"Our settlement was ambushed by Synestryn. We have no idea how they slipped past our patrols. We didn't so much as smell them coming. We still don't know how they managed that."

"How bad?"

Andreas looked to where his cousin's blood pooled on the pavement. "I saw three of our men and two women go down. They bought us enough time to get the kids out—paid for those seconds with their lives."

"Where is Carmen?"

"She's safe. I put her in one of the vehicles with the young to make sure she had the most protection possible. All of our fighters were standing between them and harm."

Joseph let out a relieved sigh. He'd claimed Carmen as his daughter to fulfill the death wish of one of his fallen brothers. He'd never wanted for her to go stay with the Slayers, but she'd given him little choice. As his adopted daughter, she was the only family he had that could serve as a hostage as valuable as Lyka was to Andreas. And Carmen had insisted in the way only a human teenager could.

"Anyone missing?" he asked.

The Slayer's tawny eyes closed in frustration and pain. "Several of the kids were doing combat practice on the far side of the settlement. Eric was teaching them. He still hasn't returned my calls."

"Did you see him get out?"

Andreas shook his head. "I couldn't go back and look. The place was swarming with demons. We're lucky to have gotten as many of us out as we did." He glanced around as if checking to see who was listening. Nearly everyone was busy doing something, and paying them little attention.

He leaned close, lowered his voice. "I've never seen this many demons in one place before. They looked almost . . . human. They walked on two legs. Had more skin than fur. Hell, Joseph, they used swords—shitty swords, but swords nonetheless."

There had been reports of those kinds of creatures being bred. Joseph's best guess was that the Synestryn were working toward creating an army that could move around in the daylight without raising human suspicion. No one knew exactly how they were doing it, but if they weren't stopped soon, they were going to win the war by sheer numbers alone.

"How did they slip past your defenses?"

"Your guess is as good as mine. Right now I'm more worried about getting the wounded to safety and getting back out there to find Eric and the kids."

"Eric?" said Lyka. "What happened to our brother?"

Joseph turned and saw her hurrying toward them. She should have been too far away to have heard any of that conversation, but Slayer hearing was good, and hers, apparently, was excellent.

She was dressed in a heavy leather jacket, leather pants, and a belt bristling with weapons. Her hair was tied back and bound out of her face, which was far too pale with fear for Joseph's peace of mind. Still, the instant he saw her, the pain behind his eyes eased and his whole world seemed to spin a little easier. He didn't know why she had such an effect on him, but right now, he welcomed it.

Andreas turned in time to face his sister. "Take it easy. It's not time to panic yet."

"What's wrong with your arm?" she asked.

"Dislocated. It'll heal."

"Good." She jabbed a finger in his chest, making him wince. "Our people were attacked. Some were killed.

Others are missing. Don't you dare tell me not to panic. Where the hell is Eric?"

"We don't know. We're heading out after him as soon as we can."

"I'm going with you," she said.

"Like hell," said Andreas, at the same time Joseph said, "No, you're not."

She glanced at each of them. "I'm not sure which one of you to smack first, but rest assured that if my brother and a bunch of our young are missing, I *will* be going out to find them."

Andreas addressed Joseph. "I guess you haven't had any more luck controlling her than I did."

Joseph wasn't going to step on that land mine, not if he could help it. Instead he turned the conversation back to safer ground. "We need to get you and your people some healing. While you do that, I'll gather up some men and we'll make plans to send out groups to help you find Eric and the kids."

"I'll figure out which of my people are fit to hunt and assign at least one of them to each group you send out. They'll know Eric's scent and will be able to follow it."

"Sign me up for the first group that leaves," said Lyka. "I'm ready to go, and I'm not injured."

Joseph knew he was going to regret this at some point in the near future, but he had no choice. "I took a vow to ensure your safety. That means you stay here."

"You can't hold me prisoner. My brother won't allow it."

"I'm sorry," said Andreas, "but Joseph is right. If you die while in Joseph's care, the treaty will be broken. I need the help of the Theronai and Sanguinar too much right now to risk that happening. I know you want to help, but the answer is no."

"You two really think you can keep me here?" she asked, her eyes narrowed in fury.

"There are prison cells beneath Dabyr," said Joseph. "I'd rather not have to put you in one of them."

"You wouldn't."

"To save your life? Hell, yes, I would."

She turned to Andreas. "You'd let him lock me up like a prisoner?"

"I'll toss you in there myself. I'm already worried I've lost one sibling. I won't lose two."

Her only response was a rough growl of anger before she turned and stalked away.

Andreas let out a low whistle. "You know we're going to pay for that, right?"

"At least she'll live long enough to make us suffer. I'm okay with that."

"You only say that because you've never had her put a scorpion in your boxers. And that was when she was four. She's had a lot of years to come up with much, much worse punishments."

"Do you think I made the wrong call?" asked Joseph.

"Not at all. I'm just saying that if I were you, I'd shake my underwear out before stepping into it. Just to be safe."

"I'll take that under advisement. But for right now, we have a crisis to kill."

Joseph found Logan and got his report. "Everyone is stable."

"Did Andreas's cousin survive?"

"He did, though it was a close call. He was seconds from death."

"How many more wounded are there?"

"Several, based on the smell of blood in the air. It's going to take Hope and I at least an hour or so to get all the healing done. I'm afraid that after that, we're going to be spent for the night."

"What about Tynan and the others?"

Logan shook his head. "They're too weak. The blooded humans have refused to give them blood. They blame all us Sanguinar for what Connal did."

"Have Tynan come see me. I'll give him the blood he needs. Andreas is playing down his injuries, but his arm is useless. He needs attention, and we need his people to have a voice of leadership. I doubt the Slayers would enjoy me telling them what to do."

Logan nodded, his silver eyes lighting from within. "I understand. We must avoid more bloodshed until Hope has a chance to replenish her power in the sun tomorrow."

"If you have to, stabilize the civilians and finish healing them tomorrow. We need all the fighters on their feet tonight. Children are missing."

"It will be done," said Logan, and he turned and went back to work.

The next hour passed in chaos as people were sorted out and given healing and shelter. Gerai—the humans who had dedicated their lives to serving the Sentinels—worked inside to provide food, beds, and a much-needed distraction for the traumatized children.

Warriors, both Theronai and Slayer, guarded the perimeter, watchful for approaching enemies. Soon, the huge front lawn inside the tall stone walls around Dabyr grew quiet and calm once again.

Joseph had worked nonstop, directing people to where they would be of the most use. Even as Tynan drank blood from Joseph's wrist, he continued issuing orders so that everyone got to safety as quickly as possible.

Once the vehicles were housed in the garage and the last civilian was taken inside, Joseph texted his warriors to summon them to his office, leaving only a few inside the gates to sound the alarm if bad things came their way.

Andreas was waiting for him, along with several of Joseph's men.

Lyka sat beside her brother, her arms crossed over her chest, glaring at him in defiance.

Fine. If she wanted to stay, let her stay. She eased his pain and helped him think more clearly, even if she was trying to kill him with her gaze.

"How many able-bodied men do you have?" Joseph asked Andreas.

"A dozen warriors and six trackers."

"Seven," said Lyka.

Joseph ignored her. "I've reached two teams in the field. They're headed this way and can meet up with your trackers. My men will pair up and tag along with the other four trackers."

"Five," said Lyka.

Again, Joseph ignored her. "Will you be on one of the teams?" he asked Andreas. "Or are you staying here with your people?"

"I'm staying until sunrise to coordinate our movements. If Eric isn't found by then, I'll be leaving, too."

"I've asked the Gerai to give you whatever supplies you need. Your road-worthy trucks are being gassed up now. It's going to take time to clean the blood out of some of them, and they'll have to stay here until they're clean, so they don't attract more demons."

"I appreciate that," said Andreas. "But I have another favor to ask of you."

"What is it?"

"The civilians and the young . . . they need a place to stay until we can relocate."

"They're welcome here for as long as you need."

Several of the Theronai shared concerned looks, but kept their mouths shut.

"I know it might cause trouble," said Andreas, "but I've warned them all that I'll punish anyone who gets out of line. We're guests here. They're all to be on their best behavior."

Lyka crossed her arms over her chest. "They're not going to like being prisoners here any more than I do."

"They're not prisoners," said Joseph.

"That's what you keep telling me, too, and yet I'm not allowed to leave. Are they?"

Joseph couldn't deal with her now—not when there was so much to do, and certainly not in front of an audience. "You know it's not safe for them to leave. We'll talk about it more when this crisis is averted."

She shot to her feet. "If you think you can push me aside like a whiny child, you're wrong. I don't need your permission to do what's right." She shifted her death-ray stare to Andreas. "Or yours."

Lyka was out the door before Joseph could stop her. He wanted to go after her, but knew it wasn't an option. He had a rescue mission to organize, a bunch of frightened children to soothe, wounded to attend and more than five hundred lives to protect. He couldn't allow the feelings of one woman to get in his way.

"I'll go after her," said Andreas. "Make sure she doesn't cause you any trouble."

Madoc unrolled a map on the table. "Let her go. How fucking much trouble could she possibly cause?"

Joseph winced.

Andreas let out a humorless laugh. "You clearly don't know my sister. I'll be back as soon as I can."

"We can't wait on you," said Joseph.

Andreas nodded at his cousin—the one who'd been on death's door when he'd arrived. He looked as strong and healthy as any Slayer alive now, thanks to Logan and Hope. "Amhas was there. He knows as much as I do."

Amhas nodded his shaggy blond head. "I got this. Good luck."

Andreas squared his shoulders. "Thanks. I'm going to need all I can get."

Chapter 6

This wasn't the first time Lyka had considered inciting rebellion and she doubted it would be the last.

She was halfway to the main room of Dabyr, where her kind was being kept, when Andreas caught up with her. He grabbed her sleeve and pulled her to a stop. "What the hell do you think you're doing?"

"You seemed to need my help, so I'm warning our people that they may be held here against their will. That way they can leave before it's too late."

"You call that help? What I really need is a sister who can listen and follow instructions. I told you to mind your manners, to be the glue that would bind our two people together, not to try to convince a bunch of uprooted, frightened people that they just walked into some kind of prison."

"They deserve to know the truth."

"They deserve to have a safe place to sleep tonight."

"You heard Joseph. He's going to make them stay here."

Andreas looked around at the clean, well-lit hallway, complete with little alcoves containing fresh plants, flowers and artwork. "It's not exactly a concentration camp. Why are you throwing such a fit? Have they been treating you badly?"

"Define *badly*."

"Have they starved you or beat you or forced you to sleep out in the cold?"

"No, but you heard Joseph. He thinks he can boss me around."

"He bosses everyone here around. That's his job. He's the reason this place is still standing, with so many juicy targets inside. He's the reason the walls haven't been overrun by demons. He's the reason our wounded survived tonight and our young have a safe place to rest."

"You make him sound like some kind of superhero."

"That's because he is." Andreas held out his hands, showing off his tattered, bloody clothing. "Look at me. I barely survived tonight. Our home was overrun, and that's my fault. Just like it's Joseph's fault that the home he protects is still standing."

"That wasn't your doing. We don't have walls like they do. We don't have magic to sling around like they do, or Sanguinar on hand to fix our every boo-boo. We survive on our own with help from no one."

"That's the problem, Lyka. We're not surviving. We're being targeted. Picked off. We've lost too many people in the past few months. I didn't realize it until tonight, but those attacks were testing our strengths and weaknesses. Those attacks were feeding our enemy the information they needed to pull off what they did tonight." He ran his fingers through his hair. "I need to know that you're doing your job here."

"What job? I just sit around, trying not to let anyone touch me. I tried to get involved with the kids, teaching them, but even that is getting shut down. Apparently, human kids are too weak to be taught how to fight."

"I know that you respect few things more than you do strength and skill in combat, but I have to side with Joseph on this one. Humans are much frailer than we are. It's our job to protect them."

"You sound just like him. It's no wonder the two of you hit it off so well. You both love getting your way and bossing people around."

Andreas stepped back, spreading his hands wide. "You want to challenge me for leadership?" he asked. "Go ahead. I'm tired. Distracted. You might just win."

No, she wouldn't. She knew better than to think she could. And the last thing she wanted was to injure her brother when he really did need to be out there looking for Eric and the kids.

"I don't want your job. Just take me with you. I need to breathe free air."

"Unless you're telling me that you've been abused here, you're just going to have to suck it up and deal like everyone else. I know you don't like the role you were given, but that's just too damn bad. It's the role your people need you to play. Both your peoples."

There were cameras everywhere. Nothing that was said in these halls was private. Before Andreas could give away her secrets, she stopped him, covering his mouth with her hand. "Shut the hell up," she said, nodding toward the closest camera.

The second she touched him, she was inundated with emotion. Hopes. Dreams. Desires.

Her gift hadn't been triggered this powerfully in so long, she'd almost forgotten about it. She hadn't touched anyone but the kids since she'd been here, and the most she'd ever gotten from any of them was a faint desire to be safe. Free.

Sometimes, when the people around her had intense needs, she could feel that, but it was a subtle thing, not at all like the raging emotions that were pouring out of her brother.

He wanted peace. Protection for his people. He wanted to find Eric safe and well, right alongside the young who had been taken. He wanted to rebuild their home and find a way to make it safe for this and future generations.

There was something else, too. Something unexpected.

A woman.

Lyka couldn't tell exactly who she was, but she could tell that Andreas wasn't supposed to be wanting her— not when he was all but promised to Faolan.

"Who is she?" asked Lyka.

Andreas jerked back out of reach. "I really hate it when you do that."

"Tell me who she is."

His face darkened with embarrassment. "It doesn't matter. It's never going to happen. Let it go."

"You can't lie to me. I know how much you want her."

"That's none of your damn business."

"Does Faolan know?"

"There's nothing to tell her. I haven't so much as touched the girl. I've barely even let myself glance at her. It's a nonissue. Let it go."

"I can't. I felt what you do. The deep yearning you have for this woman. You can't enter into an arrangement with Faolan when you feel like this."

"You think I don't know that?" growled Andreas. "It's not like I asked for this. If I ignore it long enough, it will go away. Besides, you need to be spending less time using your gift on me and more time using it on the people here. If we're to have a lasting peace with them, we need to know what it is they want, what we have to offer that is of value."

"If you think I'm going to start touching the men around here, you're crazy. You know what could happen."

"Would that be such a bad thing? Can you think of a better way to tie our peoples together than a union like that?"

She went still as a ripple of betrayal coursed through her. "That was what you wanted all along, wasn't it? That's why you sent me here when Eric was just as good a choice for a hostage."

"Eric would have killed someone here before the first full moon. You were the *only* choice."

"That doesn't answer my question. You chose me not because you thought I could keep our mother's dirty little secret safe, but because you were hoping it would come out—that someone here would figure out what I am."

Lyka felt the telltale tingling a second too late.

Joseph rounded the corner, frowning. "What are you, Lyka?"

"Pissed," said Andreas. "Disobedient. Belligerent."

Joseph's frown stayed in place as he eyed her. Clearly he wasn't buying her brother's cover. "We need you back in the war room," he told Andreas. "And you, Lyka . . . Tynan called. The Slayer children are asking for you."

She nodded, glad for any excuse to be away from Joseph right now. He was as smart as he was tenacious. He wasn't going to let what he overheard go. Escape was her only option.

She gave her brother a hard hug, reeling at the sheer scope of his want for his mystery woman. "Stay safe," she ordered. "Bring our brother and the young home."

"I will," said Andreas. "I won't rest until we find them."

She scurried off, feeling Joseph's gaze on her back. She'd escaped his interrogation for now, but she knew that once the chaos was over, he would seek her out.

She wasn't sure whether she was more worried or excited by that notion. And that terrified her.

Chapter 7

Joseph paced the halls of Dabyr, waiting for news about the hunt. He'd checked on Carmen, who was working alongside the Sanguinar to help care for the wounded. She was safe and whole, but too busy to do more than reassure him that she was safe. His people were all doing their jobs, tending the injured, soothing the children and making arrangements for everyone to have a bed to sleep in tonight. Extra perimeter guards were on patrol, protecting the walls from attack.

All that was left to do now was wait for word from those out searching for Eric and the missing children.

The teams had left hours ago, and no one had so much as found a trail. Every available Theronai, Sanguinar and Slayer was out there, searching for those kids with no results.

Joseph wanted to be out there searching with them so badly that he had to stay well away from the hallway leading to the garage. If he didn't, he'd end up behind the wheel, speeding away from his responsibilities here.

As he wandered aimlessly, his phone in his hand, hoping for a call or text, he found himself standing outside Lyka's door.

He wanted to see her again, and not just because of the mysterious comment she'd made in the hallway earlier. He needed her soothing presence, the relief she brought him whenever he glanced her way.

The pain behind his eyes was killing him, shortening his temper and making him impatient. Every second that ticked by seemed to take an eternity.

His thumb slid over the screen of his phone, itching to call Andreas or one of the others. He knew they were working and would contact him as soon as they could, but the waiting was excruciating.

He needed a distraction. Something—anything—to get his mind off the fact that he wasn't out there, at his brothers' side.

Lyka came around the corner, glowing like a beacon as she headed toward her suite. Immediately, the pain in his head eased and his cock twitched, straining against his zipper.

The feelings he had for this woman were as powerful as they were dangerous. If Andreas had even half an idea of the things Joseph wanted to do to her, the man would kill him outright. Or at least make him wish he were dead.

As soon as she saw him, she stopped in her tracks, yards away from him. "Did you need me?"

More than he dared admit.

"Has Andreas called you?" he asked.

"I'm not allowed to have a phone, remember? It's part of my being your hostage."

"You're not a hostage. You're a guest."

"Guests are allowed to leave."

He wasn't going to argue about this with her. He was

too wound up. Too on edge. If he let his temper flare, the rest of his emotions might burn out of control. He'd have that long, sleek body of hers up against a wall, feasting on her mouth before she could stop him. Once he got her there, it was only a few short seconds to having her naked in the hall while he drove his cock nice and deep.

That would definitely make the precariously perched peace treaty between their people wobble.

Joseph cleared his throat, which had suddenly gone dry with desire. "What did you mean earlier when you told Andreas that you were worried someone would find out what you are?"

"You misunderstood me. That's not what I said."

"Everything that happens in the halls is recorded. I had Morgan send me the video. There was no mistaking what you said. I want to know why you said it."

All the color drained from her face. She swayed slightly on her feet, grabbing the wall for support.

Joseph was down the hall and at her side before he could remember that she wouldn't want his help. His hands dropped before he touched her. "Are you going to fall over?"

"No," she snapped, straightening her spine.

The light caught her golden hair and made it glow. He could see in the depths of her tawny eyes—in the way she refused to meet his gaze—that she was hiding something from him. Something important.

"What did you mean, Lyka? What are you?"

Sarcasm spewed from her mouth. "A spy, sent here to take you down. Mwoo-haha."

"I'm being serious. If there's something you're hiding, you should tell me now while we can still deal with it—before it becomes too big a problem for us to face together."

"It's not a problem, Theronai. Your not minding your own business is."

"You are my business now, kitten. One of these days, you'll get used to that idea."

"Don't hold your breath. I won't be here that long." She went to her door and opened it, but rather than let him in, she blocked the opening so he wouldn't feel inclined to follow.

He opened his mouth just as his phone broke out in Andreas's ringtone.

He answered immediately. "Hello?"

"None of our trackers caught a scent."

Well, hell. He'd been hoping for some shred of good news, but he'd had too many conversations that started like this to hold out hope.

This kind of thing was best done with some modicum of privacy, so he went to the closest place open to him—Lyka's suite.

The second he marched toward the doorway, she shied away, leaving him the opening he needed to enter.

He closed the door behind him. "What about the Sanguinar? Did they detect anything they could follow—a blood trail, maybe?"

"Nothing there, either," said Andreas. "I don't know if it was the sheer number of the creatures that attacked us—too much blood from the ones we killed—or if the enemy is using some kind of magic, but it's nearly impossible to pick up on any one scent trail."

"What do you want to do now?" asked Joseph.

"I sent teams in several directions from here, hoping we'll catch a break, that they'll pick something up a little farther away from the scene of the attack. But it's not looking good. I was hoping you'd have a trick or two up your sleeve."

Joseph did his best to hide his worry. What the men needed now was strength. Confidence. Leadership. "I'll check with the warriors I have in the field and see what I can come up with. You keep at it from your end. I'll send help as soon as I can."

"Don't take too long. The young may not have much time."

Joseph braced his shoulders so they wouldn't bow under the weight of his fear for those kids. "Understood."

Andreas hung up. Joseph looked at Lyka, seeing more fear on her face than he would have thought possible.

Her chin trembled for a second before she controlled it. "They didn't find the young, did they?"

"Not yet. But they will."

"Tonight?"

He wouldn't lie to her like that. "Slayer kids are tough. Eric is with them. They'll stay safe until we do find them."

"You don't know that. You can't know any of that."

"I believe it, though. You should, too. Hope will keep us strong and positive."

She shook her head. "It doesn't matter how strong we are if we're here, sitting on our asses. We have to *do* something. You have to let me out there to look for them."

"And let you get killed because there are no warriors here who can go with you and protect you?"

"I don't need their protection, and even if I did, there are lots of warriors here."

"Those are the husbands of our pregnant women. Not one of them would leave his wife unguarded. I'm sorry."

"What about you?"

"Someone has to be here to lead the troops."

"Let one of the other men do it. Come with me. Help me find those children before it's too late."

The idea of setting out with her, of getting to spend a considerable amount of time with her, was more than tempting. He'd have her nearby, easing his headache, challenging his mind and revving his libido like a finely tuned engine.

But it was impossible. He had to make her see that.

"Even if we did leave, where would you go? There are dozens of people out there scouring the scene of the crime, searching for some clue to where the kids were taken. What makes you think you could do any better?"

"I'm an excellent tracker. And the more eyes, ears and noses we have in the field, the better. You never know what path we might cross that they haven't."

"It's not worth the risk. I'm sorry."

She went quiet for a second, but he could see the wheels in her head turning. "What if it *was* worth the risk?"

"What does that mean?"

"What if I could give you something you want in exchange for you letting me go hunting?"

She was so serious, he didn't dare laugh. But he was curious. "What could you possibly offer me that would be worth endangering your life as well as the peace treaty between our peoples?"

She straightened her spine in resolve. "A female Theronai."

Chapter 8

Lyka couldn't believe she was doing this. It was insane. Completely nuts.

She moved to the sliding glass doors on the back wall of her suite. They overlooked a parklike setting, complete with flowers, topiaries and wrought-iron park benches. Normally the view soothed her, but not tonight.

Even hinting that she knew where one of their women was located was enough to get her waterboarded. But what choice did she have? Eric was missing, possibly dead. The young still hadn't been found. Every hour that passed was one in which they were vulnerable and afraid.

Assuming they still lived.

As those dark thoughts swirled through her mind, she had to shove them away with a force of will before they could take root and fester.

She couldn't simply stay here in these safe, lush surroundings while her brother and those babies suffered. Even if it meant giving up her secret, her freedom. Irrevocably.

Joseph still hadn't said a word, making her wonder if he'd heard her.

She strengthened her willpower and forced herself to stay on the only path possible. "Your men are still dying without their mates. I know that a few of you have found women, but every one you find is a big deal, right?"

Joseph nodded slowly, eyeing her as if looking for her lie. "Huge. A bonded pair of Theronai can save thousands of lives."

"Then it seems I have something of value to you. I propose a bargain."

He stepped closer. "Don't play games with this, Lyka. I mean it."

"I'm not playing." She swallowed hard. "I'm acutely aware of the stakes." She was going to regret her actions here today, but only if her plan failed. If the young survived, their lives would be worth every day she spent in captivity. She had to believe that.

Joseph's hazel eyes darkened. His voice dropped to a tone so low, it vibrated with an unspoken threat of violence. "Tell me where she is, Lyka. This isn't the kind of secret you can keep from me."

She'd never seen him like this before. He'd always been so accommodating and solicitous. Every creature comfort she'd asked for, he'd provided. The only thing he hadn't allowed her was her freedom. She'd had no idea that what she dangled in front of him now would evoke such . . . darkness from him.

She balled her hands into fists and steadied her nerves. "First you have to promise. Bind yourself to your word. There can't be any room left for you to weasel out of your promise, or my lips stay sealed."

All the glittering light that usually reached his eyes was gone now, leaving behind the kind of darkness a man would need to have to slay beasts without mercy. She'd always seen him behind a desk, but that docile impression of him vanished. What remained was a hard, lethal warrior standing in front of her.

His voice was still low, vibrating with power, but also coaxing. "What vow do you want in exchange for this information, kitten?"

This was it. Her only chance at helping find her brother and the young.

She pulled in a long breath, giving herself enough air to state her demands without her voice wobbling. "Freedom. I want to be free to leave Dabyr whenever I want, and to go wherever I want. Alone."

He shook his head. "No. That's too much to ask of me. You can't expect me to trade your life, not even for information like this."

"That's not what I'm asking. My life is my own. Not yours. You don't get to trade it for anything."

"You're putting me in an impossible position. If I don't give you freedom, then one of our women goes unclaimed and unprotected. If she dies, so does one of my men, and untold others that a united pair of Theronai could have saved. If I do give you freedom, then you could be hurt or killed, and the peace between our people could crumble, taking countless lives along with it in future battles. How can you stand there asking me to choose from those two outcomes? Just tell me what I want to know so we can save this woman."

Lyka wasn't about to fall for it. She wasn't putting some stranger's life at stake, but he couldn't know that. "She doesn't want to be found. Outing her is a huge betrayal. If not for the lives of our young and my brother being at stake, I wouldn't even consider telling you who she is. This is a onetime offer. Take it or leave it, before I change my mind."

Joseph's jaw clenched with frustration. "If she doesn't

want to be found, then she knows what we'd ask of her. An unwilling woman is of little use. We would need her to bind herself to one of our men in order to save his soul and tap into his power."

"What if I could promise you that she would come to you willingly?"

"I don't believe you. You're grasping at straws now."

"Am I? I'm willing to tie myself to my word. I'll give you a binding vow that she will accept the collar of one of your men as long as she gets to choose which one."

"That doesn't prevent her from taking years to make her choice."

"I could make her choose."

"How?" he asked. "What does this woman owe you that you could be so certain of her cooperation?"

"That's my business. All you have to do is man up and give me your promise."

He stood there in silence for several seconds, simply staring at her. "I want proof first."

She shook her head. "No. My word is all the proof you get."

"What will your brother Andreas say?"

"If I get out there and find the others? He'll thank you for letting me go."

"And if you die while hunting for them?"

"My death is on me. Not you. I'll leave behind a note making sure he knows that you're not responsible for my choices."

"We need that woman, Lyka," he said.

"I know. And I need my freedom."

He closed his eyes and shook his head in defeat. "I know I'm going to regret this, but one female Theronai could save a lot of lives. She could save one of my men. I have to know where she is."

Victory was so close, she could taste it. "Then give me what I want."

"You swear you can convince her to bind herself to one of my men? Irrevocably?"

She hadn't even considered any other kind of bond until his comment shed daylight on the option. But that door was closed to her now, and she refused to regret it. If giving up her life as she knew it would save the lives of the people she loved, she had a duty to make whatever vows he demanded of her. "I do so swear."

"And you swear that if she is compatible with more than one of our men, she will bind herself to one of them immediately, rather than taking months to make up her mind on who she would choose?"

"I do so swear."

"I don't know how you can make this happen, but your words bind you to your actions."

"Only if you give me my freedom and fulfill your end of the bargain."

He scrubbed a hand over his face. "If you can deliver on your promises, then I free you, Lyka. I give you my word that you can come and go as you please, as long as you do no harm to anyone within these walls."

The weight of his vow bore down on her, driving her to her knees. Until this moment, she hadn't taken the time to really consider the consequences of her actions. She knew her word would tie her, forcing her to act, but the sheer magnitude of this promise was almost more than she could stand.

From the corner of her eye, she saw him reach for her. She jerked away out of reflex, even though the life of her secret could be measured in seconds.

He stepped back. Sweat beaded along his hairline, drawing attention to the tiny sparks of silver at his temples. Theronai lived for centuries, barely aging. The fact that he had even a few gray hairs was proof of just how much stress his leadership role put on him.

For some reason, the urge to ease his burden bubbled within her, making itself known.

Strange.

Joseph shoved his hands in his pockets. "I've done what you asked. Now tell me. Where can I find her?"

Lyka thought about refusing him for about two seconds before the magic of her vow drove her to act. She had no choice now. The compulsion to fulfill her end of the bargain was irresistible.

She pulled up her long sleeve to reveal the ring-shaped birthmark on her forearm—the one that marked her as a Theronai. "I'm right here."

Chapter 9

E ric Phelan woke in a cold, dark room. His head throbbed, sending wave after wave of dizziness washing over him. He tried to sit up, but even the thought of moving that much made him queasy.

A small, chilly hand was wrapped around one of his thick fingers. He cracked one eye open enough to see his surroundings.

Rock walls carved by time arched overhead. The ground beneath him was cold and uneven.

A cave.

Several Slayer children were gathered near him, piled together like puppies for warmth. He could smell their fear and exhaustion, along with the stench of hundreds of Synestryn demons nearby.

Kayla tightened her grip around his finger. She was seven, with moonlight-blond hair, huge brown eyes and the heart of a warrior. Of all the young he taught, she had the most promise.

"Are you awake?" she whispered.

"Yeah." He forced himself to lift his head enough to survey the area.

The cave wasn't very big. He doubted if he could even stand upright in the space. There were four young with him. When the attack had come down, there had been six.

Two kids were missing.

"Where are the others?" he asked.

Kayla's dark eyes hardened. "She took them. I tried to stop her, but there were too many of them."

"Too many what?"

She scowled as she nodded toward a dip in the cave wall. Eric shoved himself upright so he could get a better view. His head spun and his vision wavered, but it was still easy to see what she meant.

The dip in the wall was actually an opening—a hole leading out. Just outside of that lay freedom and more of those odd Synestryn demons that had attacked the settlement. They were far too human-looking for Eric's peace of mind, wielding steel weapons that gave them an advantage of reach. Their pale skin was covered in mangy patches of fur, but they were heavily muscled and faster than any human could hope to be.

These were the creatures that had attacked his people.

"How long have we been here?" he asked Kayla.

"A long time."

To a kid, that could be anything from hours to days. Based on the rumbling hunger in his belly, he was guessing it had been at least a day, but he couldn't be sure. The blow to his head had fucked with his memory enough that he couldn't remember the exact hits he'd taken. He healed fast, but it burned a shit ton of calories.

The other young were asleep, and he hated to wake them. Kayla was steady in a fight, but the others were more emotional. He didn't want a bunch of crying to draw attention to the fact that he was awake. "Is anyone hurt?"

"Peter was, but he's better now." She eyed the Synestryn with a death stare worthy of any fully grown woman with a bad case of PMS. "When can we kill them?"

"Not now. And not before I say. Got it?"

She nodded. "But we get to kill them soon, right?"

"Give me a minute to figure out what's going on." For all he knew, they'd have to fight their way through six levels of demons before they reached the surface. He might have risked it with a group of his brothers, but not with a few scrawny kids who hadn't even lost all of their baby teeth yet. Hell, at least two of them were far closer to human than Slayer on their best day, and those who could shift even a little had absolutely no control over it.

"I've been watching them," said Kayla. "They all obey her."

"*Her* who?"

"The ugly one—the one who brought us here—called her Treszka."

Ugly one? That rang a bit of a bell, but not enough that Eric could sort it out in his rattled skull. "How long have the other kids been gone?"

"A long time. Like, as long as it takes for Miss Carmen to read us a story."

Story time was only about an hour long—an eternity to someone like Kayla, who was pathologically incapable of sitting still. The fact that she was doing so now meant she had to be a lot more afraid than she appeared.

"I need you to be brave, Kayla," said Eric. "I need you to help keep the other kids in line. Don't let them run off and do something stupid if I'm not around, okay?"

He could smell the surge of fear waft out of the little

girl, but none of it showed on her face. "Why wouldn't you be around?"

"I need to find us a way out. If I get a chance to slip away and do some scouting, I will. But don't worry. I'll be back. I'd never leave you down here."

"You shouldn't leave," said Kayla. "Treszka is really mean. I can tell."

"How can you tell?"

"By the way she smells."

Eric had no idea how mean smelled, but he was familiar with violent, irrational and crazy. All those scents lingered nearby. And Kayla seemed certain enough about the mean thing that he wasn't going to argue with her. "Promise me you'll take care of the others. Make them stick together."

"I will. But if you don't come back, we're fighting our way out of here without you."

He resisted the urge to grin at her viciousness. She might be a handful to teach, but in a couple of decades, Kayla was going to make one hell of a fighter.

"Deal," he said.

The sound of shuffling feet and a low hum grew louder and neared the cave entrance. He had no idea what the noise was, but he doubted it was any kind of good.

"She's coming," said Kayla. "They always make that noise and bow down when she passes, like she's some kind of queen."

Now that he thought about it, the sound did hold a bit of reverence to it. And if the queen bee was headed this way, Eric was going to be ready for her with a little honey.

"Pretend like you're asleep," he told Kayla as he rose to his feet. "Don't let anything I say rattle you. Understand? I may need to lie."

Kayla let out a growl of defiance but did as she was told, like a good little soldier.

Eric couldn't quite stand upright where he was, but he found a place nearer the opening where the floor dipped lower, giving him room to reach his full height—and to fight if it came to that.

He rolled his shoulders to work out some of the kinks. All he'd been wearing during practice was a pair of faded jeans, which were now covered in dirt and dried blood—most of it his.

The humming outside grew louder and louder until he could no longer hear the Synestryn soldiers moving to make way for their queen bee to pass. He could see through the opening enough to watch the crowd part, but the reason they were parting was obscured until a woman stepped through the hole in the cave wall.

Treszka ducked through the doorway and straightened once she was inside. She was easily six feet tall, falling only a few inches shorter than Eric. She was dressed in a flowing gown of black and garnet velvet, in a style like some medieval queen would have worn. She had hip-length midnight black hair and eyes to match. Her pupils were stark white, giving her gaze a kind of weight Eric had never experienced before.

She was beautiful. Stunning. And not just for a Synestryn—which she definitely was. There was no mistaking the smell of death and pain seeping from her pale skin.

She smiled at him, displaying a perfect row of sharp white teeth. "You're awake. I'm so glad you survived."

Most of the Synestryn demons were beyond language. Eric had heard there were ones that could talk, but he'd never expected to actually have a conversation with one of them.

"Why are we here?" he asked.

"You mean why are you still alive?" she corrected.

"Whatever gets me the answers I need, lady."

"Treszka," she supplied. She lifted the hem of her skirt and stepped closer. "I really don't want to hurt you." Her black-and-white gaze bore into him. "But I will if you don't behave."

Eric could feel an acute chill coming off her skin. The stink of her flesh was almost more than he could stand. It didn't matter how pretty she was. The girl was rancid. "Where are the other two kids who were with me?"

"Safe. I thought it best if some of them were elsewhere, so you wouldn't get any ideas about escape. You don't seem the type to leave your offspring down here to fend for themselves."

She was right, but he didn't want to let her know it.

Eric shrugged. "Not my offspring."

She ran a black-tipped fingernail down his chest. It was all he could do to stand there without flinching. "No paternal instincts?"

"None."

She made a tsking sound. "That's a shame. I was hoping for more from you."

"I'd say I'm sorry to disappoint, but I'd be lying. So, step aside so we can be on our way."

Treszka laughed, and the sound was about as appealing as the squall of tortured kittens. "You know that's not how it's going to work. I brought you here for a reason."

Of course she had. "Which is?"

A slow smile stretched her lips. Her fingers slid down the center of his chest toward the button of his jeans. "I have needs."

Eric became acutely aware of the children standing

behind him. That, and the fact that the woman touching him was a fucking cold-blooded demon.

"Not only no, but *hell*, no. Not even if you were the last piece of tail on the planet and I was dying from a chronic erection."

Her smile turned into a pout. "I knew you'd play hard to get. You Slayers and your sense of honor." She waved a hand in dismissal. "It's all a big waste of time, if you ask me, but you've given me no choice but to play along. Guards!"

The second she raised her voice, a trio of those disturbingly human-looking demons piled into the room.

"Take another one of the children," she ordered.

Eric stepped to the side, blocking the path of the guard that moved to obey fastest. "Not a fucking chance, lady."

"You seem to lack a basic understanding of your situation. I am in control here. Not you. If I want you to kill and eat one of the children, then that's exactly what you'll do. Unless, of course, you'd rather I have one of my guards take them all?"

Eric glanced over his shoulder at the young. They were piled up, trying to stay warm. Kayla lay still, but he could see tension radiating through her little body. She'd heard every word Treszka had said. She may not have understood it all, but she would have absorbed enough to know that Eric had been offered a chance to save them and turned it down.

"So, Slayer, what will it be? Will you come with me, or would you prefer to stay here with your choice of three of the children? I really don't care who dies. Neither will my men. Down here, meat is meat."

What choice did he have? There was no way to fight his way free. There were too many guards outside of the cavern—and those were just the ones he could see. Chances were there were hundreds more between here and freedom.

And what about those two other young? She'd led him to believe that they were still alive. He couldn't abandon them down here.

His best option was to get her alone and kill her. Once the queen bee was dead, the drones would be distraught and confused. That's when he'd have the best chance of getting the young to freedom.

Eric held out his hand to her. "Lead the way."

Joseph was stunned speechless.

He stared at the birthmark, then at Lyka's face, then back again. He saw, but still couldn't believe. It was simply impossible. Some kind of trick.

Before he could stop himself, his hand reached toward her. He stopped in the act, waiting for her to shy away like she always did, but this time she held her ground.

"Go ahead," she said, bracing herself. "You need proof. The mark won't wipe off. Heaven knows I've tried."

His finger settled on her warm skin.

The pain he carried around with him—pain he'd endured for so long that it had become part of him—melted away. For a second he thought he became airborne, he felt so light. The shock of it rattled him down to his very soul.

He was still reeling from being pain free when the next sensation hit him. Warmth swirled up his arm, tingling his skin as it went. The streamers of heat shot straight for his chest, lingering along the branches of his lifemark before sinking into his heart. His whole body shuddered. His lifemark swayed along his skin, straining to get closer to her.

Lyka wasn't lying. She was the real deal. A Theronai.

And she was compatible with his power. She could be his.

He shoved that idea out of his head before it could take root. Most of his men were far worse off than he was—their lifemarks nearly bare. It was his duty to see to their needs first. It didn't matter if she was compatible with him or not. She needed to save one of his men.

"How can this be?" he asked, hearing his amazement in his voice. "You're a Slayer."

"So was my mother. My father, however, was a one-night stand. An Athanasian prince who came here for the sole purpose of creating me. Mom fell for his good looks and charm, and cheated on her husband. It's not exactly something my family likes to talk about."

A female Theronai. Under his roof. And he'd had no clue.

He shook his head in an effort to get reality to sink in. "Does Andreas know?"

His thumb stroked across her birthmark. His fingers had somehow wrapped around her arm in a grip tight enough that he could feel bone and muscles shifting beneath his hand. He knew he should stop touching her, but it felt so good to be free of pain. He couldn't yet stand the idea of letting the weight of his agony crush him. Soon he would let her go, but right now, he needed this respite.

She looked to where his fingers wrapped around her arm, but didn't try to pull away. That alone was a miracle.

She'd spent so much effort dodging every close contact, Joseph hadn't realized just how much he'd dreamed about touching her until now.

"He knows," she said. "It was part of the reason he sent me here. He knew that if things went to hell or you betrayed him and I became trapped here, I could always beg for mercy because I was like you. He was certain that you wouldn't kill me—not when your women are needed so desperately."

So Joseph had been tricked into agreeing to peace?

He couldn't go there. Not now. He was still trying to absorb the impact of the woman standing in front of him. "That's why you wouldn't let any of the men touch you. You knew that if we did, we might figure out what you are."

She nodded. "I'd heard the stories. I'm not exactly sure how it all works, but I thought it would be safer if none of you pawed at me."

"Now I understand why you could guarantee your mystery woman's cooperation." He paused as the consequences of her vow began to sink in. "You have to choose one of our men. Immediately."

She swallowed hard and lowered her head in acceptance. "I know."

"And you promised to bind yourself to him irrevocably."

"I know that, too." She lifted her head and looked at him. The impact of her golden gaze was nearly enough to drive him to his knees.

"I thought you hated us. Why would you willingly tie yourself to a man you hate?"

"Because I love those children. I love my brother. I'd gladly give up my life for any one of them. So I did."

He didn't like it that she thought binding herself to one of her own kind was the same thing as giving up her life, but he let it slide. There was too much to do now to worry about how she felt about her promise. She'd made it. Now all there was left was to ensure that she did as she said she would.

"You're free to go," he told her, "as soon as you choose your man. I'll summon everyone who is available back home."

"No need. I've already chosen my mate."

"Who is he?"

She closed her eyes and tensed up, as if bracing for a hard punch. "You."

Chapter 10

Lyka tried hard not to get sick all over Joseph's boots. She knew that giving up her life to save her people was the right thing to do. She also knew her path was now set in stone, and that it wasn't going to be an easy one. But she hadn't expected her decision to evoke such deep feelings of fear and trapped helplessness.

Her breathing was too hard and fast. Her stomach churned dangerously. She'd backed away from Joseph, putting as much space between them as she could, but all she'd gained was a harsh groan of pain from him. She was still just as trapped and terrified on this side of her suite as she'd been on the other.

"You can't be serious," said Joseph. "You hate me. Why the hell would you even consider binding your life to mine?"

"I don't hate you."

"Could have fooled me. Every time I came near you, you backed away like I was a demon."

"I didn't want you to touch me."

"And what about the part where you still think of me as your enemy? Your prison guard?"

"Andreas agreed to the peace treaty. I have no choice but to respect it. And once I've fulfilled my vow and let you collar me, I'll be free to come and go as I please. Remember?"

He glowered and stalked toward her. "No Theronai male in his right mind would let his woman run around unprotected."

"You don't have a choice. You promised."

"I didn't have all the details."

"That hardly matters. I don't have them, either. For all I know, I've just thrown my life away to find people who've already been killed. No one said life is fair."

"Binding yourself to one of us isn't throwing your life away. It's opening doors that you never would have had access to before. It comes with power—vast, nearly inexhaustible power. And, to be honest, I don't think you're ready for that kind of responsibility."

"Are you saying you won't have me?" she asked.

"I'm saying that you need to stay here long enough for the other single men to come back so you can pick one of them."

"I don't want to wait. Eric and the kids may not have that kind of time. I want to leave tonight."

"That's too damn bad." His face was dark red now, and the muscles and tendons along his neck stood out with fury. "You're not free until you execute your end of the bargain, which means I can damn well keep you here until the other men get home. Maybe that will give you enough time to accept that your life is different now. You can't go running off whenever you want."

Fury rose in her, bringing with it a rabid growl. How dare he try to go back on his word? How dare he try to trick her into staying until it was too late?

Lyka was many things, but passive wasn't one of them.

There was no way she was going to stay here and twiddle her thumbs while her people were out there in need. She and Joseph had struck a bargain. She got to pick who she wanted. End of story.

She lurched toward him, letting her animal side speed her reflexes. Before he could stop her, she grabbed the iridescent necklace he wore. She tried to back out of his reach, but he grabbed her before she could make her escape.

His fist closed around her wrist, sending a swarm of warm vibrations up her arm. The hot, tingly feeling swirled through her torso, hardening her nipples as it went. All that heat coalesced low inside her until her abdomen clenched against the force of it.

The slippery surface of the luceria dangled from her fingers. She could feel the warmth of his skin clinging to the supple band. It was heavier than she expected, layered with a mix of golds and greens that reminded her of his eyes.

He stared at it in shock and wonder. "What have you done?"

"I've made my decision, just like you promised I could. You can't go back on your word. You're mine now, Theronai."

His grip eased on her wrist. He took the band from her fingers and stared at her with a look she couldn't translate. It was part surprise, part hunger, part reverence. All she knew was that when he looked at her like that, it did something to her. Softened her.

"Lift your hair, Lyka."

The gentle order swept over her senses. She found herself doing as he asked without questioning it first.

He paused in the act of fastening the necklace around her throat. "Be sure, kitten. You can't take this back."

What choice did she have? She needed his power—both that of his magic and that of his station as leader of the Theronai. There was no time to waste on questioning her choices. All there was left to her now was to follow the path she'd laid out for herself and hope she could keep her regrets to a minimum.

"I'm sure," she said, gritting her teeth. "Just do it, already."

He reached behind her to the nape of her neck. The fine hairs there stirred at his nearness. No man had been this close to her in a long time, and the animal side of her perked up in acute awareness.

He touched the ends of the luceria together and they clicked shut, bringing to mind the image of a prison door clanging closed.

A bolt of panic cut through her. Before she could do anything about it, Joseph ripped his shirt over his head and drew his sword.

She'd heard stories of what would happen next—that the male would offer her an unbreakable vow. The woman would offer her own in return, and she would then have access to his power.

Lyka needed that power. She needed to have a kick-ass man like Joseph on her side in order to save her pack mates.

He dropped to one knee, slicing a small cut over his heart. The branches on his lifemark shivered in response, mesmerizing her with the wonder of the magic it represented.

"My life for yours, Lyka." He set his sword on the ground and took her hands in his. "It's your turn now. Give me your vow, kitten. Bind us together."

There was such naked want in his hazel eyes that she almost balked. There was no way a woman like her could contain whatever it was Joseph thought she had to offer him. Only ideas of fantastic power, beauty, wealth or kindness could evoke such raw emotion.

And Lyka had none of these.

"I don't know what to say."

"It doesn't have to be anything fancy. Just know that whatever you promise, you will be bound to me for the rest of our lives."

"Way to freak a girl out."

"You're the one who promised an irrevocable bond. I would have let you choose another man, but it's too late for that now."

Indeed it was.

She opened her mouth to speak three times before the words came to her tongue. "I may be a Slayer at heart, but I promise to try to be the best Theronai I can be."

As soon as she spoke the words, she knew it wasn't good enough. The promise she'd made to Joseph demanded irrevocability. Forever. She was compelled to uphold that vow now.

She swallowed and tried again. "I promise to try not to let you get under my skin or drive you too crazy, so we can be effective partners."

Again, it wasn't good enough. The vow she'd made was still unsatisfied, making her skin itch and burn with the need to promise him more.

But what more was there other than everything?

As the crushing weight of reality descended on her, she knew the truth. Everything was the only thing that would satisfy the magic of the vow she'd given him.

Lyka stared into his eyes, wondering how she'd jumped from one prison to another without even knowing it until now. She cleared her throat. "I promise you all that I have, all that I am, to fight by your side until the last breath leaves my body. Forever."

The intense sense of satisfaction she felt from appeasing the magic tying her to her vow was short-lived. Within the space of a second, the weight of her new vow fell over her, locking her inside it for all eternity.

She was Joseph's now.

Chapter 11

Lyka was his now. Forever.
  Joseph was still reeling from the shock of that when the luceria took charge and ripped him out of his own skin.

He'd heard from other men that a newly bonded couple would see a vision—some piece of the other person that the luceria thought was important, something that would help bind them together so that they could be a more effective pair.

But that's not what happened to Joseph. Instead of some kind of vision, he found himself bathed in Lyka's emotions, fears and motivations. For him, finding a woman was a lifelong dream. He'd been taught from the time he was young that he would one day be charged with the greatest gift and responsibility of his life. He would find a partner who would depend on him, who would use his strength to amplify her own. In turn, he would count on her to use his power for good, to open her heart and mind to him, and free him from his pain.

For Lyka, this union was nothing like that. It was a

tool. A means to an end. She wanted his power—both the magic that he stored within his body as well as the power of his station. She didn't want the life he had to offer her. She didn't want *him*.

She wanted freedom—to leave the walls of Dabyr and hunt unfettered. She wanted to live with the Slayers, drawing from him his power whenever she needed it. To her, this was no more than an inconvenient way of earning her freedom from him.

As soon as the luceria let go of him and he was firmly back inside his own body, he rose to his feet. Anger and frustration nipped at his heels, making his voice rough. "I won't be used."

She stared at him, wide-eyed and shaking. "I saw what you want from me. I can't do it. I'm not like you."

"What did you see?"

"You want me to be part of you, for there to be no boundaries between us. No space." She shook her head and backed away from him. "I can't live like that. I'm a Slayer. We need our freedom."

"You're a Theronai, too. You were meant to be bound to someone in our way."

"I'll suffocate."

"You'll adapt."

"You promised me freedom. You promised that I could leave here whenever I wanted."

"That was before I knew what you were. Before you tied yourself to a man who's tied to these walls."

"You can't break your promise. You won't be able to stop me from leaving."

As she said the words, he realized it was true. The magic that bound him to his word would compel him to open the gates and let her go. Unfortunately, the magic of his vow to protect her life with his would compel him to keep her at his side. "I'm the leader of this place. I can't just go off and leave."

"Then don't," she said as she went to her closet and pulled out a duffel bag, then headed to her bedroom to fill it.

Joseph was right on her heels. "What is that supposed to mean?"

"I'll be fine on my own. You just gave me access to a shit ton of power. If anything comes at me, I'll fry it."

Like hell. "You don't even know how to access my power yet."

"I'm sure I'll figure it out. I work well under pressure."

"You're not leaving." Even as he issued the edict, his skin started to itch. The blood in his veins burned as it pumped through them. His head started to pound the way it did whenever she was out of his sight. Only worse.

She paused in the act of throwing clothes into the bag. "Oh, really? You're looking a little pale, Theronai. Something wrong?"

He let out a string of curses, venting some of his frustration. "Will you at least consider the possibility that you might not be ready to wield my power without so much as a single lesson?"

"Time is of the essence."

"Yes, but what good is it for you to find the children when you don't have the power to protect them?"

She cocked one hip and stared at him in contemplation. "I'll give you ten minutes to show me what I need to know. After that, I'm gone."

"It's not enough," he told her. "It takes some women years to learn how to wield the kind of power you want."

"How do you know what I want?"

"The luceria told me. It's how I know you're just using me."

"I'm not trying to screw you over or anything. I'll be a good partner. Just don't expect me to fawn all over you the way some of the other Theronai women do with their mates. I don't fawn. Ever."

A few more of his dreams—the ones he kept hidden even from himself—shriveled and died. "Fine. You're all business. I get it. But what you don't know is that if you want to be able to sling magic around like those women do, then you're going to have to open up at least a little. This cold, I-don't-need-anyone attitude is going to get you nowhere."

"You'd hold out on me like that?"

"It's not me. It's the way the luceria works. The closer two people are, the more magic can flow between them. Those women you see fawning, as you call it, they have that kind of juice because they are as close to their men as any two people can be." He stepped up to her and gently tapped her forehead. "If you want my magic, you have to let me in here. We have to connect on a level so deep that we always know what the other is thinking—at least when it comes to combat."

She reeled away in horror. "Are you fucking kidding me? Do you have any idea how many things I know about the Slayers that you're not allowed to know? Letting you in my head would be the same thing as betraying my people."

"It doesn't matter. If you don't trust me enough to know that I'd never use that knowledge against someone you love, then you'll never be able to do more than light a match with my power."

"Bullshit."

He lifted a brow. "Think so? Let's go outside. I'll prove it."

She opened the sliders. "After you, Theronai."

He grinned at her. "Thank you, *Theronai.*"

Joseph was bluffing. He had to be. There was no way Lyka could have gone through all of that and not even earned access to his magic.

She knew how it was supposed to work. She'd heard all the stories, even seen a bonded pair of Theronai in action when she was a little girl. Her mother had done her best to warn Lyka of what she might face one day. This was the part where she was supposed to tap into Joseph's power and be able to kick ass.

He must have had some way of blocking her.

As she marched outside, she began forming a plan. She'd call his bluff and rip from him all the power she needed to rescue her people. If he was holding out on her, then she'd take it against his will.

She briefly wondered if doing such a thing would hurt him, but quickly decided she didn't care. If he was playing dirty, so could she.

He led her to the dock stretching out on the small lake behind the main building. There was a forest on the far side, and just inside the tree line, she could see small, rough cabins.

She'd been in one of those before. Naked, wearing only a sheet—an offering of peace from her brother, meant to ensure his good behavior.

For some reason, she felt far more exposed now than she had back then. Her world had been blown apart, her secret revealed and her future tied to a man she barely knew. Sure, he seemed like a decent guy, but for all she knew he was holding back his serial-killing, baby-eating ways.

Then again, if he were a monster, nothing in her vows said she couldn't kill him. He'd promised to protect her, but she'd made no such promise. If she really wanted out of this relationship, all she had to do was gack him in his sleep.

The thought turned her stomach and made her feel about as low as a pile of worm shit.

"What's upset you?" he asked as he stopped at the end of the dock.

"Who says I'm upset?"

He slid his finger along the slippery band around her neck. It buzzed and warmed in response to his touch. "This did. It connects us. It allows me to sense your emotions if they're strong enough. And what you felt a second ago was definitely strong."

The choker had shrunk to fit her perfectly. It was completely comfortable, but there was no room for her to shove her fingers under it and try to yank it off.

"It's not going anywhere," said Joseph. "Your vow to me made sure of that. You might as well get used to it. Besides, you look lovely in my luceria."

The way his gaze warmed sent a shiver through her. She shouldn't have cared about how he thought she looked, but the little thrill his compliment gave her was proof that she did. "Just show me what I need to know so I can get out of here."

He turned her body toward the lake as he stepped behind her. She could feel the hard contours of his muscles along her back as he pulled her against him. One of his thick arms wrapped around her middle, and he nestled his chin next to her ear. "See that post out there?"

All the air in her body had fled at his touch, leaving her none for speaking. Her concentration was shattered by his nearness. After so many weeks of keeping her distance and dodging his attempts to get closer, it was strange letting him touch her.

She tried to shove all thoughts of him aside and focus on her task. The water rippled under the light. A wooden pole several yards out rose from the surface about six feet. The top of it was charred black and splintered.

"See if you can hit it," he said.

"With what?"

"Fire. Force. Air. Electricity." She felt him shrug, and the power of that move rocked her body. "Whatever floats your boat."

She narrowed her gaze at the post, concentrating on it. She imagined it exploding into a million splinters. She held her breath and tried to make her vision a reality, but the post didn't so much as vibrate.

"What's wrong?" he asked. There was a smug satisfaction in his tone—a kind of *I told you so* vibe.

"Nothing's happening."

"Do you even know how to access my power?" he asked.

"I've seen the other women do it. How hard can it be?"

"Apparently too hard for you to accomplish."

She whirled on him, irritation spurring her movement. "Look, Theronai. If you're doing some kind of magical cock blocking, we've got a problem." There was something else she'd meant to say, but as she realized that she was inside his arms, practically in his embrace, all the words fell from her head.

He stared down at her—no small feat considering her height. His eyes were darker than usual, his focus gliding over her face in equal parts wonder and need. "I still can't believe you're mine."

His thumb caressed her cheek with such tenderness,

she felt her body relaxing. She may not know much about this man, but she'd seen him with the human children he protected. He was gentle, loving, even playful.

His kind had been her enemy for so long, she hadn't stopped to question whether all Theronai were the monsters her stepfather claimed them to be.

She swallowed to dislodge the lump of unwanted emotion wedged in her throat. "Don't go getting any crazy ideas, Theronai. This is a business relationship. You get to live, and I get access to your magic. Your pain ends and so does my imprisonment. Nothing more."

"You say that only because you don't know how our kind works. It's going to be my pleasure to teach you, kitten." He took her shoulders in his hands and turned her back around to face the lake. "Lesson one: tap into my power."

She was far too close to him. Her back was plastered against his chest. One of his thick arms wrapped around her waist to hold her in place. He wasn't squeezing her too tight, but she still had trouble drawing a full breath.

His mouth was right beside her ear, his voice a dark whisper of sound. "Close your eyes, Lyka."

She didn't want to. She knew that if she did, it was going to heighten her other senses. She would feel him more keenly, smell his skin and hear his voice, his breathing.

"You have to learn to trust me if you want this to work," he said.

How could she trust him? He'd been her enemy until recently.

Hadn't he?

"I'll give you what you want: power, freedom. All you have to do is trust me."

What choice did she have? Eric and the young were

in danger. They needed her to dig deep and find a way to do the impossible.

"Just close your eyes. Let yourself feel the connection running between us."

Her eyelids fell shut, and instantly she could smell him. Delicious. Intoxicating. Lickable.

A soft groan rose from her, surprising her.

"That's it," he whispered. "Just like that."

Tension ran through his limbs, as if he was struggling not to hold her tighter. Hard muscles bunched in his chest, teasing her back with a tactile treat. She'd seen him without his shirt before, but she wished now that she could feel that bare skin under her fingertips. And her lips.

No. She was not going to let herself get sucked in by hormonal urges, no matter how close it was to a full moon. This was a business arrangement. Nothing more.

"Do you feel the luceria round your throat?" he asked.

"Yes." How could she not? It vibrated against her skin, humming with the promise of power.

"The ring on my finger was once a part of that band. They're inextricably bound, just as we now are."

She wanted to disagree with that claim, but knew it was a waste of words. She'd put herself in this position. She'd agreed to the terms of their arrangement. She now had to live with her decision.

"The energy stored inside me will flow from my ring into your necklace. It will gather in you for whatever purpose you demand of it. You must give it shape, define it. Force it to do your will."

That she could do.

She focused on the luceria, trying to sense the connection he spoke of. While she could feel the warm metal and its pleasant hum, there was nothing else there. "Are you trying to stop me so I won't leave?" she asked.

"No. I want you to take my power into your body. I crave it."

Because she was touching him, she could sense another layer of want and craving coming from him. Dark, primal, sexual. His power was not the only part of him he wanted her to take inside her body.

He wanted to fuck her, fill her.

She jerked away from him, rocked to her foundation. Feeling his desire had heightened her own, making her think of things she had no business thinking. "I won't sleep with you, Theronai. Get that thought out of your head right now."

Instead of looking ashamed, he grinned. "You can sense my thoughts so soon? I never thought you'd trust me like that so quickly."

"I don't trust anything except that you want to bone me."

He frowned. "You seemed so certain, as if you knew what was in my head."

"Don't go getting the wrong idea. What I read coming from you was nothing special. I always know what people want."

Joseph grinned like he was trying to hold back a laugh.

"What?" she asked.

"It's just that I would have thought your gift would have been something a little more . . . violent. Instead, you're the perfect diplomat."

A surge of rage took over. The next thing she knew, she'd swept his legs out from under him and had him pinned to the ground. She was straddling his abdomen, her hand around his throat. "You take that back."

His grin was still in place. Her sending him to the ground did nothing to change that. "Make me."

She couldn't see his sword but knew it was there. She felt around on his belt for the hilt. The second she got close, his hand clamped over hers. He flipped her over until she was the one pinned to the ground. Even though she felt her body weight shift, there wasn't a thing she could do to stop him. He was too strong.

And he wasn't even straining with effort.

"Not like that," he said. "If you don't want me to see you as a diplomat, then let me in that pretty head of yours. Show me what a fighter you really are."

She tried to buck his weight off of her, but it was like trying to move a Sentinel Stone. He weighed a ton and was in complete control of her limbs, with her arms pinned by her ears. He straddled her thighs, rendering her legs useless.

By the time she'd given up on using physical strength against him, she was panting and sweating, despite the chilly night air.

"I told you I know too many secrets. I'll never let you in my head."

"Fine," he said, clearly not believing a word she said. "Then take a look in mine. I have nothing to hide. Maybe if you take a peek, you'll figure out how to get what you want."

The image of him naked between her thighs, his mouth and tongue working to give her pleasure, came to mind. Her arms were bound over her head by silken rope; her legs were pinned wide by his big hands. The vision was so clear and detailed, she went still in shock.

It took her a second to realize that her gift was working overtime, showing her exactly what it was he wanted. Now, in this moment. If she displayed even the slightest interest, she was certain his desires were strong enough that he would pursue them.

Something deep inside her quivered in eagerness. In desperation. Every muscle in her body softened, as if needing to give in to his fantasy.

She couldn't do that to herself. She couldn't let this man seduce her and entrench himself any deeper into her life than he already had. It was bad enough that she'd tied herself to a partner who might, at any moment, become her enemy again. She couldn't also sleep with him.

"Let me up," she demanded.

"You're strong enough to free yourself if you want to."

No, she wasn't. When it came to sheer physical strength, he outmatched her completely. If he'd been a human male, he'd already be swimming his way back to shore from where she flung him. But he wasn't human. He was Theronai. A big, irritating, muscle-bound Theronai.

"Get. Off."

"You're not even trying," he said with boundless patience. "Find the thread of power dangling from the luceria and pull on it."

She didn't know what he meant, but she was both pissed off and turned on enough to do whatever it took to put some distance between them.

Lyka closed her eyes and felt for something—anything. The quivering band around her throat was brimming with power. She could almost feel its energy glowing against her skin. Everywhere Joseph's flesh met hers, there was a hot vibration—an intense connection that was both distracting and somehow the key to her struggle.

She ignored the fact that he was a tasty hunk of man

who wanted her and splayed her hands around his bare arms. Muscles tensed in response to her touch, warming the tips of her fingers. It was there she felt the most vibration, so she slid her hands along his skin, following where the energy led.

A rough moan of desire rumbled from his chest, reminding her that he was flesh and blood. And that he wanted her.

She lost her concentration for a moment before gathering her wits again for another try. This time, she knew where to touch him—where that power was being housed.

Her fingers slid under his shirt and up over his lifemark. She could feel the branches tremble and sway beneath her fingertips. That alone was amazing enough, but what really shocked her—what pulled every bit of her attention—was the mammoth pool of power seething just under his skin.

She could sense it now, but had no idea how to reach it.

"Use the luceria," he told her. "It's the only way to get what you want."

The blasted band around her neck buzzed eagerly. As did Joseph's ring. His hand was on her shoulder, only inches away from her collar. They both vibrated at exactly the same frequency.

With one hand still on his lifemark, she grabbed his wrist and slid his fingers to her necklace. The two pieces of the luceria snapped together like magnets.

Lyka's whole world lit up from the inside out. That string of power he'd mentioned was there, dangling right in front of her. It pulsed with color and light, bulging with the kind of magic she could never have believed was real until she felt it.

"I found it," she whispered in awe.

"Yes. Now use it."

This power she had at her fingertips—this was the key to saving her pack mates. This was her path to freedom.

As that thought formed in her mind, Joseph's weight vanished from atop her. The back of her hand burned where his shirt raked against it. She heard a grunt and a heavy splash.

The flow of power cut off like a switch had been flipped. When she opened her eyes, she saw Joseph swimming back toward her, his face grim.

His power had done her bidding, and now a very wet, very angry Theronai was headed her way.

Chapter 12

Eric took careful mental notes of his surroundings as he made his way through the system of caves. His Slayer vision allowed him to see in dim light, but he also noticed that there were several torches burning here and there.

He'd been in enough caves to know that wasn't normal—Synestryn neither enjoyed nor needed light.

As he passed gatherings of those mostly furless guards, he realized that they were the ones who seemed to need the light. Perhaps whatever the Synestryn had done to create them had taken away some of their innate ability to dwell in darkness.

He spied several piles of the guards sleeping in chambers off the main pathway. Like the Slayer young, they seemed to be sharing body heat as they slept, huddled in groups for warmth.

Maybe that was something he could use against them.

He peered through every opening and crevice he could see, but there was no sign of the two children who'd been separated from the group. The system of caves was long and elaborate, leaving a lot of unexplored areas.

If he couldn't locate the kids, it could easily take him a week to find them, and that was if he didn't have to fight his way through every turn.

"Here we are," said Treszka, as they arrived at their destination.

He was too far away from the young now to do anything to protect them. They were on their own, a fact that hovered in the back of his mind like a vulture waiting for its prey to die.

He followed her flowing skirts into a large stone chamber. The floor here was relatively level, covered with rugs and pillows. A large iron bed filled half the space, leaving the other side open as some kind of sitting area, complete with upholstered furniture.

The whole place smelled . . . odd. Almost human, beneath the caustic stench he'd come to associate with Treszka.

"Have a seat," she said, waving toward a love seat.

What the hell? After hours of being on that rock floor, a soft surface looked pretty damn good.

Eric sat and was instantly surrounded by that strange human smell. It took him a second to realize that it wasn't regular leather he was sitting on. It was skin. Human skin.

Revulsion surged up his throat, but he choked it down rather than give her the satisfaction of seeing his distress.

She eyed him with an air of amused expectation.

"This is nice," he said, running his hand over the seat. "Young virgins?"

Her black eyes narrowed in irritation, but she hid it quickly. "Are you hungry?"

He stretched out on the love seat. "Sure. I could go for some tacos. Maybe a loaded pizza. There's a great little hole-in-the-wall I know of that delivers."

"Human food? I would have thought better of you, Slayer."

He shrugged. "Human food didn't make so damn many people fat by being unappetizing. You should try it sometime."

She was getting pissed. He could smell her anger falling out of her, see it in the way her white pupils constricted. "You will eat what I provide or not at all."

"Fine. Whatever." He forced himself to stare into her freaky eyes. "Just know that if you try to feed me meat from a human or one of my own, I will kill you where you stand."

She beamed. "That's what I want to see. Fire. Spirit."

"You want me to come after you?" he asked. "Hell, honey, why didn't you say so?" He stood, and several guards took a step forward, weapons raised.

"Stand down," she told the guards. "He wouldn't be able to kill me on his best day. And with that lump on his head, today is far from his best day." She clapped her hands twice, and instantly another demon entered the room, as if he'd been waiting for the invitation.

"Vazel, I'd like you to meet our guest, Eric Phelan."

Vazel loped across the room, eyeing Eric with suspicion. He was grotesquely built, with knobby patches of skin on every joint. He wore only a loincloth that shared way too much with the world. His head was bald and fleshy, with an almost reptilian texture. His thin lips were pulled back in a snarl of warning, showing off several pointed teeth as well as gaps where more had once been. His arms were too long for his frame. He had only three fingers on each hand, and two of them had an extra joint. His skin was a pale gray color, with mangy patches of gray fur.

For a moment, Eric wished he were unable to see in the dark.

"Eric, I'd like you to meet my second in command, Vazel."

No way in hell was he going to touch this demon. Instead, he nodded in greeting, pretending like Vazel wasn't the ugliest thing he'd seen in decades of fighting ugly demons.

"You should kill him," said Vazel, the words slurred through sharp teeth.

"We talked about this. He's a Slayer. I need him," she said.

"Bad blood," said Vazel. "Too far from our own. No power. He's a bad match."

They thought Eric didn't have power? That was good to know. If they didn't think he could defend himself, they might let down their guard.

"He is perfect," she said.

"I hate to get in the way of a good argument," he said, "but you promised me dinner." He didn't know how he was going to hide enough food to feed the young, but he had to make an effort. There was no way of knowing if they'd be provided for otherwise.

"Of course," said Treszka. "Send them in."

Eric smelled his kin before he saw them. The two missing young were shackled around the neck. A heavy chain dangled down, dragging on the ground before sweeping back up into the hands of one of the demon guards. Each of the boys carried a tray of food. Their eyes glittered with tears, but neither of them let those tears fall.

Eric did his best to hide his relief and the anger that followed swiftly on its heels. "Are you hurt?" he asked them.

"They're untouched," said Treszka. "And will remain that way as long as you obey."

Yeah. Obedience wasn't really his thing. It took all his

self-control to stay where he was and not rush to their sides. "Are you hurt?" he repeated, looking each boy in the eyes.

Both shook their heads but didn't open their mouths.

"They're not allowed to speak," she explained. "They know the rules. Now come and eat."

The food smelled good. Untainted. There was some kind of charred beef and even some fruit—not at all what he would have expected down here.

"Serve us," ordered Treszka.

The young scurried to obey. They set the trays down on a small table. Eric could hear their stomachs rumbling from here.

He sniffed the food carefully, letting his powerful nose search for even the slightest sign of toxin or filth. All he smelled was food. Plain, but safe.

"I won't eat until they do," he said.

"You will eat when I tell you to do so," she said.

She lifted one black-tipped finger. That was all.

The guards holding the chains attached to the boys' collars jerked on them, knocking the young to their hands and knees. One of them stifled a sob, but Eric still heard it.

He took a step toward her.

Vazel was faster than his appearance would suggest. He drew a sword and leveled it against Eric's chest, pressing hard enough to draw a trickle of blood.

"You will not touch her," said Vazel.

"Touching her is the absolute last thing I want to do, but if she hurts those kids again, I'm going to have to put her in the ground."

Vazel growled. Treszka laughed. "Boys, boys. No need to fight over me. Let's all sit down and have a nice meal together."

At the smell of Eric's blood, nearby demons became agitated. He could hear the wave of restless hunger race out of the chamber and through the system of caves.

He stared down at the grotesque demon. "If you don't take that steel out of my skin, we're going to have a problem with the other demons."

"She controls them with absolute authority."

Eric eyed the demon. "Got your dick in a drawer, too, does she?"

Vazel growled.

"That's enough! Sit!" Treszka's face darkened with rage.

Vazel sat. Eric shook his head. "I don't eat while the young suffer. Period. If you can't handle that, then we're done here."

She smiled sweetly at Eric. "You're not in charge here, Slayer. I am." Before he could react, she addressed the guards. "Feed the scrawny one to the troops. Make the other one watch."

Chapter 13

Joseph was glad the lake water was cold. It helped burn off some of his anger before he reached Lyka again.

To her credit, she didn't try to hide or run away. She stood there waiting for him, feet braced apart, like she was ready for battle.

Joseph wasn't sure his body could take another rough ride like the last one without suffering physical damage, so he stopped several feet away, dripping onto the grass. "What the hell, Lyka?"

"I didn't mean to do it." She paused, scrunching up her nose. "Well, I did, but not exactly like that. It just kind of happened."

"Is it just kind of going to happen again?"

She crossed her arms over her chest. "Depends on how pissy you get with me, Theronai." Her gaze dipped down, roaming over his torso with feminine interest.

Even with his cock being caged by cold, wet jeans, it still reacted to her look, swelling uncomfortably.

"At least you can tap into my power now. That's

something, I guess." He nodded toward the training post. "Try it now."

She squinted at the wooden post, pressing her lips flat in concentration. "Nothing is happening."

"Just do what you did before, without the whole dunking part."

She tried again, but he felt no draw on his power, no connection.

"Why isn't it working?" she asked.

"Are you too tired?"

She lifted a brow. "Do I look tired, Theronai?"

No, she looked delicious. Absolutely edible. And if he didn't stop thinking about getting his mouth on his sweet little kitty, he was going to do permanent damage to his cock. There was simply no room for it to swell in these wet jeans.

"What's different?" he asked.

"I can't feel you anymore. It's like your power is too far away to reach."

He could certainly fix that.

He stepped up behind her and slid his fingers through hers. His ring buzzed happily against her skin. The magic roiling inside him bubbled up, eager to be free.

"Try it now."

She did as he asked, but it still didn't work.

One more thing to try. "I'm going to touch my ring to your necklace. Maybe that's what did it last time."

He could have lifted her hair and touched the nape of her neck, but instead he slid his arm under hers and between her breasts. His hand shackled her throat in front, pinning her nice and tight against him.

She felt so damn good there. The sweet curve of her ass nestled against him, cushioning his erection. Lake water wet her clothes, allowing their body heat to conduct easily between them. He could feel her heart pound against his forearm, speeding the same way her breathing did at his touch.

She might not like him, but her body reacted to his touch as if she'd been made just for him. Eventually, she'd get used to his touch, his nearness.

Assuming she didn't simply walk through the gates and leave him behind.

He couldn't let her go out there alone, not with so much danger around every turn. His promise would force his hand if she wanted to leave, but that didn't mean he couldn't convince her to stay here, where she'd be safe.

He let his fingers trail over her skin, making note of how she barely reacted when he kept his touch light, but her whole body trembled when he applied a little pressure.

Joseph lowered his head so that his lips grazed the outer rim of her hear as he whispered, "Can you feel my power now?"

Her voice was faint, almost breathless. "I think so."

"Let it slide inside you. Here." He tightened his fingers around her neck, drawing her attention to the spot where his ring connected to her necklace.

Her head fell back. She let out a small moan before clamping her lips shut over it. Pleasure? Pain? He couldn't tell.

"Am I hurting you?"

She gave her head a little shake. Her golden hair slid across his chest, the strands clinging to his damp skin.

"What do you feel?" he asked.

Her voice was dreamy. "Warm. Full."

The imagery that brought to mind held a dark eroticism that made his cock throb hard against her ass. There were so many ways he wanted to fill her, leaving her warm and sated.

Down, boy. Not going to happen. Not here. Not tonight. And not ever if you don't get some fucking control over yourself.

"Open your eyes, kitten. Look at the post in the lake. Use that power filling you up to set it on fire."

"I don't know how."

"Then let me show you."

Her eyes were still closed. She was relaxed against him, accepting his hold on her almost as if she welcomed it. There was a dreamy look on her beautiful face that made him swell with pride. He'd been the one who put it there.

He knew she didn't want him in her thoughts, but she wasn't resisting him now. She was pliant in his arms, leaning on him, trusting him not to let her fall.

Once she knew what it was like to connect to him in the way they were meant to connect, she wouldn't be afraid of it anymore. She'd see that they'd be stronger when united. Unstoppable.

With the same gentle care reserved for fragile, delicate things, he found the connection the luceria forged between them and eased into her thoughts. He moved slowly, backing off whenever he hit even the slightest resistance. With each passing second, he gained a little more ground, moving deeper into her mind.

He didn't snoop or even let his curiosity gain the upper hand. He stuck to his original task and used their link to show her what she needed to do.

The instant his thought solidified inside hers, she freaked.

Every muscle in her body went stiff. She snarled, grabbed his head and flipped him over her. He slammed into the ground hard enough to rattle his bones. Before he knew what was happening, she had drawn his sword and held the tip of it to his throat.

"Don't you ever fucking do that again." Her voice was a rough growl of warning. Her pupils narrowed to slits, and her canines seemed to lengthen.

Joseph didn't dare move. Not when she was on the edge of skewering him where he lay with that razor-sharp steel blade.

"Promise me!" she demanded.

He kept his voice nice and calm. No need to rile the wild animal in her. "No. That's the way it's supposed to be between us. One day you'll see that. Until then, I'll try to be as patient as you need me to be."

She lunged to her feet and tossed the blade onto the ground. "Keep your distance, Theronai. We're done."

Lyka stalked away, making a beeline for her suite.

Joseph knew exactly what she was doing, and there wasn't a thing he could do to stop her. He'd promised her she could leave, and now she would.

But she wasn't going alone. She might not like it, but that was just too bad. She'd taken his luceria. She'd given him her vow. She was his now, and he had made a promise to protect her life with his own. He couldn't do that if she was out there and he was in here.

Joseph picked up his cell phone as he went to pack his bag. The first man on his list answered.

"I need you to hold down the fort while I'm away," said Joseph. "I'm going on a field trip."

Eric suffered through a surge of panic. The two Slayer boys both started crying.

He'd made a mistake. He'd pushed Treszka too hard, and now those kids were going to pay the price.

"No," he said, rushing to fix the damage he'd done. "Don't hurt them."

She aimed those white pupils at him, creeping him out down to his toes. "You will obey?"

For now he would. For now he would bide his time and figure out a way to get out of here without losing a single one of the young. "I will."

"Then sit and eat."

Eric sat and started eating. He didn't taste a thing. His focus was too tightly on the boys who were crying quietly on the far side of the room.

Poor kids. He had to get them out before they were irrevocably scarred.

"What do I have to do to free the young?" he asked between bites.

Vazel, the grotesque demon sitting across from him, pulled his eyes off Treszka long enough to glare at Eric. "They're ours now. We need their blood."

"Silence," she barked. "You have no idea what my plans for these creatures are."

He bowed his head in obedience, but the glare of hatred on his face was still aimed at Eric.

"So you admit you're not going to let them go?" asked Eric. "If that's the case, then go ahead and kill them now. I'd rather not see them suffer."

The boys whimpered.

"I have no desire to kill them. I will if you force my hand, but my intent is for them to live a long, healthy life. We need them down here."

That's when Eric realized the truth, and it was far worse than he'd hoped.

Slayer blood was powerful. It held the traces of magic that the Synestryn needed to live. Slayers healed fast. Regenerated blood and tissue faster than even the Theronai or Sanguinar did. And they didn't burn up any precious magical resources doing so. If fed and protected from injury, a Slayer could lose a lot of blood every day and live for decades.

That was what she'd meant when she said she wanted the young to live a long, healthy life.

She was going to bleed them to fuel her troops.

His desire to keep the kids alive warred with his need to see every last Synestryn die. He couldn't stand the thought of the young being used as food, living their lives down here, knowing nothing more than pain and imprisonment.

He'd rather see them die a swift, painless death.

"I can see what you're thinking, Slayer," she said. "I won't let you take my resources away."

"You're not leaving me much choice."

"They'll be comfortable."

"The metal collars around their necks say otherwise."

"A necessary precaution. These two tried to kill my soldiers."

Eric glanced toward the young. "Excellent work, boys. I'm proud of you."

"Take them away," ordered Treszka, clearly irritated that Eric wasn't paying complete attention to her. "Feed them. Let them sleep."

"Stay strong, boys. I *will* come for you. We'll get out of here soon."

The young didn't respond, but he knew they'd heard him. That was enough for now. They were strong. They'd survive as he'd trained them to do.

Vazel ripped a piece of meat free and shoved it into his mouth. Juices dripped down his knobby chin. "I told you he was more trouble alive. Let me take him to the pens. He's no better than the others."

"What others?" asked Eric.

Treszka's nostrils flared in anger. "Leave us until you can learn the art of silence. Now."

He shot Eric another death stare, but picked up his food in his giant fists and stomped away.

That left only her and about a dozen guards for him to take out. He glanced around the room, calculating his odds.

"You won't make it out alive," she said, as if reading his thoughts. "There are two hundred more of my men between you and the surface. You might as well get used to the dark."

The information she accidentally provided was useful. Assuming any of it was true. "I will find a way out."

She gave him a sexy smile, and for a split second, he almost forgot she was a bloodthirsty demon. Her beauty had a way of clouding his judgment, but the toxic smell coming from her reminded him of exactly what she was.

"Is that all you really want?" she asked, running her fingers down her neck to dip just inside the top of her velvet gown. Breasts were designed to make men stupid, and she really did have a spectacular pair. Especially for a demon.

He shook his head to steel his resolve. "Yes. I want the young and I want to leave. I'd also like you and every demon down here dead, if I'm being completely honest."

"I'm no demon," she said with a little pout.

"Sure as hell fooled me. If you're not a demon, then what the hell are you?"

"A Synestryn queen."

Eric blinked. "Those exist?"

"I rule this area absolutely. All of my kind who dwell here obey me. As will you."

He laughed. He couldn't help it. "You really shouldn't

say such things until you get to know a person. Makes you look like an idiot."

One second he was sitting at the table. The next, he flew across the room, coming to a hard stop as his body slammed into the cave wall. His head bounced off, rattling his brains around in his skull. He stayed where he landed, not even sliding down an inch. His feet dangled over the ground, swiftly losing feeling as the pressure holding him in place increased and cut off his blood flow.

Treszka lifted her skirts and glided over to where he sprawled, completely immobile. "And you, Slayer, should not defy a queen who possesses more power than you can imagine. It makes you look like food."

She flicked her wrist and his head jerked to the side, baring his neck. He watched in helpless horror as she tugged on her hair, pulling it back, away from her forehead. The long strands hung there by a flap of skin that had been covering what could only be called a maw. The opening in the top of her head was a grotesque black hole surrounded by half a dozen long, sharp teeth. She bowed her head, giving him a better view, and he wished like hell he'd been born blind. One bulbous eye positioned above the maw blinked at him. It was the same black iris and white pupil as her other eyes, but this one was lidded by thick, rubbery flesh with no lashes. Tears leaked from it as it regarded him.

As he watched, completely immobile, she lowered that mouth to his throat and sank her sharp teeth in his flesh.

He tried to fight her hold, tried to slow his pounding heart so it wouldn't willingly pump blood into her mouth, but nothing he did worked. With each passing beat of his heart, he fed her, strengthening her while he grew weaker.

As he became dizzy from blood loss, his eyes fluttered shut. All he could feel was the sharp sting of her teeth and the cold brush of that rubbery eyelid on his skin. Not long after that, he felt nothing as he sank into unconsciousness.

Chapter 14

Lyka surveyed the damage that had once been her home.

What used to be a peaceful woodland settlement nestled in the Ozark Mountains was now just . . . carnage. The rustic log cabins her people lived in were charred and broken. Several of them looked like they'd taken blows over and over from a battering ram. All that was left were splinters and the belongings of her pack mates strewn about like so much leaf litter.

The ground was rough with furrows dug in by the feet of hundreds of Synestryn. Those that had died had been burned off by the sun, but their primitive swords remained as a testament to how many enemies her people had faced.

It was a wonder that any of them survived.

All around her, fallen leaves and evergreens colored the area, but in the center of the clearing there was only black.

The blood of their enemy had tainted the ground, staining it and poisoning it for years to come. Nothing would grow here. Nothing would flourish here. The peaceful setting so in tune with nature would never again be the same.

Off to one side were several fresh graves dug in haste by Andreas and his men upon their return. The dirt was mounded up over those who'd been lost. There had been no time for tombstones, so all that marked their graves now were thick wooden stakes carved with the names of the dead.

A flood of anguish and grief washed over her so suddenly she didn't see it coming. The shock of the devastation was beginning to wear off, leaving behind something much more jagged and agonizing.

Her chest tightened until she couldn't breathe. She pulled in pitiful gasps of air, only to let them out in high whimpers of pain. The wind swept the noise of her grief away as if it had never been, but the marks it left on her were permanent scars of loss that would never fade.

She crouched where she stood, hearing the charred earth beneath her feet crunch with the shift of her weight. She hugged herself, praying the storm of emotion would pass and she'd once again be able to function.

She'd come here to find her brother and the children. Despite her Theronai side, she was one of the best scent trackers her people had. If anyone could find a trail leading from this place, it was her.

Tears streamed down her cheeks and clogged her nose, rendering it useless. She had to find some way to get a grip, but wave after wave of pain kept barreling into her.

So many lives torn apart. So many dead. How could she just push that aside like it had never even happened? These people were her friends, her family. She hadn't even gotten to say good-bye to them, and now they were gone.

She didn't know how long she stayed like that, crouched in the forest, surrounded by devastation and death. Her feet had long since gone to sleep. The skin under the luceria around her neck was wet with tears, as was the collar of her shirt. The angle of the sun had changed, and shadows had begun to elongate as the day neared its end.

Still, she couldn't move. She should have been here. She should have fought beside her people and helped fend off the attack. Instead she was trapped inside the nice, safe walls of Dabyr while her loved ones died.

A soft whisper of comfort brushed through her mind. A second later, Joseph appeared through the trees, heading right for her.

She'd left Dabyr alone, but she'd known he would follow her. Eventually. She just hadn't thought he'd find a way to leave his post so soon.

She wanted to be angry at him for intruding, but the sight of his tall, strong body getting closer gave her a much-needed distraction from her grief. He really was beautifully built, with just the right amount of muscle to give him an air of competence without being bulky or overblown. His wide shoulders and long limbs were just the kind of advantage a man like him would need when fighting demons. And despite all the office work he did, his hands still bore the mark of a swordsman. Calluses from hours wielding a weapon, broad palms and strong, thick fingers and forearms.

Now that she knew what his hands felt like on her—all hot and tingly—she wondered how she'd ever gone so long evading his touch.

She sniffed and tried to stand. Her legs had gone numb, making the move impossible.

Joseph was at her side in an instant, lifting her to her

feet by her arms. His hands lingered on her shoulders while his gaze settled on her neck.

She had the strangest urge to snuggle up against him and let him shield her from the carnage for just a little while.

As if he knew what she needed, he pulled her against his body in a tight hug.

She closed her eyes, reveling in the heat of his skin. He shielded her from the breeze and the stink of burned homes it carried with it. His big hands stroked her back, moving slowly enough to help unknot the tension that had been riding her so hard.

He didn't say a word or offer any empty platitudes of comfort. All he did was hold her, giving her the support she needed to find the strength to stand on her own two feet.

Lyka breathed him in, burying her nose against his chest. The smell of his skin worked its magic on her, the same way those tendrils of sparkling heat connecting the two of them did. The pale skin around his neck where the luceria used to lie was a stark reminder of their recent change in status. She was no longer hidden, holding her Theronai side hostage. It was out and free, and soon everyone would know what a freak she really was.

Maybe if she saved Eric and the young, her people would find a way to accept her.

Hunting for those kids was what she really needed to be doing, not hugging a man who seemed content to hold her until nightfall, if that's what she wanted.

She pushed away from him, forcing herself to stand on her own, face her grief.

"Are you okay?" he asked.

"I will be." Once she found the creatures responsible

for this destruction and ripped them apart with her bare hands.

He surveyed the area, his expression grim. "Andreas wasn't exaggerating. This is . . . unbelievable. How many demons were there?"

"Too many," she said, her voice rough with emotion. Tears had left cooling trails on her cheeks, which she ignored. He'd already seen her crying, but if this much death and devastation wasn't reason enough to show her grief, she had no idea what would be.

"Why did you come?" she asked. "Why did you follow me?"

"Do you want to hear what you want to hear, or would you rather have the truth?"

"I never took you for a liar."

"Sometimes the truth is too much to bear. I don't want to upset you more than you already are."

"That would be impossible."

He sighed and his shoulders bowed slightly. "I didn't want you out here alone. You and I are bonded now. As much as you may hate it, I plan to do whatever it takes to keep you safe for the rest of my life. Even if it means locking you away at Dabyr."

"Well, at least you're aware I wasn't going to enjoy hearing the truth. Points for that, I guess."

He wiped her cheek dry with his thumb, staring over her shoulder at the rough wooden grave markers. "I won't let you end up like them."

"I'm too tired to fight you, Joseph. Please don't make me."

"I don't suppose there's any sense in knocking you unconscious and dragging you back home, is there?"

She looked around at the charred logs and poisoned earth. "This *is* my home. And there's no way in hell I'm letting what was done here go unpunished. I'm finding those kids. I'm finding Eric. I'm killing those responsible. You can help or you can get the fuck out of my way."

"I figured that's what you'd say."

"And?"

"I brought enough supplies and gear to launch a small war against the Synestryn."

Relief fluttered through her, but died a swift death when he opened his mouth again.

"But it won't be enough," he said. "If you really want to be able to take these demons down, you need to use every advantage you have."

"You think I won't?"

He stared at her pointedly. "I *know* so."

"What the hell is that supposed to mean?"

"You have access to more power than most people ever dream about. It's right here." He tapped his chest. "But you don't like the way you reach it, so you're just walking away. Pretending it isn't real or that you don't need it."

"I've heard all the stories. Heard the bonded women talk. They all love their men. Trust them. You know as well as I do that I could never trust you like that."

He flinched as if she'd kicked him in the crotch. "Why not? I've never harmed you or your people. Even when we were at war, I ordered my men to defend themselves from attack but never initiate one. Never provoke the Slayers."

"Because you were afraid we'd kill you."

"No, because we're spread thin, and the only way we're ever going to beat the Synestryn is if we focus all our efforts and resources on them, rather than each other."

"Andreas feels the same way. Under his rule our people never attacked yours. It is forbidden."

"Good. Then we can move on from this animosity you've got going here, and do what we both want: find Eric and the kids."

He made it sound so simple.

Maybe it was. Maybe she was complicating it by bringing in generations of baggage.

Still, he didn't understand what he was asking. "I know things, Joseph. Secrets. Strategies and tactics. If you go poking around in my head, you're going to see them. What if the treaty doesn't work out? What if the next leader after Andreas sends us to war against you again?"

He went quiet for a moment, simply staring at her. "Which side would you take, kitten?"

"I'm a Slayer," she said, hoping he wouldn't make her be any clearer. She really didn't want to hurt his feelings, but she couldn't lie to him about it, either—not something this important. Her loyalty was to her own kind, and the little bit of Theronai blood running through her veins wasn't going to change that.

He pressed his lips together so hard, they turned pale. "We'll talk about that again later. Right now you and I have bigger problems. So do those kids. Those are the people we need to be worried about. They are the reason you need to open up a little—just enough to do what needs to be done to save them."

"You really think that tapping into your power is going to make that much of a difference?" she asked.

"It's the kind of thing that could mean the difference between life and death."

She sighed. He was probably right. "Can't I find another way to access it? Some kind of shortcut?"

"You bonded yourself to me permanently. There's no getting around that. Eventually, you'll realize that you can trust me."

But not in time for her to find her people. *That* was the part he didn't say. "Some of the other Theronai women have learned to channel magic in just a few days. I've heard the stories."

"Yes, but they let their mates in." He tapped her temple. "You won't."

"There's got to be another way."

He shifted his stance and stared past her as if he had something to hide. "There's a lot riding on our relationship, Lyka. You can't say that you haven't thought about what a union between us might mean for long-term peace between the Slayers and Theronai."

"Peace never lasts. Something always screws it up. That's why I can't let you in my head the way you want."

"Even if it means you're powerless to help find your missing brother?"

She fought against a spike of irritation. "I'm not powerless. I've never in my life been powerless. And I'm sure as hell not going to start now, when my people are missing and in danger."

"You know I won't let you risk your life, right? My vow makes it impossible for me to allow you to do anything that would hurt you."

"Theronai women go into battle all the time."

"Yes, but they also have access to incredible power and the ability to use their magic to fend off attack. You don't."

She hated it that he was right. While the idea of letting Joseph rummage around in her head was abhorrent, the thought that she could do what some of those Theronai women could was damn appealing. Slinging magic around like it was nothing . . . She could really get off on something like that.

"We should go," she said. "It'll be getting dark soon,

we have almost an hour's hike back to the road and I still need to survey the area for a clear scent trail."

"Does your sudden change of subject mean you're going to let me in, or is it your way of getting me to shut up?"

"Definitely the shutting-up one."

"You've been through hell seeing what you just saw, so I'll give in, but know that this isn't the end of the conversation. One of these days you're going to see that I hold no ill will toward you or the Slayers, and you're going to wish you'd trusted me sooner."

"Maybe," she said. "But that day is definitely not today."

The hair on the back of her neck stood up. It was the only warning she had before dark figures crashed through the brush toward them. She caught their stagnant scent on the wind as they closed in.

"Demons!" she shouted as she pulled a pair of daggers from her belt. The tips gleamed with thick black poison—one of the few known to work on the Synestryn.

Her mind rejected what her senses were telling her. These creatures couldn't be demons. The sun wasn't all the way down yet, and while the woods were growing dark, Synestryn never strayed out of their caves before sunset. To do so was to risk certain death.

Joseph drew his sword. The metallic hiss of steel on steel was reassuring.

The first shadowy shape reached them. Lyka's Slayer vision amplified the light around them, showing her a clear image of what they faced.

It almost looked human. A long, tattered coat covered its body, revealing only its face and hands. There were splotchy patches of fur on both. It wielded a sword like the ones littering the ground behind them, only this one was far more nicked and dented from use.

Its face was oddly proportioned, with a protruding mouth and nose—the clear remnants of a beast with a muzzle somewhere in its lineage. Its teeth were sharp, its eyes huge and black, with no whites showing at all. Saliva wet its chin and ran down its neck, leaving a damp patch on the front of its coat.

If not for the stench it put off, the thing could have almost passed as an exceptionally ugly human.

She tried to summon the beast inside her, but as was the case whenever she needed her tiger the most, it evaded her. It would come out and play whenever she didn't want it, but put her life in danger, and it was nowhere to be found.

Fucking pussy.

Joseph stepped in front of Lyka to take the brunt of the charge. The ring of metal on metal filled the trees. The force of the demon's blow rocked Joseph back on his heels.

"Another one coming. Get behind me!" he shouted.

Maybe he was used to most people cowering behind him, but Lyka was not most people. She was trained for this. Bred for it. Her whole family came from a long line of warriors. Sure, maybe they could shift into their animal form and she couldn't, but she was armed and wasn't about to let a little thing like being stuck in her human form slow her down.

That's why she carried poisoned weapons and knew how to use them.

As the second demon charged, Lyka shifted her stance to the left to get out of Joseph's way. She didn't want to impede his swing, and she really didn't want him fending off two demons at once. She'd never seen him in a real fight, and she didn't want to find out the hard way that he had a blind spot.

Lugging his heavy ass out of here was not her idea of a good time.

The second demon leapt over a fallen log. Its sword had the benefit of reach over her weapons, but she was faster. Once it was airborne, it could no longer control its movement. But Lyka was still firmly attached to the ground and she could.

She ducked under the creature, rolling beneath its feet. She came up on the far side, shoving one of her daggers high. The blade hit the billowy coat, but she could tell by the drag in her strike that she'd tagged flesh, too.

Now all she had to do was stay alive until the poison did its thing.

The angry demon whirled on her. She backed away, heading toward a large boulder nearby. Climbing on that would give her an advantage of height, which might be enough to keep her alive. Plus, every demon she drew away from Joseph was one fewer he had to fight.

A quick glance over her shoulder showed her that he was definitely still fighting. Only there wasn't just one creature on him; there were three.

She'd never seen anyone his size move with such speed and grace. His sword swung so fast that it was simply an arc of silver slicing through the air. Every strike hit, lopping off limbs and skewering flesh. Within seconds, he had all three of the demons in a pile at his feet.

And he hadn't even broken a sweat.

She was so amazed at his skill that she forgot to look where she was going. Her foot caught on a fallen branch and she went down hard.

The hair on her nape stood up so fast it hurt. She rolled onto her back just in time to see the demon she'd injured lift its sword to slice her in two.

Even if she got her daggers up in time to parry the attack, it wasn't going to be enough to stop the blow. There was too much power behind it, and she had nowhere to go.

She wasn't ready to die yet, but she took comfort in knowing that if she did, at least she would die at home.

Chapter 15

Joseph saw the demon's blow speeding toward Lyka's head. As it did, the end of his world played out in his mind.

He saw her die, saw her bleed out into the ground where so many of the Slayers had perished. He saw Andreas's grief and anger, and the end of a treaty meant to save both of their kind from self-destruction. He saw the clash of the races—Theronai against Slayer. Both lost as Synestryn spread out across the countryside, destroying everything they touched.

Joseph couldn't let that happen. He'd sworn to protect his woman with his life, and, in doing so, save Theronai, Slayers and humans alike.

He drew into himself minute sparks of power to speed his body. The pain of collecting that energy bore down on him, but he accepted it as the price for doing what had to be done.

His body wasn't meant for this kind of stress, and as he raced over the ground, seeing no more than a blur of movement around him, agony consumed him.

The demon's sword began its descent toward Lyka's

sweet throat. He could hear it humming as it sliced through the air.

She lifted her daggers to defend herself, but even a Slayer wasn't strong enough to stop a blow from that heavy blade.

Joseph launched himself into the air. He slammed into the demon, knocking it sideways as the heavy sword made contact with her crossed blades.

He landed on top of the demon, feeling something hard punch his stomach. He ignored the pain and wrestled his way to the top. The demon's face twisted with a grimace of agony, and it let out the screaming howl of a dying animal. Its black eyes frosted over, going snowy white. Beneath its pale skin, its veins pulsed with dark blood, which seemed to harden into stiff bulges along its limbs. Within seconds, it went limp as it died.

As soon as the threat passed, all the strength seeped out of Joseph. It took every ounce of energy he had to keep his sword in his grip.

Lyka scrambled to her feet and came to his side. He couldn't find the energy to stand or even lift his hand to ask for her help.

"Joseph," she said, her face going white and her pretty golden eyes widening. "You're hit."

He had no idea what she meant until he looked where she was looking. The hilt of a crude sword stuck out of his gut. The blade had gone all the way through him and he'd barely felt it.

He started feeling it now, though.

Joseph reached for the sword to pull it out, but Lyka stopped him, batting his hands away easily. "No. You pull that, and you'll bleed to death. We need a Sanguinar. Fast." She pulled his phone from his jeans pocket and dialed.

"Joseph's been injured. We need help. Now." Her voice shook so hard the words were barely decipherable.

He heard a man's voice come through the phone's casing, but couldn't make out the words.

"No. If I move him, he's dead. You need to send someone here."

Joseph almost asked if it was really that bad, but a cold wave of pain tore through him, forcing him to grit his teeth to hold back a cry of pain.

He didn't want Lyka to think he was weak. She already thought of him as soft from his desk job. To have her think he couldn't hold his own in battle was unthinkable.

Whoever was on the phone with her spoke again, this time with a little more concern coming through in his tone.

"I'll do what I can, but I'm no healer," she replied.

The man on the line began shouting orders, presumably to someone around him.

Lyka clenched the phone harder. "Tell him to hurry, Nicholas. Seconds count." She hung up and pocketed the phone. Her hands were shaking.

Joseph pulled in a slow breath so he'd have air to speak. "Good news?" he asked.

She knelt beside him, patting his shoulder gently. "Ronan is nearby. He's on his way."

Blood trickled down his spine, reminding him to hold very still. "Don't worry about me. Keep an eye out for more demons."

A wave of deep fear and worry flickered through him, and he knew instantly that it wasn't his own. The luceria was channeling her emotions to him, as it was designed to do.

He only wished they'd been happier ones.

He found the tiny conduit that connected them. He could sense the potential for powerful magic to flow between them, but right now, there was nothing there but the potential for more. He'd never been bonded to a female Theronai before and wasn't entirely sure how it worked, but he let his instincts guide him as he used that conduit to offer her what little comfort he could.

"I'm going to be fine," he said. "I've been through worse injuries than this and survived." It was a lie, but one he was willing to give her if it eased her worry.

She got right in his face and bared her teeth. "Don't you dare lie to me at a time like this, Theronai."

"How did you know?"

She tapped her nose. "I can smell it. I can also smell your pain."

"Sorry." He pulled in too deep a breath and his abdomen erupted in pain. "I'll try to keep my smells to myself."

Her helpless frustration churned through their link. "Is there anything I can do?"

"You've already done all you can."

"And that pisses me off." She paced a few yards away, then stalked back. With every step she became more and more furious. After a couple of minutes, she came to a stop in front of him and stared down at his wound.

Blood wet the front of his shirt. The waistband of his jeans was becoming saturated. His body's temperature had dropped, giving the cold wind plenty of room to suck the heat right out of the blood he'd shed. Each breath was becoming harder to draw than the last. He did his best to stay perfectly still, but his strength was fading, making him sway where he straddled the dead demon's body.

She took off her shirt, leaving her wearing only a stretchy camisole.

"What are you doing?"

"Tying this around your wound so the blade won't shift."

She did so carefully, moving close enough to him that he could catch the sweet scent of her skin. He honestly didn't know if he was going to make it out of this alive, but in that moment, with her so close, working to save him, he was grateful that he'd had even this much time bonded to a woman in the way he'd been born to be.

"I'm going to pull this tight," she warned him. "Tell me if I hurt you."

She tugged the sleeves of her shirt tight around his abdomen, right under where the blade protruded from his body. The slight shift of his skin was enough to make his vision waver in pain, but he held back his cry. Only a small hiss of air escaped his lips.

When she backed away, she was as pale and shaky as he felt. A line of sweat dotted her forehead, sparkling under the last rays of daylight. "I hope that slows the bleeding."

"I'm sure it will."

She stood and cocked one hip to the side. "Do you always lie this much?"

Her nipples stood out with the growing chill of night. If Joseph hadn't been skewered, he would have used his own body to warm her. Maybe even his mouth. "If you connected to me the way you're meant to do, you'd know everything. There would be nothing I could hide."

"Nice try." She backed away, rubbing her arms. "How freaking long does it take for one damn Sanguinar to get here? It's not like we're on the moon."

"The settlement is isolated. It took me almost an hour to hike here. Give Ronan time. He's coming as fast as he can."

She paced the area again, frustration rolling off her in waves. With every few breaths, his pain spiked, and each time it did, she flinched as if she felt it, too.

"That's it," she said, throwing her hands up. "I've got to do something. I can't just stand here while you die. If I allow the leader of the Theronai to die, I might as well just go and declare war against your people."

"You need to calm yourself." His words came out slower than they should have. Weaker. He was trying to appear strong for her, but it was a losing battle. "Ronan will come."

"Not fast enough." She knelt beside him. Her hands were shaking and cold as she wrapped her fingers around his. "Tell me how to heal you."

"You can't."

"You don't know that. For all you know, I'm a kick-ass healer."

His strength was fading fast. He kept fighting the urge to slump forward and rest—close his eyes for just a few minutes. "Maybe you are, but not without a source of power."

She let out a blistering string of curses, but her hold on him stayed gentle. "I will not let you die. Do you hear me?"

He heard her, but there wasn't anything he could do to help her. He was doing all he could just staying upright.

The woods were dark now. The sun was nearly below the horizon. Soon every Synestryn nearby would smell his blood and come running for him. Lyka had to be away from here before that happened.

"You should go. It's almost dark. My blood . . ."

"I'm not going anywhere, Theronai. Not while you're here, wounded and defenseless."

"There will be too many demons for you to fight."

She set her jaw. "I'm not leaving you. Stop wasting your breath."

He swayed slightly. The pain of shifting even that much sent a jolt of adrenaline through him.

"You're not going to be able to stay like this much longer. Maybe you should lie down."

She was right. His strength was disappearing alarmingly fast. If he fell over, he might do enough damage to sever an artery. Not only would that kill him before Ronan could arrive, but it would also call every demon within miles to come feast on his blood.

And Lyka's.

"Help me lie down?"

Her hands were on him in a second, easing his shoulders sideways to the ground. The move made his spine light up with pain and sucked all the air from his body, but he was finally off the dead demon, resting firmly on the cold ground.

He lay there for a while, panting for breath. Lyka kept stroking his face, biting her lip in fear. As soon as his breathing eased, she asked, "Better?"

"Not the word I'd pick, but at least now I don't have to worry about falling over."

He closed his eyes. It felt so damn good he didn't even try to open them again.

Joseph clutched his sword in one hand and prayed that by the time the demons came for his blood, he'd have regained enough strength to fend them off and keep Lyka safe.

Chapter 16

Lyka sensed the instant Joseph passed out.

He'd lost so much blood. She didn't know how he could still be alive.

Panic churned in her gut, threatening to spew out of her at any second. Her tiger paced nervously in the back of her mind, anxious to come out and force her to flee.

She fought the animal side of herself, knowing that leaving Joseph here in a pool of his own blood after nightfall was the same thing as executing him.

"Hurry the fuck up, Ronan," she growled into the chilly air.

She checked the phone. Less than an hour had passed since she'd called Nicholas for help. Even if Ronan had been on the road near the settlement, he would still be in the woods, hiking their way.

Not fast enough.

Lyka knew that some Theronai women could heal severe wounds. Maybe even as severe as this one. She didn't know if that was the kind of thing she'd be good at or not, but she did know that if she didn't try, Joseph was a dead man.

He was unconscious now. Even if he caught a glimpse inside her thoughts, he wouldn't remember it when he woke up. Would he?

It was a chance she was going to have to take. There was too much at stake for her not to act.

She picked up his limp hand and held it so that his ring touched her necklace. The two parts of the luceria locked together with an audible snap. She had no clue what she was doing, but she had to start somewhere.

Lyka closed her eyes and concentrated on the physical connection between them. His fingers were cool to the touch. The ring on his finger hummed, vibrating the band around her throat. There was power in that vibration. All she had to do was access it.

She let herself float, hoping she had some kind of innate knowledge buried within her and that those instincts would guide her now.

Everywhere his skin touched hers, she grew warm and tingly. Tiny streams of current flowed into her, gathering somewhere deep inside her chest. As they accumulated, they began multiplying, swirling around much like the colors in the luceria did. Soon there were so many of them, they grew almost painful, straining against her skin to be set free.

A new kind of panic surfaced, riling her tiger. What she was doing now was dangerous, and the animal in her wanted to take over and ensure her safety.

Run. Flee. Hide.

Fight.

That was what she needed to do now: fight.

She grabbed onto that need and channeled it, letting it strengthen her resolve.

Joseph couldn't hear her. He couldn't see her. He didn't even know she was here. There was no harm at all in letting herself sink into him just enough to do what had to be done.

She slid inward, folding in on herself until the outside world no longer mattered. There was no wind, no night, no smells or sounds. Only Joseph and the pulse of power flowing from him into her.

Lyka found the source of that power hovering within the luceria. Like a stream of light, it bubbled and churned between them. Some of it splashed into her, but only a few drops of what was available.

There was so much more she could have. So much more she needed.

The current pushed against her, trying to keep her out, but she fought it, snarling as she shoved her way through the pressure and into the source of that precious power. It took nearly all of her strength, but she made her way through until only brilliant stillness surrounded her.

She floated in that pool of light and energy, letting it soak into her cells. In some strange way she recognized every drop, as if it had been marked as hers long before her birth.

She craved it. Needed it. She belonged to it, and it to her.

A giddy sense of completion lifted her and cast her past the ocean of power into a different place. A darker place, but one just as familiar.

She looked around, wondering how she could know a place where she'd never been. Joseph stood nearby, watching her.

He was still, frowning. There was an air of expectation around him, along with a healthy dose of surprise.

"I thought you didn't want to come here," he said.

She still felt light and buoyant from basking in that

pool of power. She knew there was a reason she was supposed to be afraid, but she couldn't remember what it was. "Come where?"

One second he was on the other side of the foggy space. The next, he was in front of her, staring down at her with intense satisfaction in his hazel eyes. His fingers curled around her upper arms. Heat shimmered between them, sliding down her body until she was quivering in enjoyment.

"My home," he said.

She didn't see a home. In the distance, past the fog, she saw a fleeting glimpse of high walls like those around Dabyr, but that was all. Inside the walls, tall trees rose, blocking out the sky. They looked much like the one inked on Joseph's chest, but these were filled with so many leaves that not even the sun could filter through.

As she made the comparison, his shirt disappeared, allowing her to see his lifemark.

His jeans hung low on his hips, displaying lean muscles that ridged his abdomen and made a V down toward his groin. The tree marked on his skin had only a trio of leaves, but they swayed in time with the leaves of the trees around them.

The need to touch drew her in, taking over all rational thought. She ran her finger along his lifemark, letting the heat of his skin sink into hers. As her touch strayed down to his stomach, she felt something cold and wet.

She looked down, but saw nothing out of the ordinary except a thin scar bisecting his abdomen.

The sight tickled something deep in her mind, giving her a feeling of helplessness and fear.

"I don't like it," she told him.

He grabbed her hands in his and pressed them against

his hard chest. "It's nothing, kitten. Nothing to worry about at all. You're here now, and that's all that matters."

It wasn't, but she couldn't seem to get her mind around what was bothering her.

Joseph tilted her chin up. There was a smile in his eyes, a kind of softness she'd never seen before. "I'm so glad you're here. Where you belong."

"I can't stay," she said, knowing instantly that her words were true, though she had no idea what had spurred them.

"There's nothing to fear here. I'll keep you safe."

The walls were high. Thick. The air smelled clean and fresh, like right after a spring storm. There were no demons here. No responsibilities.

His thumb stroked her cheek. "I've watched you for so long. Wanted you. Every word we shared made me crave more. I would lie in my bed and wonder how your skin would feel under my fingertips." He trailed his fingers over her shoulder and down her arm. "How your skin would smell if I nuzzled you here." He lowered his nose to the crook of her neck and breathed her in.

A shiver tingled along Lyka's spine. Her body began to heat, and a sweet tingle of need stirred in her belly.

"There are so many other things I want to do to you," he said. "So many dreams I've had of you and me together." As he said the words, her mind was filled with a flurry of images of the two of them entwined in passionate embraces. Some of them were sweet. Others primal and raw. Each one came complete with a set of sensory details that trickled over her like hot water, stealing her breath with their intensity.

She'd spent plenty of time wondering what it would be like to be with a man as powerful as Joseph, but not one of her daydreams even came close to the potent fantasies he'd endured.

She stared at one—an image of her naked, pinned against the wall of his office by his big body. His hips were moving, thrusting himself inside her with hard, powerful strokes. He pulled her shoulders down, driving himself as deep as he could go before retreating and doing it all over again.

"I thought about that nearly every day," he admitted. "But even that didn't hold my curiosity as much as this one." He pointed to another scene.

In this one, they stood outside under the moonlight. Her arms were wrapped around him as if she never wanted to let him go. Her head was tilted up toward his, and they were locked in a kiss so passionate she felt like she was intruding on the most private of moments—far more intimate than sex against his office wall had been.

He stood beside her. The back of his hand slid up and down her bare arm. "I've always wondered what it might be like to kiss you like that. To have you kiss me back like you would die if I let go of you."

And now she wondered what it would be like, too. In fact, she wondered so much, she knew she would die if she didn't find out. Soon.

She grabbed his shoulders to pull herself up for a kiss, and before her lips could touch his, she felt something cold and wet against her belly.

Lyka looked down and saw that she was covered in blood. It stained her shirt and soaked into her pants.

Fear sank its claws into her. She patted at her body, searching for the source of her bleeding.

"It's not yours, kitten," he said, only his voice was much weaker this time—not at all like it should have been. "It's mine."

The line bisecting his abdomen had split open. Blood poured from it, soaking both of them down to their knees.

That's when Lyka remembered. She hadn't come here to see daydreams and naughty fantasies. She'd come here to heal him.

She'd come here for his power. Whatever this place was, it was the source of the energy she needed to keep him alive.

This man who stood before her, this apparition—it wasn't real. None of this was real.

"It's all real," he said, as if hearing her thoughts. "At least to me it is. Stay with me, kitten. I like having you here. You feel good in my mind. It's where you belong."

In his mind? That's where she was?

Full-blown panic crashed down on her, detonating with the force of a bomb. She flew away from him and landed with a hard thud on the ground.

When she opened her eyes, she was sitting on the forest floor next to Joseph's body.

He wasn't breathing.

Chapter 17

There was no more time for Lyka to worry about what she wanted. If she didn't act fast, Joseph was as good as dead. It didn't matter that she was freaked-out to have been inside his head, or that he might have seen things in hers that he shouldn't have. All that could matter now was the life of a man balanced in her untrained hands.

She scrambled to his side and fastened his hand around her throat. The second the two parts of the luceria locked together again, she knew he wasn't dead. At least not yet. She could feel life in him, power.

She didn't stop to think or worry. Instead she dove headfirst for his power, not caring what he might see in her mind.

There it was, right where she'd left it—a pool of energy and light so huge, she knew she'd never be able to absorb it all.

Tendrils of it rose to her call, threading their way through the link the luceria provided. The instant it hit her, she recognized it, like something she'd lost long ago that had finally come home.

She grabbed onto that power with everything in her and willed it into action. Instincts guided her way, helping her find the worst source of Joseph's bleeding. She wasn't exactly sure what she was doing, but the energy seemed to have a mind of its own.

It wanted Joseph to live.

So did she. In fact, she wanted it so much that she was holding her breath, pouring as much of herself into the act of healing him that she could.

The process quickly robbed her of her strength. Channeling so much power strained her mind and body in a way she never could have predicted, much less trained for. No drills or strength training could have prepared her for the monumental task of controlling and directing the kind of elemental force Joseph housed.

It was like trying to shove the sun into a five-pound sack. No matter how hard she tried, she couldn't control the power at her fingertips. It was burning her up from the inside out.

All she could do was let go and watch as it consumed her.

She heard deep male voices. One of them was inside her head, and still she couldn't understand it. The roar of magic in her ears was too loud.

Someone pried at her hands. She clung to Joseph, refusing to let go. A second later, she was lifted bodily and hurled through the air. When she finally hit the ground, she had a deep sense of loneliness. Emptiness.

All of her power was gone now. Someone had stolen it.

She tried to open her eyes to see who, but her eyelids were too heavy. She tried to sit up so she could regain her sense of equilibrium, but her head was spinning too fast for her to do more than flop on the ground.

Finally, a heavy wave of exhaustion sucked her under and didn't let go. She couldn't fight it. Even breathing was too hard. All she could do was relax and hope that wherever this current took her, it was someplace safe.

Chapter 18

Ronan had no patience to deal with a newly bonded pair of Theronai. His hunger was raging. He was worried about the woman who'd saved his life—a woman who'd run from him. One he was determined to find.

He'd had no time to hunt tonight upon waking. He'd used all the power the unknown stranger had given him to find her, only to come up empty-handed. His plan was to search again tonight, but the call for help had come through, thwarting his plans.

The sun had only just set, and he'd been confined to his van, unable to do more than suffer through the acute weakness daylight brought upon him. It was his bad luck to be the closest Sanguinar near Joseph when all he wanted to do was hit the road, following the faint trail of a woman who'd seemingly vanished.

If not for the blood that she'd fed him, he wouldn't have even had that hint of a trail to follow. But he did have it, and he would find her before it faded to nothingness.

He had to find her. There was no other choice. She compelled him like no other creature ever had.

He needed her.

In an effort to have this task of healing Joseph out of the way as soon as possible, Ronan raced through the trees toward the Slayer settlement. Their kind liked to be isolated and difficult to reach, which was often handy—when it wasn't completely inconvenient.

Like it was right now.

Branches slashed at his face as he hurried through the forest. There was only the slightest path left visible in the foliage—no more than a natural trail that wildlife might leave behind. But even without that trail, Ronan would have been able to find Joseph. The scent of his blood was heavy in the air, telling Ronan that the man was gravely injured.

As he came over the top of a rise, he saw Lyka and Joseph down below. Sparks arced between their bodies as she clumsily tried to heal him.

Ronan suffered a moment of surprise. Nicholas had said that Lyka had bonded to the leader of the Theronai, but Ronan wouldn't have believed it possible if he hadn't seen it with his own eyes.

Somehow, she was both Slayer and Theronai—something that definitely bore deeper investigation.

Too bad it wasn't she who needed healing, or Ronan could have used that excuse to delve into her mind and determine exactly how it was possible that she would straddle two races so seamlessly.

By the time he was at the bottom of the hill, Lyka had visibly weakened. He could smell the destruction of her body on a cellular level as she channeled Joseph's power. He was in even worse shape—unconscious, his heart stuttering against the loss of blood.

If Ronan didn't do something now, not only would

Joseph die, but there was also a chance he'd take Lyka with him.

"Stop!" he yelled at her as he made his way to her side.

She didn't seem to hear him—didn't so much as turn his way. Her eyes were closed. Sweat trickled down her temples. Her skin had gone so pale that he swore he could see through it, when the sparks between her and Joseph lit beneath her fingers.

He knew there was a chance he could injure her if he pulled her away from her task, but injury was far preferable to death. And that was exactly where she was headed.

Clearly, healing was not this woman's gift.

"You need to stop." Ronan put his hand on hers, shaking her.

She tightened her grip on Joseph, digging her fingernails into his skin. He tried to pry her fingers away, but she was far stronger than a female Theronai had any right to be—a gift from her Slayer side, no doubt.

As her body continued to suffer the ill effects of her effort, Ronan was left with no other choice. He had to separate them.

He commanded his body to strengthen so he had the leverage to tear the couple apart. It took a monumental effort, but he was finally able to use brute force to get her to let go.

She flew through the air, landing a few feet away. Ronan hoped he hadn't hurt her, but he would deal with that damage in a moment. Right now he had to concentrate on Joseph, who was mere seconds from death.

Ronan dove into his work, repairing the blood vessels and tissue the sword had severed. He slowly removed the metal blade, easing it out of the man's flesh as fast as he dared.

There was no time for him to linger in Joseph's mind and examine his thoughts, but there were some things that came through loud and clear all the same.

Joseph was burdened by his position. There were so many needs his people had—so much suffering. He took all of that into himself, putting the weight of everyone's problems on his broad shoulders. He worked endless hours, exerting himself to the point of exhaustion. The signs of it were written all through his body, all the way down to his very cells.

No wonder Lyka hadn't been able to undo the damage done to him; it was too extensive, far more than a mere battle wound.

Still, despite Joseph's fatigue, there was a growing sense of hope in him. He'd found Lyka. She'd given him something precious—something he was determined never to let go.

Ronan finished his work, restoring as much of Joseph's strength as he dared. Every bit of energy Ronan exerted was that much less he had to spend on finding his savior—and he had to find her. Joseph had lost too much blood to be of any use in helping to restore Ronan's power, which meant he would have to find the energy he needed elsewhere.

He pulled out of Joseph's unconscious body and turned his sights on Lyka.

She was young. Strong. She could feed him and give him what he needed to carry on.

With exquisite care, Ronan lifted her from the ground and carried her back to Joseph's side. The smell of blood was thick here, making his hunger rise.

He held her in his arms, shifting her weight so that her neck was exposed to him.

She groaned and opened her eyes. "Ronan?"

He stilled in the act of lowering his mouth to her throat. Light from his eyes spilled over her face, making her eyes glow like golden flames. "Yes."

She blinked a couple of times. "Is Joseph okay?"

"He will be. I arrived just in time."

She let out a long breath of relief. "I tried to help, but it didn't work."

"You kept him alive long enough for me to reach him. Without you, he would have died."

She became more alert by the second, shaking off the ill effects of her efforts to heal Joseph. She glanced over at him, saw he was sleeping, then looked back at Ronan as if realizing for the first time that she was in his arms. "You don't look so good."

"I need to feed," he said, hoping she understood that it wasn't a request.

"On me."

"There is no one else. Joseph is too weak."

She nodded, but he could smell the sickly sweet stench of fear coming from her pores. "I've never let this happen before."

"It won't hurt," he reassured her. "Just close your eyes and it will be over in a moment."

She did as he asked and Ronan took what he so desperately needed from her.

Her blood was hot, like all of the Slayers', but it had the thrumming power of a Theronai. Within seconds, he felt his body began to revive and his hunger subside. Feeding from her—being the first to do so—was a special kind of high. There was so much untapped power within her. Even as weak as she was from her ordeal, she still had more life in her than any he'd ever tasted before.

Except for the woman who'd saved his life. Drinking

from her was like consuming pure energy—sweet and intoxicating.

Before memories of that day could torment him, he pushed them aside and put his focus on Lyka.

Her mind was a jumble of emotions and fears. She'd been hiding her identity for so long, the worry of being found out had left a scar in her emotions as deep as a trench. Now that worry of hiding her Theronai side had turned to worry that her Slayer kin would shun her once news of what she was came out.

She felt like she belonged nowhere.

Ronan did what he could to ease her concerns. His people needed as many whole, healthy Theronai partnerships as they could get. Now that their men were no longer sterile, the hope of children loomed bright on the horizon. Those children were the best hope the Sanguinar had for survival. If Lyka was worried about not fitting in, she wasn't going to be as inclined to bring a child into the world.

That was something Ronan could not allow.

He was careful in his tinkering. Too much force would cause her psyche to crack. Not enough would leave her feeling like an outcast, floating between worlds but never living in either one. In the end, all he did was plant a seed of curiosity in her, giving her a desire to know more about Joseph.

Ronan had known the man for centuries. He'd been in his head often enough to know the kind of man he was. Ronan had no doubt that if she came to know Joseph, she would grow to love him. He was noble, kind and brave. He was strong, honest and steadfast. He would never leave her. He would protect her and their future children until the end of his days.

Once she knew in her heart that all of that was true—

once her love for him developed—she would open herself up to him in a way that would naturally lead to children.

Before Ronan finished feeding, he did a quick check over her body to make sure that she was whole and well. She'd taken a few scrapes and bruises, but they'd already begun to heal. Rather than waste his energy on regenerating her flesh, he would let nature take its course.

He lifted his head, willing the puncture wounds he'd left behind to close. When he was done, there was no hint that he'd fed from her—nothing for Joseph to worry about when he woke.

She opened her eyes, alertness returning swiftly. "That's it?"

"Yes."

"You're right. I didn't feel a thing. And you look a hell of a lot better."

"I'm using some of my power to dampen the scent of blood, but we need to move Joseph to a safer location so he can finish recovering."

"How long will that take?"

"You're worried about finding your brother, aren't you?" He'd sensed that worry while in her mind, but he'd learned long ago that questions would get him in far less trouble than statements.

She nodded. "Can you sense which way they went? No one else seems to be able to find a trail."

He closed his eyes and concentrated. There were hundreds of scents here—many of them of blood of the dead. "I can smell your brother, but his scent has been obscured by magic."

"Like what you're doing right now?"

"Yes."

"Is there a way to get around it? Undo the magic?"

"Perhaps, but I have other matters that demand my attention."

"More important than finding my brother and a bunch of missing kids?"

Ronan's mystery woman was still out there. For all he knew, she was in danger. He didn't know why he was so compelled to find her, but he was. And it was more than just the fact that her blood had been so exquisitely powerful. "Someone I care about is also missing."

"Who?"

"No one you know."

"Maybe we can team up. You help me find Eric. I help you find her."

Having a connection to Lyka could easily prove useful in the future. Not only was she powerful in her own right, but she was also tied to the leader of the Theronai. With all the tension between their races over Connal's treachery, it might be important to have an ally like her.

But how long would it slow him down? How much time would he be drawn away from the trail of his savior? Even one more minute was too long. He could feel her slipping farther away with every passing second.

"I'm sorry," he said. "I want to help you, but I can't. This woman's life is of as much importance to me as Eric's is to you. The best thing you can do is learn to wield Joseph's power. Once you do that, you won't need help from anyone."

"I've tried, but it doesn't seem to work very well."

"That's because you're not doing it right."

"What's that supposed to mean?"

"Trust, love, familiarity, intimacy—those are the things that strengthen the connection between the two of you and let the power flow."

She lifted her golden blond eyebrows. "You want me to fuck him?"

"That's none of my concern," he lied.

"You're no better than Joseph. Don't you guys know that we Slayers can smell a lie from a mile away?"

"Not all of you can."

"How do you know?"

"I've known your kind for more years than you've been alive. Several times over. Some of you have the gift to sense a lie, but others don't. You, my dear, are stronger than many of your ancestors."

"You're evading. Tell me why it's so important to you that I have sex with Joseph that you'd lie about it."

"Procreation, of course. The more blooded children that are born into this world, the fewer of my kind that will die of starvation."

Her stare went distant, but he could see a trail of thoughts streaming through her mind. The moment her mind touched on the idea of having a child, Ronan could smell her maternal instincts flare. It was completely involuntary, but strong enough to be unmistakable. "I barely know Joseph."

"You're the one who wanted to know how to tap into his power. I was only trying to help."

"I'm forbidden from procreating with anyone not approved by Andreas and his council."

"I'd heard. I assume that's how the bloodlines are being rebuilt."

"I'm not at liberty to say."

"Keep your secrets, Lyka. I have no need of them. I have enough of my own to carry."

She held up her hand. "Don't even go there. I've had enough secrets to last a lifetime. All I need to know is a shortcut for getting what I want. I need to be strong enough to find Eric."

"Then stop holding Joseph at arm's length. Extend some trust. Talk to him. Listen. Create a bond with the man with whom you'll likely spend the rest of your life."

"I can't think about the rest of my life right now. I only tied myself to him so I could find my brother. If having access to his power doesn't help with that, then I've ruined my life for no reason at all."

Joseph's voice was rough, but he sounded alert and fully awake. He'd heard everything, and the hurt flowing through his voice was unmistakable. "Glad to know how you really feel, Lyka."

Chapter 19

Lyka felt like a complete and total ass. She hadn't meant to hurt Joseph's feelings. Hell, the man was so big and strong, she wasn't even sure she had the power to inflict any kind of damage at all.

But she had. She could hear it in his voice and wished she could take back those hasty words. "I didn't mean for it to come out like that."

"I'm sure you didn't." He pushed to his feet with a grimace. "We should go. Too much blood here."

"I agree," said Ronan. "I'll lead the way out."

In the distance, she heard the hungry howl of Synestryn demons. "Those sound like sgath."

Joseph nodded. "Lyka, you stay between me and Ronan. I'll bring up the rear."

She almost told him that she could protect herself, but the truth was, she was tired. Her legs were shaky and her whole body felt like it had been pulled through a drinking straw. She was stretched thin. Worried. Afraid.

"It will be okay," Joseph assured her. Even with her bitchy comment, his concern was for her feelings, rather than the ones of his she'd stomped on.

"I really am sorry about what I said. You're not the one who ruined my life."

"But you do think it's ruined."

"It's only a matter of time before everyone knows I'm a freak. Part Slayer, part Theronai. When my people find out that I'm tied to a Theronai and that he might be able to take a peek inside my head, no one will ever trust me again."

Ronan winced. "You just put an entire race of people under the category of *no one*. I suggest you quit while you're ahead, Lyka."

He was right. She was so knotted up inside, so conflicted over where she belonged in the world, she kept shoving her foot into her mouth. "Where the hell is a nice, violent demon fight when you need one?" she muttered under her breath.

"How about we keep moving and stay alive instead?" said Joseph. "I don't know about you, but I've had about all the excitement I can stand for right now. I'm a few pints low."

She felt weaker than usual, too, which made her shut up and start paying attention to her surroundings. Demons were closing in on them. She could hear their howls growing closer every few minutes. If they were going to make it back to their vehicles in time to avoid a fight, they needed to pick up the pace.

Her legs felt heavier with each step. She didn't lift her foot up high enough and tripped over a low branch. If not for Joseph's quick reflexes in grabbing her arm, she would have fallen flat on her face and probably shed more blood.

His fingers tingled around her arm. Heat and tiny sparks of energy soaked into her skin, warming the right half of her body.

Suddenly, she remembered those scenes from his head—the two of them entwined, fucking each other's brains out.

She shivered at the memory and cleared her throat to ease the lump that had formed there. Part of her wanted what he'd shown her—that connection, that pleasure. She felt so alone most of the time, but when she thought about being with Joseph in such an intimate way, much of her loneliness faded.

"Are you okay?" he asked.

She could smell her arousal sliding through the air and wondered if anyone else could, too. Her Slayer senses were stronger than most, giving her hope that her secret was safe. "Just clumsy."

"She exerted herself saving your life," said Ronan. "She needs rest as much as you do. I suggest you both go straight to the nearest Gerai house and recuperate."

"There's no time," she said. "We have to keep moving."

"We will," said Joseph. "Trust me."

She wanted to, but it just wasn't in her.

He must have sensed the meaning in her silence, because he said, "You will learn to trust me, kitten. Even if it takes you the rest of your life."

"If we don't get out of here soon, that's not going to be very long. The sgath are getting closer."

"Excellent point," said Ronan. "Let's not get into another fight we're ill equipped to handle. I have other plans for the remainder of the night."

They quickened their pace and finally reached the road where the cars were parked. Ronan hurried to his van and took off with a hasty good-bye, leaving Lyka alone with Joseph.

He started stripping out of his bloody clothes so the

scent wouldn't set the demons on their trail. Even with the smears of dried blood on his skin, he had the power to mesmerize her. Watching him move captured her complete attention. He wasn't doing anything special, but there was so much graceful strength in him, she felt like she was spying on a predator.

He hooked his thumbs in the waistband of his boxer briefs and paused with his back to her. As he turned around to speak to her, the muscles along his spine and shoulders danced under his skin. His expression was flat, but his eyes sparked with anger. "You're wearing my blood. Do you have a change of clothes?"

He was so damn appealing. She didn't know what it was about him that pulled her in so completely. She'd seen a lot of half-naked, well-built men before—hell, she'd grown up around an entire pack of them—but Joseph was different. He was calm. In control. He wasn't constantly working to prove something to himself or anyone else.

Every time she looked at him, she felt like another little, missing piece of herself came home.

"Lyka?" he said. "Did you hear me? You can't go around with blood on your clothes."

She gave him a mute nod and stumbled toward her borrowed car. The scent of soap caught her attention, making her turn around.

Joseph was completely naked, with his fantastic ass facing her way. He had some kind wet wipe in his hand and was scrubbing away the traces of blood left on his skin. There was no self-consciousness in the act. He was all pragmatic efficiency and carefully banked anger.

"Are you done?" he asked over his shoulder. "The sgath are getting closer."

Her attention on him had been so absolute that she hadn't been keeping track of their growing howls.

She shook her head to get it back where it belonged and made quick work of putting on clean clothes. The bloody ones she tossed into the trees for the demons to find.

By the time she turned back around, Joseph was right behind her. "My truck is better stocked for contingencies. We'll take it."

"And leave the car here?"

"It's just a car. And I want you by my side, where you belong."

She wasn't sure what to say to that, or what to do with the little thrill of excitement his words pulled from her. "I don't belong anywhere anymore."

"You're wrong. The second you took the luceria off my neck, you made your choice. Now you have to live with it." He shot her a hard look, and some of his banked anger flared to life. "Get in."

Arguing with him now while a pack of demons was closing in seemed the height of stupidity, so she did as he asked and got in his truck.

The cab smelled like him, surrounding her with a sense of warmth and comfort that took her off guard. Before she realized what she was doing, she'd snuggled into the comfy leather seat and buckled herself in.

Joseph climbed in, his weight rocking the cab. His long arm reached behind her seat for a couple bottles of water. He handed one to her. "Drink."

She took it. "I'm not all that thirsty."

"Ronan took your blood. Drink the damn water."

She did as he asked, just to get him to leave her alone.

He cracked open the bottle and downed half of it in a single shot.

"Thirsty?" she asked.

"I feel like I've eaten a desert, cacti and all."

He started the engine and took off so fast that gravel spewed out from his tires.

"You lost a lot of blood. Are you sure you don't want me to drive?"

"I'm fine. Or I will be, once we get you somewhere safe."

Safe wasn't on the menu, at least not yet. "We still haven't found any sign of Eric."

"I told you we'd keep searching and I meant it, but we have to stop for a while."

"Every minute we wait is one too long. If you're not up to the search, then take me back to my car and I'll go on without you."

His hands fisted on the steering wheel. "Not happening, Lyka. You're not much better off than I am, not after the way you kept my ass alive so Ronan could find us."

"I'm fine," she lied. She was tired and shaky, but none of that mattered. She had to keep searching.

"You're exhausted. I can see you shaking from here. You tried to channel way too much power through what is still a tiny thread of a connection between us." Some of his fury spilled over in his tone.

"Don't get snippy with me. I had no choice."

"I understand that, and I'm grateful as hell that you took the risk. But damn it, Lyka, you could have killed yourself."

"That's why you're mad? Because I took a risk?"

"No, I'm mad because you tricked me into letting you out of Dabyr, where you were safe. Now I'm stuck watching you suffer, letting you risk your life, when we could have been back home, where you could have taken your time learning how to wield my power."

"I'm sorry it was inconvenient for you that my people were attacked."

His jaw bulged under the strain of his anger. "You

know that's not what I mean. There are a lot of people out scouring the countryside, looking for Eric and the kids. You didn't need to come out here and risk your life trying to learn on the fly."

"Yes, I did," she said. "And if you don't understand that, then you're not the man I thought you were."

"I'm the kind of man who wants his woman to stay safe—at least until she knows where her skills lie."

"I'm not your woman."

"Like hell you're not. You tied yourself to me. Unbreakable bonds. The only way either of us is getting out is through death, and I plan to keep you alive for as long as I draw breath."

"Don't remind me." She still hadn't come to terms with the permanence of their relationship. There hadn't been time.

"You're my wife now, Lyka. My mate. If you think I'm going to just ignore the fact that you almost died back there, then I'm not the man you think I am."

His throwing her words back at her pissed her off, but he had a point. She really didn't know him—didn't know what he was capable of doing. If she pushed him too far, he might get pissed enough to tie her up in some Gerai house, where she would be of no use.

She pulled in a long breath, then another. She had to stay calm here, think rationally.

He finished off the second half of the water, so she handed him the rest of hers as a sort of peace offering. "I think you're the kind of man who will respect the spirit of his vow as well as the letter. I think you're the kind of man who is torn up inside by the idea of those children suffering. I think you're the kind of man who would willingly risk his life to save someone else. *That's* the kind of man I hope I've bound myself to."

Some of his anger fell away. She could see it in the way his shoulders fell on a heavy sigh. "I can't lose you. You understand that, don't you? Even if I die out here, you have to live. You could be compatible with one of the other men—able to wield their power, save another man's life."

"I'm no more important than any one of those kids. Please don't punish me by grounding me to some Gerai house. I need to keep searching."

He flicked a glance her way, and she was sure she saw some kind of sadness in his eyes. "There are a lot of things you don't know yet. I'm happy to teach you all that I can, but you're going to have to find some trust. I told you we'd keep moving, and I meant it."

"Trust isn't the kind of thing that comes easily. You have to earn it."

"And I will. If we both live long enough. All I'm asking you for is a chance. You've got to be careful. You can't put your life on the line like you did back there. If I get hurt again, just let me go."

The idea was far more abhorrent than it would have been a few days ago. She'd grown to like Joseph since she'd come to live at Dabyr, but now that she was bound to him, she felt connected. Part of him.

She really didn't want anything bad to happen to him.

Maybe he felt the same way about her. Maybe his anger now stemmed more from the fact that he cared about her than it did from his vow to protect her life with his.

Curiosity reared its head and put the smack-down on caution. Before she could stop herself, she felt around for the link that bound them together.

It came to her easier than it had before, pulsing with heat and power. She wasn't sure how it worked, but she could feel him—his essence—in the vibration of that energy. If she'd had ten connections to other people, she was certain that she would have known exactly which one was his.

Being careful so he wouldn't figure out what she was doing, she prodded their link, searching for answers. Like some kind of schoolgirl, she wanted to know how he felt about her. It wasn't like she could ask her best friend to ask his. She had to go in search of the information herself.

She approached the conduit that connected them the same way she would have a rabid animal. She really didn't want to touch it, but she had no choice. It was the only way to find out what she needed to know.

Instincts guided her. She didn't know what she was doing, but as soon as she thought about touching his mind, she was doing so.

The luceria heated around her throat, warning her to be cautious. She could sense some thin barrier bulging between them. She could almost see through it, like frosted glass. On the other side was the information she wanted. Needed. All she had to do was find a way to break it.

The instant she thought about doing so, it exploded, letting a flood of emotions wash over her. She wasn't ready for the onslaught. It hit her hard, knocking the breath from her body.

Lyka struggled to withstand the sudden rush. She imagined herself like a tree, letting floodwaters rush by her. She stayed planted firmly where she was, feeling little splashes of his emotions as they passed.

Anger was on the surface — anger caused by a soul-deep fear of loss. He'd grieved for so many people he'd loved. No one was safe from the Synestryn. Neither was she. It was the worry that plagued him most, wearing away at his sense of calm until he was constantly fighting the urge to chain her up in a cell below Dabyr.

Below that anger was a sense of gratitude and hope. She was the focus of it, shining so bright in his thoughts that she couldn't even stand to stare at herself through his eyes. He was pinning a lot on her—on them as a team, a powerful fighting force. She knew that if she looked at that line of thought too closely, she'd freak out, developing some odd kind of stage fright that would lock her up cold.

She passed by that quickly, moving deeper. With every layer she passed, she felt more at home, as if this were a space carved out just for her.

She was warm here. Safe. Spying inside his head wasn't at all like she would have expected. Instead, she found herself lingering, practically basking inside his emotions.

Something large loomed up ahead. It was darker than everything around it, pulsing with a kind of frenetic power that dwarfed all else. As she neared, it seemed to grow in anticipation, like it had been waiting for her arrival for a long, long time.

"You're not ready for that," she heard Joseph say. The words sounded strange. Distant. Her body was so far away from her now that she barely even felt like it belonged to her anymore.

Her curiosity grew. He wouldn't try to keep her out unless he had something to hide. Whatever it was, she was going to figure it out and expose his dark secrets before they could hurt her.

He must have sensed her resolve, because she felt a growing pressure shoving her away from that pulsing, powerful secret.

She tried to tell him to back off and let her pass, but

she couldn't figure out how to speak though a mouth that was light years away. Instead she settled for showing him that she wasn't going to be deterred.

Lyka shoved forward, ignoring the resistance clinging to her, trying to hold her at bay. She pushed past the pulsing edge of the dark fog and stepped inside. It all hit her at once.

Lust. Desire. Need.

She was surrounded by it, consumed by it. This was the part of him that craved her. It wanted to possess her body and stake a claim so deep, no other man would ever be able to rid her of his mark. This part of him wanted to restrain her—not for her safety, but for her pleasure. And his. This part was pure animal instinct and raging hunger.

The fog seeped into her, becoming a part of her. It made her want, too. Made her need.

Through the faint thread that connected her to her body, she heard herself moan, felt herself shiver.

"You weren't supposed to see that," he said.

But she had. And now it was part of her, too.

She tried to back out of the dark fog, but it didn't want to let her go. It swirled around her, caressing her and whispering for her to stay. Give in. Let go.

Lyka wanted to listen. It felt so good to be here. But there was something important she was supposed to do. Something vital.

"Let me go," she begged. Even to her, the plea sounded halfhearted.

The fog tightened around her, hugging her, holding her. There was a sense of possession sliding through each pulsating swirl of power. It was careful not to hurt her, but she could sense its intent to never let her go.

With each sinuous stroke of the fog across her consciousness, the need pouring out of Joseph seemed to strengthen. She could feel his hands on her body somewhere in the distance. His fingers were on her skin, hot and strong.

She wanted to feel that touch up close—not separated and distant like she was from her body now.

Again she fought against the all-consuming need that clung to her. As much as she wanted to stay and bask in the dark power that surrounded her, she wanted to be back in her body more, feeling Joseph's touch.

By the time she clawed her way back out of his mind, she was shaking with fatigue. When she opened her eyes, she saw him hovering over her, his eyes nearly black with hunger. He'd stopped the truck and all but crawled into her seat. He had both of her wrists held in one of his big hands. His other hand had slipped beneath the collar of her shirt to splay across her chest, pinning her in the seat.

Hot waves of power tumbled out of him, sinking into her flesh wherever he touched. He was trembling with barely held control. There was a deep flush across his neck, disappearing down beneath his shirt. Thick veins throbbed under his skin, pulsing fast.

"You weren't supposed to see that," he told her.

The low, sexy sound of his voice stroked across her senses. The curve of his lips caught her attention and held on tight. Had her hands been free, she would have reached up and traced that line with her fingertip.

But her hands weren't free, and he showed no sign of letting her go anytime soon. Oddly, that gave her a feeling of safety so intense, she wasn't in any hurry for him to let go.

"I thought you were keeping secrets."

His gaze dipped to her mouth. "I was. But for good reason."

"What reason is that?"

"I really didn't want you to know just how much I'm dying to fuck you, kitten. At least not yet."

His rough words should have offended her, but instead they made her toes curl in her shoes. "So there was a time you wanted me to know?"

"Yes."

"When?"

"When I'm buried balls-deep inside that sweet pussy of yours. *That's* the appropriate time for you to know exactly how much I need you."

She had no idea what to say to that, but knowing what he wanted from her—hearing his thoughts spoken aloud—made her own sexual hunger rise, answering the challenge.

Lyka couldn't let this happen. She couldn't give in like this.

She knew that Theronai couples frequently engaged in sex. Most of them considered the bond a form of marriage—one far more permanent and binding than any piece of paper issued by some governing body. But she hadn't been raised as one of them. She didn't have to follow the path they did. She could still be connected to Joseph and mate with a Slayer male.

Couldn't she?

"If you think I'd ever let another man touch you, you're insane," he said.

"Get out of my head. I didn't invite you to listen to my private thoughts."

"And I didn't invite you to drop in on my deepest fantasies."

He had a point. "I shouldn't have done that."

"No, you shouldn't have. But you did. And now that you've opened Pandora's box, there's no closing it.

You've seen how I feel about you. Do you really think that I'd let you go in search of another man, another mate?"

"I really never considered that you had a right to *let* me do anything."

His grip on her wrists tightened. She thought about trying to break his hold, but she doubted she was strong enough, even on her best day. And today was definitely not her best day. She was weak, shaky, unsteady, both mentally and physically.

He closed his eyes, pulled in a deep breath. Let it out again. She watched as he reined himself in, shoving down his frustration and lust an inch at a time until it was all tucked neatly away, out of sight.

But she knew it was still there. She'd been inside his thoughts—felt his emotions too keenly to ever pretend they weren't real.

No man had ever wanted her the way Joseph did. It was as thrilling as it was terrifying.

"You're too weak," he said as he let her go and moved back into his own seat. He started the truck and pulled back onto the gravel road. "It's my duty to see to your care, and right now, you wouldn't be able to defend yourself if we were attacked."

"I'm fine," she lied. All that brain hopping she'd done had worn her down even worse than before.

"You can't lie to me about this. I know I'm right. You need me to revive your strength." Even though they were out too far in the countryside for streetlights, her vision was good enough that she could make out fine details in his skin. Freckles, a light dusting of hair, scars faint with age.

He really was sexy as hell—built just the way she liked her men. Tall, strong, sturdy enough to take whatever she might throw at him. Joseph wasn't the kind of man who was easily broken, not even once her two brothers got their hands on him for staking a claim on her without council permission.

"How do you do that?" she asked. "Because I'd really like to have the strength to keep moving tonight."

"I can pull power from the earth and feed it to you."

"How does that work?"

"I'm not entirely sure. I've never done it before, but my instincts are strong, and I've seen bonded pairs do it over and over."

"So, we never need to rest?" she asked.

"Not never. What I'll do for you is only temporary—just enough to get you on your feet in an emergency. Think of it like an energy drink."

"How long will it last?"

"I don't know. We're going to have to figure it out together."

"Pull over. We'll do it here." She was worried she'd piss him off and he'd refuse to work his magic on her. The longer she kept talking, the more likely it was she'd say something that would set him off. She simply couldn't take the chance that he'd change his mind.

"No. I'm not risking an experiment with something I've never tried before out in the open like this. We'll do it at a Gerai house, so that if it goes badly, at least we'll have shelter for the night."

Lyka knew about Gerai houses—safe places stocked with food and supplies, magically warded to increase their security against attack—but she'd never been to one before. "You're going to trust me with the secret location of one of your safe houses?"

His shoulders seemed to droop in frustration. "You still don't get it, do you?"

"Get what?"

"There are no secrets between us anymore. You saw my last one. Soon you'll let me see all of yours, too."

She didn't scoff, but nearly pulled a muscle restraining herself.

"I'm serious," he said.

"I know that you want us to share a brain, but I've told you it's not going to happen."

"Too late, kitten. It already has."

"What's that supposed to mean?" she asked, dread rising like a flash flood.

He turned onto another gravel road. Moonlight spilled over his face, showing her just how grim his expression had become. "You were in my head a minute ago."

"So?"

"It works both ways. While you were in my mind, I read your thoughts."

Uh-oh. He couldn't know. She kept all her secrets carefully locked away behind doors so hidden, even she had trouble finding them.

But she'd been drawn to the thing he'd tried to hide from her. Maybe when she wasn't looking, he'd been drawn to the same thing in her mind. She hoped that she would have known that he was poking around, but maybe she wouldn't. Maybe she was too new at this conjoined brain garbage to even sense his intent.

He could know. All of it. Everything.

Fear trickled through her like ice water. Her muscles stiffened against it, making it hard to breathe.

One of her hands strayed to the door handle while the other got ready to unbuckle her seat belt so she could make a quick getaway.

"What thoughts did you read?" she asked, trying to

sound nonchalant. Instead, there was a slight waver in her voice she was certain he'd heard.

He didn't look her way. He stared straight ahead, his big hands tight on the steering wheel. "I know what you're hiding."

"I'm not hiding anything," she lied.

"Yes, you are, and it's time we deal with it," he said as he turned down yet another deserted country road—the kind where no one would ever find her body. "What *it* do you mean?"

He glanced her way, his face drawn tight with intense emotion she couldn't decipher. "You killed one of my men, didn't you?"

Chapter 20

Joseph felt Lyka's panic an instant too late to predict her actions.

She sprang from the moving truck and tucked into an acrobatic roll as she hit the ground. He skidded to a sloppy stop on the gravel road and slammed the truck in park.

By the time he was out of the truck and headed in her direction, she was already on her feet, running into a nearby tree line.

Joseph couldn't leave her alone out here, unprotected. She was weak from her efforts to heal him. He'd sensed her fatigue clouding the minute connection between them. She was practically weaponless, with only those short daggers and a puny knife to hold demons at bay. And even if all of that hadn't been true, he would have been forced to pursue her because of his vow to protect her.

If she'd already become comfortable in her power, she could have pulled strength from him to speed her flight. But she wasn't comfortable yet. She probably didn't even realize that she could use him in that way.

He'd never been more grateful for ignorance in his life.

Joseph pulled specks of energy into himself, gathering them from the chilly night air. He was unable to access the huge reservoir of magic he housed, but he could make instant use of what was available to him in the environment. As he drew power into him, some of it overflowed his need and became a part of him. It wasn't fun or easy to add onto the bulging stores of energy inside him, but it was effective.

His pace quickened until he was easily gaining on her. Branches batted at his face as he passed, but she seemed to have no such trouble. She dodged and ducked, weaving through the forest with such ease, he wouldn't have been surprised to learn that she'd planted every tree and rock herself.

He finally caught up to her on the far side of a creek. She'd leapt across it, and the slick leaves littering the ground slid beneath her foot. Her arms whirled as she scrambled to find a handhold to keep her upright, but there was nothing low enough for her to grab.

She started to fall. Joseph caught her up and swept her to the top of the steep bank. She spun around, striking out at him with her bare hands. Panic still ruled her mind and controlled her actions, so he grabbed her wrists and pinned them behind her before she could draw blood—and the demons that would smell it.

The last thing they needed was another pack of sgath closing in on them.

"I'm not going to hurt you," he told her, though his words came out through clenched teeth, making them harder to believe.

"I won't let you hurt me." She snarled, baring her teeth at him as she tried to get away.

He bore her to the ground, pinning her arms with his hands and her body with his. She squirmed against his hips and thighs, lighting a fire of sexual need in his groin.

He'd spent the last few miles trying to shove all of his lust back in its box, and here she was, inadvertently destroying his efforts. Only a few minutes ago, he'd been faced with every one of the fantasies he'd had for this woman. Dark and nasty, sweet and loving . . . they were all on display, reminding him of exactly how much time he'd spent fighting his baser urges.

He'd wanted Lyka for too long to deny how he felt. There was no stopping the immediate response of his body. Despite her anger and her struggles to free herself, she felt good under him—really good when she squirmed and rubbed against him.

"Stop fighting me and listen."

"Never." She fought harder, nearly breaking his fingers in an effort to free her wrists.

He had to fuel his strength to keep her in check. He was no lightweight, but her Slayer blood made her both strong and ferocious.

It was one of the things he loved most about her.

He tried to keep his voice calm, but he was quickly running out of what little patience he had. "Stop or I'll knock you out and carry you back to the truck."

"I won't let you hit me. I'll rip you apart first."

"I don't have to hit you. I'll shove my way into your head and just turn out the lights. You don't know enough magic to stop me."

She stilled. The flush of color their chase had given her evaporated as she went pale. "You're bluffing."

"Keep being a pain in the ass and you'll find out I'm not."

Panic was still hovering inside her, looking for the

slightest excuse to come out and play. He knew she was terrified, but he had no idea why. "Why did you run off like that?"

"I don't want to die until I find my brother."

"Who says you're going to die?"

"I killed one of your men. That's not the kind of thing you can let go unpunished. Just give me a stay of execution until Eric and the young are home safe. Then I'll turn myself in willingly." Her chin lifted with an air of defiance but trembled with unshed tears.

That was why she was upset? She thought he was going to execute her?

"Lyka, even if you deserved to die, I couldn't be the one to do it. My vow to you prevents me from ever hurting you."

Some of the tension drained from her body. "So it won't happen now? You'll let me keep searching?"

He loosened his hold on her arms and stroked the inside of her wrists with his thumbs. He wasn't foolish enough to let her go, but her need for comfort and reassurance drove him to act. "Did you kill my man in self-defense?"

"No."

"Did you kill him in anger?"

"No. Even if I wanted to, Andreas forbade us from attacking your people."

"Had his lifemark fallen bare? Did you see that his soul had died?"

Her gaze moved past him to the bare branches behind his head. "No."

"Then why did you kill him?"

"He asked me to. He only had two leaves left. He was in horrible pain. He begged me to end his suffering."

Joseph understood the urge to let go. Stop fighting.

End the pain. Rest. There had been times when he'd let idle thoughts of ending his life pass through his mind. He'd always shut them down before they could take root and grow, but not all of the Theronai were as disciplined.

"Who was he?" asked Joseph.

She shook her head. "I don't know his name. I didn't let him tell me. I didn't want to know."

"How did you do it?"

"I can't tell you that. We Slayers are forbidden from talking about it."

"Let me touch your memories of the event. I need to see his face. I need to know who he was and that he met with a clean end."

"I'm not letting you in my brain again. You'll have to take my word for it. I gave him an easy death."

"How?"

She shook her head. "In the way all of your men meet their end when you send them to us."

Whenever one of the Theronai males' souls died, they were delivered to the Slayers for execution. It was a secretive affair, steeped in millennia of tradition. When he'd been young, Joseph had wondered how the Slayers managed the task, but now that he was grown, he refused to let himself think about it.

As leader of the Theronai, he'd sent too many men to their deaths. Lingering over the details of how they died was a good way for him to drive himself mad. They were dead and unable to hurt anyone else. That was all that mattered.

"I felt your guilt, your disgust. You were the one who killed him, not one of the Slayer warriors. Why is that?"

She looked away from him again.

"What are you hiding?"

"Let me up."

She thrust her hips against his in an effort to get free, but all it did was remind him that he had a soft, beautiful woman—his woman—beneath him.

He hadn't yet staked his claim in a physical way. He'd told himself there was plenty of time for that, that if he gave her time, she'd come to know him, maybe even grow to like him. After they worked together for a while, she'd learn to trust him. Maybe even with her body. He couldn't help but hope it would happen. After all, she was the only woman he'd allow himself to be with for the rest of his long, long life, and the idea of never having sex again seemed inconceivable. Especially when he would be working side by side with the woman of his dreams.

But now, with her sleek body stretched out under his, all he could think about was how fast he could get inside her. How soon he could strip her bare and kiss what lay beneath those stretchy clothes that hugged her curves.

Maybe if he gave her time to reveal her secrets, it would begin forging a link of trust between them. The man she'd killed was already dead. Nothing more could happen to him. What harm was there in Joseph giving her the time she needed to tell him what he wanted to know?

He released her wrists but didn't move his weight off her. Instead he slid his finger across her forehead in a light touch. Her skin was as warm and soft as sunlight. "You were sure I was going to kill you and all you could think about was living long enough to find your brother?"

"I can't let him die. He and Andreas are the only reason I'm alive. They protected me the whole time I was growing up. They helped me hide what I was so I wouldn't be cast out. I owe them everything."

He admired her sense of loyalty even as he cursed it. He knew there would be no stopping her, but simply coming along with her to help her find Eric wasn't enough—not when there was more he could do.

More he could give her.

This was his chance to form a bond with her—one that would start them on their journey together. Without knowing it, she was offering him the key to her trust, and he'd be a fool not to reach out and grab it.

"Then I owe them a debt, too. They kept you alive and well so I had time to find you, and now you've stopped the decay of my soul."

"But your tree is still bare. Aren't you supposed to get new leaves, like the other bonded males?"

He'd tried not to worry about that, but it had been in the back of his mind, festering. His soul was still in jeopardy until he had a fresh batch of leaves. "Not yet," he hedged. "But the more important issue is Eric. You want to find him. I want to help you."

"Then let me up. We need to get moving."

He'd wanted to wait until they were within a short sprint of a Gerai house, but his instincts were telling him that now was the time to act. Every minute he waited, she laid another brick in the wall between them. She hadn't wanted this bond, and if she didn't come to accept it, his lifemark was never again going to be healthy.

"We will," he said. "After."

"After what?"

He didn't answer her with words. Instead, he dug his fingers into the damp soil and pulled energy from the ground beneath them. As was always the case when he tapped into this kind of power, he was stunned by the sheer volume that surged under his fingertips. All he needed was a tiny trickle, but there was a river seething beneath them, eager to find a home inside him.

He resisted the urge to open himself up completely—

not while he was attached to Lyka as he was. There was too much risk involved in trying to access that kind of power. All he allowed in was a single tendril of current.

He spanned her neck with his hand, making sure both parts of the luceria connected. He directed the flow of energy from the ground, through his body and into hers.

She arched beneath him, letting out a low moan of pleasure. "Oh, my."

He imagined she'd look just like that if he ever had the good fortune to make her come. The flush in her cheeks, the way her pupils flared and lengthened, giving her a decidedly feline appearance. Her lips parted and her breath came out in short bursts.

In that moment, he knew he was going to make her his in every way possible. He was going to strip her naked, kiss and pet every inch of her. He was going to slide his cock into her as deep as a man could go and stay there until the sun burned out. It was going to take at least that long to get his fill of her. And then, when he'd wrung as many orgasms from her as she could stand, he'd let go and find his own release inside her quivering body.

He was fertile now. Tynan's serum had cured all of the male Theronai of their sterility. Joseph and Lyka could have a child—something he'd never before even dared to consider when it was beyond reach. A child would bind them together and serve as a reminder of the permanence of their connection. Surely she wouldn't be able to deny him access to her trust, her secrets, if his seed was growing in her womb. He would be part of her, and their love for their child would give them common ground.

"What the hell are you doing to me?" she asked, panting.

"Does it hurt?"

She moaned again, and there was no mistaking the sound. It was one of overwhelming pleasure. She more than liked him reviving her strength like this. She loved it.

"More." The single word was almost a plea, and Joseph wasn't sure whether he liked the idea that he could make her beg or hated that she would ever need to.

"If you want more, you have to open up. Relax. Let me in, kitten." He sent her a mental image of what he wanted. He didn't know if it would make it through the tiny conduit connecting them, but he had to make the effort.

Her body went lax beneath his. She pulled in a long breath and let it out like she was making a concerted effort to relax.

Joseph felt something between them shift. Stretch. Grow.

"That's it, Lyka. Just like that."

A shiver coursed through her body and into his.

He needed to give her more. Make her feel good. Only he would ever do this to her—fill her with power, give her the ability to wield magic. She was his in a way she'd never be with any other man, as long as he lived.

He would make sure of it—give her so much pleasure she'd never have reason to even look at another man.

Joseph pulled more power from the earth and sent it flying through their newly expanded conduit. The walls of it trembled and strained to contain what he forced on them, but they held strong.

Lyka gasped and clung to him. "Too much."

It wasn't nearly enough. There was an entire planet of pulsing, churning energy beneath his fingertips. It all wanted to touch him and become a part of him. Every spark he gave her would make her stronger, keep her safer.

"Just a little more," he coaxed.

She trembled in his arms but it wasn't from pain. Her nipples were hard enough to be visible through her clothing.

What he wouldn't give to rip her out of those clothes and have her laid out like this for him, naked and quivering. So beautiful. So his.

The sound of tearing fabric drew his attention. He hadn't even realized he'd been doing it, but he'd used minute specks of the power he pulled in to give life to his desires.

Her shirt was sliced open all the way down the front. Her bra was torn in two. All the tattered fabric was splayed open, revealing the most perfect pair of tits he'd ever seen.

He had to touch, had to lick and kiss and suck.

The flow of power cut off abruptly as he moved his hand from the ground.

Lyka's eyes popped open. The traces of the feline in her were acutely evident in the narrow slits of her pupils. As he watched, her gaze fell on his hands only inches from her breasts. Those slits expanded, telling him without a word that she liked what she saw.

Her chest rose and fell with every rapid breath. Her stare shifted to his eyes, and she watched to see what he would do.

An honorable man would cover her up. Offer her his shirt. He'd help her to her feet, see her safely to the truck and tuck her inside. He wouldn't finish ripping her clothes off and fuck her on the cold, rocky ground, especially not when even one little scratch could fill the air with the scent of blood and send demons charging their way.

Joseph had always thought of himself as an honorable

man, but as he stared down at Lyka's beautiful body and saw the naked hunger in her eyes, he knew he was wrong.

"I'm going to fuck you," he told her. His tone was too low and rough. Too much a warning and less a question. "Here. Now."

She said nothing. There wasn't even a debate going on in those catlike eyes—at least not one he could sense. She'd accepted his statement as one of fact. And she wasn't fighting it.

"Unless you stop me." The words came out of his mouth. He had no idea where they'd come from. Clearly, the honorable man in him wasn't quite dead.

Lyka reached up and grabbed his head. Her fingernails were longer than they'd been only a minute ago. Her eye teeth were sharper, longer.

None of that was right, but Joseph didn't give a shit. Everything about her turned him on. Even the freaky claws and teeth. All he could think about was what it might feel like if she used those on him, grazing them lightly over his skin.

She gripped his hair in her fists and pulled him down toward her for a kiss.

His lips met hers, and nothing else in the world mattered. She was so sweet and soft wherever she wasn't sharp and fiery. She kissed him like it was the only thing she'd been born to do. Her tongue danced with his, staking a claim.

As if any other women existed for him now. There was only Lyka.

The taste of her went to his head. He pulled her body close, getting as much of her as he could against him. Each thrusting plunge of his tongue was met with one of her own. The slick heat of their mouths grew until he could feel sparks sliding between them.

He had to have more. All of her.

He ripped the tattered edge of her shirt aside and cupped her breast in his hand. Her skin was so hot, it nearly scalded him. The urgent press of her nipple against his palm made his mouth water. He had to have a taste.

Joseph tried to pull his mouth away, but Lyka wasn't ready to let him go. Her sharp teeth nipped at his lips and tongue before licking away the sting she'd left behind. Her grip on his head tightened, and she wrapped her legs around his hips to pin him against her.

There was nowhere else he wanted to be.

A hint of blood hit his tongue, giving him a fraction of a second's pause. Something about that wasn't right, but he was drowning in Lyka and the desperate need for more of her.

She grabbed the hem of his shirt and tore it open. Her bare breasts met his bare chest, sending his world spinning. Hard nipples grazed against his skin, making his mouth water. She worked one hand between them to stroke his erection, and his cock jerked against his fly, demanding to be freed. It was so swollen and hard, he was surprised it hadn't already ripped through his jeans to reach her hand.

She drew her fingernails over the denim. He could feel restraint vibrating in her touch. "Take these off or I'm going to claw my way in for what I want."

Yeah, claws near his junk wasn't his idea of a good time, but he was so turned on, it didn't slow him down, either. Instead he rolled away from her enough to get naked without resorting to sharp instruments.

That's when he heard the cries.

Low, eerie tones of hungry demons. And they were close. "Sgath. Fuck! We have to go."

In one move he lurched to his feet and pulled Lyka along with him. She swayed for a second before regaining her stability. Her eyes widened and those slitted pupils narrowed. "It's too late. They're already here."

Joseph pushed her behind him and drew his sword just as the first demon came into sight. It was about the size of a large dog, with glowing green eyes and rows of sharp teeth. Its proportions were all wrong, like a wolf and a chimpanzee had a rabid baby. Oily black poison seeped from its pores to mat its fur. Long claws were coated with the thick goo, and would make every one of its attacks lethal.

Before the first one had time to charge, another one broke through the underbrush. Then another.

"They found us," said Lyka.

The blood he'd tasted. He didn't know if it had been his or hers, but the ferocity of their kiss had earned them this inconvenience. "I'll try to make this quick."

Then they could get back to what they'd been doing.

He launched into an attack, timing his movements to take out each one as it crossed the distance to him.

From the corner of his eye he could see Lyka with her twin daggers drawn. She'd closed ranks with a larger sgath on their right flank and was doing a great impersonation of a food processor set on puree.

He turned his attention back to what he was doing, slicing cleanly through the scrawny body of the next demon in line.

These sgath were still young. They were fast, but didn't have the power of their older counterparts. Thank goodness.

He finished off his side of the battle and was about to go help Lyka clean up her kill when the trees behind her shifted violently.

She didn't see it happen. She'd just felled the big sgath in front of her and was too busy extracting her short daggers from its body to react to the danger.

Joseph tried to call out a warning, but he was too slow.

Something dark and shiny flew out of the forest. He got a quick flash of yellow teeth and glowing green eyes before it slammed into Lyka's back and stuck there.

Its claws slid deep into her flesh, delivering a deadly dose of poison.

Rage dropped a red curtain across Joseph's vision as he barreled toward her. He cut the thing in two with one carefully placed stroke of his blade. He hadn't so much as trimmed a single hair on her head, but it didn't matter. The demon had already killed her when it subjected her to its poison. All he could do now was watch her die a slow, agonizing death.

Chapter 21

Eric had no idea how much time had passed when he woke. All he knew was that his head was throbbing and he was thirsty enough to drink whatever swill was available in the dank cave.

Kayla was by his side in an instant, her sweet face puckered with worry. "Are you okay? You've been asleep a long time. We tried to wake you up, but you didn't hear us."

He sat up a few inches, hoping it would help his head stop spinning. It didn't. "How long?" he croaked through his sandblasted throat.

She shrugged her narrow shoulders. "They fed us twice." She scurried away for a minute and came back with a plastic pitcher of water. "The ugly guy left this for you. He told us not to drink it, but I took a sip anyway, just to make sure it was safe."

Now a kid was protecting him? He must have looked even worse than he felt. "Don't do that again, Kayla. You have to take care of yourself when I can't."

"But who's going to take care of you?"

He forced himself upright, doing his best to ignore the

way the cave was whirling around him. Even if he wasn't strong right now, he had to find a way to look like it so none of the young would do anything foolish.

Kayla held the pitcher out to him. "The water is clean. You should drink. You smell sick."

"Not sick. Just a little tired." He closed his eyes to block out the spin and drank.

The cold water felt good going down. He was careful not to take too much at once for fear of puking it up.

Just the memory of that gaping maw in the top of Treszka's head was enough to make him want to vomit.

He touched his neck where she'd fed from him, but the skin was whole again. He'd been out long enough to heal the wounds she'd left behind.

And the young had been alone the whole time.

"Is everyone safe?" he asked, too dizzy to do an accurate headcount.

"Yes." She lowered her voice to a whisper. "But the boys have been crying."

"But not you?" he asked.

She bared her baby teeth. "I don't feel like crying. I feel like killing them."

Eric hoped the kid got a chance to do just that. "Tell me what happened while I slept. How many guards have you seen? Is there any kind of routine you can see to their movement? Some kind of pattern?"

She frowned at him in confusion.

He shook his head and patted her arm. "Don't worry about it. I got this." Or he would, once he had enough blood pressure to stand.

For the next hour or so, he sipped the water and held as still as possible. Kayla stayed by his side. The other young slowly migrated his way until they were all clumped up against him, shivering with both fear and cold.

He had to get them out of here. Already they were weakening. If they stayed down here much longer, there wouldn't be any fight left in them.

When he was able to stand, he slipped from the pile and wobbled on unsteady legs to the opening in the chamber.

Armed guards with patchy fur and rusty swords were everywhere. He counted at least thirty of them in sight, and could smell lots, lots more nearby. The second he approached the doorway, several of the demons bristled in aggressive warning.

Eric held up his hands and stopped in his tracks. "I need to see Treszka." He had no clue if they understood him or not. As far as he could tell, they seemed incapable of speech. All he'd heard from them were animalistic grunts, howls and that eerie hum of reverence they let out whenever Queen Bitch was nearby.

At least she couldn't sneak up on him.

"Do you understand?" he said, louder and more slowly. "Take me to your leader. Treszka."

The demons rumbled in confusion and looked at one another. Clearly, they were all idiots, incapable of a single independent thought among them.

"They won't take orders from you," said a low voice from a deep crevice in the stone.

Vazel.

He stepped out of his hidey-hole and pushed his way through the guards.

Once again, Eric was struck by how intensely ugly this creature was. He tried not to let his revulsion show on his face, but he was a few pints low and not exactly at the top of his game.

"Why do you want to see her?" asked Vazel, his words thick and difficult to understand through his fleshy lips.

"These kids won't last long down here. I thought she might show mercy and let them go."

Vazel grunted in what must have passed for laughter for him. "Treszka doesn't do mercy."

"A bargain, then."

"She has everything she wants. Why would she give up something now?"

"A woman as ambitious as she seems to be must have something else she wants. Maybe I could help." Eric probably wouldn't be able to stomach helping her reach her goals, but if it saved the young, he'd find a way to gut up.

"She's going to get what she wants from you, with or without your cooperation. She always does. So far, it hasn't mattered."

"What does that mean?"

"You haven't figured it out yet?" asked Vazel. "Maybe that blow to your head did permanent damage. Or maybe you're just not that bright."

Eric so wanted to lunge at the demon and slam him to the ground. But playing nice was in the kids' best interests, so he tamped down the urge and stayed where he stood. "Care to fill me in?"

"Treszka is the most beautiful female ever born. Synestryn lords come long distances for a chance to mate with her, but she's turned them all down."

Remembering what she had hidden under her hair, Eric did his best not to gag at the thought of what might be lurking under all those clothes. "Dare I ask why?"

"She wants beautiful children. Strong children."

All the lights went on in Eric's head, blinding him with the truth. "She told me she had needs, but I didn't realize she meant she was looking for a breeding partner."

"It is why you're here, Slayer."

He shuddered at the thought, working hard not to puke up the water he'd just gotten down. "No fucking way, dude. Chick is not only crazy, but she's got this horrible case of dandruff. Don't ever touch her head. You might catch what she's got."

"I've seen her feed before," he said, like it was some beautiful, intimate act she'd shared with him.

"On you?"

Vazel's gaze dropped in embarrassment. "My blood is not pure enough for her. It will not sustain her."

"Gee. Tough break."

His weepy eyes jerked back up at the sound of Eric's sarcasm. "You don't realize how lucky you are that she wants you. If it weren't against her orders, I'd kill you where you stand."

"So she did order you not to kill me. Good to know."

"Don't push me, Slayer. Right now the scales are balanced—I have as much reason to kill you as to let you live. If you tip that in my favor, I won't hesitate to do what I crave so deeply and empty your bones of the meat you carry."

Lovely image. "Fine, then. We'll be best buddies, because we both want the same thing: me not touching Treszka. Get me and the kids out of here and I'll make that happen."

"I would never defy her so openly. She'd kill me. Worse yet, I'd disappoint her, and that I won't do."

This dude really did have a huge crush on Queen Gaping Maw. Guess there was someone for everyone out there.

"So, what do we do? I'd just as soon keep her hands off my junk. How do we make that happen? Because when she goes slinging that magic around, there's not a thing I can do to stop her."

"No one can stop her. It is our pleasure to witness her getting her heart's desire."

"Not mine, buddy."

"You'll do what she wants. Maybe not today, but soon. You already belong to her."

That pissed Eric off more than just about anything. "I don't belong to anyone. If she pushes me, she'll learn that the hard way."

Vazel's fleshy mouth wrinkled in what Eric guessed was a grin. "I may not see you as anything more than a tasty adversary, but I will take great joy in raising your young as one of our own. Uncle Vazel."

Eric's body temperature dropped about ten degrees with the chill that flooded his veins. "Never going to happen."

Vazel shrugged his grotesquely hunched shoulders. "Resist Treszka all you like. Every Slayer child she sacrifices to soften your stubbornness is simply one fewer meal I must find to feed our troops. Eventually, you'll run out of young and she'll stop playing nice."

Behind him, the young whimpered and sobbed quietly. Except for Kayla. She ground her teeth and growled at Vazel.

"I won't let you hurt them," said Eric.

"You won't be able to stop it. The sooner you accept that, the more of your young get to live. It's your choice, Slayer. I suggest you choose wisely. She'll be coming for you soon."

Chapter 22

The howl of rage and sorrow that spewed out of Joseph scared Lyka more than the surprise demon attack had.

She'd never heard a sound like that—so raw and wounded, so hopeless and hollow.

After that observation, she wasn't given a chance for another. Her whole world was enveloped in frigid pain. It started in her shoulders and hips, where the demon's claws had pierced her skin, and swiftly traveled to every other part of her body.

She collapsed where she stood, unable to do anything more than let out a scream of agony.

More demons broke through the trees, heading straight for her. She couldn't move to defend herself. Her body was too sluggish, too swamped with pain. Every time she twitched a muscle, a burst of cold fire went off inside her nerves. She couldn't even roll out of the way.

Joseph leapt over her to stand between her and the incoming demons. He cut through them with brutal force, mowing them down like weeds. A pile of bodies covered in greasy, matted fur grew at his feet as yet another demon fell to his flashing sword.

She'd seen men fight before. Skirmishes often broke out between young Slayers searching for their place in the pack. But she'd never seen the kind of controlled violence that Joseph was laying out. There was no frenzy in him, only lethal skill delivered with cold intellect.

Beneath the haze of pain inhabiting her body, she could sense the chill of his emotions freezing the conduit that linked them. He was keeping his head and dealing with the threat to her life. Deep inside he was howling in fear and desperation, but he let none of that cloud his thinking. He controlled his emotions, not the other way around.

Lyka wanted to reassure him. He was terrified for her. In fact, he was already grieving for her, as if he thought she were dead.

She tried to send some kind of comfort through the tiny thread running between them, but her desire to ease him was too big to fit. All that seemed to trickle through was a faint strand of concern for him.

At least he'd know she was still alive.

The pain in her body began to fade as her limbs went numb. The poison was spreading through her system, making it harder to breathe.

Slayers were immune to most poisons. They'd been designed to be able to engage in hand-to-hand combat with Synestryn demons and still survive. That trait had been strengthened through the generations with careful breeding. The strongest members of the pack would reproduce, ensuring that the next generation of Slayer was tougher than the last.

Lyka's brothers had been poisoned by demons in multiple battles and survived, but they'd both been gifted with their father's genes.

Lyka hadn't. Her father was Athanasian. She had no way of knowing if the immunity to poison passed on by her mother would be enough to save her.

The last of the demons fell at Joseph's feet. Her body was so numb, it felt dead. The remnants of the pain were nearly gone now, but in its place was an empty kind of weakness—almost as if she had no body.

He was breathing hard when he turned to her. Panic lined his face, digging deep grooves around his mouth. "Hang on, Lyka."

There was nothing else she could do.

He wiped the black blood from his sword on the fur of the dead and sheathed it. As soon as his hands were empty, he bent down to pick her up.

"Don't touch the poison," she reminded him. Her voice was weak and breathless, but at least she could still speak.

Theronai weren't immune to sgath poison. If he so much as brushed her wounds, it could be absorbed by his skin and incapacitate him. If that happened, they were both as good as dead. It wouldn't be long before another pack of demons smelled her blood and came to snack on their paralyzed bodies.

He gave her a hasty nod and stripped out of his shirt. He used it to pad her wounds and keep the oily poison off his skin.

"I've got you," he said as he carried her to the truck. "Just hang on. Ronan isn't far away."

"I'll be okay." She hoped.

A pulse of grief spilled out of him.

Her words were slurred, and she hoped he could understand her. "I'm a Slayer, remember? Poison can't hurt me."

Except it had. Her brothers wouldn't have even felt the

effects of this much sgath poison. The fact that she did made her wonder just how much Slayer was really in her.

"I'm sure you're right," he said, but she could tell he was lying.

They were back at the truck. He carefully tucked her in the seat and buckled her seat belt.

She couldn't move anymore. Even her head lolled to the side.

He leaned the seat back so she wouldn't flop around so much and then hurried around to the driver's side of the truck. When he got in, he was already on the phone.

"Pick up," he all but shouted. When the person on the other end didn't, he left a message. "Call me back, Ronan. Lyka's been poisoned. I need you. Now!"

He dialed the phone again, and this time, whoever he'd called answered. "Lyka's been poisoned," he said.

There was a man's voice on the other end of the line, his tone one of calm reassurance.

"Yes, but she's also half Theronai," said Joseph.

A chill passed through her body, leaving her trembling in its wake.

"Ronan didn't answer his damn phone." Tires spun and spit gravel as he peeled out. "I don't care what he's doing. This is more important."

Another shiver racked her body so hard, it was nearly a convulsion. Every muscle in her was knotted and frozen, only now the numbness was starting to wear off and the pain was coming back with a vengeance.

Layered over that was a sharp increase in the worry flowing out of Joseph. That tiny pipeline between them was so clogged with fear, there was no room left for her to reassure him.

"I'll be fine." The words came out through her chattering teeth, robbing them of all confidence.

Joseph's hand settled on her arm, so hot it nearly burned her. She jerked involuntarily as she hissed in pain.

"It's getting worse," he said into the phone. "She's running out of time. I'm headed toward you as fast as I can go."

The truck went airborne over a bump in the road. She was unable to control her body enough to compensate for the motion, which left her slinging around in the seat like a rag doll. If not for the seat belt, she would have sloshed over into his lap.

A heavy black cloud of confusion started to form over her, sinking down to consume her as it grew. She didn't know where it came from or why it was there, but she knew that it wasn't good.

Another hard shiver grabbed hold of her body and shook her. This time, the shaking didn't ease. It got worse. Just as one wave of cold pain subsided, the next one slammed into her, stealing her breath. After a few of them, she wasn't able to breathe at all.

The black cloud expanded to fill the entire truck and swallowed her whole.

Her last conscious thought was that she'd failed. She'd failed Eric and the young by not finding them. She'd failed Joseph by not being the partner he needed her to be. And she'd failed her people by not doing her duty and killing more demons when she had the chance. She'd barely even scratched the surface on what she'd wanted to do with her life, and already it was over.

Chapter 23

Ronan ignored his phone's incessant buzzing as he raced toward the woman he sought. He'd already had to use precious power to convince a police officer that he'd imagined the pale man in the van doing 110 down the highway.

Touching the mind of a human with whom he had no blood bond, and at that distance, had been difficult but necessary.

His mystery woman—his savior—had started moving toward him.

There was no way he was going to let whatever emergency had popped up now deter him from finding her. She so rarely stopped, or even slowed down, the idea of her drawing nearer was almost inconceivable. He had to take advantage of the opportunity while it was still available to him.

A twinge of guilt over ignoring his phone hit his conscience, but he shrugged it away. If his instincts were right, then what he was doing now was far more important than anything that Joseph might want.

Normally, such thoughts would give him pause, but

his compulsion to find her was far too great for him to fight.

She'd saved his life, given him her blood. He was connected to her so acutely, he knew when she grew tired or afraid. He knew when she was hungry and when she laughed, which wasn't nearly often enough.

He'd fed from thousands of people in his long lifetime, and while he'd felt a connection to each of them, too, it was nothing like it was with her.

He ached without her. Craved her.

She was his.

When he finally found her again, he would make sure she accepted that. Make sure she never ran from him again. He would force her to answer some questions so he could understand why he felt the way he did about a woman whose name he didn't even know.

Another set of flashing blue lights appeared in his rearview mirror. He focused his gaze on the man behind the wheel, compelling him to blindness with a single, brutal compulsion.

The cruiser veered onto the shoulder and came to an abrupt stop.

The policeman would regain his vision in an hour or so—just long enough to make sure that Ronan had time to cross the state line into Nebraska.

His mystery woman was only hours away now, drawing closer with each minute that passed. Soon she would be in his grasp, and he'd never let go of her again.

Eric jerked away from the guards that had hauled his ass through the cave system back to Treszka's quarters.

She was beautiful, dressed in a green silk gown this time. It shimmered with some kind of golden thread that sparkled as it clung to deceptively inviting curves. Her breasts spilled out over the top, begging for a man's touch the way only a woman could.

Not a woman. A demon. He kept reminding himself of that, of what was under that flap of hair on her head.

A spread of fragrant food was laid out on a table set with two plates. There were so many smells bombarding him, it was hard to tell what she was serving, other than some kind of lamb.

"Hungry?" she asked, waving in invitation for him to sit.

"Not really. I'd rather eat with the young."

She glowered at him. "Sit, or they won't eat at all tonight."

So it was night now? He'd long ago lost track of the passage of days. He could barely feel the pull of the moon on him down here, well out of its reach.

Which was probably just as well. The closer it got to a full moon, the more his libido would flare, and the harder it was going to be for Eric to remember that the beautiful creature who wanted to fuck him was a demon.

Eric sat, just to get her to leave the kids alone. The poor things had already been through more than their fair share of fear and trauma down here. He'd do whatever it took to protect them as much as possible for as long as he could.

Kayla would be the first one they'd kill. She was fierce and hard to control. They'd get rid of her before she could rile the others to create trouble. At least that's what he'd do if he were in charge. The idea of never seeing that aggressive little half-pint again was enough to encourage him to behave himself.

He even pulled Treszka's chair out and smoothed a napkin over his grubby jeans, as if this were the finest restaurant in town. If playing civilized gentleman kept the kids safe for another night, it was worth the lie.

She ladled something from a pot into his bowl. He could smell about twenty different spices he couldn't name, but none of them seemed toxic.

He waited until she took the first bite, just to be sure.

"Vazel informed me that he told you why you're here," she said.

"As a sperm bank?"

"Yes."

Eric lifted his eyes from his spoon to stare at her. "Never going to happen."

"I'm unconcerned about your intent—only your worthiness."

"I'm definitely not worthy."

"Your blood says otherwise. You're stronger than your kind are reputed to be. Can you shift?"

"No," he lied a little too fast.

"I don't believe you."

"Your goons saw the extent of my ability when they attacked our settlement. I get some claws and teeth, but that's about it."

"Why do you smell like you're lying?"

"Believe me. If I could have wolfed out on your idiot brigade, I would have. The fact that they were able to capture me is proof to the contrary."

She pondered that for a minute, like she was trying to decide if she believed it or not.

The truth was, Eric could shift all the way into his wolf form, but only when the moon was full and only when Mother Nature decided it was time. It was completely out of his control.

Kayla, on the other hand, had shown some inclination toward controlling her shift. She was the generation after Eric and Andreas, and their careful breeding laws had proved to be working. Each generation was stronger than the last—more Slayer, less human. It was hard to know for sure how well she'd be able to control it until she was a little older.

He hoped like hell she'd live that long.

He'd nearly finished his meal when he felt a subtle shift in his body temperature. His kind ran hot, but he was starting to sweat, despite how chilly it was down here underground.

Treszka regarded him with a knowing smile. "Something wrong?"

His skin started to tingle, and all that hot blood began pooling in his groin. "You drugged me?"

Her satisfied grin was answer enough. "Why do you say that?"

Within seconds, he had an erection hard enough to hammer railroad spikes. "It doesn't matter what you do or how horny I get. I still won't fuck a demon."

All amusement faded from her face. She bared her teeth in a snarl. "I'm your queen."

"You're my captor. My warden."

"I'm the mother of your future children."

"I'd sooner cut off my own dick than breed you."

That was the wrong thing to say if ever there was one.

Eric flew across the room, kicking over the table and the rest of the food as he went. Soup splashed across the hem of her silk gown as he slammed into the rock wall and stayed there.

She looked down at it in fury. "See what you did?"

He didn't dare speak. Not now. Even if he could catch his breath. As it was, his ribs were being crushed by the magical force that held him in place. The pain of his bindings grew, especially against his cock, which finally decided to retreat.

Whatever she'd dosed him with had been strong, but so was the pain she inflicted. And Eric wasn't into pain.

She grabbed the front of her dress and ripped it. Then she stepped out of it, revealing a body fit for the cover of the *Sports Illustrated* swimsuit issue. She was completely naked under the silk, without so much as a thong to hide her nudity.

She was so absolutely stunning that he might have been convinced to take her for a ride. If only she weren't a demon with a maw in the top of her skull. Even the idea of getting a blow job from that monstrosity was enough to make his testicles draw up into his abdomen.

His body went airborne again, only this time the landing was much softer. He hit her mattress and bounced once before being pinned in place by an invisible force. With a slight wave of her hand, his jeans ripped open and were jerked from his legs.

She sauntered over to him, wiggling those luscious hips as she went.

His balls began to tingle, and his cock decided that maybe there wouldn't be another six weeks of winter.

Demon, man. She's a demon. Remember the teeth?

She went from furious to wearing a satisfied grin in the time it took her to cross the room. Her fingers trailed up along the inside of his thigh, tickling him with the tips of her black fingernails. "I'm trying to make this as easy on you as possible. I even dosed your soup so you'd have an excuse to tell yourself later. After I'm done with you."

He gritted his teeth and blocked out the feel of her fingers stroking his hardening cock. He wasn't going to do this. He. Was. Not.

His body had other ideas, though. It was weak. Of the flesh. It didn't care that this was seventeen kinds of fucked-up. In seconds, he was going to be erect enough for liftoff.

He didn't know how close the full moon was—how close he was to being fertile. He might still have a day or two before he could breed her, but, then again, he'd been unconscious a lot. He might not have any time left at all.

She bent down to take his cock in her mouth. Her hair shifted over her shoulder and swept across his thigh, reminding him of just what lay under those midnight tresses.

His cock deflated like an old balloon, leaving her screaming in frustration.

"You will give me what I want," she said as she increased the pressure pinning him to the bed.

"No, I won't. Kill me if you want, but I'm never going to fuck a damn demon."

Her white pupils flared, and the air pressure in the cavern changed. "Guards!"

A group of demons filtered into the room, eager to do her bidding. They barely even gave him a second glance.

"The girl. The fighter. Bring her."

Kayla. *Fuck.*

"Cover me up," he said. Nudity wasn't a huge deal among his kind, but being bound to a bed, spread-eagle, was a little different. This was not the image he wanted Kayla to have of her fighting coach or the man she was trusting to get her the hell out of this underground tomb.

Treszka regarded him for a minute, making his skin crawl. It didn't matter that her body was the stuff of legends. All he could see was what lay beneath—her cruel spirit and her demon blood.

"I had hoped to spare you more pain," she said.

"Yeah, I just bet you did."

"And Kayla. She has such a potent force of life thrumming through her. She would have done well down here in time. She might have even grown into a place of power among us. She could walk in the sun, helping me procure the human comforts that are so hard to come by." Treszka ran her fingers along his ribs, petting him. "But now that all depends on you."

Two guards came back into the cavern, dragging a spitting-mad, fighting Kayla with them.

"Cease!" shouted Treszka, imbuing her words with enough magic to force Kayla to obey.

The girl went still and stared daggers through her tangled blond bangs.

Treszka sat on the edge of the bed. Her voice was calm, as if what she was about to say was completely rational. "You're going to give me what I want. Now. Or I'm going to feed from the child until she's dead, while you watch. Which do you prefer?"

Fury lit up Eric's insides, driving away all the chill of the room. He felt his fingernails and toenails lengthen, his teeth extend down into his mouth. His pulse pounded in his ears and a low growl spilled from his mouth. "Touch her and I will kill you."

Treszka laughed and patted his arm. "You're so adorable when you're helpless."

"Let him go!" screamed Kayla. Her cheeks were red with anger, and she was doing her best to break free of the hold the demons had on her scrawny arms.

"You." Treszka pointed at Kayla. "Shut up. You." She pointed at Eric. "Decide. Watch the child die, or give me one of my own."

Eric racked his brains for some idea, some glimmer of hope that would get him out of this situation, but he could find none. He couldn't fight the magical bonds holding him down. He couldn't hope that the bitch was bluffing and that Kayla would be safe. The only ace up his sleeve was that he might not be fertile right now.

Maybe if he let her fuck him, she'd go away and leave the young alone. It would take her a while to figure out that he hadn't knocked her up.

Assuming he didn't.

He almost let himself think about the child that might result from what he knew he had to do, but stopped himself cold. If he stopped long enough to wonder what a life for Treszka's child might be like, he knew he'd never be able to make up his mind. How could he trade the life of one kid for another?

He couldn't.

She wasn't going to go away. She wasn't going to stop wanting a baby. Demon or not, the urge to procreate was strong, and he wasn't foolish enough to think it would magically evaporate because he wanted it to.

All he could do was make the choice he was faced with now and hope he could live with himself later.

"I don't want her to watch," he told Treszka. "Send her back to the others, and I'll give you what you want."

Kayla let out a muffled yell and kicked her little feet.

"It's okay," he told her. "She's not going to hurt me. I'll come see you in a little while. Everything is going to be fine."

Treszka waved away the guards and straddled his thighs. She took his junk in her cold fingers, making his skin crawl.

Eric closed his eyes. Checked out. Let her do what she wanted. Kayla was safe, and that was all that mattered.

Chapter 24

"I won't let you die," said Joseph, but it was too late. Lyka couldn't hear him anymore.

The back end of the truck sloshed around as he pulled up to the front step of the Gerai house and slammed on the brakes. He jumped out of the truck and raced around it to get Lyka to the relative safety that awaited them inside.

His shirt that was draped around her was smeared with blood and oily black poison, but she didn't seem to be bleeding anymore. For an instant, he worried that it was because her heart had stopped beating, but her panting reminded him that she was still alive.

Barely.

He was so used to feeling the potent strength of her spirit on the other side of the link, he hadn't realized just how powerful it was until it was nearly gone.

Joseph carried her to the front door and smashed the lock open with his boot. He laid her inside on the couch and pulled out his phone.

Ronan still wasn't answering, so he dialed Tynan. "Where are you?"

"I called for Logan."

"You mean you haven't even left yet?"

"I can't leave, not with so many people here to protect. Even if I did, I'm not sure how much good I could do. I'm weak, Joseph."

"I'd give you all the blood you need." Every drop, if that's what it took to save Lyka.

"And what of the pregnant women here? The children? Who would be here for them? Logan will come when he can, but there was a battle up north and several Gerai were wounded. He and Hope went to offer aid."

"Tell them to hurry." Joseph was freaked-out by the tremors that racked her body. She was pale, cold. He covered her with a blanket, but it did no good. "What do I do to help her?"

"Keep her still, calm."

"She's unconscious but still shivering."

"Did you start a fire?"

"No time. I need to burn the clothes she bled on, but I thought it could wait."

"The heat might help make her more comfortable."

Joseph set a match to the kindling that was all laid out and ready to go, thanks to the helpful Gerai who stocked this place. Lighting a fire wasn't nearly enough to ease his worry, but at least it was something—some action he could take.

"Her Theronai blood is going to kill her, isn't it?" he asked Tynan.

"You don't know that. She needs you to stay positive. You're connected to her now, remember? She may be able to sense your feelings. You must stay strong for her sake."

Tynan was right. It was Joseph's duty to see to her every need, so if she needed him to stay positive, then that's what he'd do. "I need to go. Call me if anything changes."

"You as well, Joseph."

He hung up. The fire had grown enough for him to lay a log on it. It was time to add the clothes to burn away the blood.

He made careful work of stripping away Lyka's dirty shirt and jeans. Her skin was whole, thanks to her Slayer blood quickly regenerating her skin. By the time he was done taking away all the clothes holding traces of blood or poison, she was naked except for her socks.

Joseph secured the busted front door with a chair and then lifted her into his arms. She let out a soft moan of pain and shivered.

He slid her under the blankets on a bed, then unbuckled his sword belt. The weapon shimmered a moment before becoming visible. He set it within easy reach, praying he wasn't going to need it again tonight.

He hadn't found a new shirt yet, but that didn't slow him down. She needed warmth, and his bare skin on hers would give it to her.

She shivered as he wrapped his arms around her. The fact that she was naked was not lost on him. He tried not to think about it, but the smooth skin under his hands made it impossible. The best he could do was keep his roving grasp from going too far onto intimate territory.

As he gave her his body heat, her shivering slowed and finally stopped. She relaxed in his grasp and practically melted into him. He found the conduit between them and pried his way through in order to reassure her that she was going to be fine. He was going to see her through this. She wasn't alone.

The second he entered her thoughts, he was surrounded by beauty and chaos. She was deeply confused, her dreams a jumbled mass of frenetic images. She battled sgath from all sides, her body blurring in motion. In the next instant, she was diving into a clear, moonlit lake. Her head broke the surface of the water and she looked at him with silent invitation in her golden eyes.

Joseph was already halfway to the lake to join her when it disappeared and she was standing next to a dead Theronai, tears streaming down her face.

This was the man she'd killed—the man who'd begged her to end his suffering. There was a slight smile of relief on his face. He was free of pain and fear, free from the worry that he would hurt the people he loved when the last leaf on his lifemark fell and his soul died, leaving him dark and twisted.

Inside her dreams, Lyka looked up at Joseph. "I had to help him."

"I understand."

"Please don't kill me for helping him."

"I won't. I could never hurt you."

"You already have. You've stolen me from my family, my people. You've turned me into the enemy."

"We're not enemies anymore. And you can visit your family whenever you want."

The landscape around them went dark, tossing them both to the destroyed Slayer settlement. There were bodies strewn everywhere, as if the graves had never been dug, the dead never buried.

"My family is gone. There's nothing left for me here."

"They will rebuild. We'll help them."

Her eyes narrowed in suspicion. "How?"

Joseph exerted his will over her mind just enough to show her what he envisioned. He brought the sun back, buried the dead, rebuilt the buildings and planted flowers and trees where only ash had remained. It was a beautiful place again, filled with hope and life.

"We can do this?" she asked him, disbelief clear in her tone.

"Yes. Together we can wield powerful magic."

"I don't know how."

"You'll learn. All you have to worry about is getting strong again."

She frowned as if trying to remember. "I was dying."

"No. You're going to be fine. You're just resting now."

"I can feel you holding me, but you're all the way over there. How is that possible?"

"My body is holding yours." He waved to their surroundings. "This is your mind."

"You don't belong here."

"Yes, I do. In time you'll see that."

Somehow she was next to him in an instant, without having moved. Her hands settled on his bare chest as she looked into his eyes. "You're trying to take away all the things that make me a Slayer."

"You're wrong. I've never been more relieved that you're part Slayer than I am right now. It's the only reason you're still alive."

"If I was truly a Slayer, the poison wouldn't have worked. It's going to kill me, isn't it?"

"No," he nearly shouted. He had to swallow twice to rein in his anger at the mere idea of her death. "I won't let that happen. You're strong, Lyka."

"I'm tired."

"Then draw your strength from me. I have more than enough to spare."

"I don't want to need you."

"Do you think it makes you weaker?"

"I know it does."

"Am I weaker for needing you to save my soul?"

"That's different. That's the way you were designed to be."

"And you were designed to draw power from me, even if you don't like it."

She was silent for a minute before she spoke. "I don't want to die. I need to find my brother and those children."

"Then use me. Use my power. Open yourself up and take what you need. As soon as you're strong again, we'll go find them."

He could feel her need to go hunting rise within her. It was so powerful, it was nearly a compulsion. The animal inside her reared its head, demanding she obey. It wanted to be set free to hunt. It wanted to survive, no matter what it took.

She took his hand and brought it to her throat. The luceria glowed in swirling gold and green that brought out her eyes and warmed her skin. Once the colors were fixed and were no longer in motion, their bond would be complete. Until that time, if she died, he would survive until his lifemark was barren and he met his death at the hands of a Slayer, or until he found another mate. But he didn't want that. Even if it was likely he'd find another woman compatible with his power—which it wasn't—he wanted Lyka. She was beautiful both inside and out. She was strong and brave and fearless. She was smart and loyal in a way rarely seen in this day and age. And once he got past her prickly exterior and into the heart of her soul, she was kind. Generous. Loving.

Joseph wanted her to pour all of that on him—to let him bask in everything that made her who she was all the way down to her core. He'd never seen a more stunning, glorious creature, and he wasn't ready to let her go.

He circled her slender neck with his fingers, connecting both parts of the luceria. "Take what you need, Lyka. Whatever you want."

A slow, steady trickle of power began to flow out of him. Her head fell back, and a soft moan of pleasure rushed from her. When she lifted her head again, her eyes were glowing with heat.

"Go home, Theronai," she said. "When I'm done here, I'm coming for you."

He didn't know what she meant, but she was now strong enough to cast him out of her thoughts and shove him back into his own skin. He lay on the bed next to her naked body, his hand on her neck as it had been in her dream. The deadly chill of poison had left her skin, and she was now covered in a warm pink flush.

Energy began flowing from him at a faster and faster rate. The pressure inside his body began to ease, giving him room for a deep breath. He hadn't felt this good in years—not since the power he housed had grown out of control.

She was bleeding that off now, freeing him from centuries of discomfort.

A fizzing, tingling feeling spread across his chest. Her bare nipples hardened in response, as if she felt it, too. Her hands snaked around him, holding him tight against her lithe frame. Her toes curled against his calves, and her fingers dug into his back.

Joseph wanted to stroke her from head to toe and back again, but he dared not let go of their connection. She wasn't experienced enough to pull power from him without the physical contact of ring on necklace. Soon she'd be able to reach the magic inside him from miles away, but not yet.

The idea that she needed him this close gave him a

rush. To be needed by a strong woman was a potent thing, one he wasn't sure he'd ever get used to. But he wanted to.

He wasn't sure exactly how, but he felt her shed the effects of the poison, felt her strength return. She opened her eyes and stared into his.

She was, without a doubt, the most beautiful woman ever created. And she was all his.

"Better?" he asked.

"Not as good as I will be once I get your cock inside of me."

Raw, physical need flared in his gut, setting him on fire. He wanted to stop her and ask why she was so turned on—to make sure she wouldn't regret her actions later—but he wasn't that strong a man. Every action he'd taken in his life had led him to this moment—claiming his mate. He knew the luceria wouldn't have chosen her for him without a reason. He had to trust that that reason would make itself known at some point along the way. Until then, he was going to give her what she wanted and make her the happiest woman on earth.

He cradled her face in his hands and kissed her the way a woman this rare and precious was meant to be kissed. He took his time, savoring each sweet flavor and texture her mouth had to offer. He fed her his breath while he feasted on her, showing her with lips and tongue what he had in store for the rest of her sleek body.

His skin heated until he couldn't stand the blankets cloaking them. He shoved them aside and rolled her beneath him, pinning her to the mattress. She tried to get the upper hand and fight her way to the top, but he wasn't having any of it. He liked her beneath him, all soft and writhing with need.

She was naked. He needed to be, too. Their skin was

meant to be touching, as often and as much as possible. Who was he to deny either of them that pleasure?

He moved off her just enough to rid himself of his jeans. By the time he did, she had slid over him, straddling his thighs.

His erection rose in front of her, thick, dark and throbbing. The tip was shiny with pre-cum, proof of his lack of control when it came to this woman. He'd wanted her for far too long to hold himself back now.

Indecision warred on her face as she stared at his cock.

He hoped she hadn't changed her mind, because if she had, he was still going to take her. Lyka was his. It was time she understood exactly what that meant.

Chapter 25

R onan skidded to a stop outside of an airport.
    She was in there. Somewhere.

He parked his van and rushed inside, following the call of her blood in his veins. He'd made it almost all the way across the parking lot when he felt her move again, only this time the sensation was bizarre. He'd never felt anything like it before.

She was moving toward him, but she was also ... above him.

Ronan's woman had boarded a plane and was flying away from him.

A large jet buzzed by overhead, and he knew that she was on it, completely out of reach.

A sense of failure and loss swept through him, but he reined it in enough to plan his next move. Just because she was flying away didn't mean he couldn't still find her.

He hurried inside and checked the terminals for recent takeoffs. He made note of the destinations of those flights and went to the ticket counter.

Ronan wasted no time trying to convince the young woman across the counter to help him. He simply exerted his will over her, took control of her mind and compelled her to print him a copy of the manifest of every flight that had left in the past ten minutes.

Something she did must have triggered an alarm, because there were several uniformed men converging on his location.

Rather than spend precious energy trying to stop them from coming after him, he simply ducked behind a thick column that held up the vast ceiling and shielded himself from human sight. By the time he was on the other side of the column, he was completely invisible to every person around.

Hiding himself like this was burning power fast, so he broke into a run and headed for his van. It wasn't until he was miles away from the airport that he allowed himself to stop at a local mall and read over the papers he'd collected.

Two of the three manifests were for small planes. The last was the only one with enough passengers to fill an aircraft the size of the one he'd seen pass overhead. He crossed out all the male names, which left just a little less than half of the passengers. Too many.

There was one man he knew who had a knack with computers. If anyone could find pictures of the women remaining on this list, it was Nicholas. But if Ronan called him, he was going to catch hell for all the missed messages the irate Theronai had left on his phone.

Still, what other choice did he have? He needed to know where she was going before she got so far away he could no longer feel her. If she ended up in Europe, he was going to have to make careful plans to follow her. He absolutely could not be caught on board an airplane when the sun was up. Even if a single Warden was summoned, it would mean the death of every living soul on that plane. He couldn't risk that many lives—not even for her.

Ronan picked up his phone and dialed Nicholas, bracing himself for the penance he was going to have to pay for being AWOL. Whatever he had to do, he'd do, as long as it got him one step closer to his mystery woman.

Chapter 26

Lyka wasn't sure if she wanted to suck Joseph's cock or ride him first. Both were such tantalizing options.

She'd felt sexual need before, but never the way she did now. It was a living, breathing thing that crawled through her body and demanded action. She was just glad that he was already hard and ready for her, because if he hadn't been, she wasn't sure she would have survived making him that way without combusting.

She could still taste his kiss on her lips, all hot and sweet. The man knew what he was doing with his tongue, and as soon as she could stand being in her own skin again, she was going to convince him to use that tongue between her thighs.

Just the thought had the slick heat of arousal spilling from her core.

She was so empty there, so hot. She needed him to put out the fire and give her relief.

Pulling his power inside her had been far more erotic than she could have imagined. One moment she'd been hovering on the verge of death. The next, she was consumed with a potent rush of possessive need. She knew it wasn't hers, but it hardly mattered. The fire his power had lit in her was blazing out of control and had to be extinguished.

Only he could give her relief.

Lyka had no idea how she'd gotten naked, but she was glad for the convenience now. With one graceful shift of her body, she lowered herself onto the tip his erection.

Wetness bathed him as she moved her hips, working to adjust to the thickness of his cock. His big hands grabbed her hips and held on tight. With slow, steady pressure, he forced her down until she was full.

Wicked, delightful sensations winged through her limbs, stealing her breath. The sweet stretch and pressure inside her was almost enough to set her off. All she needed was a few strokes, and she knew she'd come screaming his name.

"I need you to take all of me, kitten."

She didn't understand what he meant until she reached between their bodies and felt just how much more he had to give her.

The idea made her whimper, but even she couldn't tell if the sound was due more to apprehension or excitement.

"I'm full," she told him.

"Not yet, you're not. But you will be."

His powerful body moved, taking her with him. She found herself flat on her back, her body pinned by his hips and arms.

There was nowhere for her to go to escape his massive presence, nowhere for her to hide from his hot hazel gaze.

He eased forward, stretching her until stars danced in her vision and her whole world shrank down to the flesh connecting them.

It was too much and yet still not enough. She grabbed

his shoulders, unsure if she wanted to pull him closer or push him away. In the end, it didn't matter what she wanted, because he gathered her hands and pinned them over her head.

Her first instinct was to fight the restraint, but after a second, she realized that it arched her back in such a way that his cock stroked a whole new and delightful set of nerve endings inside her.

Hot, strong fingers cupped her breast, catching the sensitive peak between them. He pinched and rolled her nipple with the skill of a master safecracker, unlocking every bit of resistance left in her.

Her body went limp beneath his, accepting his weight, his heat, his hold on her wrists, the intrusion of his erection pressed deep inside her core.

"That's right," he crooned. "Just let go. I have you."

She believed that. As stupid as it might make her, in this moment, she trusted Joseph completely.

He let out a low, rough groan of approval. "Sweet kitten. I'm going to make you purr."

He covered her mouth with his and began moving his hips in earnest. Each steady thrust filled her, stretching her more than she thought possible. All conscious thought of what he was doing seemed to vanish, leaving behind only the fog of acute pleasure he'd laid over her body.

Her deep want, combined with his relentless skill and gentle force, sent her over the edge. Her world shattered in golden shards of heat and light as her orgasm took her. Her body clenched around Joseph's cock, flooding him with slick wetness. She tried to hold on to him, but he was too strong to be trapped by her grasp.

He kept moving, riding her hard to prolong her orgasm. After it passed and she was lying there, quivering and boneless, she opened her eyes to find him watching her.

"How many more times can I make you do that before you're spent?" he asked.

"None," she said on a weak breath of air. "You nearly killed me."

A dark smile curved his lips. "That sounds like a challenge to me, love. By the time I'm done with you, you're going to forget what it's like to not be writhing in the throes of orgasm."

There was no way she could take more. He hadn't come yet, but there wasn't much she could do about that until she caught her breath. As it was, she was already shaking from the force of being loved by a man as potent as Joseph.

No, not love. Sex. That was all this was. She couldn't let any girlish fantasies cloud her judgment. A few short months ago, they'd been enemies. To think that he'd come to love a woman like her was foolish. Wanting him to do so would only weaken her.

And she was already too weak to see straight. The man had blasted her world away, leaving behind a filmy haze of sexual satisfaction. She could have basked in it for hours if not for more pressing matters.

Lyka shifted in silent request that he move off her. Instead he hooked her ankles over his shoulders and drove deep.

Sparks lit high in her abdomen, where the tip of his cock had settled against some exquisite spot. She could feel a trickle of energy pouring from him into her. Every tingling strand of it seemed to coalesce at her core, relighting the fire he'd just put out.

"I'm not done with you yet," he said with a hint of a growl in his voice. "And I won't be until I flood that sweet pussy of yours with my seed. But first, I'm going to make you scream again."

She shivered at his statement, given with such confidence that she could only accept it as fact. It didn't matter that she'd just gotten off or that her body had started to cool down. He was going to take what he wanted from her and make sure she enjoyed the ride.

One of those erotic images from his mind flashed behind her eyes. She saw it in full, living color— his powerful body bent over her, his cheeks hollowed out as he suckled her nipples. His hand was between her thighs, stroking her clit until she was whimpering with need.

Her skin heated as he played the scene out for her. Just like that, she was right back on the edge, fighting the keen bite of arousal as if she'd never come.

He found her mouth with his and kissed her like the world was coming to an end, like he'd die if he didn't breathe the air from her lungs. Possessive aggression was coming off him in waves now. The rough edges of it grated against her, making her wonder how he could even imagine her with another man after the way he made her feel.

Another of his fantasies played out between them. This time his dark head was between her thighs. His thick fingers were clenched around her hips, holding her tight as he licked and sucked her. She could feel his deep satisfaction, his need to pin her in place and feed from her, pleasure her, like this.

Beyond their minds, her body was straining to take everything Joseph wanted to give her. Every heavy surge of his hips sent him gliding against parts of her that had never before been touched. Her womb clenched and pulsed as she veered toward release.

She arched her back, causing Joseph to dive down to

nibble and suckle her hard nipples. He reached behind her, grabbing a handful of her hair, forcing her to arch her back more. She couldn't move her head, couldn't move her hips. All she could do was lie there and let him take control.

The instant she yielded, her mind melted and her body went off, bursting into the kind of pleasure so acute, it was nearly pain. She heard herself cry out, felt Joseph tighten around her, swell inside her.

"So fucking sexy," he growled. "Can't wait any longer, kitten."

She didn't understand what he meant until she felt his semen erupt deep inside, so hot and powerful that she knew she'd never again be the same. Even in the depths of her climax, she knew her world had just changed. As the last waves of intense pleasure settled into quiet ripples, as the last pulses of his semen filled her, she knew what it was to belong to someone.

Too bad it was the wrong someone. None of her people would ever understand her binding herself to a Theronai like this. She was his in every way that mattered. She even smelled like him now.

She hadn't realized it before, but up until this very moment, she'd been holding out a little sliver of hope that one day her life would return to normal. She'd go home, be with her family and friends. This whole brief interlude where she played Theronai would be over.

That dream was dead now. She'd given herself to the enemy, body and soul. There was no undoing that.

Chapter 27

Justice stepped off the plane on shaky legs. She'd thought she could outsmart the fates or God or whoever it was that compelled her by flying halfway across the country.

She'd been very, very wrong.

She'd felt Ronan growing closer to her. She knew he was hot on her heels, searching for her with endless determination. It didn't matter how far she went or how fast she went there; he was always only a step or two behind her, giving her no time to rest.

As soon as the fates demanded that she move toward him, she was out. Done. Finished being their bitch. Let them do their own damn dirty work. She quit.

Only that's not the way it worked. Much like the Mafia, there was no getting out unless it was feetfirst. She was trapped in her job, chained to it for life.

Assuming she lived.

"Are you okay?" asked one of the attendants at the end of the jetway.

Justice eyed the perky blonde and nodded. "Airsick."

She needed to turn around, get back on the flight and

go back to the fucking Midwest. *That* was what the fates wanted of her, and those bitches always got their way.

Justice stepped out of the path of unloading passengers and planted her feet. She breathed through her nose, hoping the urge to go east would fizzle out and leave her alone. That was where Ronan was. And if he found her, she was sure the bloodsucker would be the death of her.

She wasn't ready to die. She hated her life and the way she was tossed about like a corked bottle on the ocean. Still, she was too scared to face what might lie on the other side of this place to do anything about it.

She'd already woken up once naked, alone and with no memories of a former life. She really didn't think she could take doing so again.

The urge to obey bore down on her, making her head throb and her gut churn. Her skin had constricted to the point that she wasn't sure how she was going to find the space to pull in her next breath. As it was, she was panting and sweating, taking a lot of stink eye from the people passing her.

She couldn't stay here, whatever she did. She had to move. Do something. The itch inside her was too extreme to just stand around and be tortured. At least if she were moving, she'd be distracted from the way she was slowly dying inside.

Justice found herself in baggage claim, retrieving her hard-sided, cherry red suitcase. Her next stop was a rental-car agency, where she got the fastest set of wheels they had to offer.

Ten minutes later, she was behind the wheel, flying down the highway.

An interstate junction loomed up ahead. She could go left and head for California, or right, back to Ronan

Land. Left was freedom and excruciating pain. Right was elation, followed by a bloodsucking vampire.

In the end, there really was no choice. There never had been—at least not for her. Justice had no free will. She was a tool. A pawn. She went where she was told and did what was expected of her, no matter how cruel or disgusting it might be.

Her only hope was that wherever the fates sent her this time, Ronan would be far, far away.

Chapter 28

Joseph realized the instant he could breathe again that he'd made a fatal mistake.

Lyka hadn't been ready for sex. It was too soon, and now she was shutting down, closing up shop and boarding all the doors on her thoughts so he couldn't see a single one.

He should have waited. Given her time. Let her accept the fact that she was irrevocably bound to him — that she wasn't going back to her old life once Eric and the kids were found.

But, no, his dick had to get some, and now he'd potentially ruined his relationship with his mate for the rest of their long, long lives.

How the hell could he have been so stupid?

She slipped from the bed and wobbled to the bathroom. The door shut behind her, blocking off the sight of her lovely ass, as well as any chance he had of reading her thoughts.

He poked at the connection between them, hoping for even a slight glimpse of her feelings, but all he got was a cold, blank wall.

He fell back against the pillows and covered his eyes with his forearm. The longer he waited to bridge the gap that was forming between them, the wider it would become.

The only thing he could think to do to draw her back to him was to help her find her brother, but they'd been working on that with little success so far. So had a lot of other people. Whoever, whatever, had the Slayers, they were covering their tracks well. Not even the best Slayer noses had been able to follow the trail.

Then again, not one of those Slayers had the power of a Theronai at their disposal, either.

Joseph thought about waiting for her to come out of the bathroom, but every second that passed was another chunk of ice clogging their connection. It was time to melt that all off.

His legs were a bit unsteady as he slid on his jeans, but he forced his shaky limbs to carry him to the bathroom door. "Lyka, are you okay?"

"Fine. Just cleaning up." Her tone was sharp with irritation.

He'd left a hell of a mess inside that sweet body of hers when he'd come, but she'd seemed to like it at the time. Maybe she was one of those OCD chicks who just couldn't stand a man's semen touching her.

If that was the case, then she was just going to have to get over it, because he planned on messing her up again. Frequently.

Whoa. Down, boy. Getting pissed over something he didn't even know was true was not the way to get Lyka to open up to him.

He put a muzzle on his irrational burst of anger and forced his voice to come out nice and calm. "Can I come in?"

"Isn't there another bathroom?"

"Not one with you in it."

She let out a long, agitated sigh. The door opened to her gloriously naked body posed with one hand on her curvy hip. He was sure her expression would have shown him just how pissed she was if he could have found the strength to lift his eyes past her flushed breasts.

He loved the way her nipples felt against his tongue, the way she squirmed and panted when he applied just the right amount of suction.

How in the world was he going to concentrate on work now that he knew just how she tasted, how she sounded when she came?

"You wanted something?" she asked.

He had wanted something—something that had nothing to do with spinning her around and fucking her against the bathroom sink.

Joseph closed his eyes so his brain would start to work again. This was important. Whatever it was.

As the sight of her beauty moved from reality to memory, he remembered why he'd knocked on the door in the first place. "I thought of something we could try."

"I'm not having sex with you again, Theronai."

"Not that." Though heaven knew he had about a million fantasies stored up—things he would so love to try with her. "I mean that there's something we can try that none of the others searching for Eric and the kids can."

"What?" Her tone was skeptical, but laced with enough curiosity that he knew he'd at least piqued her interest.

"How good is your sense of smell?"

"Very."

"Compared to other Slayers?"

"I was one of the best trackers in the settlement. The

fact that I couldn't find a trail leading away from the attack meant there wasn't one."

"What if there was?"

"Are you saying I missed something?" She pushed past him.

He opened his eyes just in time to see her wrapping the top sheet around herself. He knew it wouldn't take much to have her naked again, but he was going to find a way to resist the urge. Somehow.

Joseph cleared his throat and stared at the wall behind her head. Nothing sexy there. "I'm saying that you have access to a whole shit ton of power now—power you could use to amplify your natural tracking abilities."

"You think that if I tap into your power, I might be able to find the trail leading to Eric and the young?"

"It's possible. Andra has an uncanny ability to find lost children, and she follows a path of fear they leave behind."

"Why the hell isn't she out here helping us?"

"Because she's pregnant. It's too great a risk to her unborn child for her to put herself in danger."

"We could have at least asked her to help."

"I wouldn't do that to her. It would tear her up inside to know that some kids were missing and she couldn't help."

"You didn't even ask her?"

"No, I didn't. Be as pissed at me as you like, but all it's going to do is make it harder for you to get what you want. Anger doesn't help our connection grow, and if you want to use my power to find that trail, you're going to need all the help you can get."

Lyka poked him hard in the chest—hard enough to leave a bruise. Even so, the branches of his lifemark swayed and whipped around in an effort to get closer to her touch. "Don't think I'll forget this."

"Neither will Andra, once she finds out that I was hiding this from her. You'll have to get in line behind all of the other people who are pissed at me on any given day. Comes with the territory of being a leader."

"Yeah? Well, as your *wife,* I get first dibs on thrashing your ass."

He grinned and covered her hand, pressing it flat against his chest. "So, now you claim the position as my wife?"

"If that's what it takes to get to beat the shit out of you first, absolutely."

Venting her anger was one thing. Letting it fester and grow was another.

He grabbed her wrists and pinned them at the small of her back. She struggled against his hold, but only for a second.

Joseph leaned down, putting his lips close to hers. "Feel free to try your hand at that whenever you like, kitten. You may be a Slayer, but I'm still more than strong enough to restrain you until you calm down."

"What if I never calm down? What if I'm pissed at you for the rest of our lives?"

"Then I guess you're going to spend a lot of time like this." He tightened his grip and pulled her hard against his frame.

Her pupils lengthened, making her eyes dim to dark gold. Her lips parted, and her nipples beaded up beneath the sheet. The flush of her skin beneath the luceria had started to fade, but it was back now, proving just how much her body responded to his.

"You think you can control me?" she asked.

"Why would I do that when I like you out of control so very much?"

She closed her eyes. "I'm not going to let you do this again."

"Do what?"

"Turn me on. Fuck me when there are lives at stake. We don't have time for this."

"Maybe not, but what we shared wasn't a total waste of time. If you would let go of your anger for a minute, you'd feel what I did right before you shut me out."

"What's that?"

"You trusted me. It might only have been for a second, but you let go of your animosity long enough to let me in. That's the kind of thing that strengthens the bond between us."

She opened one eye to peer at him in skepticism. "So?"

"So the stronger our bond is, the wider the conduit connecting us becomes, the more power you can channel out of me, the more magic you can wield."

She frowned. "I don't trust you any more now than I did before."

"You're lying. I know what I felt."

Her gaze went distant. He could feel the ice between them melting by slow degrees as she studied their link. Her body began relaxing in his arms, but he couldn't bring himself to let her go. He loved having her against him, close and safe.

After a moment, her presence was hovering between them, right on the threshold of his mind. She hesitated there, but even so, he could tell how much easier it was for her to reach him now than it had been before.

"You're always welcome, Lyka."

"It's too weird."

"It won't always be."

"I lack your confidence."

"I have enough for both of us," he told her. "Come. See how I think we'll find your brother."

The lure of that knowledge must have been too much for her to resist, because he felt her the instant she entered his mind. So fierce, so bright. Her energy was unlike anything he'd ever experienced before. He doubted she had any idea of just how precious she was.

"I'm just a mutant."

He didn't dare argue with her now—not when she was exactly where he wanted her to be. Instead, he opened himself wide and let her feel the way he did about her. He let her see how strong and fearless she was in his eyes, how beautiful.

Her body shivered in his arms, and a small sigh escaped her lips. "Show me."

Joseph did. He guided her to the part of his mind that had been working on the problem since it had come up. The mechanics of it were a little fuzzy, but the theory was strong.

"You clearly have never followed a scent trail before, have you?" she asked.

"Not one that was any longer than it took me to reach a Dumpster."

"It's like another kind of sight—like a strand weaving through the air or along the ground. In order to be able to follow it, you have to understand the way the wind blows, how breezes flow past objects and swirl in corners and crevices. You have to understand how scents combine and alter one another, and how to separate them out again, the way a cook does when trying to re-create a recipe."

She shared with him her experience with tracking by

scent. It was unlike anything he could have imagined. There was so much more complexity to it than he'd ever thought. It was more an art than a science, and, from what he could tell, Lyka was one heck of an artist.

"Do you think it will work?" he asked.

"It's worth a shot. How far are we from where Eric and the others were abducted?"

He didn't want to go back there. It was too dangerous.

"You can't lock me in a box," she told him. "We're out here to do a job. I can't do it without taking some risks."

His first thought was that he'd find a way. His second was that she'd read his mind without him forcing her to do so.

"It's not like you're all that complicated," she said. "And if digging around in your skull is what it's going to take to find my kin, then that's what I'll do. Now take me back to the settlement, or I'm going without you."

"You won't be able to channel my power if I'm not there by your side."

She lifted a golden brow. "And you won't be able to stay away, knowing that place is rife with demons and I'm there, in danger."

Touché. The woman definitely knew his weakness.

Chapter 29

Eric couldn't look any of his students in the eye when he was tossed back in the stone room where they were being held.

Treszka had given him a sheet to cover his nudity, but she'd taken away a hell of a lot more. Promised she'd do it again. Soon.

He wasn't going to think about that now. Hell, he wasn't going to think about it later, either. It was over. Done. Time to move on.

He tore a strip from the sheet and scrubbed himself with it the best he could, then tore off another and fashioned himself a loincloth.

His feet were bare now, though he couldn't remember how that had happened. Maybe his shoes had been torn off at the same time as his jeans. Right before—

Nope. Not going there.

"Anything new to report?" he asked the young.

Kayla didn't even glance his way. Her head was down and she was hugging her knees—not at all like her.

"We've been trying to count demons," said one of the boys, "but they all look the same. There seem to be about twenty in the next room all the time. We can hear and smell more, but we're not sure how many."

He tossed the rest of the sheet to the boys and said, "Tear this into strips. The thinner, the better, but not so thin they'll break easy."

The boys went to work. Eric crouched beside Kayla, facing the same direction so neither one of them would have to look at the other.

"You okay?" he asked.

"Fine. They took me right back here, like you said."

"Why are you off by yourself like this?"

Anger flooded her words, making them sound much older than her years. "You let her hurt you."

"It wasn't that bad," he lied. "Do I look hurt?"

She barely flicked a glance his way. "I can smell you, you know. You're lying to me because you're ashamed. You didn't smell like that before she sent me away."

Eric had no way to explain reality to a seven-year-old. Not without fucking her up irrevocably. "Listen, kid. We all do things for the good of the pack. That's all I did. I just wish she hadn't taken my clothes away. That's why I'm ashamed."

"You're lying again, but it's the good kind."

"What's the good kind?"

"The ones for birthdays and not hurting people's feelings."

He nodded. "Maybe I am lying a little, but there really is nothing for you to worry about. I'm not hurt. You're not hurt. And we're going to fight our way out of here."

That sparked her interest. She turned to him, her eyes bright with excitement. "We are?"

"I'm done playing by Treszka's rules. It's not going to be easy, and it's dangerous as hell, but I'm not going to stay down here and never see the sun again. You with me?"

She nodded eagerly, making her moonlight-blond tangles bob. "What do you want me to do?"

"Gather up some rocks the size of your fist. We need to make weapons."

Lyka ignored the carnage as much as she could this time. Seeing her home in this state was almost more than she could stand, but Joseph was nearby, and for some reason that helped.

He kept soothing her through the connection they shared, and, strangely, when she let him, the thin pipeline between them seemed to expand.

She still hadn't forgiven herself for taking the time to fuck him when her people were in danger, but at least the outcome had been a good one. Besides the mind-blowing orgasms.

Whether it was pleasure or trust or some other magical power his cock possessed, their bond had strengthened. If not for the lack of time they were dealing with, she might have even experimented with taking him for another spin, just to see if her theory was right.

She paced the perimeter of the area where the ground had been disturbed by battle. With every deep breath, another bundle of scents came to her. She blocked out the smells created by the surrounding forest and concentrated on those that didn't belong. The rancid stench of oily demon fur. The sweet smell of sunshine on children's skin. Blood of both her kind and Synestryn. Beneath all that was the acrid scent of fear and hunger. Desperation.

Exhaustion bore down on her. Another night had passed and she hadn't slept nearly as much as she needed to, especially with the strain she'd been putting on her body. The worry over missing children and trying to learn new magic was more than enough to wear out even the toughest girl.

She'd tried to sleep in the truck on the drive here, but every time she closed her eyes, she imagined another horrible fate for the missing young. And Eric. He was as badass as they came, but even he had a breaking point. Her only hope was that the Synestryn had taken prisoners for a reason, rather than simply killing them outright, as they had so many others. Surely if there was a reason to abduct them, they were still alive, right?

"I'm sure they're fine," said Joseph, obviously sensing her anxiety.

She still wasn't used to sharing such a deep connection with anyone, but she had to admit that it was nice to have someone propping her up right now. If not for the thin thread of hope she held on to, she was certain she'd be a complete basket case. Joseph's nearness and natural optimism helped her cling to that hope a little easier.

"Anything new?" asked Joseph from a few feet away. His sword was drawn and his watchful gaze was on the land around her.

"I'm finding the same scents as before."

"Try using my power this time."

"I'm not exactly sure how."

"You're smart. You have good instincts. Just listen to them."

The truth was, she didn't like the idea of becoming dependent on another person. She'd already tied her life to his. Asking her to lean on him for things she'd always managed on her own grated against her sense of independence.

He let out a faint sigh of impatience. "You're the same woman you were before you took my luceria."

"Will you please get out of my head?"

"Not a chance. You were born for this, Lyka. There's no shame in doing what you were created to do."

"It's a lot easier to say that when you've grown up knowing what your position in life was going to be from day one. I grew up thinking I'd find some way to be a Slayer—stay with my own kind."

"You are with your own kind. You were just wrong about who that was before."

If they went down this road, she was going to get pissed, and right now she couldn't afford to get angry at the man who held the power she needed. Like it or not, she had to suck it up, lean on Joseph, and take the blow to her ego. She might not be able to find Eric on her own, but she would find him. As long as that was the outcome, she could accept whatever she had to do along the way. That's what Eric would have done for her.

Lyka closed her eyes to focus her senses. Just beneath the skin under the luceria, she could feel Joseph's power sparking and eager to do her bidding. She'd grown used to the soft warmth coming from the necklace, but now that she gave it her attention with the intent to use it, the supple band began to heat.

She shivered against the sensation and immediately tried to block it out. Instead, she concentrated on the dancing strands of magic waving around, trying to get her attention.

Lyka grabbed onto a bundle of them and pulled them into herself. Instantly, her body let out a giant sigh of relief, as if she'd been starving to death and had just put the first bite of steak in her mouth.

As her cells rejoiced at the fuel she fed them, she pulled in a deep breath through her nose.

The difference in her sense of smell was like the difference between jumping through a backyard sprinkler and shooting down a three-story water slide at an amusement park. Everything was amplified, nearly choking her with the potency of it.

She gagged on the stench of demon, but forced herself to take another breath.

Eric. His scent was everywhere. And now that it was amplified, she could smell something even more familiar than her own brother.

Herself. Parts of his scent were identical to hers, thanks to their shared maternal blood.

She dropped to the ground and sniffed again. Eric hadn't been here for the battle. There wasn't enough of his essence here for him to have fought to protect the young here. He'd been taken from somewhere else.

Lyka pulled in more of Joseph's power, revving up her senses even more. The animal in her was unfamiliar with what she was doing, and that made it uneasy. Fearful. Angry.

She felt her teeth lengthen, her skin tingle and itch, her fingernails grow and thicken into sharp claws.

"Lyka?" Joseph's voice was filled with worry. "Are you okay?"

Her voice sounded odd, coming out around too many teeth. "You've been in my head, Theronai. You know what I am. What I can do."

"Yes, and I accepted that, but this is not . . . normal. Even for you."

She looked down at her hands. Her fingers were short and thick, tipped with sharp claws. A fine layer of golden fur covered her skin. She'd seen some of her kind shift this far into their animal forms, but she'd never been able to do so. Until now.

Joseph's power. It had to have something to do with her sudden change.

She looked up at him, seeing surprise and a huge helping of worry in his hazel eyes. He tightened his grip on his sword as if she might lunge at him at any time.

Lyka tried to tell him that she wouldn't hurt him, but the wind shifted, and she caught scent of something.

She took off toward the woods, ignoring Joseph's worried voice behind her.

A few hundred yards into the dense woods, there was a clearing. In that clearing was the nexus of smells she'd been hoping to find. Eric, several children, fear and determination. Plenty of demon blood.

This is where he'd fought the demons to protect the young. And based on the bloody drag marks through the brush, this is where he'd fallen.

She took off, following that path at a dead run. The sound of her clothes ripping distracted her, but she didn't slow down. Thorny branches tugged at the loose fabric, but she didn't dare stop, not when she was hot on the right trail.

There wasn't enough blood lost for Eric to have died. And the young were mostly unharmed. She couldn't smell much of their blood, though she could detect the distinct stench of fear next to the sweet innocence on every leaf and twig that had grazed one of the young's skin.

The trail went on for a mile through the woods before it emptied out onto an old farmer's road. She'd lived in this area long enough to know the terrain, and this road hadn't been used in years. Deer had woven a narrow trail along the road, but there were small trees growing up to reclaim the path. Those trees had been knocked down recently, and the tire marks of some kind of all-terrain vehicle were visible in the mud. She could smell exhaust fumes and rubber tires trampling over the scents of grass and trees.

Joseph ran out of the woods behind her, breathing hard. He came to a dead stop, his jaw slack with shock. "Lyka? Are you in there?"

She had no idea what he meant for a second. And then she saw one of her hands. It wasn't a hand anymore. It was a paw. A big one. She had four of them, along with all the other parts of a tiger.

A little streak of panic lit through her. She tried to open her mouth to ask him what had happened, but all that came out was a mewling growl.

"It's okay," said Joseph, sheathing his sword. "I can feel you freaking out, but I'm sure this is all completely normal. Just keep those claws and teeth to yourself, and everything will be just fine."

He reached through their link with a timid kind of reluctance, as if worried what he might find on the other end. When his thoughts touched hers and that instant flare of recognition lit between them, his shoulders drooped in relief.

"Okay. That's good. My girl is still in there." He moved toward her slowly, hands lifted in front of him. "Can you change back?"

She wasn't in control of such things. Even when it was only her teeth and fingernails that shifted, they would always go back to normal when they wanted, not when she did.

Lyka tried to convey that information to him. It must have worked, because he nodded.

"Then we'll wait. No worries." He stroked her head, sliding his fingers through her fur.

His touch felt good, reminding her just how much she loved feeling his hands on her. The purr she let out was beyond her control.

Joseph laughed. "You know, when I pictured what my

life would be like when I found my mate, this was not at all what I imagined."

That made two of them.

"I saw the tire marks," he said. "I've heard of demons using vehicles lately, but it could have been humans. Dorjan."

Lyka had never seen one of the human blood servants the Synestryn sometimes used to do their dirty work. Unlike demons, Dorjan could move about in the daylight, making them a useful tool to have.

But that's not what happened here. There was no recent scent of human around, even one who fed off the blood of demons. At most she detected a faint hint of human, likely coming from whoever had once owned the vehicle.

It's not like Synestryn could walk into a dealership and fill out loan paperwork. Chances were they'd killed whoever had owned it and taken it from them.

She shook her head, hoping he would understand.

"We've been seeing this for a while," he said. "The demons have been stealing human children and altering them so they can breed with them. There are more and more sightings of human-looking Synestryn all the time."

Lyka had heard rumors but wasn't sure they were true until now. This knowledge was the kind of thing that could cause a panic among humans and Sentinels alike. If a demon couldn't be recognized on sight, then that gave it more time to get close enough to kill.

Do you think that's how those things were able to attack us before the sun had set all the way? she asked through their link. She hadn't even stopped to think that it wouldn't be possible for him to hear her, which made her realize just how much her instincts were running the show right now.

"I do." Joseph kept idly stroking her. His fingers worked magic along her neck, lingering over the luceria as they passed. Every time he touched it, crackling shards of power sank into her skin, making her tingle. "And I have to admit, it's more than a little creepy knowing that we're no longer safe in the daylight."

Slowly, as her body relaxed and the adrenaline rush of the hunt faded, she felt the animal in her subside. The change was fast—faster than she would have thought possible. One minute Joseph's hand was sliding over her fur, and the next he was stroking the bare skin of her back.

She was on all fours, naked except for the luceria. Her hair fell around her face, hiding her blush.

"Guess I lost my clothes along the way," she said, remembering the sound of tearing fabric and the feel of the bramble tugging away the shreds.

She sat up and covered herself with her hands.

Joseph wrapped his fingers around her wrists and pulled her hands wide. His eyes had gone dark with desire, making her wonder if this man would ever be sated.

"Don't," he said. "You're too beautiful to hide from me. And when it comes to you, there is no such thing as getting my fill."

Her skin began to heat under his gaze, but she tried to play it cool and not let him know just how much she liked the way he looked at her. "This mental-connection thing doesn't leave much room for privacy."

"Maybe not, but it does come in handy in a fight. One day, when you've had plenty of time to practice wielding my power, you'll know what I mean."

"Does that power include being able to magically fabricate clothing?"

He grinned and stripped off his shirt. His bare chest

was such a thing of beauty, she forgot all about being naked. Her hands were on him, stroking his lifemark, before she even had time to question the sanity of such a move.

Small, fuzzy buds lined the once-bare branches.

"Your leaves are coming back," she said.

"Because of you." He wrapped the shirt over her shoulders and used the open edges to pull her toward him. The journey ended at his mouth and the hot, sweet kiss that awaited her there.

Since when did she let him kiss her whenever he wanted? Then again, how had she gone so long without this exact thing?

She spent so much time overthinking it that by the time he pulled away, she'd hardly had time to enjoy the ride. She felt cheated and would have gone for seconds, but there were people counting on them.

"What was that for?" she asked.

"Because there was no other option. I see you and need to kiss you. I've been holding that back for way too long to keep it in check now. I hope you understand."

She did. She felt that way now—like she had to hold herself back from taking what she wanted.

What was it about this man that ignited her? She'd always been curious about him, but she'd thought it was because he represented the thing she feared most about herself. Now that her secret was out, she didn't have to fear him—at least not that he'd out her—anymore.

He slid his finger along her brow. "There's way too much going on up there. I think it's time we plan our next move so you can stop worrying. I say we follow these tracks and see where they lead."

"Just like that? No discussing what just happened to me?"

"You shifted into a tiger. I didn't expect it, but I've adjusted."

"How is that even possible? *I* haven't had time to adjust, and I'm a Slayer. Nearly everyone I grew up with would die to be able to do what I just did." For generations, Slayers had bred with humans, diluting their bloodlines until their powers faded and only a very few could even display animal traits. About a hundred years ago, the Slayer council decided to create breeding laws that were designed to strengthen the best genetic traits. Lyka's mother was one of the strongest Slayers born in generations. So was the man she'd married. Both of Lyka's brothers had shifted into their animal forms, though neither could control it.

She knew now exactly what that was like.

"I think we've found another of your gifts, kitten."

"What's that?"

"You used my power to amplify your Slayer abilities, not diminish them. That's got to make you feel better about that pesky Theronai blood in your veins."

She hadn't thought about it that way, and, truth be told, she was getting used to the idea of being able to sling magic around. If she was even half as good as some of the women in the stories she'd heard, walking around attached to a magical battery wasn't going to be all that bad.

Especially one built like Joseph, with the skills to make her purr.

"As much as I like where your train of thought is headed," he said, "I think we need to get moving. We'll go back to the truck and grab a change of clothes for you so you don't freeze."

"I'll be fine as long as I keep moving. Let's just go while the trail is hot." She buttoned up his shirt, which protected her all the way down to her knees. He'd found her shoes a few yards back in the woods, but they were shredded almost beyond use.

"You're going to be a bit high maintenance in the clothing department, aren't you?" he asked.

"For all I know, shifting was a onetime anomaly. I may never be able to do it again."

"Don't you want to?"

"It's not that. I've spent my whole life wondering if my father's genetics had ruined me as a Slayer. Now that I know that isn't the case, it makes me wonder if my mother's genetics ruined me as a Theronai. What if I can never wield your power the way another woman might have been able to do? I've bound us together, so you're stuck with me. That kind of sucks for you."

He grabbed her arms and pulled her close so she had no choice but to look at him. "Listen carefully. Despite your motives at the time, what you did when you bound us together was save my life. You took away my pain. You got me out of that damn office, so I can remember what it's like to be a warrior again. Whatever else you are, however you may compare to other female Theronai, I will always be grateful to you for what you've done."

She'd always thought of the Theronai as the enemy. Power-hungry, egotistical jerks who thought they were mankind's salvation. She'd never considered that they would hurt or dream of a different life. And she sure as hell hadn't thought that one of them would lay so much gratitude at her feet, as if her mere existence were the best thing to ever happen to him.

Her throat tightened with emotions she dared not name. Her eyes burned as she fought against tears. She couldn't speak. All she could do was nod and pull away before she humiliated herself.

Joseph let her go. Maybe he could tell she was on the verge of tears and decided to take pity on her. Whatever the case, she was able to pull herself together once she wasn't looking into his eyes.

"The trail leads this way," she said, stating the obvious.

Light trickled through the trees. Another day was passing, and her loved ones were still in harm's way. Nightfall would be here soon, and with it, another night of terror for the young.

That was what was important. Not her recent ability to shift. Not her feelings for Joseph or vice versa. Everything else going on in her head was just going to have to sit back and wait for its turn.

His warm hand settled on her shoulder. "We'll find them."

She closed her eyes and nodded. "Soon, Joseph. We have to find them soon. I don't even want to think what will happen to them if we don't."

"Then lead on, Lyka. Find me something to kill."

Chapter 30

Ronan was beginning to understand how crazy felt. His mystery woman had no sooner stopped moving away from him when she started coming back toward him again. He had no idea why she'd run like she had, but he was tied to her closely enough to know that the only reason she was coming back now was because she was in pain.

That was something Ronan could not tolerate.

He'd headed toward her as fast as he dared, stopping only when he ran out of fuel or when the sun was high and robbed him of all ability to drive safely. The last thing he needed was to crash his van, break the magically enhanced glass that blocked the sun and accidentally summon a Warden to kill him while he lay pinned or unconscious—an easy target.

The drive exhausted him, but not nearly as much as it did her. She rarely stopped and never for more than twenty or thirty minutes. She didn't sleep, didn't slow, didn't veer off course.

He wasn't sure exactly where she was coming from, but she moved like death itself was nipping at her heels.

Then she stopped. A huge flood of fear spilled out of her, followed closely by disgust and, finally, resignation. Acceptance.

She was tired. Hungry. Hurting.

Ronan followed his instincts, taking as many back roads as he could to reach her. She had left the interstate miles ago, moving north on country roads, right before that spike of fear had slammed into her. He had followed, heading west toward her.

The magically treated glass in his van kept him safe, but it did nothing to ward off the weariness from being awake during the daylight. If not for the potential prize at the end of this ride, he would have found a nice, dark cave and slept in it until sunset.

She was close now, barely a mile away. He didn't let up on the accelerator until he saw her car. A rental with Arizona plates, right inside a metal outbuilding.

That's where she'd gone—a place with so much sun, he'd never survive.

Ronan doubted her destination had been an accident.

There was a giant metal barn with a door large enough for a tractor to pull through. It was open. She was inside. He couldn't see her, but he could feel her.

She was afraid of him. Her heart was pounding, and fear was leaking into her veins. She was hiding something, but he had no idea what.

He pulled his van through the opening, adjusting his vision to search for any potential traps she might have laid for him.

The pair of windows on the western side of the building was boarded up. As soon as he cleared the threshold, the retractable door slid down behind him. The building went dark, but he could still see well, despite his powers being muted by the sun's rays.

She was there, standing next to her car. She opened one of the back doors to activate the dome light, which cast a pale glow over a body even more beautiful than Ronan had remembered.

The first time he'd seen her, he hadn't exactly been at his best. He'd been nearly dead, starving for blood, animalistic in his hunger. He'd attacked her, fed from her, held her against her will.

It was no wonder she was afraid of him now.

He took in the curly black hair that fell just past her shoulders, gleaming in the dim light. Her skin was a deep tan that made her silvery green eyes stand out like faceted gemstones. Signs of weariness stained her face but made her no less lovely. All those marks did was increase Ronan's need to see to her care and safety. If she was his, she'd never suffer again. He would make sure she was rested and fed, comfortable and warm—whatever she needed, he would provide it.

But she wasn't his. Didn't even want to be near him. At least she hadn't until now.

Ronan pulled to a stop and turned off his engine. He turned on the headlights to help ease her fears, and then stepped out of the van inside the protective confines of the metal building.

He would be more careful this time. Be gentle with her. Respect her wishes.

Everything in him that was ravenous and demonic laughed at the idea that he would be anything more than his true self.

As he stepped around to the back of the van, she held up her hands. "That's far enough."

Ronan forced his feet to stop. It was an act of willpower, but one he made for her comfort.

"Who are you?" he asked.

"Justice."

Ah, so she was here to inflict some kind of punishment on him. At least she was honest about her intent. Even though he hated it that she wanted to hurt him, he had to give her credit for owning up to it.

"What is your name?" he asked, clarifying his question. "Mine is Ronan. I should at least know the name of the woman who's come to mete out justice."

"No, Justice *is* my name."

"I didn't see it on the manifest for your flight."

She frowned. "I have no idea how you got your hands on that, but, for your information, I flew under an alias."

"So, your friends call you Justice?"

"I have no friends."

He couldn't help but feel the sting of pain saying that caused her. Protective instincts rose to the fore, and all he wanted to do was take her in his arms and soothe her hurts. "I will be your friend, Justice."

She laughed, and the sound was so musical, he wanted to dance. "Nice try, bloodsucker. But I think I have enough friends."

"You just said you had none."

"Exactly."

"Why are you still here?" he asked. "Why didn't you run from me the way you have every other time I've come close to finding you?"

Her mouth tightened in anger. "They wouldn't let me."

"They who?"

"No one you know. Now, let's just get this over with so we can both go on with our lives." She stepped out from behind her car. Bruises darkened her arms, along with what looked like scabbed-over cuts.

Ronan was at her side before he realized he was moving. Magic fueled his speed and scared the living hell out of his woman. She wheeled back from him so fast, she left a dent in the metal siding of the outbuilding.

"Do not touch me," she said. "The last time you did, you nearly killed me."

How could he explain to her the hunger he'd felt at the time? He hadn't meant to take so much of her blood or to be so rough with her. If he'd been in his right mind, he would have been gentle with her, cherishing the gift of blood she'd given him.

But he hadn't been gentle, and she had no way of knowing that he didn't make a habit of ravaging women who showed up out of the blue to save his life. All he could do now was respect her wishes and hope that in time she'd find some sliver of trust for him.

Because he really did need to get his hands on her again, feel her warm skin against his lips and taste her sweet blood as it flowed over his tongue, replenishing his cells with the magic they craved.

Ronan held up his hands and backed away a step. "I'm sorry about that, Justice. I deeply regret how I treated you that day. If you'd stayed, I would have explained that I'm not usually so rough with—"

"Your prey?" she supplied.

"I don't see you like that."

"No? So if I tilted my head and pulled my hair out of your way, you wouldn't come after me again? Tear into my skin with your teeth and drink my blood?" She angled her head so that her hair fell away from the smooth lines of her throat.

He could see her pulse pounding beneath her skin, feel the power of the magic that beat there, rich and intoxicating.

She was meant to sustain him the way Hope sustained

Logan. He was certain of it. Why else would she compel him so completely?

Ronan had expended a lot of energy chasing after her, and more healing Joseph. He was still functional, still strong enough to keep going despite the hunger rolling around in his empty belly—a hunger human food couldn't touch. Nothing had eased that bone-deep, gnawing starvation the way her blood did, and now she was posed as if offering him another taste.

He saw the glow his eyes cast as his gaze slid over her body, homing in on her throat. His mouth watered for her. His chest worked overtime trying to draw her scent into his lungs and hold it there. Normally, his sense of smell was much stronger, but the sun had weakened all his abilities. Until it set, he would never be able to get enough of her scent.

He needed this woman in a way he couldn't understand or describe. The urge to feed from her nearly overwhelmed him, but he reminded himself that this was about the war, not the battle. If he was to win the woman, he had to let her think he was nice and safe, not the ravenous predator that lurked within him.

"I would be so very gentle with you," he told her. "I could make you feel so good, make your whole body shimmer with pleasure."

She swallowed hard, the movement a helpful distraction from the hot pulse pounding along her neck. He was able to break the spell her blood held over him and look into her beautiful eyes. Midnight pupils ate up the silvery green ring. "Yeah. Not going to happen. Ever. Keep your damn fangs to yourself."

He was losing ground with her. He could feel her slipping away, feel her nervousness rising with every passing second. If he didn't do something fast, she was going to bolt.

Ronan forced himself to back up and put a vehicle between them. That seemed to ease her nerves and got her to move away from the dented wall.

"I understand," he said. "If you didn't wait for me here to feed me again, then why?"

"I have something for you. Something important. I don't know why, so don't ask. All I know is they made me bring it here and wait for you."

Curiosity sparked beneath his skin. He would cherish any gift this woman offered him, but he thought it might not serve his cause to say so. "What is it?"

She dug in her pocket and pulled out a key fob. One push of the button unlatched the trunk of her rental car. The trunk lid popped open, and Ronan knew instantly what lay inside. He could smell the demon lurking there, one she'd hidden from him until just now. If he hadn't been so consumed by her scent, if the sun hadn't diminished his powers, he might have detected the stench of demon earlier. But he hadn't, and now he was trapped in an enclosed space with a woman who wanted him dead and a demon that wanted his blood.

Apparently, his first instinct had been right. This had been a trap all along.

Chapter 31

At the end of a hike that lasted several hours, the trail finally came out on a rural blacktop road a few miles from where Joseph's truck was parked. On the road there were some muddy tracks that cut off abruptly, as if the all-terrain vehicle that had made them had been loaded onto a trailer.

"This is it," said Lyka. "This is as far as the trail goes."

"You can't smell them anymore?"

Her shoulders slumped as she shook her head. "I can smell diesel exhaust, but that's not going to get me far. I can't separate one vehicle out from another. Whatever they did with Eric and the young here, they were no longer leaving behind a scent trail. No blood, no dead skin, no hair . . . nothing."

"They could have been loaded into the back of a truck."

She paced the area, her hair glowing in the last light of day. Night would be on them soon, and when it came, he needed to have her safely behind protected walls, or at least in his truck, where he could see danger coming for her.

Frustration and a steadily growing sense of failure and fear were tumbling out of her. The pathway between them was wider now, leaving room for him to better sense her emotions. And as much as he loved knowing how she felt, he hated that she suffered and there was little he could do to stop it.

This wasn't a problem he could kill for her. This was a battle of stamina and keeping her hopes up high enough that she could continue searching for her family.

Joseph went to her and took her hand in his. "This isn't our last hope."

"No?" she asked. "Then tell me what our next move is, because I've only got one more idea, and you're not going to like it."

"Tell me what you're thinking," he said.

"Do you remember how I told you that I always seem to know what people want?"

"Yes."

"I think it works with other creatures, too. Not just people."

He blinked at her. "What makes you say that?"

"I knew about the woman Ronan is looking for—about how he'll stop at nothing to find her."

"Okay, but Ronan isn't a demon."

"No, but when that sgath attacked me, I knew it wanted my blood. I knew it wanted to eat me."

"Honey, I hate to break it to you, but sgath feel that way about all Sentinels and blooded humans."

"I realize that, but I *knew* it. Felt it. The way I do with people. I'd never been touched by a demon before, so I was a little shocked when it hit me."

"Okay, let's just say that it does work. How does that help us?"

"If we can find one that wants to capture more Slayers, then maybe we can follow it home or find some way to interrogate it."

Joseph's instant reaction was a swift, harsh denial, but he held that in and gave himself a minute to calm down before he spoke. "Let's pretend that your idea will work. How are we going to capture a demon without killing it?"

"Leave that part to me," said Lyka. "I'm the one who can physically touch their skin without being poisoned. I'll figure out something."

"You're right," he said. "I don't like it. In fact, I hate it. I don't want you getting close enough to a demon to see it, much less touch it."

"We can't just sit around waiting. If you've got a better idea, I'm all ears."

"I'm sure I'll come up with something," he said.

"Fine. You hop right on that, brainiac. In the meantime, we should head back to the truck. It's getting dark fast."

Joseph went through about twenty different scenarios to trap a demon—and not just any one, but the right one. Each scenario that ran through his mind ended in utter disaster. If he had more time and some welding equipment, he might have a shot, but without those, he was screwed.

"The frustration I feel sliding off you is not exactly instilling a lot of confidence in me," she said. "And we're almost back at the truck."

"I'm still thinking."

They rounded the bend, back to where he'd parked the truck, a little ways down from where they'd left her car. Lyka was half a step ahead of him and came to a complete stop, sucking in a shocked breath.

An instant later, he saw what she had: the vehicles

had been totaled. The tires were shredded, the axles bent so that the wheels sat at an awkward angle. Both hoods were ripped open, and the guts of the engines were spilling out onto the pavement. Their spare clothes were now tattered strips of cloth and leather.

"New plan," said Lyka.

"What's that?" he asked.

"We're screwed."

Chapter 32

Justice watched the bloodsucker's face fall with disappointment. In fact, if she wasn't mistaken, he was actually hurt by her offering.

For some reason, that upset her.

What a ridiculous reaction. The man had all but killed her, and she cared about hurting his feelings? Since when?

"I'm on a schedule here," she said, "so can you please just take this to Joseph, whoever he is, and I'll be on my way."

"How do you know Joseph?"

"They told me."

"Who is they?"

She rolled her eyes. "I don't know. All I know is they won't leave me the hell alone until you take the damn monster and give it to Joseph. Can you do that or not?"

"I can." He peered into the trunk to see the unconscious . . . thing she'd captured.

"How did you manage this?" he asked.

"I hit it with my car, fought it into submission, tied it up with rope and shoved it in the trunk."

"By yourself?"

She widened her eyes and looked around. "Do you see anyone else?"

His gorgeous face paled even more than it had before. She could tell by the compulsion the fates had given her that the dude wasn't a fan of the sun, but she'd never seen anyone go this white. "You touched this creature? Is that where you got those scratches?"

He started coming after her again, and she stepped around the car to put some nice, sturdy metal between herself and him. "Don't come any closer."

"This demon is poisonous. My intent was only to help. I didn't mean to scare you."

"You didn't," she lied. "And I'm fine." Or she would be once she got back behind the wheel and down the road again, away from him.

"How were you injured?"

"The thing's fingernails. I knocked the sword out of its hands with the car, but it still put up a hell of a fight."

"And you won," he said, stating the obvious. "How did you win?"

She patted her ribs and the semiautomatic pistol she kept strapped there, hidden under her jacket. "I shot it."

Ronan eased closer to the creature, gliding over the dirt floor with the grace of an Olympic ice skater. "It's still alive."

"I wasn't supposed to kill it."

"Why not?"

"Hell if I know. Are you going to take it to Joseph, or do I have to do the job myself?"

"What does Joseph want with the demon?"

"I've never met the man. For all I know, he's going to cut it open and study its parts. I really don't care. The only thing that matters is getting it to him. Will you help?"

She was starting to get frantic now. The fates were nipping at her heels, urging her to hurry. If she didn't, she might well become incapacitated with pain right here, completely helpless to stop Ronan from sucking out all her blood.

He stared at her for a few uncomfortable seconds. That familiar pressure was closing in on her, bringing with it a mountain of fear.

"If it's that important to you, I'll call him."

"Now," she urged, hoping she didn't sound like too much of a bitch. She really needed the vampire to play nice.

"If it pleases you, yes." He pulled out his phone and dialed. An angry male voice answered.

"I know I didn't answer earlier," said Ronan. "I was otherwise occupied."

The man on the line, presumably Joseph, went off for a full minute while Ronan winced and held the phone away from his ear. "I understand. It won't happen again. The reason I called was because I have something I think might interest you. Do you have need of a live Synestryn demon, by chance?"

"As a matter of fact, we do," said Joseph into his phone. How the hell had Ronan known? Freaky Sanguinar trick, no doubt.

"Where are you?" asked Ronan.

"Standing outside of what used to be my truck."

"Used to be?"

"Yes. I'm afraid you're going to have to come to us with your present."

There was a slight pause before Ronan answered. "We can do that."

"We?"

"Long story. It's getting dark out. Where will you shelter?"

"I'm in Slayer territory. There are no Gerai houses near enough to make it on foot. We'll have to find a defensible position and sit tight until someone can pick us up."

"I know a place," said Lyka.

"Where is it?" Joseph asked her.

"Less than a mile on foot."

"Come to Andreas's settlement. Call when you get here, and we'll meet you at the road."

"I'm hours away from there. Are you sure you'll be safe that long?" asked Ronan.

"We'll have to be. I doubt anyone is closer than a few hours out. We're stretched thin with so many pregnant women stuck at Dabyr."

"Stay safe. We'll hurry." Ronan hung up.

Joseph looked at Lyka, who was biting her plump bottom lip in anxiety. Before he could think better of his actions, he pulled her into his arms and kissed away the dent she'd left behind.

As always, she went straight to his head, making his blood sing in his veins. He didn't understand how she had the power to rock his world so hard, but he was starting to like that she could.

"Where to?" he asked, eager to get her out of the open, where they could be attacked from all sides.

She was a little breathless from their kiss, her cheeks flushed, but that worry he'd felt coming out of her had abated.

She gave him a devilish grin. "How do you feel about heights?"

A demon's howl, answered by one of its kin, echoed through the woods.

"It doesn't matter," said Joseph. "We need shelter. Fast."

"Follow me." She took off at a jog, making a beeline through the trees.

Joseph stayed close, sword in hand. He tried to push power through their link to help fuel her body, but it wasn't working. Something was blocking him, so he sought out what it was.

She was exhausted, worried, a little afraid. She was concentrating on leading him through the woods in the quickest, safest manner while simultaneously extending her senses so she would be able to detect a demon before it pounced.

There was no room in her thoughts for some new way to use his power. She was already handling as much as she could.

Joseph sent her as much reassurance as he could muster, but it wasn't much.

Her long legs ate up the distance, moving effortlessly over rocks, logs and fallen branches, despite her bare feet. She was naked except for his borrowed shirt, and her curvy bottom kept peeking out to tease him.

His balls tingled and grew heavy. His cock started to swell and throb.

He knew he shouldn't be thinking about such things at a time like this, but he couldn't help it. He remembered all too well how perfectly her ass fit his hands, how smooth and soft her skin was there. And the shadowy perfection hidden between her thighs . . .

His foot caught on a tree root hidden under the leaves and he fell flat on his face. His sword landed a couple of feet away, protruding from a fallen tree.

Lyka skidded to a stop and turned around to help him.

He pushed himself back to his feet before she reached his side and made his humiliation complete by offering him a hand up. It was bad enough that he'd been clumsy; she had to come to his rescue, too.

"Think about my ass later, Theronai," she said. "We have ground to cover."

She'd heard his thoughts? He couldn't help but smile at that. They were making progress, which meant that somewhere deep down, she was starting to trust him, even if only a little.

"Don't get your hopes up," she said. "Your thoughts about my ass were just really loud."

She spun on her heel to take off again when Joseph saw the glow of green eyes in the woods on the other side of her.

He instinctively amplified his vision to see what was hiding, and drew power to his eyes to turn night into day.

A sgath was there, lurking in the darkness.

It leapt toward her.

Chapter 33

Lyka felt Joseph's burst of panic and knew instantly she was in the way. She wasn't sure how she knew that, but she followed her instincts and dove to the side, away from his swinging blade.

Moonlight bounced off steel and muscles gleaming with sweat. Shirtless Joseph was a wonder to behold, complete with the kind of potent strength that made a woman's knees turn to liquid, along with the rest of her.

The new leaves on his lifemark were shiny, though she had no idea how that was possible. They trembled with the force of his blow as he jumped into the air, meeting the charging sgath head-on.

His sword sliced one leg off the demon. It howled in pain and skidded to a clumsy stop, where it began licking the blood flowing from its wound.

Joseph didn't pause for a second. He walked right up to the thing, half-naked and deadly, and finished off the demon in one hard stroke. Its head flew into the woods, coming to rest at the base of an old oak tree.

Two more demons charged in, and he dispatched them with the same brutal efficiency.

Lyka hadn't even made it to her feet yet before the whole thing was over.

She'd seen a lot of men fight, but none had the same kind of controlled grace that he did. Slayers were much more emotional when they fought—filled with a feral kind of berserker rage—but Joseph's mind had been completely calm the whole time. At least it had been once he knew she was out of harm's way.

He was fast, powerful and nearly silent in his attacks. Hell, the man wasn't even breathing hard.

He offered her his hand and pulled her to her feet.

"That was beautiful," she told him.

He lifted a dark eyebrow. "Beautiful?"

Embarrassment washed over her. She shouldn't have said such a thing. Men didn't want to be beautiful. They wanted to be handsome, masculine.

Joseph was all of that, too, but she was always stunned by the way he fought, as if he had all the time in the world.

It was so freaking hot, she just wanted to run her hands over him and feel that strength firsthand.

"Are you okay?" he asked. "I'm getting a weird vibe from you."

"Then stop poking your nose in where it's not welcome. We're almost there."

He cleaned his sword and motioned for her to lead on.

At least now she had her back to him, so he couldn't see her cheeks burning with embarrassment. She had no idea what was wrong with her or why seeing him fight had suddenly rattled her so deeply, but it definitely needed to be fixed. Fast.

Lyka led him the rest of the way to their temporary hiding spot. She hadn't been in this tree house since she was a child, but it had been kept in good repair, used by Slayer young who, like her, had needed some time alone away from the settlement.

The climb was longer than she'd remembered, and her muscles were burning by the time she'd made it all the way to the top of the rope ladder.

Joseph crawled up through the trapdoor of the tree house right behind her. He pulled the ladder up so demons couldn't make use of it, and shut the wooden door in the floor.

They were alone now, relatively safe, and it struck her that if she had to be holed up with someone, she was glad it was Joseph. He was easy to be around and such an intense distraction, she was able to let go of her worries, if only for a few seconds at a time.

Shadows draped across his face as he settled back against some cushions that had been left here recently. He was such a powerfully built man, with the kind of broad shoulders that looked like they could carry the problems of the world. Smooth, tan skin stretched over his muscles, delighting her with the kind of masculine contours that made a woman remember just how differently men and women were built. And why.

It was hard not to think about how well they fit together and whether she'd ever again allow herself the pleasure of his body.

A breeze slid through the gaps in the wooden shell, stirring dust through the space. She could smell the scent of teens and the hormone overload they left behind. Beyond that was the darker, more mature scent of Joseph's skin, luring her to reach out and touch, taste.

"Hell of a climb," he said.

She spread out a couple of cushions to pad the wooden floor and stretched out on them. It eased her sore muscles, but did nothing for the deeper, hungrier ache growing in her abdomen. "The tree wasn't this tall when I was a kid. Guess they had to get a longer ladder."

"I'm not complaining. Demons with enough claws might be able to make the climb, but we'll definitely know they're coming from all the heavy breathing."

It was dark inside the space, lit only by the glow of the rising moon.

That's when it struck her. The moon was full. That's why she'd gone all mushy watching Joseph fight. That's why she wanted him. This was the time of the month that Slayers became fertile and hormones ran rampant.

Hers were about to get out of control. It was probably already too late, but once the moonlight hit her skin, she would be lost in need, desperate for sex from a man who lit her up.

She'd never been with a man at this time of month before—at least not with one she wanted. Many of the Slayer males would lock themselves away until the full moon passed, rather than take a chance that they might ravish some unwilling female. And the women ... they would band together, the older ones helping keep the younger ones in check until the need had passed.

It was definitely an interesting time around the settlement, and not one she missed.

But here she was, back home, trapped with a man that called to her senses, with a rising moon and little time to find some control.

"What's going on, Lyka? I can feel you freaking out."

"Just stay away. Don't touch me." She wanted him to touch her so badly, she nearly grabbed his hands and put them on her. And he was going to know it, too, if she didn't find some way to keep her mental shields nice and high.

"What did I do?" he asked.

She closed her eyes to block out the concern on his handsome face, but it didn't work. She could still see him, all gleaming in the moonlight, his muscles the color of burnished bronze. Those broad shoulders of his would look so good between her thighs, and what his mouth could do to her while he was there ... pure heaven.

"Talk to me, Lyka, or I'm going to shove my way in your head. I feel you throwing barriers up. You're not going to like what I have to do to tear them down."

She didn't know if she was strong enough to keep him out or not, but what she was going through was private, for Slayers only to know.

He pushed against her mind, trying to find some way in. The pressure made her head throb, and she knew she had to give him something or he was going to learn everything.

"Tell me what's going on," he insisted.

She hugged her knees and rocked. "Full moon."

Cool air blew past her. The fact that she wasn't wearing panties—that they'd been shredded when she'd shifted—made it all that much harder to forget that her pink parts were steadily warming.

"So?"

"Promise you won't fuck me."

His tone was the same as if she'd asked him to cut off his own dick. "Hell, no."

"I'm not ready to have young."

"Okay. Good to know. But I'm still not following why you're suddenly freaking out about this now."

She opened her eyes and knew what he saw. Her pupils had lengthened as the animal in her prowled around, demanding that she take action and claim her mate.

No, not her mate. He hadn't been approved by the council. She might have tied herself to him for life, but that didn't mean her people would approve.

"Promise me you won't touch me, no matter what I do. Even if I beg."

He shook his head. "I won't make that promise. I will always give you what you need, Lyka. There's no shame in needing me to touch you, comfort you."

He didn't understand, but how could he? He wasn't a Slayer. He'd never felt the consuming desire to give in to the needs of the flesh. To release the beast and let go.

Moonlight shone through the narrow window, growing closer to the corner where she now cowered. "Just give me some space. Please."

He moved closer, intoxicating her with his scent, making her want with such desperate force, she was certain it would tear her apart. It was beyond arousal, beyond desire, causing her physical pain. The need had never been like this before, clenching her womb like a vise.

She curled up on her side in the hopes of making it stop, but all it did was remind her that she was naked beneath Joseph's shirt.

Her mental walls began to crumble. She did her best to reinforce them, but she wasn't experienced enough in such things to be sure her patches would hold.

"Trust me," he told her as he stroked across her mind, coaxing her to give him the knowledge he wanted. "Tell me how to ease your pain."

She hated it that he knew she suffered, that she was weak. She hated it even more that he was more than capable of taking away the pain. All she had to do was spill her people's secrets to an outsider.

"We're bound now, Lyka," he said as he pulled her into his arms. "Family. I'm no outsider."

He was so warm, so strong and solid. Just touching his skin seemed to ease some of the tightness in her chest.

"Get out of my head," she said, though her words lacked any real fire. How could she be angry with a man who was trying to offer her comfort?

"Is it some kind of sickness?" he asked.

"Call it temporary insanity."

"It looks more painful than that. How long does it last?"

"Until the moon is no longer full." *Or until the fire is quenched.*

"Ronan will be here soon. I'm sure he'll be able to ease you."

"No!" she shouted. Everything inside her rose in denial at the idea of another man touching her. Just the thought of the Sanguinar's hands on her was enough to make her want to vomit.

"Wow. Okay. Violent reaction noted. I'll make sure Ronan keeps his hands off you."

She relaxed a little in Joseph's embrace. His fingers stroked up and down her arms and across her back, soothing her enough to ward off the worst of the pain.

"But we have to do something, Lyka. You're in no condition to fight like this. And the chances of us being attacked out here aren't exactly slim. You have to be able to run away, at the very least."

She couldn't even think about that right now. Standing was inconceivable. Fighting was as likely as her flapping her arms to fly to the moon and giving it a good gut punch for making her miserable.

"I'm sorry, honey," he said, "but we really don't have a lot of options. You're going to have to trust me to help you."

"You don't even know what to do," she said between clenched teeth.

"Maybe not, but your brother will. I'm calling him."

Oh, hell. The only thing worse than suffering through a violent storm of sexual need without relief was letting her big brother know it was happening. "He's going to be dealing with his own issues right now. It's a Slayer thing."

"Good. Then he'll be able to tell me what to do."

Another wave of pain ripped through her, making every muscle in her body clench. She heard Joseph dial his phone, but there was nothing she could do to stop him. She couldn't even find enough air to beg him not to make the call.

Dark spots rippled in her eyes, adding more proof to the pile that she was in no condition to fight.

"It's Joseph," she heard him say. "Lyka's in pain. Some Slayer thing, she says. What do I do to help her?"

Andrea's voice came through the line, angry and indecipherable.

"I can't lock her in a room. We're not at Dabyr. We're out looking for Eric."

Joseph stroked her back as her muscles squeezed down to fit someone with a much smaller frame than hers. She tried to pant through it, but it didn't do squat to help.

"It's a long story," said Joseph. "All I need to know is what to do for her. She's suffering. As her mate, it's my duty to make it stop."

Joseph paused while Andreas went on a furious rant.

"You knew this could happen when you sent her to me," said Joseph. "You knew she was a Theronai and didn't tell me. I'm the one who should be pissed that you hid what she was from me. She and I could have started bonding weeks ago."

Andreas's rant continued, but he was losing steam fast, likely dealing with his own need.

"No, it's permanent. No way out."

After a few seconds, the tone of Andreas's voice changed to one of weary acceptance.

Joseph's hand involuntarily tightened at the back of her neck. "Seriously? That will fix her?"

"Yes." The word came through loud and clear, and, instantly, Lyka knew her brother had ratted her out.

Chapter 34

Joseph had always known that the Slayers were private people, keeping to themselves and protecting their secrets with an almost cultlike ferocity, but even that hadn't prepared him for what Andreas had told him.

"You're mated to my sister now, so you might as well know how to deal with this. It's going to happen every time the moon is full, at least when she's not pregnant." The Slayer's voice was tight with pain. "She needs sex."

"Seriously?" said Joseph. "That will fix her?"

"Yes. If you do it right, it will. But she's fertile now, so unless you're both ready for young, wear a fucking rubber." There was a muted groan of pain, as if he'd covered the phone with his hand.

"Is that's what's wrong with you, too?" asked Joseph.

"Yeah, but I'll live. Just take care of my sister and you'll live, too. I don't like it that you let her leave the protective walls of Dabyr."

"Neither do I, but it wasn't exactly my decision. She tricked me."

"Lyka is good like that." He sucked in a sharp breath.

"Gotta go, man. Hurt my sister, and I'll kill you." Andreas hung up.

Joseph looked down at Lyka, who was doing her best to absorb her knees into her chest. Pain trickled out of her through the luceria. She was shaking, pale.

He couldn't stand to see her like this.

"Andreas told me what to do," he said.

She opened one eye, revealing a narrow pupil and plenty of fury. "Keep your hands off. I'll be fine."

She looked anything but, and even if she hadn't, he could feel a little sliver of what she did.

It wasn't good. It reminded him far too much of the pain he carried around before she'd taken his luceria and freed him of it. The least he could do was return the favor.

And if it got his hands on her sweet body in the bargain, then all the better.

"I know why you're afraid," he said. "You don't have to be. I'll protect you." If she wasn't ready to have a kid, then he'd respect that. He didn't have any condoms, but there were other ways to take care of her. "I won't come inside you."

She looked up at him with a feral light glowing in her catlike eyes. "You don't understand," she said. "But you will."

And then she pounced.

She shoved him back to the floor of the tree house in a move that was far more suited for combat than foreplay. She landed straddling his hips, her hot hands splayed across his naked chest. Her mouth covered his in a kiss so demanding, he could feel the air being pulled from his lungs. Her tongue thrust into his mouth, giving him a taste of wild need.

The mental shields she'd been using to keep him out

crumbled, and a torrent of emotions came spilling out. All the pent-up desire that had been rolling around in her for hours broke free and invaded him, becoming part of him.

He was instantly hard, aching with the need to bury himself in her over and over.

This was no gentle desire. It was all jagged angles and hot, sharp edges. There was nowhere to touch it without feeling its sting, and the only way to ease it was to give Lyka everything she wanted. This was her need, her lust. And he was going to sate it.

She was naked beneath his shirt, and so scorching hot and wet, it was a wonder she didn't burn him. Her deft fingers had his fly open in seconds, and an instant later, she was sliding her tight, slick pussy down over his erection.

He let out a rough groan and tensed every muscle in his abdomen to keep from coming right then and there.

She rode him in long, slow glides that had every inch of him sliding out and back in again. Then, when he was seated fully inside her, she rolled her hips until his cock hit a spot that made her breath catch in her chest.

"I need it," she demanded. "Don't you dare hold back on me."

He wasn't sure what she meant, so without thinking, he slid into her mind as easily as he had her body.

This was the first time he'd come across this part of her. It was more animal than woman, guided solely by instinct and urge. It was ferocious and hungry, unwilling to take no for an answer.

It wanted his seed. It wanted him to breed her. Give her a child.

The idea that part of her felt that way gave him a visceral thrill, but he knew better than to let it go to his head. It wasn't what Lyka wanted. She wasn't ready. She'd been very clear. Whoever—whatever—was in charge now, it wasn't the woman he loved, the one he'd promised to protect.

And that was exactly what he was going to do. He'd waited centuries for children of his own. He could wait a little while longer—as long as it took for her to be ready.

"You can't deny me," she said as she unbuttoned his shirt and pulled it away from her breasts. "I know what you really want—the binding tie of a child uniting us as one, a sweet little life in your arms to protect and raise to be kind, strong and noble. Your eyes looking back up at you." She brought his hand up to her abdomen and held it there. "I know you want to give that to me. I've felt your desire running deeper than even you realize. You've waited so long." She leaned down and slid her tongue across the outer rim of his ear and whispered, "You don't have to wait any longer."

She made use of the luceria, sending him an image of him holding their child.

The instant, potent emotional reaction that caused in him was completely unexpected. He needed what she showed him. Craved it. He hadn't realized until now just how long he'd been rejecting the notion as impossible. Not only had there been no woman in his life, but also all of the Theronai males had been cursed with infertility. A child of his own was an impossible dream.

Until now.

"That's right," she said, her tone coaxing as she lifted her hips and slid back down onto him again. "Give me what we both want. Give me a child."

She began to move in earnest, riding him with purpose. He was bathed in her slick heat, and every nerve ending was lit up with pleasure.

His hands spanned her waist, urging her on. She dug her fingernails into his chest and tossed her head back with abandon. Delightful, sexy noises echoed against the wooden walls, reminding him of just how beautiful she sounded when she came.

He needed to hear that again.

Her breasts jiggled, begging for his attention. They filled his hands perfectly, her hard little nipples grazing against his palms. He had to taste, so he rose, arched her back against his arm and drew one nipple into his mouth.

Sweet heaven, and the moan his suction pulled from her went to his head. His cock jerked inside her, demanding more.

He rolled her over onto the cushions and pulled one sleek leg over his shoulder.

She let out a sound somewhere between a sigh and a command. "More."

With each stroke, he drew closer and closer to orgasm. His skin tingled, his balls drew up tight and sweat broke out along his spine.

If he didn't stop her now, he was going to lose control and fill her with his seed. And why not? It's what she wanted, what she'd begged him for. Wasn't it?

You don't understand. But you will.

That's what she'd been trying to warn him about. Whatever the full moon did to her, it was artificial—some bizarre Slayer insanity that would pass. And when it did, her life could be altered forever if he didn't protect her.

Joseph gritted his teeth and pulled his cock from her body before he lost himself in the moment and forgot what she really wanted. "I have to stop now, before I can't."

Lyka went berserk. She screamed in frustration and came at him, launching herself from the floor.

"You will fuck me, Theronai," she growled.

His erection was in wholehearted agreement, but he was too busy controlling her body to give in to it.

He didn't want to hurt her, but she was strong. It took all his combat ability to pin her to the floor without breaking bones or skin.

"You don't really want this," he told her, giving her a little shake.

"I need it. Please." Her fury turned to desperation and left tears pooling in her eyes. "It hurts."

He couldn't stand to see her cry, see her in pain. Not his Lyka. He'd made a vow to protect her, and if that meant never coming again, then he'd find a way to do that, too, no matter what it cost him.

Her arms were pinned by her ears. His body held the rest of her down. She was squirming beneath him, but it had migrated from a way to escape to something sinuous and needy.

He didn't dare let go of her, for fear she'd attack him again. The last thing they needed was for someone to draw blood and alert every demon for miles that there was prey up in this tree. But he also couldn't simply hold her down for the rest of the night.

"I'm going to put you to sleep," he told her. "Don't fight me. Just let go. I've got you."

"No. Please. Don't leave me like this. The dreams . . ." She swallowed hard, and her pupils narrowed in fear. "The pain."

He touched her mind just enough to get a hint of what she meant, and wished he hadn't. Pain had been part of his world for longer than he could remember. What she suffered now was shorter in duration, but more acute. He couldn't leave her to deal with it on her own, not when he could ease her.

She needs sex. That wasn't exactly the kind of thing a brother would tell a man about his sister unless it was important.

Joseph wanted nothing more than to give her what she needed. All he had to do was find a way to maintain control and keep all those pesky sperm of his to himself.

She squirmed against him, grinding his hot cock against her soft belly. He nearly came right then, but managed to pull himself back from the edge.

Joseph tightened his grip on her wrists so he could hold on to her if she tried to bolt. "Spread your legs, Lyka. I'm going to make you come."

She obeyed eagerly, writhing against him until their bodies meshed seamlessly. So fucking good. So perfect.

He closed his eyes and savored being joined to her for a moment before he put on his game face.

Joseph was a man on a mission. He used every bit of sexual skill he had to gauge her reactions and find just the way she liked it. Unfortunately, the way she liked it was also what worked for him, and he was biting his lip just to hold himself back while he pushed her toward release.

She fought against his hold, but he didn't dare let her up. Her pupils were elongated and that feral light was glowing in the depths of her golden eyes. The animal in her was steering the ship now, and he didn't trust her not to do something she'd regret later.

Her breathing sped and her heart pounded hard, making her pulse beat in her wrists. A pretty pink flush spread out across her face and throat. The little panting breaths she took became soft cries, wordlessly begging for more.

Both parts of the luceria sparked in the darkness. The tiny strands of lightning joined forces in a miniature display in the air between them. Pale golden slivers of heat and light spread out over their skin, caressing them with tingling energy.

She arched her body beneath his, catching and holding her breath as she did. Her pussy fluttered around him, and her abdomen clenched hard as she peaked. She cried out as her orgasm rushed through her in waves.

Joseph had never seen anything more beautiful in his life. It was so fucking sexy, he felt his balls tighten in anticipation of release. He used every technique he could think of to keep from coming right along with her. Instead he kept doing what had set her off, stroking just the right spot, nice and deep inside her.

Finally, as her body relaxed beneath his, he pulled out from her silken depths and let go of his seed, spilling it onto her soft stomach. His orgasm went on for fifty years, and by the end of it, he could barely hold up his head.

He rolled to his side, keeping hold of one of her wrists in case she decided to go all wildcat again.

"I'm okay now," she said, a little breathless. "The storm has passed."

It took him a couple of minutes to catch his breath. "For how long?"

"I don't know. I've never gone through the need before with a man. It's hard to say how I'll be with you."

"If it starts up again, I'm going to tie you up with my belt before you can draw blood."

"I understand," she said, sounding a little regretful. "Do what you think you need to do. I trust you."

And she did. He could feel the truth of her words vibrating through their link.

He rolled onto his side to kiss her, thanking her for such a precious gift, and saw the luceria had changed. It was barely swirling with colors, almost a solid band of shimmering, iridescent amber.

He slid his finger over the warm band. "Soon you'll be known as the Amber Lady," he whispered, reverence in his tone.

She lifted his hand to look at his ring and saw what he did. The strangest look crossed her face. "Pretty soon there will be no getting away from me, or you're a dead man."

He smoothed her hair away from her damp forehead as he gently probed her thoughts. "That bothers you, doesn't it?"

Her mental barriers slammed into place so hard and fast, he was practically caught in them.

"Stay out of my head," she told him as she ripped a strip from the hem of his shirt and used it to clean away his semen.

"I thought you trusted me."

"With my body, yes."

It wasn't enough. He wanted all of her. All of her trust. Anything less would never be enough.

"I'll give you time," he said, hoping he had the patience to follow up those words with actions. "But you need to learn to let me in before you'll be fit for battle."

"You think I don't know how to fight?" she asked.

"You know how to fight like a Slayer."

"We Slayers have kicked our fair share of Theronai ass over the years. Don't go getting all superior on me."

He was tired of her prickly side, tired of her showing him all those barbs when he knew what a sweet, kind woman was lurking beneath the surface.

Rather than let her go on with her tirade, he rolled her back beneath him, where she seemed to let go of some of her aggression. "Have I hurt you? Have I belittled you or your people in some way I don't know about? Have I disrespected you?"

"Well, no, but—"

"No, I haven't. Why the hell do you insist on casting me in the role of the bad guy?"

"Because I don't want to be what you are. I want to be a Slayer. I want to be normal, like one of my own kind."

"And I don't want to sit behind a desk all the time, making life-or-death decisions for thousands of people who don't even know I exist. We all have our burdens to bear."

She stopped cold, blinking at him in shock. "You don't like being leader of the Theronai?"

"I want to help, but, yeah, I'd much rather be doing it with a sword than a pen."

"And now that we're bonded? Will it be someone else sitting behind that desk, making those decisions while you and I go out and kick ass?"

"My term isn't up yet."

"What if someone else wanted the job?"

"Anyone who would want the job isn't fit for it. That's why we volunteer one another—whoever gets the most votes loses."

She grinned at that. "How many votes did you get?"

He let out a weary sigh. "All of them. Except my own. It was a conspiracy."

Lyka stroked his cheek. "They made the right decision."

"How do you know?"

"I've played around inside your head, remember? I know the kind of man you are. Strong, smart, determined, selfless. They're lucky to have you."

He wanted her to feel that way about being tied to him, but he didn't dare voice his desire and look like some kind of a loser. She'd made it clear that being with a Theronai had been her last choice. She would have much rather been with a Slayer—a man she saw as her own kind.

Rather than say something stupid, he settled with, "Thank you."

She frowned at him. "You don't believe me?"

"It's not that. I'm just thinking ahead a little to how you're going to feel once you're grounded again."

"Why would I be grounded?"

"Because I have to go home soon and do my job. Nicholas can only hold down the fort for so long before he's going to want to get back out there and fight."

"Are you forgetting your promise to me—that I can leave Dabyr whenever I want?"

"No. I just thought things would be different now that we're bound. Theronai couples almost always stick together."

She squirmed out from under him. "And you assumed that I would stay there with you."

"Well, yeah."

Lyka shook her head, making her wild, golden hair dance about her shoulders. "I keep telling you, I'm a Slayer at heart. I can't live cooped up like that for the next ten years."

In all the chaos of searching for Eric and the kids, Joseph hadn't really stopped to think about what their life would look like after they found them. He knew she needed to feel free and that she wanted to fight, but until now those pieces hadn't coalesced in his brain to form a solid conclusion: his mate was going to be miserable living his life with him.

"I understand," he said. And he did. He was going to have to choose between his duty to his people and his duty to his mate. He couldn't break his vows to any of them, which left him only one option. "I can't break the bond you and I have, but when this job is done and Eric and the kids are safe, you're free to go. I won't hold you at Dabyr against your will."

"What will you do?"

"What I always do," he said. "My duty."

Chapter 35

Ronan tried several times to compel Justice to do his bidding. Each time, she did exactly as she pleased.

He was a powerful creature, centuries old and with ancient and mysterious abilities. She was supposed to at least pretend to fight the magic he was working on her.

"Will you stop!" she snapped at him as she drove over the backcountry roads like they were her own personal racetrack. "You're pissing me off with all that buzzing in my head."

Ronan hadn't dared let her out of his sight. He'd insisted that if she wanted the demon delivered to Joseph, she was going to have to be the one to do it. And the only way she could was if he guided her to the meeting point.

Surprisingly enough, she'd relented, agreeing to drive while he navigated.

"Who are you?" he asked. "Where did you come from?"

She shot him a surly glance and readjusted her grip on the steering wheel. "Are we there yet?"

"Almost. You didn't answer my questions."

"No. I didn't."

"Will you?"

"No. I won't."

"Why not?"

"Listen, vampire," she began.

"Sanguinar. Not vampire."

"You stalk the night, drink blood, are all pale and far too pretty for your own good. If the shoe fits . . ."

"Too pretty?"

"Sorry. Did I step on your pretty little vampire toes? Should I have called you handsome?"

He would have enjoyed that. Instead, he was unsure of what she thought of him, and that made him flounder in insecurity. Did she like the way he looked? He certainly loved looking at her.

"Take a left at the next intersection," he said.

"You didn't answer my question." She shot his words back at him with a mischievous glow lighting her silvery green eyes.

"You answer one of mine, I'll answer one of yours."

A wide grin spread across her luscious mouth. "I love games. But I get to go first."

"As you please."

"How are you able to find me?"

"I drank your blood. It's a part of me now. So are you. I'll be able to find you wherever you go for as long as you live."

She shivered, and he had no idea if it was the good kind or the bad kind. "Does that upset you?"

"Yes," she said. "Next question."

"But it's my turn."

"You just asked yours. You wanted to know if I was upset. I told you. Thus, my turn."

Clearly, he was going to have to be more careful in his dealings with this woman.

"Is there any way to hide from you?" she asked.

"No," he said, being as curt as she'd been, with no explanation. "Why do you keep running from me?"

"Because I really don't want you to bite me again. It was . . ." She trailed off, leaving him squirming with curiosity.

"It was what?"

"Unsettling." She turned where he'd indicated, putting them only a couple of minutes from their destination. "Next question."

"You tricked me. That isn't fair."

"File a complaint with my supervisor."

"Fine. It's your turn again."

She turned and captured his gaze. He truly couldn't ever remember seeing a more beautiful woman. Even Athanasian women were average compared to her, and they were utterly stunning.

Then she asked, "How do I kill you?"

"Why would you want to do that?"

She shook her head. "My answer first. Then yours."

"I bleed much the same as any other creature. Or you can cut off my head. Just don't try sunlight, unless you want to die right along with me." Giving her that knowledge had been easier than he would have thought. He wasn't sure if it was because he trusted her, or if it was because he'd given it within the context of a game. Or perhaps it was something else entirely.

He pointed to a wooded patch containing a row of trees with purple paint marking their trunks, along with several prominent No Trespassing signs. "Park here. I'll text Joseph and tell him that we've arrived."

"It doesn't look like anything," she said.

"That's rather the point. The people who live back in these woods don't want to be found." He sent Joseph the text, telling him they were waiting for him at the entrance to the Slayer settlement.

When he was done, he said, "Now answer my question. Why do you want to kill me?"

"Because you're interfering with my work and slowing me down. You have no idea how . . . upsetting that can be for a woman like me. If I thought I could just ask you nicely to stop following me, I would, but something tells me that the only way you'll stop is if you're dead."

"Your assessment of the situation is accurate."

She nodded and reached under her seat. "That's what I thought you'd say."

Ronan didn't see her next move coming. One second she was sitting beside him, playing their little game. In the next, she had a heavy flashlight in her hand. She smashed it into the side of his head with a numbing impact. The blow was so hard, his head hit the glass, shattering it.

Warning bells went off in his mind, clanging about his impending doom. Sadly, he was too stunned to do more than make note of them as he fell unconscious.

Chapter 36

Justice hated breaking open such a pretty head, but she had no choice.

The fates giveth, and the fates taketh away.

She had no idea why they were so fickle, driving her to save his life one moment and demanding that she smash his head the next, but she'd learned long ago that there was no point in fighting it. Every time she did, she suffered.

Before the smell of his blood could draw any nasty monsters, she used a roll of duct tape in her ready bag and bandaged him up so well, it was going to take him days to cut through all the layers, and even more to get the adhesive out of his luxurious hair. No way were demons smelling anything through that.

Then she went around to his side of the car and eased him onto the ground. The demon in the trunk came out next, and it was all she could do not to puke as she made contact with its rubbery, cold skin.

Once her cargo was unloaded, she got back into her rental car and headed north, at the urging of the fates.

She had no idea what was up there waiting for her,

but it really didn't matter. One direction was the same as another.

Every journey ended in suck.

Lyka was so stunned by Joseph offering to let her go, she hadn't thought of a single thing to say to him for the past thirty minutes. She kept running over the conversation again in her mind as they hiked back to the road to meet Ronan. His timely text had saved her from saying something she'd regret, but only because she'd started thinking about what was on the other end of this hike.

A demon awaited her—one she was going to have to touch.

She shuddered just thinking about it.

"Everything is going to be fine," said Joseph.

She'd been so focused on the task ahead and his proclamation that she was free that she hadn't been able to juggle keeping her mental shields up, too. But now that she was thinking about it, she could feel his warm presence hovering in her mind, keeping tabs on her without being intrusive.

She wasn't sure how he managed the delicate balance, but it was something she was going to have to watch out for if she ever needed some privacy.

Right now, there were too many things spinning in her head for her to worry about that.

"What about the treaty?" she asked. "I'm supposed to be acting as your hostage to ensure that my brother upholds his end of the deal."

Joseph hiked a few paces in front of her, giving her a lovely view of his broad shoulders. He shrugged as he walked. "I'll release him from that part of the treaty. I don't need a hostage anymore. I trust him to do what's right."

"And us?" she asked. "You Theronai are all about your bonds. You're going to just let me walk away without a fight?"

"There's nothing I want more than for us to be the kind of partners we were meant to be, but I made a promise to you. If you want to leave, you can. In time, your abilities will grow and you'll be able to channel my power from a distance."

"And your vow to protect me? How will you uphold that if we're not together?"

He went quiet in a way that told her she wasn't going to like his answer.

"Spill it, Joseph. I have a right to know how you're going to manage this feat."

"You've backed me into a corner, Lyka. I promised to lead my people for twenty years. I promised to give you your freedom if you bound yourself to one of us—which you did. Then I promised to protect your life with my own as any Theronai worth his salt would. How do I do all those at once?"

He couldn't. Not unless she stayed with him at Dabyr. The problem was, he would be compelled to honor all of those promises. If he didn't, the magic binding him to his word would begin acting on him in negative ways. It might be little, annoying things at first, but eventually he would be driven to do what he promised he would. He would have no choice.

"Do you have a plan?" she asked.

"I do."

"And it is?"

"Every time you leave Dabyr, it will be with an escort of my choosing. Most likely a contingent of Theronai and Sanguinar. Slayers, too, if Andreas will assign some to your security detail."

Lyka stopped dead in her tracks. "What?"

"You heard me."

"I demanded my freedom from Dabyr so that I'd be free of it, not so you'd send it along with me."

"It's the only way to ensure your safety. I may not always be able to go with you, but I can protect your life with the power that comes with my position."

"It's not what I want, Joseph."

"It's not what I want, either. I guess that means it's a fair compromise."

Frustration tightened her skin. She stormed off, slashing the brush as she went.

There was no question at all that he'd do what he said. The problem was, she'd pushed him back into this neat little corner that had also trapped her, too.

"And if you're thinking about trying to slip away from your protection," he said, "don't. Every one of my men would give his life for yours or for mine. Irritating the piss out of you by sticking by your side won't even make them break a sweat."

Lovely. At least at Dabyr, she had the privacy of her suite. With an entourage of armed men following her, she'd never get even a moment alone.

Lyka was just about to turn around and force Joseph to promise not to do that to her when she cleared the trees.

One of those human-looking demons was lying by the road, bound so tightly with duct tape that it looked like a silver caterpillar as it wormed its way toward Ronan's unconscious body. He was also bound with tape, but only around his head.

From behind her, she heard the sound of steel on steel as Joseph drew his sword and charged.

"Don't kill it!" she yelled, rushing to grab his arm before he could ruin their chance at using the demon to find Eric.

Rather than slice it in two, Joseph kicked the demon away with his boot. Then he crouched beside the Sanguinar and felt for a pulse.

Ronan groaned and his eyes fluttered. Silver light spilled out, casting long shadows along the ground. "Justice."

"Yes," said Joseph, clasping the man's shoulder. "We will find justice for what was done to you. Hang tight."

"No," said Ronan before he conked out again.

Joseph got on his phone. "Nicholas, Ronan is hurt. We have no wheels. Send the chopper to my phone's location." He hung up and looked at Lyka. "Do whatever it is you're going to do with that demon so I can kill it."

She nodded and hurried to comply before he quit indulging her experiment and did what he'd been born to do: kill demons.

The creature had not been cowed by the kick Joseph had given it. It had already started inching its way back toward Ronan and the easy prey he provided.

Whoever had captured it had tied a gag in its mouth. The red fabric was dark and wet with saliva as it tried to chew its way through. Patches of wiry black fur splotched its face, reminding her of a spotted dog. Long claws at the tips of its fingers barely peeked out between layers of tape. It was trying to scratch its way free, and, given enough time, it probably would succeed.

The idea of touching the thing was repulsive, but she had no choice. The only time her gift had ever worked with a demon had been when it had come in physical contact with her. Being close wasn't going to cut it. As horrible as the idea was, she didn't doubt for a second that whatever Eric and the young were going through was much, much worse.

Lyka planted a knee on the thing's chest. It lunged for her, bowing awkwardly in an effort to bite her. She increased the pressure and held one of her daggers against its cheek, right under its eye. It looked past her to where Joseph stood. A quick glance over her shoulder told her that his sword was drawn and ready for use, poised right above the demon's groin.

"If you don't move your weapon, all I'm going to feel this creature want is your sword away from its balls."

Joseph backed off, but only a couple of inches.

Lyka pulled in a deep breath and put her hand on its pale, greasy, furred forehead.

Instantly, she felt its desire to feed, to kill, to rip flesh and bone apart and lap up blood before it could soak into the earth. The feeling was so strong and so real, her stomach growled with the need to feed on human and Sentinel flesh.

Sickened by the sensation, she pulled away and breathed through her nose so she wouldn't vomit.

Behind the gag, the demon's mouth widened in a smile. It knew it had upset her.

"This is a waste of time," said Joseph. "All it wants is to kill."

"If you don't like it, stay out of my head while I do this."

"Not a chance in hell, kitten. You're not going into that pile of filth without backup."

For some reason, that reassured her and eased her nerves. Knowing he was there was going to make this easier the second time around.

She hoped.

Lyka braced herself and laid her hand on the demon again. This time, she was ready for the horrible hunger and need for blood. She let all of that pass over her, digging deeper into what the thing really wanted.

She wasn't exactly sure what she was looking for or how to draw from it what she needed to know, so she tried forming a mental picture of Eric and showing it to him.

The instant it touched her thoughts, she felt a dark stain spread through her. Something wild and vicious took root, growing so fast, she was certain it would take over her entire world.

She didn't know how to fight it. There was no defense against something so sick and tainted. It seeped through the cracks in her mind, twisting her as it went.

"Not my woman," she heard Joseph growl.

A warm light suffused her, burning away the filth. She opened herself up to it, blasting away every mental barrier she'd erected. She needed Joseph inside her mind— needed his warmth and goodness to drive away the evil that had invaded.

The luceria hummed around her neck, growing hotter with every passing second. Tingling sparks of power showered down over her skin in a visual display. Everywhere the sparks touched the demon, its skin burned and blistered.

The thing howled in pain and retreated from the bright glow of Joseph hovering in her mind like some kind of avenging angel waiting to strike. It cowered in fear.

That's when Lyka charged.

She shoved her way into the demon's thoughts, digging deeper for what she needed to know. Eric and the young had been taken for a reason. They hadn't been killed like so many others. They'd been kept alive, and this creature had to know why. Its reaction to Eric's face had been far too strong for it not to have seen her brother.

Lyka's head began throbbing. Sweat trickled down her body. She felt Joseph's bright fury protecting her, but he was quickly losing patience. She had to work fast.

Not knowing what else to do, she found the trickle of power flowing into her and pulled on it. Maybe if she had more juice, she could find what she needed to know.

Then again, maybe she'd just burn this demon's brain to mush and lose her chance altogether.

As soon as she called on Joseph's power, it leapt to do her bidding. She felt it fill her, strengthen her, warm her. She was surrounded by it, filled with it. He had so much strength, and it was all hers for the taking.

She grabbed the demon's face in her hands and showed him the image of Eric again.

This time, Joseph's power amplified the vision, giving the demon no choice but to let her see its reaction.

It knew Eric. He was to be protected. Kept safe.

Why?

She shoved the question into the demon's head. It flinched, but there was an image of a beautiful woman blazing in its memory. She had long, black hair, pale skin, and the kind of body that would make men kill just to be near her. Surrounding this woman was a feeling of reverence, obedience.

She was the demon's queen. She was the one who wanted Eric.

Where is she?

There was no response, only the picture of cave walls and the shared warmth of its fellow demons piled together in sleep.

Joseph's words came out through clenched teeth. "You need to stop now, Lyka. I can't hold back its poison much longer."

Poison?

"It's trying to infect your mind. Can't you feel it?"

She had, but now Joseph was holding that at bay, and from the strain in his tone, it wasn't easy.

Still, she couldn't stop yet. She still didn't have the information she needed.

Lyka pushed harder, digging deeper into the thing's thoughts. Its desire to please its queen washed over her, nearly knocking her out of its head with sheer force. She held on to her position, clinging tightly to the ground she'd gained.

What do you want? she demanded.

The image of that beautiful woman filled Lyka's head again, along with a low, almost worshipful hum.

This demon didn't just want to please its queen; it wanted her. Wanted to possess her, fuck her, consume her flesh and blood.

Lyka shivered in revulsion and tried not to let her disgust wash over her. Some of it clung, but she managed to shed enough of it to concentrate.

I can give her to you, she whispered to the demon's mind. *Take me to her and she will be yours.*

The creature didn't believe her, so she drew more of Joseph's power into herself and pushed harder. The mental compulsion wormed its way into the demon's mind and found fertile ground. She urged it to grow, to consume his every waking thought.

Take me to her and she will be yours. I swear.

"No!" shouted Joseph.

She didn't understand what had upset him until she felt the weight of her vow to this creature crash down on her. She'd been so swept up in winning the war waging in its mind that she'd forgotten to guard her words. The vow she'd made was binding. Unbreakable. She would now be compelled to uphold her end of the bargain.

What had started as a lie to gain this demon's cooperation has now become an imperative. She had no idea how she would manage it, but she had to find some way to deliver a powerful Synestryn queen into the hands of a demon who wanted to eat her.

Chapter 37

Joseph tried to rip Lyka out of the demon's thoughts, but he was too late. She'd made her promise and was now bound by it.

How could he have been so reckless? He should have sensed her intention before she acted. He should have stopped her. Protected her.

All he could do now was damage control.

He physically lifted her away from the demon, breaking her connection to it. She fought against him, but he used brute force to control her flailing limbs.

Because he'd stayed tied to her mind, he could still feel the taint of the demon sliding around in her, causing her to experience an artificial cascade of fear and anger.

Her arms were pinned at her sides, and she tried to claw at his thighs to free herself. Her fingernails had started lengthening into claws, and in a few more seconds, she was going to be ripping through a lot more than just denim.

"Calm the fuck down, Lyka." He gave her a squeeze to emphasize his order and to rob her of just enough air to weaken her. She was incredibly strong, and it took every bit of power he could muster to keep her under control.

He did his best to stroke across her thoughts and calm her mind. She was a total wreck upstairs, thanks to that rabid taint the demon had infected her with.

Slowly, she began to stop fighting, partly because she was starved for oxygen, and partly because he was working hard to burn every speck of demonic stain from her thoughts.

When she went totally limp, he let up enough pressure so she could breathe normally again. He didn't dare let her go, though—not until he was sure that this wasn't a trick.

Joseph stayed firmly in her mind, giving her no chance to put up those giant mental barriers again. He was staking a claim on this territory, too. Putting down roots. Settling in for permanent residence.

"I didn't invite you," she told him.

"Too damn bad. You opened yourself up to that thing. You let it in. If even one shadow of that fucking demon is left in your head, I'm going to be here to kill it. Don't even think about trying to lock me out again, or you're going to have a headache for about a year. Understand?"

She nodded. "I hear a helicopter coming."

Joseph's hearing apparently wasn't as good as hers. Something else that was a gift from her Slayer side, no doubt. "Are you calm now? Can I let you go?"

"Yes, but the second you do, I'm cutting the tape away from that demon."

"I should just kill the fucker."

"You do that and we've lost our last chance at finding Eric and those kids."

He knew that. He hated it, but he knew it was true. "I

can't let you run off after a demon without me, and I can't leave until I know Ronan is safe."

"Then you'd better hold on tight, because I can only fight the compulsion to fulfill my vow for so long."

Joseph watched the chopper land in a nearby clearing while he kept a tight hold on Lyka. It was no hardship having her in his arms, but he would have much rather had her there because she wanted to be than because she had to be.

A couple of minutes later, Nicholas came through the brush and found them. His phone was in his hand, its screen lighting up the scars crisscrossing his face.

"It's nice that not everyone disables the trackers in their phones," he said as he approached. "This is why I put them there. So I can find you when you need help." He eyed Lyka. "Looks like you need help."

"I'm good," said Joseph. "Ronan isn't. I need you to take him to Tynan."

"I thought I'd be bringing you two back, too. That's why I came with an empty chopper."

"We can't go yet," said Joseph. "We have a demon to follow."

Nicholas lifted his brows. "On foot?"

"I doubt it has a car," said Lyka.

The demon grunted and gurgled behind its gag as it tried to chew through the fabric.

"We really can't lose it," said Joseph. "You don't happen to have a spare tracker on you, do you?"

"Always. Hang tight." He jogged off toward the helicopter and came back a few minutes later with a black backpack. "I assume you're going to let this thing loose?"

"Yes," said Lyka as she tugged against Joseph's hold, as if testing to see if he was still in control. "The sooner, the better."

Nicholas turned the demon onto its stomach and sliced through several layers of duct tape to reach its skin. He used a small tube of superglue to adhere an electronic gadget about the size of a dime to the center of the creature's back. He then glued a scrap of leather over it. "So it won't try to scrape the thing off on a tree trunk."

"Can I pick up the signal on my phone?" asked Joseph.

"Use the app I installed last year. I'll text you the code to this tracker." He gave Lyka a meaningful glance. "You need a hand with anything else?"

"Just Ronan."

"I can come back after I drop him off," said Nicholas.

"Itching to get away from the desk?"

"Hell, yes."

"I'll be home soon and free you."

"You'd better. I need to be out there looking for Torr."

"Do you have any leads?" asked Joseph.

"Still looking. I don't think the magic that zapped him was evil."

"Then he'll turn up. Have a little faith."

Nicholas picked up Ronan's limp body. "Call if you need me. I'll be on standby."

"Will do."

Nicholas disappeared through the brush with Ronan in his arms.

Lyka jerked against Joseph's hold. Her tone was nearly frantic. "Need to go now. My skin is burning."

"Just hang on, honey. Once Nicholas is in the air, I'll cut the demon free."

As soon as the chopper flew over the trees, Joseph dragged her away from the demon and loosened his hold. "Stay here."

"I don't know if I can, but I'll try."

He let go of her. She hugged herself, rubbing her hands over her arms like a junkie in need of a fix.

Joseph made quick work of cutting the tape restraining the demon. He left a few loops of it—just enough to hold it in place for a few seconds while he went back to Lyka.

He got a firm hold on her with one hand while gripping his sword in the other.

The demon broke free and started toward them. It stopped cold as Joseph lifted his sword. "Run or die."

Apparently, the thing understood him, because it hesitated, then turned and sprinted through the brush so fast, it seemed to disappear.

Lyka lunged after it, but Joseph held her back. "Not yet. Let it think it's free, or it will never return to its queen."

"I need to go. Need to follow it."

That damn vow was riding her hard, making it impossible for her to think about anything else. He could feel her frantic sense of panic flowing through their link.

He took her by the shoulders and gave her a little shake. "Look at me. We're going after it. It can't get away. We can track it, remember?"

She either didn't hear him or didn't believe him, because that sense of panic grew until she was shaking with it.

He couldn't wait any longer. It was too much to ask of her to suffer like this.

Before he could let go, he felt a huge draw on his power. As he watched, her eyes changed, becoming those narrow, feline pupils. Bone and tissue surged beneath his hands as her body began to shift. It took less than three seconds for the change to be complete.

She fell to the ground in the form of a fully grown tiger, wearing the tattered remains of his shirt.

"Lyka." Her name was a plea. "Don't do this."

Of course she said nothing. Instead, she gave him one last golden stare, then turned and leapt into the forest on the heels of the demon.

Lyka had never felt so free in her life. Her body was strong, moving easily over the rough ground. Her senses were running hot, picking up even the slightest traces of the demon where it had passed.

She had no idea how long she ran—time meant nothing in this form. All she knew was she felt like she could keep going for days like this.

The demon slowed as it dipped down into a ravine. She held back, staying hidden in the thick undergrowth of the surrounding forest. There were hundreds of scents here—both demon and Slayer.

Eric had come this way. So had several young.

She was close.

Moving silently on four paws, Lyka eased down toward the origin of all those scents. Whatever magic had blocked them before was missing here, giving their presence away.

The demon stood next to a narrow opening in the rock, waiting for her. It looked at her with its dead black eyes and pointed.

Apparently, the connection she'd made with the thing had lasted. It knew she'd vowed to help it claim its queen, and, even from this distance, she could feel that it wanted the woman more than it wanted to drink Lyka's blood and eat her flesh.

She went where it pointed, slipping into the low mouth of a cave.

It was brighter inside than it should have been. She'd been in plenty of caves in her life, and there was no darkness that was quite so deep and impenetrable as that of the belly of a cave.

Still, the light flowing down the tunnel here told her that this was no ordinary cave.

The demon eased up beside her, keeping a safe distance. It knew not to trust her any more than she trusted it. Still, they had reached some odd kind of agreement that stemmed from her promise to help it get what it wanted.

It went to all fours, moving easily along the low tunnel. She followed it, pausing only when she saw what lay ahead.

There were more demons like it milling about—dozens of them. Some of them were piled in sleep, while others were tearing raw meat from cow bones.

At least it was cow and not people.

As they neared the gathering, the demons began noticing her presence one at a time. There was a moment of confusion—she doubted any of them had ever seen a tiger before—but it passed as they realized that whatever she was, she was still made of meat.

They closed in.

The demon escorting her hissed at the others, warning them away. It made a strange clicking sound for a few seconds, then a series of short hums. After that, the horde began going back about its business.

Miraculously, she'd been labeled as *not food*. And it stuck. Hopefully, it would stick long enough for her to gather her kin and get out of here, because there was no way she was going to be able to fight this many demons and survive.

The system of caverns and tunnels wound around in

a wide spiral. As they neared the center, Lyka could smell Slayer young. They were hungry, afraid. She could smell their tears.

A rough growl rumbled in her chest.

The demon stopped and looked at her, baring its teeth in warning.

She held perfectly still, waiting for the thing to make up its mind whether to attack or keep moving. Finally, it turned around, giving her a view of the leather Nicholas had glued to its back as it moved deeper into the spiral.

The ceiling of the cave shot up high in this area. The tunnels curved so tightly that she could see only a few yards before her vision was obscured by more rock wall.

The demon pushed open a pair of solid wooden doors, stirring the air.

Eric's scent hit her with such force, she felt her eyes tear up. He was here. Alive. But something was off. He smelled wrong. Broken.

The demon pointed, indicating she should go through the doors. She did, and stepped into a lavishly decorated room fit for any queen. There were thick, ornate rugs; elaborately carved furniture; and a line of wooden wardrobes, one of which stood open to reveal several velvet gowns.

Lying in the center of a giant bed, bound hand and foot, was her brother Eric. He was naked, covered in ragged bite marks like nothing she'd ever seen. Infection burned red around his wounds, especially at his groin. It looked like animals had been gnawing on his genitals.

His body was lean, almost gaunt—proof that he'd burned a lot of his reserves trying to heal himself. Sickness hovered about him, and a heavy layer of that wrongness she'd sensed earlier.

She raced to his side, shifting back into her human

form as she did. The second she reached the bed, his eyes popped open.

He blinked several times as if to clear his vision.

She went to work loosening the ropes binding his wrists over his head. "I'm getting you out of here. Just hang on."

"Lyka?" His tone was heavy with confusion, so she took a couple of seconds to ease his mind.

"It's okay now, Eric," she said. "Everything is going to be okay."

The smell of his fear was so strong, it gagged her, but his gaze wasn't fixed on her. He was looking past her to something behind her.

"She's here." His voice cracked with terror. *"Run."*

Chapter 38

Lyka turned in time to watch the most beautiful woman she'd ever seen let go of her velvet skirts and lift her hand.

"He's mine."

A crackling electrical charge filled the room an instant before power exploded out of the woman.

Lyka instinctively pulled on Joseph's power to shield her while she covered her brother's body with her own.

The force of the blast hit her back and knocked the breath out of her. It shoved the heavy bed several feet across the stone floor, where it hit the opposite wall hard enough to shatter the wooden frame. Heat spilled out around her shield, burning precious oxygen from the air.

When the pressure of the magical attack faded, Lyka could feel Joseph's panic vibrating through their connection. He was desperate to reach her, exhausted from running, but refused to slow as he rushed to her side.

He wasn't going to make it to her in time. He was too far away. She could tell by the way his thoughts were a distant echo, rather than a powerful mix of emotion and images.

She was on her own.

Lyka spun around to face her attacker while she shifted into her tiger form. The change was instantaneous, easy. Shock rattled around in her, until she realized that she'd managed the feat only because she'd drawn power from Joseph.

She prepared to launch herself at the woman, claws extended, teeth bared. She was going to rip this woman's throat out for what she did to Eric.

Her body coiled to attack, but she couldn't pounce — not at this woman. She'd made a promise to a demon to deliver her, and she was bound by the magic of that vow.

Lyka couldn't kill the bitch. Her own words had tied her hands.

Eric, however, had no such constraints.

She slashed at his ropes, freeing him in a few quick strikes. Her fur stood up on end, warning her of an incoming attack.

In a heartbeat, she resumed her human form.

Once again Lyka used her body and a surge of magic to shield them from the blast. As heat and light washed over them, they were pushed back until they were smashed flat against the stone wall of the cavern.

"No one takes from me what is mine," screamed the woman.

"Treszka, stop!" yelled Eric. "You don't even know if you're pregnant yet. You might still need me."

"I have from you everything I need now."

Confusion cast a fog over their words for a second before Lyka realized what they meant. He hadn't been bound to the bed, naked and chewed on, because he'd been serving as food. This Treszka woman had been raping him.

Lyka's stomach turned at the implications. She tried

not to think too hard about what her brother had been through—at least not now. Now all that mattered was getting the hell out of here.

Treszka's blast of magical force faded again, leaving behind the smell of ozone. It was hard to breathe. Lyka's body felt weakened from the lack of oxygen.

Eric was trembling, reeking of stunned regret, infection and weakness. They couldn't stay in here much longer. They needed an exit strategy.

Lyka pulled power from Joseph to strengthen her body and used every bit of muscle she had to flip the monstrous bed onto its side. It leaned against the wall, forming a tight shelter for her and her brother.

The scent of demons grew stronger, and the sound of their footsteps got louder as they approached the chamber.

"Any other way out?" she whispered to Eric.

"Not that I saw."

"Where are the young?"

"Separated in two groups. You should have passed one on your way in."

The smell of the young had been present on her path here, but it had been faint. Hours had passed since they'd gone that way. Maybe days. "I didn't."

"Then I don't know where they are now. I'll keep her busy here. You go find them and get the hell out. I'll just slow you down."

"We leave together."

If they left at all. As of now, Lyka couldn't think of any way past the woman and her sledgehammer magic.

I'm coming, Joseph whispered in her thoughts, faint and distant.

It's too dangerous. Stay away.

Not going to happen, kitten. Hang on.

She had no choice. She couldn't even fight back against this woman.

But perhaps she could restrain her. Once Treszka was bound, Lyka could deliver her to the demon she'd made a promise to. What it did with her after that was none of Lyka's concern.

She had no clue what she was doing, but she had to try something. She pulled a steady stream of Joseph's power into her, letting it build inside her. In less than a couple of seconds, the pressure of the magic became too much to bear. She had to let it out. Now.

"Stay here," she ordered Eric, and then she grabbed a sheet and darted out from behind the bed so she could see what she was doing.

Power bulged inside her body, pressing against bones and organs. With every passing fraction of a second, more energy collected in her, demanding to be set free.

Lyka tossed the sheet toward Treszka, imbuing it with a living kind of magic. The sheet flew through the air and wrapped around the woman's legs like a boa constrictor.

She toppled onto her hands and knees. Her black hair fell over her face, and she brushed it back, giving Lyka a murderous look. As those inky locks pulled away from her forehead, they took with it a flap of skin that covered a gaping maw filled with wicked teeth and a single, weeping, bulbous eye.

Suddenly, the woman wasn't so beautiful. She was all demon.

Treszka ripped the sheet from her legs as it if had been tissue paper. The hem of her velvet skirt was shredded. Her black eye burned with hatred. "What are you?"

"Fifty percent Slayer, fifty percent Theronai, one hundred percent Gonna Kick Your Ass."

"Guards!" Treszka screamed, and lifted both hands. Every loose object in the room became a projectile weapon, flying right toward Lyka's head.

Chapter 39

Joseph wasn't going to make it in time to save Lyka's life.

He used every trick he knew to fuel his body and give himself a boost of speed. Both she and the demon had moved far faster through the woods than he could, putting him at least a couple of miles behind her.

His lungs burned. His legs were on fire. His body was covered in hundreds of little cuts that branches and brush had left behind. He knew his blood was calling every demon around for miles, but there was no time to slow down and bandage himself.

As it was, he'd already wasted precious seconds calling for backup. His only hope was that other allies in the field would be closer to Lyka than he was and would make it to her in time.

He kept trying to get her to tell him what was going on, kept trying to see through her eyes, but she didn't understand what he wanted, wasn't able to comply or didn't want to. All he got from her was an occasional pull on his power and a whole lot of emotion. Fear, shock, fury.

Whatever was happening to her wasn't good.

Joseph did what he could to feed her the energy she needed so she wouldn't have to work so hard. With each passing minute he drew closer to her, easing the strain of drawing strength from him over a distance.

He should have taken more time to teach her how to use his power. He should have insisted that she let others find her brother. He should have found some way to control her before she'd bounded off into the woods, hot on the trail of a demon.

At least Joseph knew where she was headed. The tracker Nicholas had installed had worked like a charm—right up to the point that the signal vanished altogether.

Joseph hoped that the signal loss was due to the demon going underground rather than to the tracker being destroyed.

He slowed just enough to check his phone again and make sure he was still headed in the right direction. The screen was bright in the darkness of the forest, drawing a tiny swarm of bugs within seconds.

The last known location of the tracker was just up ahead, on the other side of a hill.

As he cleared the hilltop and looked down into the ravine below, he came to a dead stop.

There were demons down there. At least a dozen of them, all pale and naked, wielding those rustic swords. They scrambled toward a narrow opening in the rock like someone inside had wrung a dinner bell.

That wasn't good. Based on Nicholas's tracker, this was where that demon had gone. And that meant Lyka was inside.

Apparently, she was dinner.

Chapter 40

Eric grabbed Lyka's arm and jerked her back behind the heavy bed. Several bits of wood, metal and stone embedded themselves in the mattress. A small knife slammed through and gouged into the bedpost, sticking there.

He tugged it free and looked at the choker his sister wore. "Let yourself get collared, did you?"

"I did it to save your hairy ass, so keep your opinions to yourself."

Another volley of magic hit them, shoving the bed a few inches closer to the wall. There was no room left here to maneuver anymore. They were trapped, easy targets for Treszka to finish them off. They had to get out before she could do the job.

"You call this saving me?" he asked.

When she showed up, he'd never been so happy to see anyone in his life. And then he realized what it meant: she was stuck down here with him, too.

"Working on it," she said.

"The bitch has dozens of demons under her control. I'm in shitty shape for a fight, and you didn't even bring weapons."

"Yes, I did," she said. "You just can't see them right now."

"Then what are you waiting for? Kill the cunt."

"I can't."

"Can't?"

"Long story."

The smell of demons assaulted his nose. He could hear their steps grow closer. They were in the room now.

"Might as well tell me now. We're going to die down here."

"Speak for yourself," she said. "I just learned some new tricks, and I really want to live long enough to practice and get good at them."

"Now works. You can practice now."

The heavy bed was ripped away from the wall by a mass of demons. Treszka stood a few feet away, her hands on her hips.

She was carrying his young. At least that's what she'd said. He didn't want to believe her, but part of him must have, because he actually hesitated at the thought of killing her.

Then he remembered what she'd done to him. How she'd violated him. Hurt him. Left him bleeding, fevered and helpless, tied to her bed.

Just when he'd thought he was safe, she'd come back for more. She'd forced herself into his mind and made him burn for her. Made him beg.

Vomit crawled up his throat. Rage tingled across his skin.

"You think you can kill me?" she asked, a little smile playing about her lush mouth. She spread her arms. "Go ahead and try."

Eric's body tensed, preparing to charge, but that was as far as he could get. Whatever she'd done had cast a web of control over him, forcing his feet to stay planted where they were.

"We have a problem," he told Lyka.

"Just one?"

"Are you sure you can't kill her?" he asked.

"I'm sure."

"Well, that sucks ass, because I can't, either."

Treszka laughed. "I'm done with both of them," she told her demon guards. "Kill them."

Chapter 41

Joseph slipped in behind the demons as they went in the cave. They were all too busy rushing to wherever they were going to pay him any attention. Even the ones who looked his way, nostrils flared at the scent of his blood, simply licked their lips and kept moving.

Whoever or whatever controlled them must have been more powerful than their constant hunger for Sentinel blood.

Lyka was in here. He could feel her presence nearby, growing stronger with every step. She was tired. Afraid. Without hope.

He'd let this happen. It was his job to ensure her safety, and here she was in a demon-infested cave, as far from safe as she could be.

I'm coming, love. Hold on.

He wanted nothing more than to rush to her side, but if doing so got him killed, he wasn't going to be any help to her at all. It was better to be smart. Be careful. There was no way of knowing if one of the demons' hunger would outweigh its obedience. But if it did, he'd be ready.

He followed the demons as they converged on a central location. He couldn't quite see what it was—there were too many bodies in the way. But he could hear this strange, low hum spreading outward.

As it finally reached him, he realized that it was the demons making this noise.

She's headed your way, Lyka whispered to his thoughts.

She who? His question reached her easily. She was no longer trying to keep him out. In fact, she seemed to welcome his presence, clinging to it like a lifeline.

Queen Bitch, Lyka answered.

He shifted his grip on his sword and amplified his vision. There was plenty of light in here for him to see, but a heightened attention to detail was definitely in order. When a man was on a mission to save the woman he loved, he needed every advantage he could get.

Love? Her shock rang through the question, making it clatter in his thoughts.

Now wasn't the time for such confessions, but he was acutely aware that he might never have another chance to let her know how he felt. So rather than hold back, he opened himself up and let her feel what he did. He let her see the way he saw her—beautiful and brave, fierce and loyal, sexy and sweet. She was everything he could have ever hoped for in a mate, in a wife, and he felt like the luckiest man alive to be with her for whatever time they had together.

Something in her fluttered. Expanded. He felt her absorb his love and let it strengthen her. *If you want more time with me, you'd better hurry. Eric and I are about out.*

That was all the motivation he needed to change tactics. He was done with sneaking around. It was time to attack.

Joseph rolled his shoulders and started hacking his way toward his woman.

Chapter 42

Eric and Lyka backed into a corner where the demons could come at them from only one side. She lifted her hand and drew on Joseph's power with the idea of defense in mind. A shimmering film of pale light appeared around her and Eric, protecting them from the slavering demons.

Some of them were weaponless and clawed at the luminous barrier, but most of them wielded rusty, primitive swords that looked like they'd been banged out in haste. The blades were thick and heavy, and she felt each one strike the wall she'd erected.

"Nice trick," said Eric.

Sweat was already forming on her forehead. As much as she loved the feel of Joseph's power running through her, it was exhausting as hell. "It won't last long."

"Can you move it?"

She had no idea. "Why?"

"If we can get to the door, we might be able to trap a metric shit ton of these fuckers in here. I've had plenty of time tied to this bed to study the place. The doors are solid. It will take them a while to chop through. It's the only chance I see of getting out of here."

It was worth a shot. There was a man out there who loved her, and she really wanted to know what that felt like for longer than the time it took her to die.

If Joseph had given her only words, she never would have believed that he loved her, but he'd done more than that. He'd let her in, let her feel what he did. It was beautiful, warm, safe. She'd slipped right inside his thoughts and basked in the glow of his love.

And she really wanted to do it again.

The only way to manage that was to survive, so Lyka mapped a path from the corner where they were trapped to the doorway. They had about thirty feet to cover and several pieces of furniture to go around—no small feat.

She took a step to her left and forced the barrier to slip around to cover Eric's flank. He was weaving on his feet, doing all he could just to stay upright. If he took a hit now, she didn't think he'd be able to stand, much less walk.

The shield moved with them, but dragging it was as hard as lifting a bank safe with one hand. She had no idea how she was going to make it thirty feet.

You can do it. I'm with you every step. Joseph's comforting support settled over her. He was waging battle, slicing his way through a hallway stuffed with demons, and yet he still took the time to ease her worries.

Because he was the prize for survival, Lyka gathered her strength and took another step, then another. Sweat poured off her body and her legs were shaking with weakness, but she kept moving.

Eric started to go down. Lyka grabbed him before he could, but the shield faltered and a rusty blade made it through the hole before she could plug it.

She didn't even realize she'd been hit until she felt the blood trickle down her arm.

You're hurt. Joseph's worry came through loud and clear.

She gritted her teeth as the pain hit her. *Keep your nose in your own combat, Theronai. I'm fine.*

Her blood excited the demons, making their attacks come at a frenzied pace. With each hit the barrier took, she felt herself wobble, weaken. She really didn't know how much longer she could keep this up.

As that thought passed through her mind, she felt a rush of power flowing into her. Joseph was pushing it her way, trying to ease her burden.

She was floored by his thoughtfulness, by his care of her. She didn't know how to repay him other than to keep fighting. Refuse to give up. When this was all over, she'd work on paying off all the debt she was racking up.

No debt. We're one now.

And they were. She could feel everything he did, hear every thought that passed through his mind. He was with her, in her, his power flowing through her. She'd never felt anything half as intimate as the connection they now shared. It was so beautiful that she had to blink tears from her eyes.

Cry later, kitten. Fight now.

For him, she would. For *them.*

The conduit between them opened wide, giving her a rush of power. Her skin tingled as it raced over her. Her bones vibrated with the strength he housed. The air around her crackled in anticipation.

Lyka shoved her shoulder under her brother's arm and bodily hauled him along with her. He did his best to support his weight, but he was in bad shape. She could feel his strength fading.

She had not come all this way just to watch her brother fall now.

Joseph's power seethed and boiled at his end of their connection. She didn't know how much more she could take, but if ever there was a time for her to get tough, this was it.

She sucked a huge mass of power into herself and used it to clear their path to the door. Demons flew back as if they were bowling pins struck by a wrecking ball. Their bodies hit the opposite wall with a wet thud, splattering reddish black blood everywhere.

The remaining demons smelled the blood and went berserk. They turned their attention toward the new source of food and descended on their kin like vultures.

Lyka used the distraction to jerk her brother through the doors and slam them shut.

Joseph was just outside the doorway, finishing off the last of the demons left alive. There were piles of dead foes in his wake. His sword was bathed in their blood. He was shirtless, his muscles glowing with sweat. With each heavy breath he took, his lifemark swayed.

She rushed into his arms, leaving her brother to hold himself upright. Her naked flesh felt good against Joseph's, like she was finally coming home after a lifetime of being without one.

He pulled away and inspected her wound. Concern lined his face.

"It's not that bad," she said.

"It's not good."

"I've had worse from sparring practice. Let's just find the young."

Eric limped toward them. She hadn't noticed it at the time, but he'd taken a hit to the leg from one of those swords. Blood seeped down from his thigh to his foot.

"How bad?" she asked.

"No worse than yours," said Eric. "They split up the

young. I know where some of them are being kept, but didn't see where the two boys were being held."

"I'll find the boys," said Joseph. "You and Eric get the rest of the kids and head out."

"There are too many demons here. And Treszka's still out there."

"Treszka?"

"The demon-queen bitch who rules this place," said Eric. "She's got juice, so be careful if you see her."

"I can't kill her," said Lyka. "My vow forbids it." Even now her vow to that demon was pounding on her, demanding that she hunt the queen down and deliver her.

A strange look crossed Eric's face. "How long have I been gone? Is the moon full yet?"

"Yes."

He nodded slowly in resignation, but refused to look her in the eye. "I don't think I can kill her, either."

It must have torn up Eric to admit that he was too weak to do the job. Her brother was a proud man, a strong warrior. For him, being unable to fight meant he really was as bad off as he looked.

"I'll take care of her," said Joseph. "But first we find the kids and get them to safety."

Lyka didn't want to split up. She didn't want to be separated from Joseph and unable to help him when he ran into trouble again.

He gave her a smile that brightened his eyes. "We'll be together soon, love. Until then, I'm still here." He stroked her temple, then pressed his hand over her heart. "And here."

If he kept this up, Lyka was going to disgrace herself by crying in front of her brother. It was the kind of thing he'd never let her live down.

She sniffed and turned to Eric. Standing right behind him was Treszka.

A dozen of those disturbingly human-looking demons appeared behind her, gathering around their queen. One of them had several short strips of silver duct tape clinging to its patchy fur—the remnants of its bindings.

It was the one she'd vowed to help claim Treszka as its own to possess as its mate. And now Lyka's chance to fulfill that promise was standing right in front of her.

Treszka flipped back her long black hair to reveal that gaping mouth in the top of her head.

Before anyone could react, she sank her black fingernails into Eric's shoulders and bit him with that horrible maw, ripping a chunk of flesh from his neck.

A look of shocked horror covered his face. She let go of him. Blood spurted several feet into the air with each beat of his heart. He fell to his knees, bleeding to death fast.

Eric's blood trickled down Treszka's pale temple as she looked at Lyka. "You're next."

Chapter 43

Joseph shoved Lyka aside as he charged Treszka. No way in hell was he letting this demon get his hands on his woman.

Eric's hot blood hit Joseph as he passed. The man had only a few seconds to live, and Joseph wanted the Slayer to know he was avenged before he died.

Before he could reach the demon, a blast of searing power hit him, slamming him back into the stone wall of the cave.

Joseph shook his head to clear it, but everything was a little slower and hazier than it had been a minute ago.

"Really?" she said. "You really think it would be that easy to kill me?"

She stepped over Eric. Lyka was at his side, frantically trying to save his life. Blood surged out from between her fingers. She was drawing power from Joseph at a steady rate, fumbling to find some way to slow Eric's bleeding.

As much as Joseph wanted to help, he didn't dare let his attention slip from the demon queen headed his way.

She looked him up and down with approval. "I had

considered using a Theronai to father my offspring. Now that I see you, I almost wish I had. If only your kind was as hearty as the Slayers. I really didn't think a Theronai would be strong enough to survive playing with me, but now I wonder if I was wrong." She lifted a hand. "Perhaps next time."

Her attack hit him with an invisible force.

Joseph's world exploded in pain. He felt like his skin was being ripped from his body one cell at a time.

He couldn't think, could barely see. His hearing was fine, filled with the sound of his own voice lifted in agony.

Run! he tried to tell Lyka, but nothing got through. Their connection was already full, roaring with the flow of power.

Then suddenly, the pain was gone. He slid down the wall, rocks scraping his bare back. Even that felt good by comparison.

When his eyes finally started working again, he saw Treszka lying on the floor, pinned in place by an iridescent band of energy. Lyka's hand was raised, bloody and trembling as she held the demon down.

"She's yours," said Lyka to the demon wearing bits of silver duct tape and hovering tentatively nearby.

It eased from the group, moving closer to its queen.

The tracking device was still glued to its back, where Nicholas had put it.

Treszka screamed and thrashed against Lyka's bonds.

Another rush of power flowed out of Joseph as she strengthened the magic holding the demon in place. It was already wobbling, weakening with every passing second.

That's when Joseph felt what she was doing with his power and realized that not only was Lyka pinning Treszka, but she was also using a tiny shield to patch Eric's artery and slow the bleeding.

She was still new to wielding magic, and multitasking was draining her fast.

Joseph didn't have much time left to act before his window of opportunity closed.

Tracker Demon inched closer to Treszka's feet and pushed her velvet skirt up her legs. It lowered its mouth and a long black tongue spilled out to lick its queen's skin.

Revulsion churned in Joseph's gut, but he didn't let it slow him down. As long as this demon lived, Lyka would be bound by her vow to it. She'd be trapped by her word, unable to kill the demon queen that was hell-bent on taking all of them down.

Joseph pulled sparks of power from the earth surrounding him to fuel his body. His skin tingled and glowed as he attacked, slicing off the head of Tracker Demon in one single blow.

The instant it died, Lyka screamed and siphoned off a huge rush of energy. Joseph fell to his knees under the strain of providing what she needed. A couple of seconds later, he saw Treszka's head twist hard and keep twisting until her neck broke. Her body went limp and the taint of power around her dissipated.

The rest of the demons that she had controlled paused for a second in confusion before they realized they were free.

No longer held by the will of their queen, the demons charged.

Chapter 44

Lyka was better at killing than healing, but for Eric, she was determined to learn the skill fast.

As soon as she knew Treszka was dead, she popped a shield over herself and her brother and went to work.

Demons were scrambling outside the shimmering dome, but Joseph was on the job. Even though there were a ton of them, confidence radiated from him, reassuring her that he was in complete control.

She'd never seen a man fight like him. So much skill and carefully contained power. No rage or berserker attitude—just calm competence.

His confidence flowed around her, giving her the peace of mind she needed to focus on the task at hand.

She really didn't know what she was doing, but she'd studied a little anatomy and knew that all she had to do was line up Eric's tissues and keep him from bleeding to death while his body did the rest. Slayers healed fast, and while his body was taxed from what he'd been through over the past few days, he was strong.

"You can do this," she told him. "Just close your eyes and relax. I won't let you bleed out."

Treszka's bite held some kind of poison. Lyka wasn't sure how she knew, but it must have had something to do with the connection she now had with her brother. Part of her consciousness was in him, monitoring his body for signs of what she needed to do next.

Joseph kept cutting down foes one after another. Reddish black blood spattered his skin, leaving angry welts wherever it touched.

Synestryn blood was toxic, and Joseph had only his jeans to protect him from the spray of his killing spree.

Inside the dome of protection, Eric shivered and panted, struggling to stay alive.

"That's it," she said as she kept pressure on his wound. "You're almost out of the woods."

At least she hoped it was true.

One of the demons got a hit in on Joseph, slicing his arm with a rusty blade. She felt the sting as if it had been her own flesh, but he didn't so much as flinch. Each stroke of his sword was as graceful and smooth as the last.

Eric sucked in a long, shuddering breath and opened his eyes.

"Welcome back," she said.

"Just in time to join the fight."

"Joseph's got it," she said. "Just stay here and relax."

"Hell of a fighter you've got there."

"He sure is. And that's not all he's good at, either."

"TMI, Sis. I really don't want to have to kill him."

Joseph cut down the last of the demons in the area and surveyed the room, looking for more. His gaze met hers, and she felt his love for her spill over her, warming her soul.

"If you two are done making googly eyes at each other, I'm ready to go," said Eric.

She helped him to his feet, bracing his weight. "He needs some rest, but he should recover."

"We'll grab the kids and head out," said Joseph.

Eric nodded. "I saw two of the young go that way." He pointed to the opening on the far side of the cavern. Then he nodded to the door nearest them. "The rest are this way."

"I'll head to the west," said Joseph. "You two start toward the exit and pick up the kids on the way out."

"I don't want to separate," said Lyka.

Joseph glanced at Eric. "He won't make it much farther. You have to get him out."

"I can go as far as I need to go," said Eric.

Lyka knew it was a lie. He was in bad shape—way too close to death for her to take any chances.

She nodded at Joseph. "We'll meet you outside."

"I love you," he said, then ran off before she could recover from her shock of hearing the words aloud, much less say them back.

"Come on, Sis," said Eric. He stared at the motionless demon queen, looking at her with an expression of loathing and regret. "I need to get out of this fucking place."

They wove their way back toward the exit, passing piles of Synestryn bodies as they went. There were two more still alive, guarding the cavern where the young were being held, but Lyka made quick work of them, slamming them together so hard, their heads caved in against each other's.

The young rushed out, hugging the adults and crying tears of relief.

Except for Kayla. She went to the demon bodies and began kicking them in fury. A string of filthy words poured from her mouth, but Lyka gave her a pass. After what they'd been through, the girl deserved a bit of lee-way to vent her emotions.

Got the boys. Joseph's thoughts filtered through her head easily now. She didn't even think about fighting him. This telepathy stuff was way too handy for her to shun it. *Sending them back to you while I guard their escape.*

Through his eyes, she could see that there were still dozens of demons alive in this system of caves, and they were all gunning for Joseph. The scent of his blood was pulling them out of the shadows, but he was still going strong, holding them off with the help of the narrow tunnels to funnel them to him one or two at a time.

Lyka turned to Eric. "The young will help you get out. Joseph found the other two boys. I'm going back for them."

The kids realized that this was their chance to shine and crowded around Eric to help him stay on his feet.

Lyka picked up the swords of the dead demons and handed them to the young. "Don't be afraid to use these. Scream if you run into trouble. I'll hear you."

To be certain she would, she amplified her hearing with the help of Joseph's power, and set out after him.

A few minutes later, she ran into the pair of Slayer boys. They still wore metal cuffs around their wrists and ankles, attached to broken chains. They were a little scuffed up, but basically both still in one piece.

"Is Joseph behind you?" she asked.

The older boy shook his head. "He had to stop before the cavern and hold them off. There were too many left for him to risk them surrounding him on all sides."

Lyka reached out to him, but all she got was a sense of weariness and growing concern.

"How many were there?" she asked.

The boys shared a frightened look with each other. "Hundreds."

As strong as Joseph was, as skilled as he was, and even with the advantage of the tunnels limiting his foes, there was no way he could defeat odds like those.

You need to hurry, said Joseph. *I can't hold them off much longer.*

She opened herself up to him and, sure enough, she saw the kind of odds he faced. There were demons as far as the eye could see, their bodies pressing together, trying to force Joseph back into the giant cavern a few yards behind him.

Lyka looked at the boys. "The exit is clear. Put your left hand on the wall and don't take it off. Keep moving upward. Eric and the others are already on their way out."

"We can't go alone," said the younger boy.

"Yes, you can," she told him, giving him a little shake. "Go now. Hurry."

The boys took off on scrawny legs, kicking up dust behind them.

Don't you dare come back here, Lyka, said Joseph.

Don't you dare die before I get there, Theronai.

It's too late. I can't hold them. Run!

Chapter 45

One of Joseph's greatest fears had been that he would die behind a desk. Now he knew that wasn't going to happen.

He'd served his people well, fought hard and found true love. It was more than most men ever got, and a life he was lucky to have led. His only regret was that he wouldn't live long enough to let Lyka know just how much he loved her, how precious she was and how honored he was that he got to call her his, if only for a little while.

I'm not done with you yet, she told him.

He knew he wasn't getting out of here alive. He'd known it from the time he'd sent those boys running while he held off the demons on their tail. There were too many Synestryn for him to defeat alone, and there was no way he was going to call Lyka for help.

She needed to survive. His people needed her. There were so few female Theronai that every one was precious.

She more precious than most—at least to him.

There was no sorrow in his sacrifice. He could not

think of a more noble death than defending innocents and protecting the life of his mate. It sure beat the hell out of dying of boredom in his office back at Dabyr.

He could feel the powerful flex of Lyka's muscles as she ran toward him. She'd shifted to her tiger form and was rushing headlong into danger.

Don't do this, Lyka. Please. Turn around.

Not going to happen. If you don't want me to die down here, then keep your ass alive. I'm almost there.

Tell Nicholas that my death wish is for him to lead the Theronai.

Do I look like your secretary? she asked. *Tell him yourself.*

The demons were bearing down on him. One had already slipped around behind him and left a deep gash on his back.

At least those swords weren't poisonous. His body was still going, despite the pain of his wounds. But it wasn't going to last much longer. It was simply a matter of numbers.

Fatigue weighed down on him. Even using the trick of pulling power from the earth, his cells were starting to rebel. His reflexes were slowing, his muscles burning. Every slice his sword made was doing less than the last. As the sheer mass of demons pressed him, his only choice was to take a strategic step back now and then to avoid taking damage. Each step gained his enemies ground toward the cavern that was only a few feet behind him.

And once he was in there, he was dead. No amount of fancy sword work was going to keep them from attacking him from all sides.

Another attack shoved him back a step. He could hear the echo of steel on steel bouncing off the cavern walls behind him.

One slippery little fucker slipped past his guard and popped up at his back. There was nothing Joseph could do to stop the impending blow—not without giving another three demons his back.

That move would kill him for sure.

So he braced himself for the blow, searching for a single second's opening to turn and deal with the demon at his rear flank.

A feral growl sounded behind him. Then a demon let out a hissing scream of pain as it died—a familiar sound now, after the dozens he'd killed so far.

Got him, came Lyka's satisfied tone in his head.

He caught a flashing image of a demon's limp body being shaken in the teeth of her tiger form before she tossed it aside.

A flash of movement warned him a second too late that an attack was coming. His sword was already engaged with another, blocking it from reaching his flesh. He tried to avoid it by taking another step back, but it was too late. There was nowhere he could go to stop the blow.

He felt Lyka's alarm, felt her siphon off a huge surge of his power.

A pale, shimmering light appeared in front of him as she erected a shield wall. The momentum from combat rocked him back on his heels. He lost his balance and fell back into the cavern opening.

Something was wrong. His body wasn't responding right. He looked down to see what was the matter.

Protruding from his chest were four inches of rusted steel—the tip of one of the demon's swords. It had been severed by the shield, which left the blunt end glowing orange where it had been sheared.

Lyka was beside him in an instant. She looked down

at him with the eyes of a tiger, but he saw fear glowing in those golden depths.

Don't move, she told him, panic filtering through with her words. *The sword is near your heart.*

Was it? He couldn't tell. He couldn't feel anything but a faint flutter in his chest and a chill racing through his lifemark.

That was probably a bad sign.

"You need to leave," he said. "My power won't be available to you for much longer. Once it fades, you'll be trapped in here with all the demons behind your shield."

Your power isn't going to fade unless you die, and I won't let that happen. Her tone was confident, but the feeling of panic scampering through her proved it a lie.

His heart fluttered again, only this time it felt like a fist being shoved through his chest. He clamped his lips around a scream of pain and was left panting by the time it passed. "Go, kitten. Please. Before it's too late."

I will, but you're going with me.

The feeling of rock-solid resolve coming out of her was the last thing he felt right before his heart fluttered, stuttered and then stopped.

Chapter 46

Joseph wasn't breathing.

Panic engulfed Lyka, making her shake so hard, she was kicking up dust under her paws.

She didn't know what to do to save his life, but she knew she had to.

She loved him. She couldn't let him go. Not before she at least had the chance to tell him how she felt.

She'd been an idiot not to see it before. It had been huddled there, cowering inside her, afraid to make itself known. He wasn't her kind. He wasn't what she'd wanted for herself.

None of that mattered. Love didn't care about artificial boundaries. It laughed at the plans of Slayers and Theronai alike. Love did whatever the fuck it wanted, and turned the lives of everyone it touched upside down.

But accepting it . . . that was the sweetest feeling in the world.

If only she'd done so sooner. If only she'd realized how she felt sooner and told Joseph, maybe something would have ended up differently. Maybe he wouldn't be lying there with a sword sticking out of his heart and blood trickling across his flesh.

A feeling of denial boiled up inside her, burning off everything else.

Screw all the *if only*s. Fuck all the *maybe*s. She was going to change reality to suit her, dammit.

Lyka pulled magic from Joseph and used it to reach inside him and squeeze his heart, forcing it to pump. Wherever there was a cut in his veins, she patched it with a tiny force field. He wouldn't heal anywhere near as fast as Eric, but she'd find a way to keep the magic flowing for as long as it took for his body to do its job.

She was handling a lot of different tasks, and the shield holding the demons at bay began to fizzle out under the stress.

Before it failed, Lyka had to get Joseph out of here.

She needed to keep him as still as possible, so she formed another thin film of power beneath him. His body hovered off the ground a few inches atop the stretcher she'd made.

Still in her tiger form for speed, she grabbed the edge of the barrier with her teeth and shoved him forward. She moved faster and faster as she got the hang of it.

Joseph's power flickered as he teetered between life and death. She managed to keep the thin film of energy solid beneath him, but that was all. The wall behind her—the one holding back all the demons—fell.

The sound of excited clicks and yelps grew louder as the demons gained on them.

Within minutes, she was past Treszka's remains and able to smell fresh air. Up ahead, the entrance to the cave was nearly blocked. Only a small hole remained inside a wall of rubble.

Someone had collapsed the entrance.

Lyka shoved Joseph through on his shimmering stretcher. She was right behind him, but her big tiger's body wouldn't fit through the hole.

She shifted back to human form and wiggled through just as the first of the horde of demons cleared the corner.

"Plug it!" shouted Eric.

The young scurried to obey, working together to lever a huge rock into place with a sturdy tree branch.

The stone wall wasn't going to hold them for long. She could already hear them scratching at the rocks on the other side, trying to claw their way free.

A familiar noise beat in the background, but Lyka didn't pay it any attention. Her complete focus was on Joseph.

She knelt by his side and laid her hands on his chest. Blood was everywhere. There were still hours of night left, and any demons nearby would be headed their way as soon as they smelled it.

"You need to take the young and leave," Lyka told Eric. "They can't be near him with all this blood."

"What about you?"

Joseph was still alive but only barely, and only because she was forcing his heart to beat. The power flowing out of him that was usually as strong as a river was barely a trickle now. She was struggling just to keep in place the tiny shields that were preventing him from bleeding out altogether.

They'd escaped the cave, but she had no idea how she was going to keep him alive long enough to reach help.

Lyka bowed her head over him, pressing a kiss to his forehead. "Please don't die, Joseph. I need you. I *love* you."

A flutter of something flowed through their link, but it was so faint, she couldn't decipher it.

The noise she'd heard earlier began to get loud. The wind picked up. She covered Joseph's head with her body as dust and leaves whipped around them.

Eric put his hand on her shoulder. "It's going to be okay, Sis. The cavalry is here."

Lyka looked up to see what he meant. A helicopter landed a few yards away in a space barely big enough for the job. Out jumped Nicholas and two other burly Theronai, swords in hand. They made a beeline for the cave entrance, taking up a fighting stance, ready for whatever made it out.

Behind them was a tall, lean man, his dark head bowed against the wash from the rotors.

Ronan.

He lifted his head as he neared Joseph, and a pale silvery light spilled from his eyes. His expression was harsh, his face gaunt. "I'll need blood if I'm to save him and still find the woman I seek. Lots of blood. And I don't have the strength to mask the pain."

"Yes," she said without hesitation. "As much as you need. Whatever it takes."

The glow in his eyes brightened. "Deal."

Ronan grabbed her, bent her head back and bit her neck.

She was so shocked by the sharp sting of his teeth sinking into her skin that her control faltered. The power she'd been channeling to keep Joseph from bleeding to death slipped from her grasp.

She tried to find the strand of energy again, but there was nothing there anymore. The connection was severed.

Lyka was alone.

Without her there to keep Joseph's heart beating, it stuttered once, then fell silent.

The luceria opened and slipped from her neck. She

moved to catch it, but Ronan was in the way. She fought against his hold, using all her strength, but no matter how hard she thrashed around, she couldn't break free of his grasp.

Sleep, he ordered as he continued to drink from her neck. He shoved the command directly into her mind, leaving her no choice but to obey.

She lasted all of ten seconds before fatigue sucked her in and stole all her strength.

Chapter 47

Vazel found his queen on the dirty cave floor. With her neck twisted at such an odd angle, she was no longer perfect, but she was still beautiful.

Her breath was so shallow, he almost thought she was dead. But the faint beat of her heart had called to him, summoning him as powerfully as any verbal command she might have uttered.

He stroked her hair, straightening the tangled locks to cover the maw in the top of her head. Why she covered herself like that, he never understood, but he knew she liked it better when no one could see what she really was.

"I can't save you," he said.

Her eyes opened slightly, but that was the only sign she gave that she'd heard him.

"But your blood will live on." He cut open her gown with a knife, baring her abdomen. It was smooth and flat, but he could still sense the life that pulsed within her, struggling for survival.

The Slayer's seed had taken root, just as Treszka had hoped.

"It should have been my child," he told her. "And now it will be."

There was a flicker of terror in her black eyes, as if she realized what he intended to do. He hated her fear, but he wasn't going to let it stop him. Not when he knew this was the right thing to do. How else could she live on?

Vazel summoned every bit of power he possessed and used it to speed the flow of time within her body. Her abdomen grew with the child, but there was no pain. His mistress couldn't feel anything below her broken neck now.

By the time he was done and felt the first contraction ripple through his queen's belly, he was exhausted. Sweat rolled from his skin. His body shook from the strain of wielding more power than he ever had before.

With trembling hands, he carefully cut into Treszka's body to retrieve its fruit.

The child was perfect. Beautiful.

"You should be proud," he told his queen, but she didn't hear him. She'd bled out from what he'd done and was gone from his reach forever.

Vazel cut the cord and wrapped the child in a strip of velvet from Treszka's gown. A sense of pride filled him as he cradled in his arms the thing he'd dreamed about most since he'd first laid eyes on his queen.

He looked down at the remains of the woman he'd loved and smiled. "We have a son."

Chapter 48

Lyka woke up in her suite at Dabyr as if nothing had happened. She was whole and safe. All her wounds were healed. She was clean and naked in her own bed.

Completely naked.

She reached for the luceria, already knowing that it was gone.

A deep sense of loss consumed her, driving her from her bed. She slipped into a bathrobe and made it as far as her living room before coming to a dead stop.

Joseph sat at the desk in the corner of her living room, working.

He stood up as she came out of her room but didn't come toward her. Instead, he gripped the back of the chair like an anchor. "You shouldn't be out of bed yet. Ronan said you'd sleep for another day."

"Guess he was wrong."

The luceria was back around Joseph's neck again. It looked like it always had, like it had never graced her throat.

His hand rose to touch the band. "You're free."

"How? I didn't leave any room for a way out of our bond."

"Except death," he said. "I died for a minute or two before Ronan brought me back."

That's why she hadn't been able to reach his power, why she hadn't been able to reach him.

That moment had been the loneliest of her life. Truth be told, that feeling wasn't much better now. The only consolation was that Joseph no longer had any way of knowing what she was thinking. She couldn't be ashamed of her weakness.

"So, what does that mean?" she asked him.

"It means you're off the hook. Eric and the kids are safe. Andreas and the rest of the Slayers are staying here until they can rebuild and reinforce the settlement. I told him that you're free to go with him when they leave."

He didn't want her to be here anymore? Had she done something to upset him? Or was it just that he'd seen the person she really was and wanted nothing more to do with her?

No one else had ever connected with her like he had. If he didn't like what he saw, then maybe there was something wrong with her.

"What about you? What about your pain?"

"You funneled so much power from me that I'll be fine for a while."

"Your lifemark?"

"Still has three leaves. The others fell when we separated."

"So, you're fine without me, huh? What about me? What about *us*?" she asked, her tone a little sharper than she'd intended.

His gaze dropped to the floor. "I can't put you in danger like that ever again. I have no clue how the other men do it."

That pissed her off.

She marched up to him and got in his face. "Really?" she asked. "We have one little bump in the road and you call it quits?"

"Little bump? I fucking died, Lyka. If we'd been together much longer—if the colors in the luceria had stopped moving—you could have died right along with me."

"You only died a little. And Ronan patched you up. You can't let that get in the way of doing what you were meant to do—and I don't mean sitting behind a desk."

"I'm needed here. Someone has to sit behind the desk."

"Then take turns. You deserve to get out there and fight just as much as the next guy. And so do I."

He frowned at her. "You want to fight?"

"Honey, I was born for this. I may still need some practice at the magic part, but I've never in my life felt as whole and satisfied as I did when I was working side by side with you."

"You don't have to do this," he said. "Or you could take your time and see if you're compatible with any of the other men."

"Screw that. I've found my partner. You're the man I want. You're the man I love."

His smile was slow to form, but once it did, it stretched all the way to his eyes. "Damn, I love hearing that. Say it again."

"You first."

"I love you, Lyka. I have for longer than I'm willing to admit."

"I love you, too, Joseph, but it's still pretty new, so don't push it." She grinned and reached up to pull the luceria off his neck. It opened easily, wrapping around her hand as if needing to get closer to her. "This is mine. And so are you."

He kissed her until her head spun with desire. When she pulled away, she could feel the heat of the luceria back where it belonged, around her neck.

"And you're mine," he told her. "My life for yours, kitten. All of them."

She placed her hand on his lifemark, feeling the slight pucker of the scar he now wore over his heart. "Forever, Joseph. Whatever comes our way, we face it together."

Read on for a sneak peek at the final book
in Shannon K. Butcher's thrilling Edge series,

ROUGH EDGES

Available in August 2015 from Signet Eclipse

April 28
Dallas, Texas

After two weeks of sleepless nights, little food and endless hours spent working beside a man who lit up her libido like the surface of the sun, Bella Bayne wanted nothing more than a little quality time with her vibrator and a solid eight hours of shut-eye. In that order. Instead, what she got was the man of her fantasies—highly inappropriate ones at that—standing on her front porch, making her mouth water far more than the fragrant bags of Indian food he was toting.

"Thought you might be too tired to cook," said Victor Temple, the most perfectly formed male of any species ever created.

He stood a few inches over her five-foot-ten-inch frame, blocking out the streetlight behind him. He had aristocratic features that were made more interesting by the three scars decorating his face. They were small but broke up the sea of masculine beauty enough that she could look at him without sunglasses to mask the glare of perfection. His dark blond hair was cut with military precision, falling in line exactly as he pleased. After several missions with this man, she'd learned he defied the laws of helmet hair in a way she still couldn't understand. Blood pact with dark forces, no doubt.

His clothes were casual but neat and extremely high-end. Victor came from money. Old, refined, nose-in-the-air money, yet she'd never once seen him flaunt it. No diamond cuff links, flashy cars or pricey watches for this man. No, Victor Temple had way more substance than that, which was another reason she wished he was anywhere other than standing on her front porch. It was his substance combined with those stunning good looks that made him dangerous to her professional ethics.

"Hungry?" he asked.

Bella was hungry, but not for what was in those sacks. If not for the fact that she was Victor's boss, she would have feasted on him weeks ago. But her strict no-fraternization policy meant she had to keep her hands and mouth off. Way off.

"You should be at home, asleep," she said, forcing censure into her tone. "If you think I'm giving you the day off tomorrow so a pretty boy like you can get his beauty rest, you're wrong."

"I slept more than you did while we were away. And when one comes bearing gifts, Bella, it's customary for the receiver to at least pretend to be gracious."

"Sweetheart, I don't like pretending. And I'm not gracious."

He smiled as if he found her amusing. "Only because you're hungry, which I have learned over the past few weeks makes you cranky. Now step aside, Bella. I'm coming in to feed you. Then we have to talk."

Talk? At this hour? That couldn't mean good news.

He didn't give her time to move. Instead, he stepped forward, and she had no choice but to step back or she'd feel his body collide with hers. As nice as his body was, as off-limits as it was, she wasn't sure she'd survive the crash without tossing him to the carpet and riding him until she got off. At least twice. Maybe then she wouldn't be so cranky.

"Talk about what?" she asked as he strode past her as if he owned her home, heading unerringly to a kitchen he'd never before even seen, much less navigated.

"It can wait until after food."

His clean scent lingered in the air around him, crossing her path and making her drag in a deep breath to capture it. For a moment, the urge to bury her nose against his chest took over and she forgot all about why she didn't want him here. She had to shake herself to get her brain working again. "You're *my* employee in *my* home, honey. If I tell you to talk now, then that's what you'll do."

He glanced over his shoulder at her, daring to give her a grin. "I'm off the clock. You can't order me around. Deal with it."

Fury struck her for a second before turning to lust. She had no idea what it was about this man. She was the owner of a private security firm. She worked with badass men all day long, every day. None of them had ever held her interest for longer than it took her to flatten them in the sparring ring.

But Victor Temple was different. He got under her skin and made it burn. It didn't matter that he was her subordinate, or that he was on loan from the U.S. government to help her deal with a situation of nightmarish proportions. She couldn't seem to be near him without wishing they were both naked, panting and sweating.

Maybe it had something to do with the one and only time she'd taken him on in hand-to-hand-combat practice. They'd both been panting and sweating then, and while they hadn't been naked, she was acutely aware of just how skilled he was. How perfectly built he was. Not overblown or bulging with showy bulk, but his big frame was wrapped with sleek, functional muscles that rippled with power. She had fought bigger men than him and won, but only Victor had been able to pin her to the mat.

She was a strong, independent, kick-ass woman, but even she had to admit she liked that in a man.

"I was half hoping you wouldn't answer the door—that you'd be asleep," he said.

"I needed to unwind a bit first."

He lifted a wayward lock of damp hair that had escaped her haphazard ponytail. Only then did she realize just how close he was standing. Too close.

"Shower didn't do the trick?" he asked.

No, but her vibrator would have if he hadn't shown up. After all the time she'd spent with him recently, she wondered if she'd still be able to keep his face out of her fantasies. "There's a heavy bag in the garage. A little time with that would have worn me out."

He stepped away, leaving her feeling adrift for a second before she caught up with reality. She could not be drawn to Victor. She had to lead by example, and fucking her employee on the kitchen floor, whether he wanted it or not, was not the kind of tone she wanted to set for her workplace.

"You're worried about Gage, aren't you?" He glanced over his shoulder as he washed his hands. Muscles shifted beneath his tight T-shirt, adding fuel to the naughty fantasies she already suffered for this man.

Her gaze slid past him to the window over the sink.

She didn't want him to see how he affected her. Even more than that, she didn't want him to see her fear for Gage. He had willingly walked into the hands of a monster in the hopes of taking her down for good. No one had heard from him since. Bella had to stay tough, appear confident and provide leadership for her men. That included Victor.

She straightened her spine. "Gage has been gone for weeks. He was ordered to make contact with me as soon as he could. The fact that he hasn't is more than a little concerning. Sweetheart, any sane person would be worried."

Victor turned back toward her as he dried his hands. A flicker of sympathy crossed his features, making him even harder to resist. "He's smart. And tough. I'm sure his silence is a sign that he's working an angle with Stynger, not that he's in trouble."

"Easy for you to say. You weren't the one who sent him into that crazy bitch's hands."

"He volunteered for the job. He knew exactly what he was doing when he let her men take him into custody."

"He did it to save Adam from taking his place. I know Gage. The second he learned that Adam was his brother, his decision was made."

"Are you saying that he wouldn't have volunteered if it wasn't to save Adam?" asked Victor.

"No, he was on board the whole time, but now that he knows he has a brother, there's no telling what kind of sacrifice he's making to keep Adam safe."

Victor stepped closer, easing into her personal space like he belonged there. "There's more at stake here than one man. Gage knows that. He's smart enough to realize that the only true way to keep Adam safe is to take Stynger down for good."

"That's part of what worries me. It's personal for Gage. If he gets the chance to kill Stynger, he'll do it. Even if it means sacrificing himself." Maybe he already had, and that was why no one had heard from him.

Victor must have read her mind. "He's still alive, Bella. You have to believe that." He came toward her, compassion shining in his bright eyes. One lean, hard hand was extended. She knew he meant to offer comfort, but she was too fragile for that right now. She had to stay strong, stay tough. As tired as she was, as worried as she was, it would have been too easy for her to crack under the strain and let her emotions run free. One touch from him might be all it took to shatter her self-control.

She hadn't cried in years—not since the night she'd killed her husband in a blind rage. She wasn't about to start now.

Bella moved away before he could reach her. "I'm sure he's alive," she lied. "I'm also sure we'll find him soon. I just have to stay vigilant and keep looking for even the smallest signs of his whereabouts. We've been on enough missions together that I know how he thinks."

Victor's hand fell to his side. "You'll be a lot more vigilant after you get some food and sleep. You know him better than any of us. If we're going to see some obscure sign he left behind, you're the most likely one to spot it. But only if you're not exhausted."

She gave him a pointed stare. "I'd sleep better without one of my men in my kitchen, honey."

"When was the last time you ate?"

She couldn't remember, but that didn't make him right. "If it's that important to you, then feed me already so we can get to whatever it is you need to talk about. I'm wrung out."

"Maybe the talk should wait until tomorrow."

"I'm busy tomorrow. Talk now."

"I don't think so. Your blood sugar is too low for my peace of mind. It'll take only a minute to warm up the food."

She watched him move around her kitchen, opening cabinets and finding what he was looking for. The smell of curry filled her kitchen, making her stomach rumble.

He set a plate of food in the microwave, pushed some buttons. Nothing happened. He frowned as he checked to make sure it was plugged in. "It's not working."

Bella went to his side and tried to make the appliance work, with no luck. "Sorry. It's one of the few kitchen tools I know how to use. I must have worn it out."

"No worries. We have other options." He opened her oven door and pulled out her box of business receipts, staring at them as if they might bite. "You keep paperwork in your oven?"

"It's a handy spot. Nothing blows away when I open the windows."

"What about when you cook?"

She laughed. "Honey, I work eighty-hour weeks, minimum. I spend more than half of my time out of the country, run a reputable business where lives are on the line every day, and you think I have time to cook? You're adorable."

A blush brightened his cheeks and made his glacier blue eyes stand out. She knew he was a poster boy for the military, all upright and honorable, but there was something about the clarity of his eyes that really sold the whole look. She swore she could see right through him, like he had nothing to hide.

No one was that honorable. Especially not her.

"Does your oven even work?" he asked.

Bella shrugged. "Who knows? Never tried it."

He turned a knob to get the gas-fueled contraption working. She probably should have been paying attention to how he operated it, but all she could concentrate on was the way his fingers gently gripped the knob, giving it the slightest twist.

Her nipples puckered in response.

After a few seconds, his brow scrunched up as he turned the knob again. "Your pilot light's out."

"I didn't want to set my receipts on fire. The IRS frowns on excuses like that during an audit."

"Got any matches?"

She pulled a lighter from her junk drawer and handed it to him. He knelt down, making his jeans go tight over a manly ass carved by God himself. She was so busy admiring him, she barely heard his question.

"Did you move the oven out recently?"

Bella shook her head to get it set on straight again. "Why on earth would I do that?"

"To clean under it."

She grinned. "So adorable. I just want to pinch your cheeks." His ass cheeks, if she had her choice.

"Right. Got it. You don't clean, either."

"I have a housekeeper who comes in once a month to keep the place livable."

"When was she here last?"

"I don't know. While we were gone sometime. Why?"

He pointed to some crumbs on her floor next to a rusty brown smudge line, his face taut with concern. "Scuff marks. Someone's moved your oven."

Before she had time to follow why he was upset by her oven's position, he turned on a flashlight app on his phone and directed it behind the oven.

"Bella," he said, his tone eerily calm, as it was during

a firefight, "turn around and walk out the way I came in. Don't touch anything."

Serious worry settled in between the cracks in her arousal and fatigue. "What's going on?"

He took her arm and forced her to start walking. "Someone tied what looks like an explosive device to your gas line. Time to go and call the bomb squad from outside."

Also available from
NATIONAL BESTSELLING AUTHOR

SHANNON K. BUTCHER

They are the Sentinels: three races descended from ancient guardians of mankind, each possessing unique abilities in their battle to protect humanity against their eternal foes.

THE NOVELS OF THE SENTINEL WARS

Burning Alive
Finding the Lost
Running Scared
Living Nightmare
Blood Hunt
Dying Wish
Falling Blind
Willing Sacrifice

**"Enter the world of Shannon K. Butcher
and prepare to be spellbound."**
—*New York Times* bestselling author Sherrilyn Kenyon

Available wherever books are sold or at
penguin.com

S0337

M883G1011